MW01222912

RED
SKY
FALLING

Also by Christopher G. Moore

Fiction

His Lordship's Arsenal
Tokyo Joe
A Killing Smile
A Bewitching Smile
Spirit House
Asia Hand
A Haunting Smile
Cut Out
Red Sky Falling
Comfort Zone
The Big Weird
God of Darkness
Cold Hit
Chairs
Minor Wife
Waiting For The Lady
Pattaya 24/7

Non-Fiction

Heart Talk

RED
SKY
FALLING

A NOVEL BY
CHRISTOPHER G. MOORE

Heaven Lake Press

Distributed in Thailand by:
Asia Document Bureau Ltd.
P.O. Box 1209
Bangkok 10110, Thailand
Fax: (662) 260-4578
Web site: www.heavenlakepress.com
E-mail: editorial@heavenlakepress.com

First edition 1994 by Heaven Lake Press
Trade paperback edition: copyright © 2005 Christopher G. Moore
Printed in Thailand

Jacket design: Jae Song
Author's photo: copyright © 2004 Pamela Hongskul

Author's web site: www.cgmoore.com
Author's e-mail: chris@cgmoore.com

Publisher's note: This novel is a work of fiction. Names, characters, places and
incidents either are the product of the author's imagination or are used ficti-
tiously, and any resemblance to actual persons, living or dead, events, or locales
is entirely coincidental.

ISBN 974-92385-7-5

Hell is full of musical amateurs: music is the brandy of the damned.

George Bernard Shaw
Man and Superman

1

Not that anyone in the business remembers the Harvey Trio or the few who remember shake their heads and laugh like they've heard the punch line to some old joke. It doesn't bother me they forget. I don't care if they laugh. We once had it together. The billboards in the nightclub lobby announced the Harvey Trio were playing and had our pictures. That was me at the piano and Jack with the violin and Saint Anne holding the mike. Two brothers and a sister who had a look you couldn't quite place by nationality or ethnic background. But we fit in and had a rap like someone you knew from America. At least that was the way we were raised. We might have played in a hotel lounge while you were stirring your martini after a convention, talking with your friends. You are excused if you didn't catch our act; a lot of people fall in that category. But give us some respect. We were in show business; but not everyone who is an entertainer is noticed. A handful get recognition; most are lucky to pay the rent. We were once good. I know that is true. But what is good? In the real world there are a lot of good acts. You can get lost just being good.

Once we opened for Ray Charles in Tokyo. And for Muddy Waters, in Singapore I think it was. It might have been Hong Kong. Enough time has passed that my mind is fuzzy on time and places. I remember the entertainers, though. The great ones. And they showed me the difference between great and good is about as big as between day and night and black and white. Saint Anne would become famous. It is a strange, American word.

But Saint Anne was to become famous for the wrong reason. Some say this doesn't matter so long as the fame comes out of talent. There is an American fame that comes out of killing. Murder, even in America, isn't the best way to get yourself in the newspapers and on television. And given the competition among all the murderers in New York the chances are you're not ever going to be all that famous. Murder is like the music business, you might be good but the chances are you aren't ever gonna be great.

It started like this. On Thanksgiving, Elizabeth had walked out of the kitchen with a wry smile on her face, her brown eyes wide with fear and moist and watery. She wrapped a Band-Aid around her left index finger. Little splatters of blood were flecked on the front of her white apron as if she'd been splashed. When she saw me holding the camera waiting to take a candid photograph, her lips formed the shape of the Holland Tunnel entrance off Broome Street.

Not long afterwards, my brother, who'd cornered Elizabeth in our kitchen as she sliced carrots and onions, appeared with that look of someone who has showed up at the wrong address. Jack was rarely shy. But that moment, with tiny drops of my wife's blood seeping through the Band-Aid and falling on the wood floor, Jack sniffed he had caused the misfortune. Of course, his motives had been entirely inspired by curiosity. He had miscalculated the timing of his question to Elizabeth. Like a blunder in billiards when the miscue drives the cue into the green velvet like a spear into the flesh of a 50s movie monster. Only in this case it was a small paring knife into the flesh of Elizabeth's finger.

"What is the color of your daughter's nipples?" Jack had asked, as he pushed the buttons of the microwave.

"Why ever would you want to know?" asked Elizabeth, the East Midlands inflection rising in her voice.

"Are they dark brown, light brown, pink, or . . . ?"

"I don't know."

"And what is the color of your nipples, Liz? You must at least know that."

Elizabeth mistook her finger for a carrot. Disbelief can cause an error in perception. Just as a misunderstanding can change a paring knife into a weapon. What something is, or becomes, as Father would say, was a matter of pure chance. Or bad management, bad manners, or—this accounted for most domestic encounters which finally evolved into combat operations—simple bad luck.

SUCH an inquiry would not normally have surprised Elizabeth. She had been a part of the family for years. She knew we had some mixtures in our genes that made skin color, hair texture, eyes, nose, difficult to judge. Someone once said the Harvey kids looked like skid road cake ingredients that never got stirred right. Jack had some yellow blood, I had a few quarters of black blood and Saint Anne had enough water running through her veins to irrigate a desert. She was half-Vietnamese. We were a trio of half-breeds. Jack was playing around in the kitchen because he wanted to know whose blood had won the gene war, creating the shape, color and size of little Lucy's nipples. When you have mixed blood you are sensitive to the small victories like the shape of a nose or the texture of a nipple. That was part of the beauty of that Thanksgiving, remembering how Elizabeth had recovered so fast. We all had a good laugh until tears fell down our cheeks. But after that day, Jack became less inclined to apply his version of Freud in our kitchen. Jack's theory was simply that a daughter and mother with the same color nipples were in a lifelong competition over men. Freud occupied a minor role as prophet in Jack's world. My brother was far more absorbed with his enormous collection of needles, Hong Kong stocks, and local Triad friends. He had a fascination with the sea. His original interest began with Father who taught him the finest details of the English defeat of the Spanish Armada. The year 1588 was magical for Jack. He played in the lottery in whatever country we used to play in. 1588 was the year that proved the whole body of military judgment was blocked against the edict of chance.

That following summer, Elizabeth, as has been her practice for many years, left Manhattan for July and August and spent them in England. Our nine-year-old daughter, Lucy who, since the subject has been raised, has small, pink nipples unlike the light brown aureole of her mother's, accompanied her, leaving me to fend for myself on Wooster Street. Lucy's nipples, come to think of it, are a shade of color much like those of her paternal grandmother who lives in Seattle. And that is strange since I was adopted.

Before Elizabeth left for England, Jack asked her, if it wasn't too much trouble, to find one of those wonderful old prints of Martin Frobisher, a very important figure (on the English side) in the English battle against the Spaniards, and a dead white man whom my brother has adopted as one of the true Gods. Wagner, Mozart, Freud, Nietzsche are a few of the other altars at which Jack has worshipped; however, his greatest of Gods, Kong Zi, or Confucius, topped his all-time list of starters. A kind of quarterback of all the Gods, who threw the I Ching against the wall of time. Anything was possible for a human being. This was another reason I never got that photo from Muddy Waters.

Chance gave our daughter Lucy two wildly eccentric grandfathers. Both grandfathers had lives devoted in an odd twenty-four-hours a day way to entertainment. Though neither ever achieved anything beyond local celebrity. Her maternal grandfather, a song-and-dance man, used magic, card tricks, one-liners, and small, white pigeons in his act. My Father, who was my step-father, and adopted all of us through a Seattle lawyer, had a dream we were going to be a great trio one day. Only one thing he didn't figure on. My heart wasn't in it. Neither was Jack's. He spoke Chinese better than he did English. Saint Anne, now that girl, she had the heart for it. We were the product of a social experiment that shaped our heads and hearts. Unaware for the most part, like livestock, we were only partly conscious of the disturbances we stirred, emitting an odd tangle of complex signals about things that seemed obvious and apparent to us. The fact that from an early age our brother Jack decided to abandon the ways of the west and become Chinese was accepted by the family before we had even grasped the full meaning. He was half-Chinese so it just seemed natural though he had been raised by white middle-class folk. In many ways a complete conversion in manner, speech, and dress suggested adherence to a cult. Jack appeared as a kind of secular Moonie. He attended a private Chinese school in Vancouver. Jack bowed to Father and Mother with his hands clasped in a prayer-like formation at chest level. My earliest image in life was sitting in a window and watching Jack in a red silk shirt and pants bowing to my Father as he walked up the driveway carrying a briefcase. The top of life had been twisted so that the lid didn't fit. And I kept Ray Charles posters on the wall of my bedroom. What leaked out and ran down the sides were those silences when everyone in the family appeared in costume—Saint Anne dressed like a Viet Cong, Jack dressed in red silk and I dressed in leather with Ray Charles sunglasses. We moved around the room with brilliant, deep smiles.

After a long interval—even before Jack had moved to Manhattan—something outside of himself caused him to join the west. Not overnight, but over months and years, in a thousand little ways, he became the custodian of knowledge that defined modern western man. He soaked himself in this wisdom. The western way of thinking was like an aquarium of exotic fish, and he couldn't take his eyes away. And he still can't completely. But his conversion was incomplete. He fell in between the cracks. Out of the blue he'll start speaking in Chinese, or begin in English and finish the sentence in Chinese. All the laws of syntax dumped into a cement mixer and poured out gray and hard on the surface of the night. Thoughts subverted by the very material which served to construct thoughts. Thoughts with oddly shaped doors and windows; floors unsupported by walls. As a result others were, in Jack's mind, constantly stumbling and falling over things, not seeing what was plainly in front of them.

His memories of childhood read as subtitles to the movie which now ran inside his adult head. As Alex once said of Jack, if you aimed him in the right direction, he was moderately capable of staying in the game. But the main point about Jack was that, like the dead, he lived outside of time.

ON Bastille Day the heat blasted like someone had turned on a giant blow-torch and pointed it through the downtown canyons of Manhattan at two in the afternoon. A white haze fogged midtown, making it fuzz-ball gray. Ghostly structures dissolved in the sweltering heat. Elizabeth and Lucy had been in England for two weeks and I had begun to settle into my annual routine of fending for myself. After my morning photo sessions, I walked out into the blast furnace of the afternoon for a large Coke at the Mexican place on the corner of Canal and Wooster. At the bottom end of SoHo, the street vendors drank beer from bottles wrapped in brown paper bags, drooping against old cars and trucks, weighed down by tropical weather they thought had been left behind.

My ice melted into the watery Coke two minutes out of the Mexican deli. Ali, a street vendor from Morocco, with fifteen kids scattered like bird droppings between here and North Africa, hid out from eight different mothers in an ugly, battered van which he parked in the shadows across from our building. I walked past the books, records, clothing, lamps, and tools Ali had set up on the sidewalk.

"Where's Star?" asked Ali. He'd given this nickname to Lucy.

"In England," I said.

"That's a bullshit country, man. I had a wife there once. And two boys, I think. And they don't like blacks. You know that, man?" Whenever anyone said something like that I wondered if someone had told them I had lived in England. Ali scratched the beard on his chin, narrowing his shifty eyes. As if he was trying to remember faces erased long ago from his mind. He kicked a metal box of magazines with his boot and cursed under his breath. Whatever was inside his head snapped into place with a bolt.

"Why you let her go off to England just like that? She don't like the heat?"

I sipped my Coke, chewed a piece of ice. "It's cooler," I said. But I was thinking the heat was making him crazy and mean.

Ali rolled his eyes to embellish his disgust for such a lame excuse. He mouth softened slightly, and that meant a business transaction.

"Got something special I kept back for you, man," Ali said.

He held several frayed ties for me to examine. But what caught my eye was the tie Ali had wrapped around his large mongrel dog.

"The Parrot's real fucking hot," he said. He brushed the dog's thin, floppy ear out of the line of foot traffic. With Parrot's ears pulled back you could see the dog was wearing a tie. Parrot was the neighborhood watch-dog that no one seemed to own, but everyone fed. On that 14th of July, Ali dressed Parrot as a kind of makeshift model.

"How much for the tie?" I asked. Ali, like most people, saw only patterns and colors, shape and material, when he looked at a tie. One of the few advantages of an English education is the ability to recognize that many ties are encoded with important social significance. It was a knack to put a name to a private school, a university, a regiment, a members-only club etched into the narrow strip of material worn around the necks of lawyers, brokers, and civil servants. On this occasion a King's College tie had been knotted around the neck of a hot, panting mongrel.

"How much, Ali?"

"Man, Parrot likes that tie very much."

"How much? Two dollars?"

"Five."

"For five it looks better on the dog," I said.

We settled on three-fifty, and Ali tossed in an old copy of Life magazine with a photograph of Margaret Mitchell, the author of *Gone with the Wind,* on the cover. That was a little surprise for Saint Anne. Ali usually gave me, or Saint Anne, or our brother Jack—who had a standing order for Chinese artifacts—a break on the price. He particularly liked the blond wig Saint Anne sometimes wore. He knew that she was a singer. Ali told her she was more beautiful than Madonna and had a better voice, too. He laid it on how our sister Saint Anne ought to be in the movies. She had the looks that melted the eyes out of the heads of millionaires. Saint Anne scoffed, blushed, and overpaid for second-hand magazines she never read.

Jack teased Saint Anne—a habit left over from our childhood—that Ali was looking for the mother of number sixteen. But with Peter Montard proposing marriage to our sister right in the nightclub, going up to the mike and asking her in front of the audience if she would marry him, despite the fact she was already married, not even Ali's flattery could compete with that act. Jack said that Saint Anne had lost her sense of humor. And all of our spirits had slumped with the summer departures. Elizabeth and Lucy, of course. Saint Anne's husband, Alex Walker, had bet himself away on the winds of chance.

I loosely wrapped the King's College necktie around my neck.

"You gonna kill the ladies with that tie, man!" said Ali, scratching at his crotch.

I looked up to the fire escape of our building where my corn and tomatoes were growing in large plastic pots. The corn was doing exceptionally well in the heat. Growing inches every day now. Norman Hedgecock, who lived in Seattle, sent me the seeds by regular mail along his handwritten detailed instructions about their planting, care, and harvesting. He ended the letters in the same way. "You reap what you sow." Or another he liked was, "What goes around comes around." All of which leaves out earthquakes, tidal waves, floods, tornadoes, avalanches, midair collisions, train derailments, highway snipers, not to mention black holes and volcanoes. In the frenzied activity of the day, everyone needs something to hold onto in the morning. What old Mr. Hedgecock thought left out certain conditions. The main feature of uncertainties when cause didn't add up to effect. Not the sort of thing that was worth expressing to an old man whose passage on his final voyage was gardening in a city where the growing season lasts about as long as a fruit fly.

If the weather held and the insects missed the fire escape this year, then the harvest of vegetables might well be devoted to a celebration of Saint Anne's divorce from Alex and her wedding to Peter. Grafting a two-for-one ceremony into this summer of our lives. I fingered my new tie. It smelled of Parrot. Bits of dog fur covered the tie. I plucked off a few mangy long hairs, flicked them into the wind, which had blown them back into my Coke. The morning of Bastille Day had blown a hot wind across the city as if history roared through, leaving a few fingerprints of the past here and there.

Wearing that hairy King's College tie made me feel at once regal, expansive, and generous like an African dictator who had just crushed a coup and decided to have a party. It also reminded me of Englishmen drinking pints, playing cards, and the sound of Elizabeth's father playing Gilbert and Sullivan at the piano curved around inside my mind and filtered away into someone I once heard very drunk singing the Marseillaise at the bar inside La Coupole in Paris. I missed Lucy's looking down from the fire escape, waving as she watered Mr. Hedgecock's seeds in plastic buckets. Instead, I had only an image of her in my mind through the monotony of the heat. And Elizabeth slapping at a mosquito buzzing at her neck.

Above me in the street, on the fire escape, my plants, in them I drummed up the faces of my family. Because I wanted them nearby at that very moment. In such a climate, only the faces of family keep one sane and alert. Fifteen kids, I thought to myself. That wasn't a family; that was showmanship, like pitching a perfect baseball game. Civilization wasn't about being famous. It was about belonging. And conjuring up Elizabeth and Lucy kept me part of something that mattered. Yet, to be fair, Ali and Parrot, his dog, on Bastille Day created an epic feeling; more a feeling of portent, of distant thunderclaps on the Jersey side of the Hudson River. Maybe it was simply that I feared Saint Anne's ultimate marriage to Peter would shift things forever. One of those random thoughts flying off some remote runway of the mind. The pilot lifts off and flies through the consciousness, dropping a few bombs over familiar terrain. That's called fear. Amazing how it came out of the interior spaces at near the speed of light.

Peter Montard—who had been born in Paris and had lived in New York since age seven—was the pilot I saw in the cockpit of that plane, flying at treetop level, red lights flashing danger, thousands of horsepower, and diving straight through one pocket of dreams and crashing like a nightmare into a hairy spider body of flames. In an odd way, Heather said, we should be grateful to Peter. Heather, Jack's second wife, soared on cocaine. She said that the whole family made you want to find the melting pot that everyone always bragged about years ago in America and smash it before any more people got melted and formed into the twisted shape of the Harveys. This came from a woman who had the guts to trap a large rat in the basement of our building with her bare hands while a group of about thirty illegals were screaming and climbing the walls. Heather had the habit of getting to the bottom of things. A no-bullshit lady. The worst thing about Heather was her near-perfect record for being right on such matters. We were the beginning of a new hybrid of race, tribe, and creed. We were chosen to be part of an arrangement in living that Father called a dangerous experiment. No one had wanted us. We had been abandoned by mothers and fathers we never knew. They threw us out like some of Ali's junk which he couldn't sell. Father picked us up and gave us a home. We were grateful for that chance.

Like his father, our father waited for death in a self-imposed exile. All he really asked of us was that we never let the others die

9

alone. That we never do to each other what our natural parents had done to us. That seemed fair. We were a three-brick wall with a turnstile for others to pass through the front door and out the back. That included Elizabeth, Lucy, and Heather. Alex was the first one ever to threaten to walk out. Of course it wasn't exactly that simple. Like a Chinese water torture, Alex's leaving appeared a drop at a time, as beads of sweat on Saint Anne's forehead and neck. Drop by drop, she ran for the first shelter. Peter Montard.

2

Several years ago, not long after Father had turned seventy-six years old, he got himself drunk, finishing half a bottle of Johnny Walker Red on the balcony of his one-bedroom apartment. He leaned over the railing, the whiskey bottle in one hand, smudged glass in the other. Below him was a paved parking lot off an alley in Kerrisdale—a neighborhood in Vancouver. Father felt himself getting sick and thought about throwing up on either the yellow Mazda or the red TransAm, but being dazed, so drunk he couldn't decide who he hated more, the Japanese or the thick-necked teenagers who drove a red TransAm, he twisted himself around, staggered inside, and spewed in the kitchen sink which was loaded down with a week's worth of unwashed plates, glasses, and cutlery.

Mother said about that time Father had started to look like what she imagined Truman Capote might have degenerated into had he lived that long. Part of Father's resemblance to Mr. Capote had to do with the hats he had begun to wear. Hats collected from the Salvation Army. He wore them in summer even though the combination of drink and sun made him sweat. He looked a little crazy in a beret. In a photograph sent to us, I thought Father looked more like Hemingway than Capote. Maybe it was the photo which caught his blood-shot red eyes along with his safari hat and pipe.

Father lived in a corner one-bedroom apartment on the second floor of a building containing twenty other units. He had lived there for many years after his retirement from the university. After he and Mother separated, his routine stayed much the same. In the mornings, he huddled over tables of second-hand sheet music sold

11

in several local shops. He salvaged scraps of Wolfgang Amadeus Mozart, Ludwig van Beethoven, Gioacchino Rossini, Carl Maria von Weber, among others. He searched for the soiled, torn, ripped copies. Copies smelling of damp cellars. They sold at a fat discount. He loved a bargain. Father lingered over the music, tracing the notes with his fingers, moving his head and breaking out into improvised melodies. He returned to his apartment with the smelly sheets of music and began drinking. In this drunken stage Father made airplanes from paper ripped from old sheet music. He sailed the paper airplanes across the narrow walkway between his building and another apartment building identical to his own. On the wall of his apartment was one of those promotional photos of the Harvey Trio. It was the only thing he ever put on his wall. When we were in the business, we did Blues, Jazz, Rock 'n Roll, and Pop. We never did any classical. Not professionally that is.

In his old age, Father's hair grew wild and bushy in his ears like some kind of wiry climbing vine. In his right ear was a plastic hearing aid; the old-fashioned kind, flesh-colored and oblong, the shape of a coffin for a cockroach. But as I child I thought of it as an undyed Easter egg that you got a prize for if you pulled it out. When he wanted privacy, Father simply flicked the control gizmo and signed himself off the air, as Jack put it. Saint Anne once asked him what he heard when the power was down. He smiled at her and said, "White noise." A white noise which erased all the sound in the world, and left Father to tune in the sounds which knocked about inside his head.

He spent his old age making musical paper airplanes. The wind carried his missiles through the open window onto the balcony table of a young newlywed couple opposite. The wife in her Laura Ashley dress, her long, blond hair blowing softly in the wind, reached down and picked up a Gounod or Mozart airplane, unfolded it, with a happy smile on her face. As if she had received a personal invitation to dine at a grand house in the country. Then she carried the crumpled paper into the sitting room, and read it to her husband, a young lecturer in the English department. Father's message to his young neighbors was always the same, "Is there danger?" That's all it ever said. A three-word question sailing out of the blue from a loony old white man who lived alone.

The most difficult part of Father's old age had been this virtual confinement to quarters with no one to listen to him rap. Half of the time now he would not know whether he had his hearing aid turned on or off. The world had grown silent, cold, and lonely. Would he come out to New York and live in our building? We asked him. Not a chance. I suspect it was his disappointment with the Harvey Trio. We were his hope and we had failed him—and he never really got over the sadness of our disbanding, giving up music, that is, except for Saint Anne. Keeping his mind just this side of alcoholic paralysis, he spent hours writing letters to Mother. Letters he never sent. More letters to relatives in New York and Montreal he had not seen in forty-odd years. Father said he had always been afraid the twentieth century was either a mistake or a joke. He did everything in his power to revert to the earlier age of chamber pots and handwritten letters.

Neither Mother, Jack, Saint Anne, nor I seriously tried to interfere. Our function had ended years before. We were the live audience for his questions, observations, quotes, and theories. Father had married and had adopted us to create a permanent rehearsal group. Then, in his old age, he found himself alone, his old colleagues dead or living up-country, or out of the country, his family like swallows had circled back to the south to roost in the States. Growing elderly, knowing his time was closing down, Father had become keenly aware that the questions which had obsessed him for a lifetime remained unanswered, and more than that, the present generation thought that certain types of questions which he pressed on others made him whacky. Why was this deaf old man spending his last years bothering everyone? Reworking worn-out material that belonged somewhere between the whirlpool of therapy and the mess in the kitchen sink.

The young couple ignored Father as they grilled hamburgers on the opposite balcony. Father, wrapped in an old bathrobe and his feet in sandals, leaned over the railing. He waved with both hands. He yelled at the couple. Finally, he folded a piece of sheet music from the great Charles Francois Gounod into an airplane and sailed it across the open space, landing it belly-down on one of the plates. This strange old man with nothing to do but make paper airplanes out of sheet music while he waited to die. That was why they ignored him. Watching this death-dance out of the corner of their eyes as they slowly turned their hamburger patties on a warm August evening. The young lecturer, though he probably was unaware of it, picked up part of a great opera—Gounod's Faust—squeezed the music into a ball, and dropped it on the hot coals where it exploded into a ball of orange flame. That must've made our Father smile from ear to ear. The professor of philosophy smiled, all full of rank, privileges, and rights. All of it ashes and smoke.

THE hardest thing for Father wasn't growing old in exile; it was being totally ignored. The tables had turned without him knowing what had happened. The world had switched him off; treated his ramblings as white noise mingling among the traffic, the sound of laughing voices in the distance, a television or radio playing, a telephone ringing, a dog barking. And for once, Father could not vault over those barriers, demand, attract, and retain the attention of his audience. His whole life he had had an audience. His students and colleagues, to whom Father was an important scholar in the philosophy department. Mother listened to his lectures until she knew them by heart, read his scholarly papers. Saint Anne and Jack, his two eldest children, were an unruly, often unpleasant audience. All that pinching and punching. Their behavior convinced Father that children were an inappropriate audience for his deep insights into the meaning of life. We hid downstairs behind the furnace at the first sound of the clasp opening on his briefcase, the distant sound of rustled papers, or the peculiar way he warned the world of his intention when he cleared his throat. By that time we were long gone.

"Why doest thou persecute me?" Father asked, before switching off his hearing aid and retreating back into the inner sanctum of his study. This was a question for which no one in the family, including Mother, had an answer. Anyone who truly understood the question had died before our century had been born.

SAINT Anne was the eldest at thirty-four years old; one year older than Jack, and two years older than me. About the circumstances surrounding our adoptions. The fact is our stepparents could not have children of their own. Children of academic families are not often recruited through a back-channel lawyer. Arnold Keene, Esq. delivered us to the Harvey family. We emerged from the haze of addicted prostitute mothers into the lap of a university professor and his wife. Keene, the lawyer, got all the right paper work so it was legal. We were allowed to keep only one thing from our past. Our first names. Our Father had made up his mind that he wanted a harmonic connection with a certain period of his past and decided that the best way of accomplishing his wish was through shaping the minds of his children.

Our parents met by accident in Blackwell's book shop, off Broad Street, in Oxford, England. Mother had bent down to retrieve his hearing aid, which had fallen behind a row of philosophy books. She had looked at that device and it was a crucial moment. What does a young girl do? Two years later they were married. Father had accepted his first teaching position as an assistant professor in the philosophy department at the University of Washington. Mother's pregnancy began in Seattle early that spring of '61. But the child was born dead. Mother had her female parts removed and almost died.

Father insisted they adopted immediately. Fair enough. They had gone through some major pain and loss, and replacing the dead baby with a live baby seemed the right thing to do. Arnold Keene had promised to handle everything without any delays or problems. At first Mother protested. She wasn't sure about adopting children from what she called broken homes. The fact is, we had been abandoned, we never had a home to break. Saint Anne was the first adopted Harvey.

While Mother remained flat on her back in the hospital, Father came into her room with Saint Anne gently cradled in his arms. She watched as he held the bundle out to her. "It's for you," he said.

She didn't know whether to cry or laugh. She knew her baby was dead.

"It's a girl," he said.

"What's her name?" asked Mother.

"Saint Anne."

"Funny name for a child."

"A gift from God," said Father. "I think she's a start."

With a shy gesture, Mother took Saint Anne into her arms.

"The start of what?" she asked.

"A family."

"Where is her mother?"

"Our lawyer says the Mother's gone back home. Signed the baby away before she went. So she's ours. All you have to do is say you want her. Otherwise, I take her back to the lawyer's office. There are other people waiting if you don't want her."

"Where is her home? The mother?"

Father looked down at the baby. "Vietnam."

"Isn't there a war there?" asked Mother.

She stalled for time; Father stood at the foot of the bed as a duty nurse came into the room. It seems that Mother and the duty nurse had developed a close personal bond. Mother expressed her uncertainty, her pain, rage, and confusion, and all the time she was holding Saint Anne in her arms, thinking, do I keep this baby or do I give this baby back? This wasn't a hearing aid. This was a flesh and blood child like the one she had lost. She wasn't ever having another; that much was for sure.

Before Father could get an answer, the duty nurse asked him to leave the room. He had no choice. Mother's blood pressure and other vital signs had to be checked in accordance with strict hospital procedures. That meant, she told Father, absolute privacy—meaning no guests could be present. Father retreated, and Mother and the duty nurse had a heart-to-heart talk about babies and life.

"She's a pretty thing," said the nurse.

"You think so?"

"Kind of looks like you, too."

Mother folded back the blanket and looked closely at Saint Anne's face. She was looking at her the way you look into the mirror, thinking about how the eyes, nose, and mouth belong to you. Saint Anne's eyes were wide open and staring straight back like she was auditioning for a part.

"You really think so?" asked Mother.

"Look at the mouth. Looks like yours."

Saint Anne got the call-back. She got the part and because of her Jack and I had it easier getting adopted into the Harvey family. That made Saint Anne special.

"She's got a strange name," Mother said to the nurse. "Saint Anne."

"It's a message," said the nurse, crossing herself.

"She's an orphan and a refugee."

"Not anymore," said the nurse, smiling. "She's got herself a family now."

Saint Anne started in the business real young. It was in her blood.

When Father was ushered back into the room, he didn't really have to ask Mother what she had decided. He could see it in the way she held Saint Anne, pursed her lips up to Saint Anne's and kissed her cheeks.

"I guess she'll do," Mother said.

A year later, when bringing Jack home, Mother carted him off to the same hospital. She checked in like it was a hotel. Her friend Dorothy, the duty nurse, who had been to many backyard barbecues. She had bought Saint Anne many gifts, and had just finished redoing her basement with her husband, Carl. She had rushed to the hospital, even though it wasn't her shift, and even though she'd worked twelve hours straight through, to help Mother witness the kind of baby mother would deliver under the name of Harvey.

"That baby got a liver complaint?" asked Dorothy.

"He's got some Chinese blood," explained Mother.

Dorothy stared at Jack.

"The eyes don't look Oriental," said Dorothy.

"You didn't think Saint Anne looked part-Vietnamese," said Mother.

"True. I would never have guessed with that baby. But this baby is different."

"What do you think?" asked Mother, holding Jack up between her outstretched hands and then lowering him down, giggling, to touch her nose against his nose.

"I think that baby's already chosen you. So why are you asking me?"

"Because you're my best friend."

"And what if I said throw that one back in the tank?"

Mother put her hand around Jack's.

"You'd not say that, Dorothy?"

"Only if I thought it was the right thing. But I think you ought to keep this one. He kind of grows on you with that soft, black hair and black eyes."

When Father came in to the room he looked at Mother and Jack, and then over at Dorothy who gave him the thumbs-up sign.

"What's his name?" asked Dorothy.

"Jack," said Father.

"That don't sound Chinese."

"He's assimilated," said Father.

Mother ignored them, playing with Jack like he was her own.

"You think he's musical?" asked Mother, after their conversation died down.

"The child has perfect pitch," said Father. "I tested him against Mozart and Jack didn't come out wanting."

"Jack, you are gonna be a great man some day," she said, kissing him on the forehead. They watched her looking with that look only a mother can have.

"It's fine, Dorothy," said Father.

Dorothy wasn't so sure. "You got any more orphans up your sleeve?"

"That's the same question my wife asked."

Saint Anne had already demonstrated her musical talent from an early age. She sang and danced like she was auditioning for a Broadway show. She was a star already and she was still a child. Saint Anne was a hard act to follow. Mother wanted more than the music business for her first son so that he would always be eligible for living in a single-family zoned neighborhood and anyone who was different—unless they had some talent going for them—would be disqualified for life from such a place and would end up living in squalor in some run-down Mexican village, drinking beer in the hot sun, and picking off blackflies hovering over the front porch with a handgun.

The year after Jack came into the household I was born. On 22 November 1963—that's right, the day John F. Kennedy was assassinated by Lee Harvey Oswald in Dallas, Texas. Everyone claims to know what they were doing and where they were doing it when Kennedy was shot. All I know is that I was in a warm liquid place, dark, silent and suddenly someone pulled the plug. It is a burden carrying around the birthday of a famous dead man. You know what goes through people's heads as they clock you? "Hey, man if Kennedy were reincarnated, then . . ." They never quite finish the sentence. Because I ain't no reincarnation of Kennedy or anyone else as far as I know. I don't vote; I don't even like politics. So about the time of Kennedy's funeral it was my turn to make my debut at the hospital where Mother was waiting for me. Chance had finally waited out the Harvey family that hot day in Seattle, a place which never gets hot. By rights, I'm the child who should've turned to a lifetime of I Ching study rather than Jack. When my time came, my momma gave me over to Arnold Keene for adoption and he called Father. Dorothy and her husband Carl were on vacation in Denver. Mother, holding me in her lap, frantically tried to reach Dorothy at the Red Deer Hotel outside Denver, and ask her. . .ask her what? So she put herself into the hands of chance. As she squeezed her arms tightly around me, she said to Father, "But this is the last one." She was watching the funeral on the television set and crying at the same time.

"I promise," said Father.

She had stripped me down on the kitchen table and looked me over with a flashlight.

"He's got some black blood in him," she said. "But Kennedy tried to help the black people." She blew her nose and dried her leaky eyes.

"That boy is going to play the piano like no other boy ever played on this earth," replied Father.

"I don't want an orchestra," she said.

"A trio is fine," he replied.

So I pushed and kicked and fought against that flashlight inspection of my arms, legs, neck, face and body. I passed and became Gideon Harvey, the only name I have ever known. I know what you're going to say, because I've heard it ten thousand times before. Gideon, like the guy in the Bible. The man who was the judge of Israel. At three, I was playing the piano. My memory of Seattle ends the summer of my fifth year when Father was appointed to a full professorship at the University of British Columbia. That summer the whole family moved to Vancouver. Distance wise it was a two-hour plus drive. But Canada was a different country. This strange family crossed the border into a country where there were almost no black people. It was one of the first things I noticed. Everyone was white except for a few Chinese and Japanese.

FATHER would appear at the edge of the sitting room, his right side tilted against the French doors, a faraway expression on his face, as if he was looking at all the tubes, microchips, and wires, the whole electronic circuitry inside the television, as his three children sat in a semicircle watching television. "Do your ears ring from the pipes of socialistic pipers, who want to make you wanton with mad hope?" Father would ask.

The sight of his children watching television stood in stark contrast to his vision of the new world. He watched us as if we were some kind of paleolithic creatures more interested in advertisements about cigarettes, beer, and car tires than the inner landscape of man. He turned off his hearing aid and waited, and waited.

In the 1970s Father underwent a conversion. He felt that he had found an important missing link in the theory of philosophy. That link was Drake. It began as a hobby. Nothing more than a way to distract himself from his serious articles and books; an historical figure who became a sort of intellectual companion. Although, Father may have been among the first to think of Drake as an intellectual. People read into the lives of others the strengths and conditions they wanted to find in themselves. Father had been passed over for the deanship of the department the same year that Drake began appearing in his dreams. The rejection of his department was a challenge. Father wanted more than anything to rehabilitate his reputation. And Drake, so he thought, was exactly the man who could help him do it.

He began a buying binge of every book he could order in Canada or abroad on the Spanish Armada; maps, engravings, anything remotely connected with the 1588 naval battle. He opened accounts with Christie's and Sotheby's in London. Their brochures and catalogues filled our mailbox, coffee tables, scattered like a trail from Father's study into the kitchen, sitting room, bathroom, and upstairs bedrooms.

Father knocked on the bathroom door, where Saint Anne had locked herself in smoking cigarettes and reading teenage girl magazines with a mud mask over her face, a towel wrapped around her head. She wouldn't open the door at first. But Father wouldn't go away; he persisted, shifting from his knuckles to his elbows to the heel of his shoe, and finally Saint Anne, smoke billowing from her lips, the only flesh in all that mud, swung open the door, and Father said something like, "Are you co-conspirators in the current folly of nations who want above all to produce as much as possible and to be as rich as possible?"

Saint Anne started crying, and Jack came out of his bedroom shouting something in Chinese. Being the youngest, I walked into this scene, and took Father by his hand, and led him back into his study, sat him in his chair, and asked him to tell me about Drake. Jack bowed as we walked past. Saint Anne wadded balls of tissue and let them slip from her hand onto the carpet. "Gideon, why are you the only one in this family who cares about the most famous white man to ever set sail on the troubled waters of this world?"

"Because my ancestors were carried as slaves in those ships. And if you want to know why Saint Anne's crying, it's because someone called her a gook at school."

"I will write a note to the principal."

"When someone called me a nigger you wrote a note. And all that happened was that I got beat up. So writing notes don't help much as far as I can see. Unless you got a fleet of ships and a lot of guns like Drake, don't go writing any notes."

Father saw Drake as the master of his own world. When the world was small, underpopulated, and heroes didn't have to give interviews on televisions or go before congressional hearings, Drake captured, defeated, stepped on, however one wants to cut it, the Spanish fleet. Overtook them; boarded them; blew them out of the water; burned their wooden boats to the sealine, and then chased the rest of them back to Spain. Drake had been in a difficult situation, but rose to the challenge; he grabbed his moment, and passed

21

into legend. That's why Father liked him; admired him, wished he'd been there at Drake's side in 1588, rather than fighting with a daughter covered in mud and a son speaking a foreign language he couldn't understand. And Father had convinced me that the raw material of history and philosophy was all connected to the ships, the blood, the guns, the winds off the coast of England. It was only much later that I learned about how Drake's victory was just another fight between two slave empires, seeking to make a bundle off the back of black and brown people.

One day, years later, the last time, in fact, I saw him, Father laughed about the money spent, the hours wasted, the passions fueled by Drake's 1588 battle. Father said, "Don't ever forget that every man mistakes the limits of his vision for the limits of the world." I knew that Father had taken the quote from Schopenhauer, but I said nothing. I also knew that had been the real reason Father had never been chosen as Dean. He could perfectly quote what had been written on the plates of time; he just didn't understand what was vapor and what was heavy water.

Peter Montard, Saint Anne's boyfriend, a Wall Street investment banker, believed that he had never made a mistake, that his ability to see into the future time and time again to determine capital and earnings was a natural condition. All he needed was to activate the right switches, and it was no more difficult than sexual intercourse. As much fun, said Peter, as fucking in a strange bed. When he was killed, I thought about which of his switches were the last to close down. That afternoon of his death, the world continued to go on and on and showed little interest, really no interest, in the fate of Peter Montard. Even on the 14th of July when he lay broken like a twig. Cast out of this life without a serious thought or close relative, or even a friend at his side. What lurked in his brain at that precise moment? A thought about our sister? The Dow Jones Average? An old Rolling Stones song? Fucking in a stranger's bed as his blood cooled in the hot sun.

3

Two weeks before Peter was killed, he dropped around to my studio out of the blue. Peter wasn't the kind of guy who went anywhere without an appointment. He invested money for the top ten recording artists in America. He was their Wall Street man who made them even richer than they already had any right to be. Peter became one of those fringe players on the edge of show business along with the accountants, lawyers, and managers. I was surprised and he could see that as he stared at me across my desk for a long time. He said he wanted to ask me about something, something important. Something that as the future husband of Saint Anne he was entitled to know. He wasn't asking much, he said. He wanted to ask a few questions that had been troubling him. How had we been raised in Seattle and Vancouver? What happened to us in Asia? Why did we have so much money and no one in the family ever seemed to work? If he was going to make Saint Anne a household name, a brand product, then he had to anticipate the negative spin people might want to put on her.

And one other thing bothered him, "Why is Saint Anne obsessed by water, sailing and death?"

"Her mother died in a boating accident," I said.

"In Vietnam?" asked Peter Montard.

"In Peugeot Sound. That's off Seattle."

I found out a long time ago that it is hard to dissolve the truth from the hard rock of the past. A few pebbles stood out but the rest was like a mountain sucked into outer space. He said to take my time, and he wasn't going anywhere as I thought about things.

An octave in a raised voice there. An earache at seven years old. A collection of caresses, disappointments, imagery, grudges. It is less a place in the past than a lighthouse, with a beacon throwing light in a narrow pinpoint, around and around, but at the end the sea and the land remain mostly in darkness.

"Did you know that all three of us were adopted?" I asked him.

He didn't know.

"We were babies at the time," I said.

"Saint Anne never knew her real parents?" His mouth was hanging ajar like someone had slammed him hard on the back of the head.

"Nope. None of us did. All we know is that our mothers died in a boating accident." And that was the truth.

"Saint Anne never tried to find her father?"

"We had different mommas and papas," I said. "Jack, too. But to answer your question, Saint Anne never had any desire to look for her father. Though sometimes she wondered if she inherited her singing talent from her mom. The Vietnamese have a talent for music."

"This could be damaging," he said.

Of course this information floored him, frightened him. I told him how a Seattle lawyer named Arnold Keene had arranged our adoptions. He got all the legal work done real fast; we were processed off the books, so to speak. When I was eight or nine I once asked Jack how Keene was able to get things done so fast and he said it was because Keene had a judge in his pocket. For a couple of years I had these dreams about a finger-sized judge inside Keene's suit pocket. This tiny judge had the power to hand out throwaway kids and every time Father and Mother wanted another baby, they phoned Keene who opened his pocket and ordered up one from the judge.

MOTHER really tried to learn from her mistakes. Child rearing is a system of trial and error, an experiment, with some small and large testing, and the failures mark the character, the moral and ethical features of the child. Or so it was to be in our family. Beginning with the eldest—Saint Anne had perfect white teeth, almond-shaped black eyes, wore her black hair in long locks which spilled over her shoulders. She always had freshly ironed dresses and white socks. The early photographs of Saint Anne with Mother showed a shy, dusky skinned child with her thumb sticking to the roof of her mouth like a National Geographic photo of a healthy half-breed kid in the tropics. She clung to Mother with her free hand. In those early pictures the only time she wasn't sucking her thumb, brooding, or covering her face, was when she was blowing out the candles on her birthday cake.

Saint Anne's thumb-sucking condition was largely the by-product of Mother's golf game.

Mother once leashed Saint Anne to an old oak tree in the back-yard, near the fence in the rear. Of course, from Mother's point of view, it was summer, there was plenty of grass, birds sang in the trees, we lived safely in the bosom of a middle-class neighborhood near the university, where nothing bad ever seemed to happen. Saint Anne was within reach of the swing set, sandbox, and Mother left out red apples and a jug of water just in case Saint Anne got thirsty. This abandonment sent an electric charge through Saint Anne's soul, roughed up her view of the universe, created a disordered state of mind when it came to nature and the outdoors. It was a violation, a war crime, in Saint Anne's memory. The Vietnam War was still going on and there is my younger sister tied up like a Viet Cong to a tree awaiting interrogation.

Her fear of indoors activity arrived in a slightly different fashion. Mother decided Saint Anne needed new shoes. Buster Browns. The store that sold them was downtown. She was five. Mother dressed her in a frilly white dress with matching white socks. When the salesman leaned down and tried to put on the right shoe, Saint Anne withdrew her foot. She pulled her leg up on the chair, and put her chin on her knee. It hurt, she said, there was a nail inside. Mother took the shoe from the salesman and put it on her foot. A few moments later, blood leaking from her foot had soaked through her perfectly white sock, and Mother held her in her arms waiting for the ambulance to take her to the hospital.

❖

WITH Jack, Mother changed her pattern of child care. From infancy Jack was taken out on the golf course with Mother. Mothering had taken on a natural rhythm; each morning she dropped Saint Anne and Jack off at school with a bag lunch made of the finest cold cuts, the next stop was the day-care center for me at the university, and she would be on the first tee by nine. She hired Mr. Ling to teach Jack how to play golf on the weekends. Mr. Ling was a Chinese short-order cook, who worked the night shift in Chinatown and during the day speculated by selling and buying shares on the stock market. He had been a high school math teacher before the '49 Revolution. About the time of Jack's eighth birthday, he had become totally fluent in Chinese. He dreamed in Chinese. Mother sent him to a special private school in Chinatown; he was the only non-Chinese, except for the Russian Consulate's kid, in the entire school. From ages nine to eleven, Jack spoke Chinese more than he did English. He bowed to his elders, prayed for his dead ancestors, and refused to open Christmas gifts. Mr. Ling also taught Jack the ins and outs of inside trading, hedging, commodities trading and how to launder money.

It was impressive to have a brother who spoke another language; but to have a brother who sounded like a real alien was something of a novelty to friends and neighbors. Personally I was more impressed that my brother had his life charted at age eleven. Jack's firm desire was to become a monk and play professional golf on the PGA. A kind of Arnold Palmer in silk robes, burning incense as he walked from hole to hole and throwing the I Ching to select the right club.

Mother and Ling put a nine-iron into Jack's hand. Father countered with a violin in Jack's other hand. By the time Jack turned ten, he could play the violin and use a nine-iron on the University of British Columbia Golf Course with deadly accuracy. At 150 yards out he could put the ball within a foot of the hole. Mr. Ling told Jack that nine was a lucky number in China. Given that the revolution which left Mr. Ling homeless, without a bean to his name, and a price on his head ended in 1949, I had my doubts that nine was good luck. But at Jack's age, he trusted Mr. Ling completely, and took "nine" as magic, and refused to use any other club. As far as I know there isn't a nine wood.

My ten-year-old brother, nine-iron in hand, conferred in Chinese with his caddie, as Mother waited beside her cart. He leaned over the ball, head down, and with a nice, firm, solid swing placed the ball pin high, then bowed to Mr. Ling, then to Mother, before he took out his putter and with a light, sure stroke knocked the ball into the hole for a birdie. Mother couldn't stop talking about Jack's score the first time he broke ninety with the nine-iron and putter. She sent his score card, an affidavit signed by Mr. Ling, and a letter to the Guinness Book of Records. But they turned Jack down. There wasn't a category for a ten-year-old Chinese-speaking half-breed using only a nine-iron and putter to break ninety in Vancouver, British Columbia. Father suggested under his breath that he wasn't surprised. At the same time Father had Jack on local television playing the violin. It was a war between instruments: clubs and violins. Jack never chose sides in these family disputes. By age thirteen he was trading shares part-time in Mr. Ling's brokerage house. No more short-order cooking for Mr. Ling who was shorting the market and cooking the books and making a ton of money.

Saint Anne, though, that girl, she was a singer from day zero; the day that judge in the pocket of Arnold Keene said Father and Mother could keep her.

I was spared the consequences of Mother's golf game on the development of my character. After she had given up the game, Mother took up photography as her main interest and reason for being. At the time of her shift, I had already been playing the piano for two years. My childhood was spent at a piano or inside the darkroom, pouring solutions, emptying trays, and developing negatives. Music and darkness. The evening of the day that Mother threw her Spalding bag, Wilson clubs, and Philip's white-fringed spiked shoes into the lake which guarded the sixth hole, Father consoled her over the dinner table.

"But no more of this indecent serfdom, no more of this becoming sour and poisonous and conspiratorial!" said Father. Whatever that meant no one ever seemed to care. It was just the way Father talked.

But whatever it meant seemed to make her feel slightly better as she spooned out mashed potato onto Jack's plate. She even managed a feeble smile. Early that afternoon, Jack, with only his nine-iron and putter, had beaten her in a head-to-head eighteen-hole match. Ling and about a dozen of his cronies from Hong Kong followed them around the course, waging bets, spitting in brass jars, and arguing in Chinese, and, most of all, shouting encouragement to Jack.

None of this information did Peter Montard the slightest bit of good. He didn't ask many follow-up questions at the time. Everyone else's family upbringing seems culled from the Middle Ages. The bulk of our childhood was cut from older, denser wood. I told him about our first time out as the Harvey Trio and how we got paid and were allowed to keep the money. And I told him about the years we spent on the road before we packed it in as a trio and Saint Anne went on as a solo act in nightclubs, always thinking she was going to make it real big. Secretly she thought Jack and I held her back. Not that she ever said this to our face. One of her friends said it for her and she didn't know I was listening. Saint Anne said, "I couldn't ever tell that to the boys."

Peter did coax a few more details about the nail which required three stitches in Saint Anne's foot. And asked whether she could still wriggle her toes. That, I thought, was an odd question. I assumed that she could. The world is full of these kinds of worries. And if she couldn't wriggle all of the toes on her right foot? That was the question I wished I'd asked him. If I could bring him back from the grave, I'd ask Peter why he'd brooded over that question.

4

Now there are some things you should know about the man who got himself killed. Peter Montard's great passion in life, other than predicting capital market changes, was wind-surfing. Perhaps in the seed of such passion is a tiny, grimy cell of destruction. As Mr. Hedgecock used to say when I was a kid, "You reap what you sow." And I would add you can never be certain what trouble lies within the inner cells of the seed. Or so it ultimately proved to be for Peter. Since Saint Anne abhorred sports—Mother had cured her early on—it was something of a surprise that Peter's obsession with wind-surfing didn't bring back memories of the old oak tree.

Peter wanted her to stay on the shore. Watching him. Applauding him. There was a touch of our Father in Peter's checkerboard of desires. For hours Saint Anne watched him sailing across the bay, singing to herself, rocking herself like she were on stage and the sea was her audience. She saw him out there. His body against the sky and the bay, at times no more than a dot against the horizon, gave Saint Anne a sense of security. With her naked eye, she watched the sunlight dance on his board. He played like a child with a child's love of the water and speed. Wind-surfing gamblers came to the bay to challenge him. A stream of them, mostly young men, locals who lived full-time on the Island. They bet twenty, fifty, sometimes a hundred dollars a race. A fortune for one of them. Not enough to bait a hook in the stock market for Peter. Saint Anne liked the personal satisfaction Peter got from winning. Something a nightclub singer could understand better than others. Because every night you had to win the audience. If you didn't win and had that audience against you, then you were in trouble. With her voice—she could do Billie Holiday, sending a chill down your spine—and her looks she always won over the audience. But she was insecure, thinking she was too fat, or she was getting too old to make it as a star.

I guess, in part, Peter's desire to take her along to the bay to watch him sail back and forth for hours on end made her feel secure. She knew exactly where he was, what he was doing, and where he was going. One indisputable fact about our planet is the problem with the ozone. I never really thought much about the ozone until I met Peter. You take certain things about nature and the environment for granted; the sky, for instance. Whoever thought of the sky as a filter on the lens of the sun? Suddenly there were holes in that filter; and Peter over the years had done a fair amount of wind-surfing under one of those holes over the south shore of Long Island.

Skin cancer, if treated at the outset, isn't often fatal. Peter Montard had been treated eleven times. In each instance, there was a red, circular spot, say on the calf of his right leg. The doctor's treatment resulted in a disklike brand. After a few months all that remained was a patch of scar tissue. By the time you have eleven of these distributed over your body, they are difficult to cover up. Like an old gunfighter who had always won with the faster draw, but over the years had been nicked a few times. These tiny propeller-blade-like nicks accumulated like the teeth marks left by old enemies. I only mention the exact number of skin cancers to illustrate Peter's dedication to wind-surfing and partly out of rationalization—I bore only partial responsibility for his death.

The chances were that sooner or later, as the surface of his body (if he had had a little black blood things might have been a lot different) became used up, one of the cancers would beat him to the draw. Then Peter's death, though not natural, would have been less dramatic. Like the old Viking funerals we could have wrapped his body in a plain, white sheet on the wind-surf board, set it ablaze, and as all the young locals stood about in a circle with tears in their eyes, pushed it out into the Bay. But I'm less concerned with the methods of disposing of the dead, than the causality of sudden, unpredictable death.

One thing should be made clear in advance. Neither Saint Anne nor Jack ever accused me of killing Peter. But Jack hinted that in a wider sense, of course, I had been responsible.

"Why not just admit it? Get it over with. Purge it from your system," Jack said.

"But Peter's death was an accident," I said.

"There are no accidents," he said. "It's all fate. Believe me, I know about these things. And so does Saint Anne. That's why we're a family." Jack was theatrical but serious about my hand in the killing. The man who puts the rope around the prisoner's neck is as much an executioner as the man who pulls the lever that drops the floor out from under the condemned.

WHAT I remember best about Peter Montard was how skinny and pale and small he looked. He looked like a high school student who lived on popcorn and Coca-Cola. Next to Saint Anne's husband Alex Walker, Peter looked like he could walk out of a doll house without having to duck his head. As if Alex could pick him up, and walk the little Peter wind-surfer doll up the stairs and tuck him into bed. Investment bankers talk mostly on the phone; no one really knows what they look like. It was hard to imagine people giving someone who looked fifteen all that money to play with.

Mainly his shoulders narrowed in, creating a sort of Grand Canyon around his chest cavity like the man had had open heart surgery. Also he had a stiff bristle of a mustache which covered his upper lip. On Peter the lip hair looked phony. Like a pimp's lip rug. He kept his hair cropped short to reduce wind resistance. And most of the time, when he wasn't walking around in a black wet suit, he wore baggy shorts that fell to the knee, and a powder blue T-shirt. But his main physical idiosyncrasy was his legs. Peter was bowlegged. He looked as if he had just dismounted from a horse. A cowboy who had somehow fallen on the wrong side of the branding iron about a dozen times. It was a physical condition that was directly at odds with his class in Manhattan. He was powerful, rich, and he was going to make Saint Anne a star.

But we've already established that class is a difficult quality to determine for the working rich of Wall Street. Behind a phone or computer, class was simply a by-product of predicting well with numbers. Only in the Hamptons on his wind-surfer, his black wet suit glistening in the hot sun, did the mind wander to whether this bowleggedness was the result of a childhood disease or whether he'd inherited it; still carried the gene, ready to pass it. Not the best motive for an illegal act, let alone murder, but deep down I had some deep, unresolved hostility towards Peter. He was one of those people with an instinctual need to win at any cost. And he had a way of grasping other people's dreams, hollowing them out, then refilling the dream with his own promissory notes for the future. He did that with Alex. And he did that with Saint Anne. I suspect that's pretty much the way he made his living.

WE had known Peter for years. I met him at a time when there was still an ozone layer over Long Island. Before there was a consensus that America's decline was gathering speed like a log off a high-rise building and millions of people would end up no better off than Peter Montard. Before Bill Clinton went to the White House. Before the homeless in dirty rags wandered the streets begging, singing, talking to themselves, sleeping in doorways, on park benches, against a gate or fence. I met Peter in a different world than the one he departed.

The reason Saint Anne had not made a play for him earlier was that she was married to Alex Walker. Alex was born in San Francisco and was raised in the Bay area. He met Saint Anne in the lounge of the Hilton where we were playing in between gigs in Asia. He heard her sing and fell in love. That happened a lot with Saint Anne; only this time she saw something in this man that made her want to love him back. Alex had the body of a professional football player. Muscles in the upper legs that rippled in a dozen spots with each step. Upper shoulders and arms that looked as if they'd been cut out of redwood trunks. His blond hair curled over his ears. And Alex had alert blue eyes, eyes which seemed opened out on some perpetual circular pattern from the line of scrimmage, waiting for the ball and watching the defense. Eyes that projected motion, concentration, and suspended fear.

Alex played three seasons with the Oakland Raiders as a wide-receiver. In that respect Alex and Peter were very much alike. Competition was the centerpiece of their life. The hologram of a geological time was alive inside their minds. Inside their dreams. Then he got injured; a knee injury and he was out of his football uniform and into a suit and tie job at a public relations firm. You see the idea in the back of Saint Anne's mind was that Alex, being a football star, was going to give her the lift, the exposure to hit the big time. Only he got injured before that happened. It changed things between them. I could see that but I never said anything to her. Injury or not, Alex had had one thing Peter envied. A glorious past. A reputation as someone who had played in the big leagues that counted in America. Alex had had more than his fifteen minutes of celebrity status.

He missed playing the game. When his life folded over like a newspaper, it never occurred to him that football would not be written on the other side. That Alex Walker would not have some chance of remaining connected to football. Of course, he played in pick-up games of old-timers on Saturdays in Central Park. But he had to be careful of his knee and that slowed him down. But it did not matter. He lived a lifetime on those afternoons in the park. Elizabeth and I would take Lucy to watch Uncle Alex run his patterns from the wide-receiver position. Then Alex left New York suddenly. He became a person Saint Anne only talked about in the third person. Never using his name, never wanting any of us to mention Alex. Even little Lucy was not to ask after Uncle Alex. He had gone to Paris, alone, with only a carry-on bag, and a job as coach of a start-up football team in a two-bit league. Alex left these shores in mid-May, reappearing on the Rue du Renne as the genus North Americanus Footballis. He had done what Father had sworn us never to do: he abandoned the family. Alex had done what her momma and papa had done and Saint Anne could not forgive him for that hurt.

Peter saw his opportunity, picked up the fumbled football, so to speak, and continued the play-by-play with Saint Anne. For a long while Saint Anne was like a wary, fine-boned exotic bird afraid to fly; afraid of entanglement; worried about getting caught in the wires of another marriage. Alex had gone through a mid-life crisis; and, as far as we knew, he was doing diagrams of plays on napkins at Le Dome. But then we were shut out. Saint Anne wanted it that way. After Memorial Day, Peter, who had always been very proper with Saint Anne, made his play on the beach, beside his wind-surfer, on the Bay side of Dune Road, on a cool night not long after Alex split. And for a while both Jack and I felt that Saint Anne had found some solace in the difficult time after Alex, to use Saint Anne's words, fled with his ego and a few shirts and socks.

Peter, to give him his due, was instrumental in her recovery. He guided Saint Anne through the natural disaster of Alex Walker's departure, but never disclosing his own complicity. Because Peter spoke English like any other New Yorker from the 212 exchange, it was difficult to remember that he came from France. That most of his family was still in Paris. That he had an uncle who thought if the no-nonsense English could go mad over American football, then why not the French? Peter had played his cards close to his chest; and he played them well, knowing exactly what was at stake. In effect, he exiled Alex and his beleaguered dreams for selfish reasons. He wanted to beat Alex. Take away something that had been his for a very long time. His wife, our sister, Saint Anne, with the six-inch scar on the sole of her right foot. A fact that wouldn't come out until the end of the summer. And by then Peter was dead and no one wanted to speak ill of the dead.

THE building we owned in SoHo was built in the nineteenth century for manufacturing. That meant it was built for machines and people who worked on machines. Those who built it never thought that one day the machines would be unbolted from the floors and ceilings and people would pay huge sums of money for the privilege of living on a renovated factory floor. When we bought the building, the last owners were needle manufacturers and merchants of other people's needle products. Needles are the oldest technology. With computers evolving every few months it is difficult to believe that we still have tools that have barely altered over thousands of years. The old owners told us there would have been no progress without the needle. We'd still be swinging from trees, painting our faces blue, and living off berry bushes. Baying at the moon. The computer and the space shuttle came about through the eye of the needle, they said.

The evolution of man leaped forward with the discovery of fire, the wheel, and, of course, the needle. We heard hours and hours of this theory of humanity from the owners as we negotiated over the price. When the old owners finally had gone, we discovered left behind, piles of samples. An entire history of needles in the cupboards on the ground floor. They'd been the American distributors for James Smith & Sons, an English company established in 1698, at a time when there probably wasn't a single steel needle in all of Manhattan.

The jargon of needles rivals that of the law. There are Sharps, Betweens, Milliners, Crewels, Cotton Darners, Tapestry, Chenille, Yarn Darners, Long-Eyed Bookbinders, the saddlers' awl, the stabbing awl, curved harness needles, curved billiard needles, sail needles, shoemaker's needles, sack needles, elliptic gold eye needles, beading needles, mortuary needles, tattoo needles. Before the computer and the information age, clearly the needle held most things together, from our shoes to ships, bags, clothes, curtains, to name a few. Sometimes one can have a little too much inside information about things.

For example, the intimate relationship of all manner of different needles to the preparation of dead bodies for burial. When Peter Montard had managed to get himself killed, Jack went to the cupboard and sorted through the large boxes of discarded needles. He knew he had the right sample right away from the large red cover and the words "Made in Germany" on the front. Unlike the English companies which always put the name of the needle above each page of samples, the Germans used simply a number. The "B/6545" or "B/6526" for the purpose of ordering over two dozen different mortuary needles. There's something very German in such precision, about knowing the exact number of stitches you need to sew up slaughtered bodies.

Until one flips through all the needles used to deal with the dead, it's not possible to have a good idea of the range. At the end when there's no one else around watching; when there aren't professional mistakes per se that mean anything. The night Peter died, I caught Jack downstairs in his bathrobe, holding a flashlight over the German mortuary needle samples. He pulled out the largest—the B/6545—a needle which vaguely resembled, in size and shape, the curved wing on a pair of eyeglasses. The last inch tapered to a precise, sharp point. The eye of the needle could be stuffed with thread which almost crossed the line into the smaller sizes of rope.

"That's the one they'll have to use on Peter," Jack said, shining the flashlight on the needle. "I've looked through them all. I'm quite certain it must be this B/6545. Of course, I could be wrong. But I don't really think so."

"God, it's horrible," I said. That was one of the biggest motherfucking needles I had ever seen.

"I just knew you'd agree with me. I told Heather you would. I can't tell you how delighted I am. Not about Peter, of course. Although we both know he was wrong for Saint Anne. But finding this exact needle is significant, you know."

"I don't get you."

Jack looked at me, his skin coppery color under the flashlight. He seemed wounded that I didn't understand why at two in the morning I found him roaming through my studio looking at needles.

"Because, at the funeral, we'll be—just the two of us, though, with your permission, I want to tell Heather—we'll be able to know how they did it. That is, assuming they have an open coffin service. Which I think they should. If you have any influence on Saint Anne, please suggest an open coffin. Peter's friends can't pay their proper respects with the lid closed. You want that last look. Not out of curiosity; that's morbid. But just to say good-bye. And, of course, when you and I look, we can give the mortician a little nudge and whisper B/6349."

"B/6545 is the right number."

"Yes, you're quite right. I was just testing you to see if you are still awake. I think I will play that number on the lottery."

"Sometimes, I think you're twisted, man."

Jack stared down at the needle again, grinning and carefully put it in the pocket of his Chinese silk shirt. Then he repeated the number B/6545 to himself several times. Finally, the number still on his lips, he disappeared up the stairs, shining his flashlight like a beacon and murmuring the number to himself in Chinese. Only then did the function of the object become real.

PETER Montard, that one time he broke his rule about always making an appointment, dropped past my studio without any warning. He sat on my well-worn sofa, leaned forward at the waist, and examined the contents of a large glass which served as my counter. Inside, I displayed a collection of antique cameras.

"Who's hot?" he asked.

I am thinking he didn't come around to ask me a question which he could have asked over the phone. But I decided to play along.

"Magritte uses lots of fire," I said.

He shook his head, smiling. Then came a variation of his usual question. "You know what I mean, Gideon. What's a good investment? You see, the stuff coming in and out, who's the next Jasper Johns? The next Magritte?"

"Hey, don't ask me, man. I don't have the inside track. The stuff comes in. I photograph it, and then it's gone. Down a rathole somewhere in Jersey or the Lower East Side."

"Keep an eye out for me. For a star-to-be. I'd like to get something special for Saint Anne. A surprise gift for your sister. Before I get her face on the cover of People magazine."

Given the nature of Peter's death, I often thought about this conversation. Especially the part about "a surprise gift." That was my first reaction. Peter had been expelled from life in midtown Manhattan by a kind of surprise happening. But Saint Anne didn't see his death as a gift; she saw in her mind People magazine without her picture on it. I saw a kind of genius for dying. That surprised me most about Peter Montard, looking back on the events preceding his final day on earth. Bastille Day. Perhaps that was the only genius left in the twentieth century. An instant, smooth way of cutting out. Without going through all the halfway houses. Dwelling for a while in pain, then hope, checking into despair, descending bit by bit, into the shadows which had no names.

Red Sky Falling

IN the hallway of our five-bedroom house that overlooked English Bay in Vancouver, Father had hung a framed original letter written by the hand of Napoleon. Behind glass and with a delicate cherrywood frame, the letter was short and to the point. And at the very end was Napoleon's signature. Across the hall was a grandfather clock that chimed, and when I was small I'd stand on tiptoes and look at the reflection of Napoleon's signature inside out on the tiny bodies of pink faced cherubs. The content of the letter was mundane; like most of Napoleon's life, the fine details of running an army. On our wall an obscure French officer named Louis Lacharite had been granted a commission in the army. It was the one thing from the house that Saint Anne wanted after Mother and Father died. Saint Anne's nature drew her to the idea of artifacts from famous people, thinking, like a lot of people, that if you own such objects the fame rubs off on you. Perhaps it was Napoleon's ability to be in control and get himself famous at the same time. She hated the notion of chaos and being ordinary which was the same thing in her book. Random, irrational arguments, theories, or people. So the way Peter died engaged a deep loathing, and made her vengeful.

The day Peter Montard dropped past the studio unannounced and began asking about fast access to the new masters, I mentioned the story about the Napoleon letter. If he really wanted to work up a little surprise, something a little special for Saint Anne, I suggested that a rare letter, preferably by a famous singer, would do the trick nicely. I had seen some framed letters written by the likes of Janis Joplin and Billie Holiday and I knew that Saint Anne would have loved anyone who bought her a letter by one of those singers. And I gave him the address of a specialist, a collector who had his offices in midtown and sold rare books, prints, and letters. Someone totally reliable. His prices were fair, and his knowledge comprehensive. As it turned out, I sent Peter Montard to his death.

5

Jack was fond of saying that he lived outside of time. He refused to wear a watch. He ignored clocks and other people's watches. That's the main reason I never got a signed photograph from Muddy Waters. Jack had been four hours late. The concert was long over by the time he showed up. Ignoring time was Jack's thing. Only he had two exceptions to his time phobia—around the World Series and the opening and closing of the Hong Kong market—then he would ask what time it was. In Jack's first marriage, his wife never adjusted to the complex qualities of a life devoid of any concept of promptness. Jack lived like ancient man who tracked the stars, moon and sun. Heather said he figured out the time in large blocks like the seasons.

He might eat dinner at ten or at three in the morning; he might fall asleep on the sofa in my studio, with nineteenth-century samples of needles spread out all over the floor. Everyone else in the world moved from the present into the future according to measurements of minutes, hours, and days. Without any structure, schedule, or regularity, Jack came and went according to his instincts, driven by his senses, and totally absorbed with any person or object—much like a child—which he happened to find in his way. Elizabeth believed that, in substantial ways, our daughter had no better playmate than her Uncle Jack.

No one in the family ever waited a meal for Jack to show up. Whenever the urge of hunger crept over him, he fired up his wok in the kitchen and stir fried vegetables, cooked a pot of rice, or wandered through the house with a bowl beneath his chin, using chopsticks like a shovel. Jack was forever late for movies, plays, airplanes, dates, concerts, and each time he offered the most sincere, impassioned apology. There was always a compelling reason for his lateness or his failure not to appear at all. Invariably someone or something distracted his attention.

A typical Jack excuse for being late happened on his twenty-first birthday. He decided that it would be absolutely wonderful to celebrate the big event at the place of his conception.

"And how do you know where that was?" asked Saint Anne. "You don't even know who your real mom and dad were."

"Dear girl, I asked a professional seer. And why not? Aren't you curious? Whether it was in the back seat of an old Buick? Against the kitchen sink? Inside the fridge? Behind a rice paddy?"

"Man, you know I don't believe in that seeing into the past, peeking into the future trip. Those guys are grifters, fraud-slime. They take your money and tell you any old story. You know that, Jack," I said.

Jack turned around to face me, with a broad smile. "I didn't ask just anyone. I asked Arnold Keene to find out and told him he would get a lot of money if he helped."

Wowee, I thought. The Seattle lawyer with the judge in his pocket was still alive and coming up with schemes to make money. Jack had tracked him down, and Keene never had thrown out a single file in all his years of practice. He must have figured that one day there might be another pay day lurking inside one of those manila folders and Jack proved him right.

"You know about my mom?" asked Saint Anne.

"I got the goods on all of us."

"You should have asked before you started digging. Maybe I don't want to know about those people who threw me away," said Saint Anne.

"Then I won't tell you," Jack grinned.

Everyone was interested in their roots, where they came from, who were those people who brought them into the world before they drove off into the sunset. Saint Anne was no exception though she pretended she was. I didn't have her kind of pride.

"You're playing with our heads, Jack," I said. "Come on, tell me where I was conceived. Not that I believe for a moment Keene ever knew that."

"Let's forget it. It doesn't matter."

"Okay, okay. You're playing with us, Jack. Let's get it over. Where was I conceived?" asked Saint Anne

"Playing? I am having a birthday party."

Saint Anne rolled her eyes. "Have it your way, Jack. We don't want to know."

He giggled, trying to draw out the tension.

"In a brothel. We were conceived in a house of prostitution," he said.

Everyone went kind of silent, wondering whether Jack was sad or happy about this place of origin. And Saint Anne and I weren't any too sure about what he had to say about us either; we weren't exactly the All-American example of conception places—whoring, fishing and watching the movies.

"Keene might have lied to you," said Saint Anne. "Fed you any story just like Gideon said."

"I checked it out with some other people and they confirmed the basic facts. Not every last detail, mind you, but the essence of the story and that is what counts. And that cost a lot of money but I think it was well spent," Jack said.

"You mean you know who those people are?" I asked.

Jack shrugged. The question didn't seem important to him but I could see from the way that Saint Anne was shifting her weight from foot to foot that she was dying to find out about who her real momma and papa were.

SOME of my artist clients squeezed paint directly from a tube onto the canvas; others used a knife, a teaspoon. One used a tuning fork. While others used their fingers, toes, elbows, lips, hair, cigarette holders, and the occasional light concealed weapon. Were they any good? Black people who did this kind of thing on subway walls or private buildings got their ass hauled away to jail. These people, most of whom were white, called it art and took what they had done as seriously as any minister preaching at the front of a church. Lucy had a better eye for design, color, and composition than most of the people calling themselves artists. After a couple of years looking at this stuff through a camera lens, I admit that my line of judgment had gone blurry. One never knew what the wind would blow in. A caricature. A kite cut loose from a light pole. A bundle of old newspapers pasted together and framed. A soccer ball with darts glued in. Cookies made of marble. Scissors of glass. What was in the stores one year appeared on canvases the next. Some of the pieces I had to keep in the fridge so they wouldn't melt and turn to goo.

"You don't believe in genius?" Peter asked that afternoon, sipping coffee from a paper cup.

"I believe there is a difference between good and great. I can't tell what genius has got to do with it and I don't think anyone knows. Artists want to be stars. Like Saint Anne wants to be a star. She's real glad that you are going to help her get her face in People magazine. Maybe get her on MTV with a video."

"You think she's great?"

Man, I hated that question, especially about my own sister. How can you make a judgment about someone you grew up with? You either know too much about them, or not enough. Peter had another fresh orange-colored disklike patch on the top of his left hand. The afternoon light hit it like a bicycle reflector as he smoothed down the ends of his mustache. He was waiting for an answer.

"Only time will tell. It ain't up to me. It's for others to say. She's my sister, man. You ever hear anyone admit they thought their sister was great?"

From his attitude, those slightly moist wind-surfer eyes, he appeared to disagree. He took in my worth, assuring himself that anyone who invested so much faith in instinct over reason probably was not a reliable source of investment information.

FOR Jack's twenty-first birthday that year he bought Saint Anne and me first-class tickets to Seattle. With Keene's help —we found out later Keene wasn't required to do a lot of digging—Jack had located the old house where he had been conceived and since he had hit some money in gold futures and was flush he had decided this was the way to have to some fun. He rented the entire house—which was no longer a brothel—for us to have a party.

The two-story white frame house with a large, gray porch, the paint peeling off and exposing the wood beneath, was still a rundown rental property. It had not been a brothel house for years. It was in a bad neighborhood which looked like it could be the location for a TV-movie about drive-by shootings. Seattle had changed, the power structure, the power brokers, who could be paid off and what judges were in whose pockets—none of it was the same. The old house was now occupied by an extended family of Mexicans who worked as gardeners on the grounds of some of Seattle's most distinguished homes. Jack paid the Mexicans a large sum of money to clear out for two days and two nights. Keeping their part of the bargain, the Mexicans slept in cars, under makeshift tents, and wrapped up in wool blankets under the wide open skies in the back garden. We were forever stepping, climbing, or jumping over Mexicans for the entire stay. None of us had been back to Seattle for years. The city had grown. Most of the houses looked about the same. Except our house had been painted gray, the front garden had been covered with pitch.

Jack had got the idea of meeting up in Seattle one night from a fortune-teller who said one of his ancestors had a restless soul. This ancestor had been murdered in a country where the long-nose people lived. That was America.

The three adopted Harvey children returned to that strange old house stinking of stale beer, cat piss, and walnuts—the shells were scattered everywhere. We celebrated Jack's birthday in the exact fashion that he'd wanted. A local bakery made a three-layer chocolate cake with thick, white icing, and Saint Anne and I stuck on twenty-one tiny candles. Jack sat on the edge of the bed with the lights off, watching the candles burn; Saint Anne knelt on his left side, and I on his right. He chanted a prayer in Chinese, and we watched, without saying a word, as the candles burned down on the cake. The smell of burnt icing filled the small bedroom. One by one, the candles extinguished themselves and melted through the icing. At that moment I felt that something had changed in Jack; maybe in all three of us, but this new mood didn't stop Jack from carrying out some rituals—ones he had picked up from Mr. Ling who had spent a couple of years in a Buddhist temple after he fled China.

"What are you doing, Jack?" I asked.

"Making merit for all the whores who once lived here," he said.

"How you gonna do that?"

"I thought about burning a candle for each of the girls who worked here. But that could be a ship load of candles. So I decided to set birds free instead. That way they will be reborn into a better life. Three girls in particular."

I thought about this for a while. "Why three girls, Jack?"

His face looked like a Cheshire cat after it had eaten a big rat.

"Gideon, my brother, nothing much is ever lost on you."

Now Saint Anne was listening, drumming her fingernails on the window pane.

"Aren't you going to answer him?" she asked.

"For each of our mothers. My Mother, Gideon's mama and Saint Anne's mum, all were working girls. They were friends. More than friends, they were like sisters. Like we are brothers and sisters."

"You mean my mother . . . ?" Saint Anne couldn't finish her sentence.

"Yes, your mother."

"She was a . . . ?"

Before Saint Anne could say whore, Jack held up his hand.

"Stop. Don't say it. She was your mother."

"Jack, man. Don't fuck with us like this. If this isn't true, then it's a bad thing you are doing." I meant it, too.

He looked a little hurt.

"You think I would lie about something like this?"

Saint Anne was crying, rubbing her eyes with her fists balled up like a baby's.

"I thought Mother said we had been abandoned," She sobbed. "At least that was romantic."

And there I was thinking that I had been thrown away and the Harveys had rescued me from a garbage can where my real mama had left me.

"Family histories die hardest of all histories written by the winners," said Jack. "But there's nothing to cry about. We should celebrate these noble women."

"What's noble about being a whore?" asked Saint Anne, finally finding a way to work the word into the conversation.

"You judge too quickly," said Jack. I must admit I was on Saint Anne's side, thinking noble had to be a bad choice of words. I wanted my parents wicked, evil, unfeeling creatures who had conceived me in passion and then didn't take any responsibility once the passion had cooled. Jack was right—this was hard to let go of and feel anything but full of rage at having believed in a lie all those years.

"These three women stood up to the brothel owner." Jack was feeling our hostility but that didn't stop him from explaining what was on his mind. "Other women who worked here had become pregnant. But these three were the only three who didn't get rid of their babies. Abort the occupational problem. Keene was not just a lawyer. He was a property owner. He owned an interest in a company which had title to this house. He told our mothers they didn't have to go through with an abortion. But. And this was a big but, they had to give up their babies and keep on working, or it was out on the streets. I would say, that was no ordinary love. By making a stand and giving us life, they acted in a noble fashion. It's how Saint Anne got her name. According to Keene, some of the other girls who had worked in this house with her said that having that child had cost her a lot of money. That must be some kind of a special child to throw away so much cash. 'Not a child, but a saint,' one of them had said. 'Yeah,' your mother agreed. 'She's a saint. She's Saint Anne. And she's gonna do good and be famous and rich and happy, not like her real mother.'"

Whether Arnold Keene ever heard such a conversation is open to question. Jack swears the old man told him. I believe he likely did but that doesn't mean Keene was present when those girls were talking—because it sounded like the kind of girl talk that women don't use around men—or if he had been around the brothel all those years ago, the events and conversation would have become confused, blurred, running together over time. Jack had paid Arnold Keene a lot of money for this information. Why wouldn't he want Jack to feel he had received value? These were some of the questions I had and kept to myself. Because Saint Anne liked the story. It was better than the one Mother had told her. That her mother was Vietnamese and that she had once been a famous singer in Saigon.

What was likely true, however, was that the Harvey Trio had sprung from the same whorehouse. And we were standing in the very room where our mothers had likely worked. That was something. I started looking at everything differently, the carpets, the wallpaper, the lamps and the bed. We sat on the edge of the bed, wondering how much of this Father and Mother knew when they adopted us. In the end, it didn't much matter if you were conceived in a short-time sex-for-money transaction or in a traditional family, you have a life, one you carry on your back into the future, one you make yourself.

About a hour later a delivery truck from a pet store arrived with bird cages. There were about forty cages stuffed with exotic, foreign birds—parrots, parakeets, finches, cockatoos, a falcon, two pelicans, humming birds, and some nightingales. There were other rare birds I didn't have a name for and only glimpsed as they fluttered past in a whirl of feathers and screeches into the hallway. The men in the truck carried all those cages up to the bedrooms. Jack gave them a large tip.

"What are you doing with all those birds?" asked Saint Anne.

"I am going to give them freedom. That's how you make merit. After I saw the fortune-teller I took the advice of a monk on how to release the wandering spirit of my mother."

"But those song-birds don't want freedom," said Saint Anne.

Wowee, I thought. Was that a telling remark from a singer!

"Every living thing wants to be free," said Jack.

"They'll die out in the open. Cats will eat them. Other birds will kill them. You will have murdered them."

"That's up to them," said Jack, opening the window in one of the bedrooms and opening the cage door to let a half dozen nightingales fly out.

"The fortune-teller said an ancestor's spirit, he didn't say anything about your mother being dead."

Jack had been waiting for this moment, planning for it ever since he got on the airplane in Singapore. "She was murdered."

"Jack, that's not funny," said Saint Anne.

"Some say it was an accident."

"Don't fuck around with us like that, Jack," I said.

He pulled out a stack of newspaper clippings and laid them out on the bed. They were old and yellowish. I picked one up and started to read a story about how three prostitutes from Seattle had died in a sailing accident in Peugeot Sound. It had been real foggy, there had been a squall out of the northwest. Other reports were about the police investigation and the possibility of robbery. A medical expert found bruises on two of the bodies which had suggested a struggle and violence. Another article raised speculation that the women, who were local prostitutes, had been part of a drug ring and had been killed by foreign smugglers. Looking through all the clippings with Saint Anne was one of the hardest things I had ever done. She was sobbing, wiping away the tears.

"That is a picture of your momma," said Jack, pointing at the photograph of a young girl in one of the newspaper clippings.

It was the first picture Saint Anne had ever seen of her.

He didn't have to point out mine; I saw her, also for the first time, a beautiful black girl with big, laughing eyes.

"The authorities finally ruled it death by misadventure," said Jack.

"Meaning that they decided to stop asking questions and close the case," I said.

"My mother was murdered," sobbed Saint Anne.

Jack put an arm around Saint Anne.

"I talked with one of the girls who worked here with our mothers. Her name is Janet. She's fifty now but she remembers them. She remembers the night they died. She said those girls had gone to some lawyer on a Monday asking to get their babies back. They had made up their minds they had made a bad mistake putting them up for adoption. The next thing she knew it was Friday and they were dead. Drowned in the sea. Janet thought someone killed them. She didn't say anything to the police. She was real sorry she had kept quiet all these years. But then she was young and all she knew was if someone could kill three girls just like that, they wouldn't have any trouble killing her. And what would have been the point? Who would have believed her? No one."

"Who was the lawyer?" I asked.

Jack stopped smiling. "Janet couldn't remember. I know what you are thinking. I asked her if it was a lawyer named Arnold Keene. Her face was blank. She never knew the name to forget it, she said."

"What can we do, Jack?" asked Saint Anne.

"Make merit to release their spirits," he said.

"I'd rather release the spirit of the asshole who did this," I said.

The next morning when Saint Anne and I had our bags packed and at the door, Jack was still cross-legged as we'd left him the night before. The rooms smelled of bird shit and there were feathers all other the place. Some of the birds were flying around inside the rooms and hallways, others perched inside their cages. Something in the merit-making scheme didn't seem to have gone quite as Jack had planned. His stubble of beard glistened in the sunlight. That huge bulbous forehead was reddish, small veins near the surface pressed against the skin like some kind of underground irrigation system. The sort of head that appeared to most like an oversized mental storage tank, filled with calculations, information, facts, objects, perceptions, and instincts. Jack's looked like they'd been generating extra power throughout the night. A solar panel groaning with energy.

As we walked back into the bedroom, Jack looked up at Saint Anne for a moment, reached out and touched her hand. Jack was wearing an old cloth cap which made him look like a gamekeeper. The gray speckled wool cap, with a cloth bill, was on the back of his head.

"Come on, Jack, let's get out of here. Go back home."

"Not till they are all free," said Jack. He was in one of those moods where you would have needed a forklift truck to get him off the bed.

"Saint Anne's right, some of these birds don't want to go outside, Jack. They are inside birds." No amount of argument was about to change his mind.

"There's another flight tonight. I don't want to go this morning." His eyes shone with happiness.

"But the place is going to be crawling with Mexicans in about an hour," said Saint Anne. She started to pick at the fleshy part of her right palm; a nervous tick of hers whenever she sensed danger. "Some of them might be bird eaters."

"Don't worry so much, Saint Anne," said Jack, looking at the uncut birthday cake. "And by the way, thank both of you for an excellent birthday party last night. It was truly wonderful. I could feel the spirit of our mothers very close."

"I'm not going to let my mama down," said Saint Anne. "I'm gonna be famous just like she wanted. Then I'm gonna use the money to find the cocksucker who killed her."

"Of course you will," said Jack. "It's your destiny."

With the sound of walnut shells breaking underfoot we left the house and Jack inside.

To my way of thinking, it was not in anyone's cards to be famous. Most of the time it was blind luck. Being in the right place, at the right time, with the right friends and a teaspoon of talent. That's not saying someone who is great doesn't make it despite the odds. But I have never been able to figure out where that greatness thing comes from—destiny, genes, brain chemicals, or a way of dealing with some big hurt that swells up inside like a mountain and the only way to level off that mountain of pain is to develop greatness.

Several days after Saint Anne and I returned home, we still hadn't any word on Jack's travel plans. Finally, Susan, his wife, flew out to retrieve her husband. She found him cooking Chinese food for a dozen Mexicans ranging in age from three months to eighty-one years old. One of the Mexicans had taught a parrot to say "Jack" with a Mexican accent. Another freaked out finding a pelican under his bed. One of the Mexicans' dogs had jumped on the bed and eaten the birthday cake; but not before smearing icing over the walls and floors. Several cats had eaten a few birds.

The Mexicans loved him nevertheless and told him about this young guy they did gardening work for who had all these comput- ers. The guy was Bill Gates, and Jack bought about ten thousand shares of Microsoft when no one in America could have told you whether it was an ice cream or panty-hose company.

The odd thing was that Jack had no sense of how long he'd been in Seattle or how long it had been since Saint Anne and I had left. He had had a birthday party, bought out a pet store, purchased shares in a software company no one had heard about. But he felt refreshed. After Susan washed him up, dressed him, and got him out to the airport, they had a fight over birds he carried on as hand luggage. He had this idea of setting them free in Vancouver. Jack insisted on holding the cage; Susan insisted it was dirty, the birds were diseased. A few thousand feet over British Columbia, Susan told Jack she was leaving him for good. She didn't care if her

Uncle Ling lost face—he had arranged the marriage over Father's objection that Jack was too young—and nothing or no one was going to change her mind.

"She told me, poor girl, she couldn't live this way any longer," Jack reported to us over a week later. By then the decision to divorce had become official. Susan had all of her things in Vancouver shipped back to Hong Kong, and we never saw her again.

"What the hell does that mean?" asked Saint Anne.

"Susan thinks my sense of reality is unhealthy," he said with a smile. "What a silly girl. You would never know that she was mainland Chinese. Still, there are other fish in the sea."

PETER'S death was so spectacular that it was carried on the six o'clock news. The anchor woman squirmed in her padded swivel chair. A slight shiver. But visible enough in the muscle along her neck to send a chill through the viewing audience. By news time Saint Anne had taken four Ativan and watched the story in a stupor. Jack had the Mets baseball on television and was talking Chinese to a broker in Singapore. He watched the local New York City news like it was a movie of the week. He said that Asians didn't have the same hang-up about death; dead bodies were something to be marveled at closely. A Korean greengrocer mugged in Harlem, a shooting on the IRT, a baby dropped out of a window on Flatbush Avenue, an old-age pensioner stabbed with a switchblade knife for her handbag. These scenes put Peter's death in a broader context.

As I watched the news report, I felt Peter's blood on my own hands. Television witnesses death in a special way. The camera lens feeds on the mess surrounding sudden, violent death. A still body collapsed in an odd angle. Pools of blood. Stained, rumpled clothing. In most cases the only suggestions of death that remain are the police chalk marks outlining where the body had come to rest. The camera eyes the empty shadows, and homes in on people milling around the moist red spot leaked by the victim. The body was hauled to the morgue.

But Peter's body, warm as a freshly slain bird, lay still on the sidewalk. A cluster of people stood heavily on their feet, their hands deep in their pockets. A chilled, perplexed expression on those street faces. Here and there an upper jaw extended; a cluster of small black children, hugging tightly to their mother's waists; with sweaty faces and watery eyes. A nervous kind of laugh that death can elicit. What distinguishes our species from most is that half-embarrassed, half-comic look on the faces of witnesses who have seen death close-up. An expression you'd never see on a spearfish circling a dead spearfish; a lion crossing the path of a dead lion, and so on. But in defense of the species, I'd say that we among all creatures understand that ordinary life is filled with many near misses. And when someone doesn't get out of the way in time. Well, there's a mess, and a body, a crowd, and television cameras, and those silly near-collision reports. Peter Montard had become the kind of New York televised death which stayed in the memory for a long time. The TV people played up Peter's show business connections. They got someone from the Estate of Jimi Hendrix, a spokesman for Sting, a guy who looked like Perry Como, and a new, hot rap group to come on camera and say how much Peter Montard was going to be missed, and what a good friend he had been and not to miss buying their new album. No one said they were going miss him making all that money for them but no one ever says that kind of thing when someone gets himself killed by a log in midtown Manhattan.

For the eleven o'clock news which recycled the earlier report, Jack had set up the VCR. He thought Saint Anne, not right away, of course, but one day, would want a permanent record of Peter's departure. She would have time to reflect on what Father used to say, that "danger alone acquaints us with our own resources."

I sat in Jack's sitting room beside Heather, his wife, who was smoking a large joint rolled from a dried banana leaf. The smoke rolled out of her nose and mouth, thick and gray and heavy. Tilting my head to the side, I watched the camera zoom in on Peter's body which was covered by a white sheet. I found myself looking at the creases made by his legs (everyone else was looking at the head). And I found myself thinking that if you turned him upside down his legs looked like a goal post. For a moment, I thought of Alex Walker, in full Oakland Raiders' uniform kicking a field goal through those legs. Three points. Not that he ever kicked field goals for the

Raiders but I saw him kick the ball through goal posts once in a pick-up game. I wondered if Peter's uncle had broken the news to Alex in Paris. The only other time I can remember Jack getting so excited over something on television was when the Toronto Blue Jays won the World Series for the second time.

Some hours after we had watched that news report, Heather switched on the all news channel by mistake (she had intended to watch Midnight Blues on Channel J). For a moment it was difficult to distinguish the two channels, because the news channel was running footage of bodies all bloodied in some marketplace. It looked like a crowd of peasants had got in the way of a mortar. Then the news reader cut in and started talking about how women and children had been killed. As Heather was about to flip over to Channel J, Jack, who, just at the crucial moment wandered past the television, asked her not to change the channel. He immediately phoned me.

"It's four in the morning, Jack," I said, looking over at the alarm clock and the empty spot left by Elizabeth. Two hours earlier I had phoned her with the news of Peter's death.

"Peter's no longer news. There are piles of bodies on the screen. Many in much worse shape than his. I wanted to pass that thought on to you, Gideon. I know that Peter's death and police questioning you and going down to the station was very trying for you. I thought this would cheer you up."

I was depressed, putting down the phone, thinking that Jack was never going to understand that foreign dead bodies don't matter all that much on American television. Living in those foreign countries they deserve to get themselves killed. That's what it comes down to. But Peter, he lived in America, and was just walking down the street and zap, a log put out his lights. That's not supposed to happen in America where you've got building codes, laws, regulations, inspectors, and skilled labor. When your time was up, then no amount of law or safety was going to protect you or give you a second chance. Jack kept saying that no amount of law was going to deprive fate of its due.

A few moments later Saint Anne phoned, her voice raw from lack of sleep, cigarettes and pills.

"You awake, Gideon?"

"Jack just phoned about some bombing overseas," I replied.

There was a long silence. Not one filled with tears for Peter Montard or sniffling or moaning. But the silence of the V2-engine cutting out over London during World War II. One of my lecturers talked about that silence and the pause between movements in music and how silence creates an expectation.

"I want my revenge. I want that kicker. Someone killed my momma and your momma and Jack's. No one ever paid for that crime. Someone is gonna pay this time. This one doesn't get away. You understand what I'm saying?" All I heard for the next moment was her inhaling on a cigarette.

"Don't let me down, Gideon."

I know what was going through her head. No MTV deal, no cover of People magazine, no big break into greatness. She was just gonna stay good, stranded on the fringe of show business like a kid with her nose stuck against the window of a candy shop. She was halfway into the shop when the door got slammed on her and now she was mad as hell. She was starting to sound like Father. When he would talk about the need for an instinct which delighted in war. Sir Francis Drake had it. Victory over pleasure was the motto. Saint Anne wanted the kicker. When Alex had been out of her life for nearly six weeks, she continued to exhibit the linguistic effect of a four-year marriage to a former professional football player.

6

One August afternoon, when I was still a kid, we had a family picnic on Spanish Beach. The Harvey family camped out on some blankets on sand. The summer sun warmed the inland waters of English Bay. We ate tongue sandwiches Mother had made and washed them down with cherry Coke. On the surface, we behaved at the beach like any other normal Canadian family. The Lion mountains, across the Bay, were mostly covered in a lush sea green. Here and there, were ugly mud-colored stains left by loggers who chiseled gorges along the mountainsides. Small clouds rolled a carpet of shadows over West Vancouver. Clusters of dense light edged against a swiftly moving gray, slender field of shadows creating temporary moments of twilight followed by bright sun. The land, sea, and mountain blended into shades of day and night.

Near where we sat, sea gulls circled near the water's edge, waiting to greedily devour any scrap of food left after a picnic. In the distance, on Grouse Mountain, the red gondola cars moved slowly along the trail of steel pylons anchored in rock and stone. Before us the sea, dotted with small sailing boats, remained a translucent greenish blue like you find on the scales of a carp if the sun hits it just right. Father, uncomfortable in a swimming suit, rested his chin on his knees as the sun beat down on the back of his neck. He slapped at a blackfly and missed, hitting his leg and leaving his fingerprints outlined in red. Mother rubbed more sun tan lotion on his neck and on his bulbous forehead.

His large friendly head turned red in the wind and sun. At age thirteen, I thought that ideas had coagulated in the membranous structures, bloated the network of fibrils and granules of the brain, and naturally pushed Father's head into a podlike shape. On the beach, with the angle of the sun overhead, I thought of the small waves sluicing against the shore as roughly equivalent to the tides inside Father's mind. Unless Father drained the right side of his brain daily, his cranium would burst and spew brains and gore half a mile. As my tension built, I asked Father what was on his mind. And his answer on that Sunday afternoon came as no surprise. He'd been watching the ships on the Bay and thinking of Drake. He got my attention by saying he thought Drake had some black blood in him but the historians had hushed it up. Wowee, I thought. This Drake was like me, so I listened to what Father had to say.

One thought had a hard, steel-like rind around like a shell, closed and mysterious. And that thought which exploded inside his enormous forehead was about Drake and the day he delivered his defiance to the Admiral of the Spanish Fleet immediately before the battle began.

"What's a defiance?" asked Jack, pouring a handful of sand over one foot. His English was more basic than the rest of us. That summer his habit was to ask for a definition, then translate the answer aloud to himself into Chinese and nod sagely.

"It's a challenge, stupid," said Saint Anne, sneaking another sandwich from the wicker basket on Mother's blind side.

"But what kind of a challenge," I asked Father.

"Yes, that is the question. What was the challenge?"

We all expressed mild surprise (though deep down, at least for me, it was a valuable insight that Father didn't know every single thing associated with Drake). Everyone had their turn at a guess about Drake's defiance. Apparently the answer had been lost to history.

"Someone slapped the Admiral's face or spit in his soup," said Saint Anne, chewing as she spoke.

"Don't talk with your mouth full," said Mother, biting into an apple. Saint Anne flushed, twisted away slightly, and with a troubled expression, began picking at the bright orange scar on the bottom of her right foot.

"Being English, maybe someone delivered an insult. Vile and disgusting like an American hot dog. History might have changed with the delivery of a bowl of healthy rice noodles." Jack looked up at Father, and from the squint of his eyes saw that Father was unimpressed.

"He was an Englishman," said Father. "Not an ex-monk, Chinese stockbroker."

"If you ask me, it was a threat. Someone threatened to hurt him, expose him. Blackmail and humiliate him into extinction," said Mother, pieces of McIntosh appleskin caught between her front teeth.

That made everyone laugh. Except for Father who sat grim faced, his hands shaking and staring straight at Mother, unable to chew or swallow what was in his mouth.

Finally he managed to say, "Blackmail is the most foul of all evil deeds."

The pressure of his question aggravated the tension between our Mother and Father, gathering force around the blanket, and the focus came to rest on one fixed point. I was half absorbed by a large flat-bottomed cloud curved at one end like a saucer gliding in from the sea, wondering how much black blood Drake had and whether it was from his mother or father's side and so I wasn't immediately aware that everyone was staring hard at me. I wrinkled my nose toward the sea breeze coming off the bay and reached down, picked up a small stone, and threw it into the water. When I glanced back at Father, he was waiting.

"Well, what do you think, Gideon?" he asked.

All I could see was a plumage of blue veins in Father's head. His chest swelling in and out. Sweat dripping down his side from beneath his arm. I stared at him for a long moment.

"Bad music. Someone played some bad music for the man. That was Drake's defiance," I answered. It was the first thing that popped into my mind and to this day I have no idea where it came from.

The tension evaporated and everyone was happy again. Jack doubled over with laughter on the blanket, balancing the weight of his body on his forehead. Saint Anne dissolved into giggles and dropped the rest of her secreted sandwich into the sand. Mother laughed so hard that she got goose flesh on her arms. At age thirteen that kind of laughter feels like pitching headfirst into the jaws of irredeemable shame. A two-dimensional universe where the worthless, useless, and brainless people are sucked into once they've been found out. In that knot of laughter, it took a few moments for everyone to realize that Father wasn't laughing. He sat upright on his knees, his hands outstretched to me. It was as if he'd looked at me for the very first time.

"How good bad music and bad reasons sound when one marches against an enemy," Father said, quoting Nietzsche. He reached over, extended his hand and patted me on the head.

"Of course, Gideon. That must have been it."

Jack punched me on the leg.

"You read it somewhere."

"Bet you did," added Saint Anne.

"That answer comes from Gideon's natural insight into the nature of man," said Father. "Mother, this boy is destined for a proper English education. I've been feeling that for some time. It won't be wasted on Gideon." If that wasn't a parental defiance cast among his children, it would be difficult to know what would be. I had proved myself—not just a man—but a scholar and classical musician in the eyes of my Father, and in the presence of my elder sister and brother. At thirteen I became Father's heir apparent. I was anointed as leader of the trio. I was the man. I was going to learn to play the piano for the concert hall and not for bars and lounges. Sibling rivalry being what it is, Saint Anne said one day everyone was going to be real sorry when she was famous and she wouldn't answer our letters or phone calls. That day on the beach in Vancouver, however, became a saddle that we all rode. Had I dropped out of eighth grade and become a lifeguard on the beach, somehow my position as the Harvey child who instinctively knew the right, off-the-wall answer to gothic questions was undisputed.

My acceptance, like an idiot savant whose only talent was playing the piano, changed the pattern of our expectations. Like a troughlike blade that scooped notes out of space, fully scored and arranged. So the notes registered in words became my specialty.

UNTIL the eighteenth century, revenge had the smell of old castle entrances and courtyards about it. Brown, yellow and black people never got any chance for revenge; they just had to take what happened when ships came and planted flags in their gardens. Revenge had a tinge of the Middle Ages; from a time when rank, title, dignity were hereditary. This was a time of ornamentation; of medieval craftsman. If life were the melody, then revenge functioned as the harmony in the daily sonata. Accepted as part of the messy struggle, with both sides committed to honor. Then the duel yielded the solution. In more ill-tempered, dangerous times, the grudge or quarrel has no place to go. Most of the theories on who killed John Kennedy and why were based on revenge. The day of my birth was a major revenge day event because of that man's death. Modern revenge was like jazz; it belonged to everyone all over the planet and everyone was taking their turn; it wasn't just the white people who had the right to avenge disrespect. When I had a phone call from Saint Anne a few hours after Peter's death and the subject of revenge came up I wasn't all that surprised. Born when I was, it seemed that revenge was my destiny. And I finally had got the call that I had been waiting for all my life.

She asked for my help. Who wouldn't throw a life preserver to their own sister? We'd always been there for the other person. Our loyalty was rooted in similar attitudes, values, and upbringing. Most of the time, except for a few odd cosmetic wrinkles, and although we were orphans delivered by a judge in the pocket, we thought alike. Saw things much the same way. Believed in the same components of daily living. This time Saint Anne and I were on different wavelengths. She desperately wanted revenge, and she tossed into my lap—as Father had done years before—the job of coming up with a sudden hard stroke of genius. Saint Anne, no doubt about it, wanted a life for a life. Not entirely different from Old Mr. Hedgecock's what-one-sows-one-reaps kind of reasoning.

The day after Peter's death, I headed down Broadway to Trinity Church, passed through the main gate about ten in the morning. Then cut across the cemetery and finally knelt down beside the marble bunker with Alexander Hamilton's name, date of birth, and death. He'd been killed in a duel with Aaron Burr. Hamilton had been only forty-seven years old. This illegitimate son from the West Indies had enough honor to face his opponent eye-ball to eye-ball. The man had black blood. He had been thrown away, too. He knew the pain of that, the burden of carrying yourself around with the knowledge those who gave you birth treated you like garbage. He died looking down the barrel of Aaron Burr's dueling pistol. What would he have done in my case?

❖

IN our age, the music changed when the duel was outlawed. Would Alexander Hamilton have invoked some higher law to write a new score? What would Alex Walker do? If he hadn't gone to Paris in the first place none of this would have happened. At that point, I started to feel self-pity. Hamilton's dust had lain undisturbed for years. No amount of beating my chest would raise an answer from his tomb. I lolled about for another thirty minutes in protracted confusion. Thinking first that Saint Anne was overreacting to the emotions of the moment, and once she had some distance from Peter's death, then she'd change her mind. At the same time, I had this desolate, lonely feeling of being on the edge of understanding something in her would travel beyond the full hurt she nursed at the moment. And I thought about the person who'd ended Peter's life as if it were a bad telephone connection.

When I told Jack about Saint Anne's decision to avenge Peter's death, he was in a deep tantric trance. I waited for a while and all he did was merely shrug his shoulders.

Then his eyes opened and he looked straight at me.

"I never figured you for a Jack Ruby type," Jack said.

"I'm being serious, Jack. The girl wants this done," I said.

He sighed, knowing full well the utter determination of Saint Anne once she had decided she wanted something. "It's not like ordering a Chinese take-out," he said. "But it can be arranged." The eyebrow over one eye arched. He had some Triad connection I didn't want to know about and told him so.

Jack pointed out the risks. And the duties. In Drake's time the warrior used a sword or spear. He wore armor into battle. A professional warrior didn't sneak up on an enemy and thrust the spear into the back.

"A defiance preceded the gore of a revenge," continued Jack. He sat back into the wheelchair, assuming his yoga position. Doing yoga in a wheelchair was a recent affectation. After an hour of deep meditation, Jack's eyes popped open, he rolled from one end of the loft to the other at maximum speed. Jack used the brake on the wheelchair to make a sharp right turn into his kitchen, and appeared a moment later peeling an apple. He stood up, the apple peel in one, long thin piece trailing behind him, and moved over to the window.

"I don't think that Saint Anne has a duel in mind," I said.

"She wants to hire an Italian thug who comes to our nightclub. The gangster has a crush on her. Why not let him take care of Peter's killer? Slice this person up into tiny bits and dispose of the bits. There is a good reason. It would be bad for business. The police might come around and ask questions. I don't want that, Gideon." Jack fed himself a piece of peeled apple off the knife blade.

"She wants us to do it," I said, sitting down in the wheelchair, and rolling it forward to the window next to Jack. In the street below, Parrot was barking at a beggar who had tried to piss against the side of our building.

"She wants you to do it." My brother looked at me with a wide smile. "She thinks blacks are better at this than Chinese."

"Don't give me that jazz. What was it that happened over there at Tiananmen Square? The Chinese machine-gunned a couple thousand dead in the street."

"That was politics, Gideon. This is revenge."

IT had been Jack's idea to take a taxi to Wanchai district for dinner even though we were all tired from three long sets at our hotel and Saint Anne and I wanted to stay in our rooms and order hamburgers and French fries from the room service menu. The owner of the restaurant, a friend of Mr. Ling, had invited Jack and he wanted his family with him, or it would be a big loss of face. So we went along, went into the small, dirty place with a few tables. Saint Anne and I looked at the menu, thinking about what to order, and seeing right away there were no hamburgers or fries. In Asia it was difficult to know if the menu was a bad translation of the local language or a literal translation and people really ate what the menu said.

"What is fat poured squid?" asked Saint Anne, screwing up her nose.

"Forget that, look at the special. Mixed frozen meat," I said. "No bun, no mustard, just frozen meat."

"What kind of restaurant is this?" asked Saint Anne. From the way that girl ate you would never have guessed she was half-Vietnamese.

Jack was lost in a serious Chinese conversation with the owner, and didn't acknowledge our questions over the menu.

What really caught my attention was something called crab soup with fish-sounds. Wowee. You can't make up anything that weird. About then some little Chinese guy with a dirty apron comes screaming out of the kitchen and shouting that the PLA was machine-gunning people in Tiananmen Square. I tried to order the crab soup with extra fish-sounds but no one was paying me or Saint Anne any attention. And I was thinking this is the one soup a musician should try at least once in a lifetime but it ain't gonna happen tonight. As it turned out Saint Anne and I ordered hamburgers and fries at our hotel. Jack stayed behind. He disappeared the night of the massacre, leaving no word with us and he didn't surface for five days. While Jack was gone, I played the piano and Saint Anne sang for five nights as the lounge filled up with foreign correspondents trying to get into China.

When Jack showed up at the hotel, he was all smiles, saying how he and brother time were never all that well-acquainted which was Jack's way of explaining why he was always late and could disappear for days without telling anyone. Then he told us that some changes were necessary.

"Like what?" asked Saint Anne.

"We are moving to New York," he said.

Saint Anne started to cry and he put his arm around her and told her that he was going to buy a nightclub for her in downtown New York so that she could continue her singing career in the Big Apple. "You want to be discovered, don't you?"

She nodded.

"Where better than New York City?"

"What about you, Jack? What are you going to do?" asked Saint Anne.

"Help my people find the American dream," he said.

WHAT Jack meant was that he had started a business smuggling boatloads of illegal Chinese immigrants into New York. And he had bought a club for Saint Anne and a photo studio for me. Jack said it was his mission in life to see that everyone's dreams came true. I believed him. And so did Saint Anne, until she started to doubt whether Jack and his nightclub was going to do the trick. That was a big trick, too. But years after Tiananmen Square she wasn't any more famous than the night we looked at a menu with crab soup with fish-sounds.

Jack was good at smuggling Chinese into America. We kept illegals in our basement as part of the underground railway, allowing the Chinese a way into the American dream. Jack sometimes reminded me that my mother's ancestors had used a similar pipeline around the time of the American Civil War. In America, it's not always easy to separate making a buck from doing the right thing. The thing Saint Anne wanted didn't have anything to do with profit making. She wanted to murder someone only to do the right thing. That seemed real American, too. But why would Saint Anne choose me as the instrument of her treachery? I didn't particularly like Peter Montard in the first place. What did I owe Saint Anne that hadn't been paid for many times over in the past?

"You must admit, Gideon. That on Saint Anne's side, Peter hadn't been given a defiance, either. And because she's a girl, and we are men, the duty falls on us. So shouldn't you avenge her? Look, I'm in a wheelchair." There was a slight tremor in his voice as he finished.

"Nothing wrong with your legs, man. You've been in the wheel-chair since Peter got himself killed so you'd have an excuse," I said.

"It's karma," said Jack.

"Fuck karma. I ain't killing anyone."

Saint Anne had been crippled by Mother and by school kids calling her a gook. And Jack had reversed his culture and raised himself on symbols and coordinates that isolated him from the mainstream west. I was the only one who hadn't been cramped or injured by what people said about me. "Hey, you boy." Or sometimes, "If you don't like it, you can go back to Africa." I ignored them and being good at the piano gave me a lot of slack with people. You get people singing and snapping their fingers, they aren't going to call you names, try and fight you. And because of that one small talent, one that had been improvised more than intended for me, it fell on me to help Saint Anne, and this was one way I could make right all the bad things and wrongs that had been done to her.

Sitting beside Alexander Hamilton's tomb in the churchyard of Trinity, I had remembered one very important historical fact. Hamilton, though he lost the duel, has gone down as the hero; and Aaron Burr lies dead in the earth as the villain. But I knew enough about life to know the seeking of revenge had lost any sense of heroism. All that remained was a mixture of warfare and community living. I thought about all those dead people killed in cities, villages, streets in Europe, Africa and Asia. There was murderous, hateful revenge on the television every night. Where had it gotten anyone in the world? What I couldn't decide on in the warm temperature at the graveside was the extent to which my sister's revenge of Peter's death was a hostile act towards his killer or towards the person who had killed her own flesh and blood momma. Those three young girls had gone sailing for a day and they never came back. No one ever revenged those girls because they were colored prostitutes. Jack's momma had been an illegal and so had Saint Anne's. My momma's people had been in America four hundred years but she had lived and died like an illegal. For Saint Anne it was time to make things right, to take a stand.

THAT same evening, I found myself at the Roundabout Theater with an extra ticket which a friend couldn't use. It was a play that Elizabeth particularly liked. Her father had a bit-role in the very same play in the mid-60s, and she had gone backstage where all the lead actors had made a great fuss over how beautiful she was.

During the intermission of Tom Stoppard's Rosencrantz & Guildenstern Are Dead, I went downstairs and into one of those old-fashioned restrooms the size of a football field. Huge white marble urinals that looked like converted pharaoh tombs carved out of solid granite. It always seemed like pissing on the dead. I retreated into one of the stalls, locked the wooden door behind me. A moment later, I noticed some writing on the wall. Writing in a sort of tomb scrawl.

Someone had written in neat, precise letters above the toilet paper dispenser in my stall:

"I was held at gun point for six hours. Now I will be forced to tell my therapist that wrote this on the wall."

What would the white Founding Fathers have made of this cry from the heart? Inside this small shelter to stumble upon not just a tangent of modernism, but the main shock wave of modern man. Pure helplessness. Alexander Hamilton had at the bare minimum laid claim to classical tragedy. All that this anonymous writer had spinning in the center of his cortex was a few gems from Freud. Instead of revenging his lost honor and attaining some value of what it meant to be a human being, he mortgaged his spirit to his shrink. At that moment, the answer to Saint Anne's question came to me. Just like it had that August Sunday on the beach in Vancouver. She had regulars who followed her around to the various clubs where she sang. You don't have to be famous to attract groupies; though it improves the quality of the groupies, that can't be denied. One of Saint Anne's admirers was a guy in the mob. The unions were controlled by the mob. One of those unions run by an ex-cop with an Italian name and who came to listen to her sing with a gun in his pocket. He always requested her to sing Sad Songs Make Me Cry. He gave her twenty dollar tips. He asked her out after she finished a set. She would go and sit at his table. He would ask her why she's not doing the ballrooms in Las Vegas, and why she wasn't on TV and in the movies. She had the looks and the voice for it. Asia was in and she should take advantage while everyone was looking for the first Asian mega-star in America. Wasn't she interested in applying for the job? Of course she had heard this kind of crap a couple of thousand times. It didn't mean anything for a customer who wanted to get in her pants to tell her how great she was. But being great was a whole different thing. Being good, you let cocksuckers like this Frank Cora into your pants. One night he told her not to worry about his gun. He saw that she was clocking the bulge under his arm. Packing a gun was an old habit left over from his twenty-six years on the police force. He didn't go anywhere without his gun.

"Does that include the shower?" she joked with him.

"It has rubber bullets for the shower," Frank Cora said. This was the one man who knew how to find the kicker.

"I thought they used rubber bullets in Northern Ireland and the Gaza Strip," said Saint Anne. "But I never heard of them in a shower."

"She's got a sense of humor," he said to his friends. They laughed because he told them to laugh.

She watched them laughing, thinking these are the same kind of guys who used live ammo in mother's homeland. But no one had lifted the embargo on the American desire to avenge that lost war.

7

Think of this Frenchman, Peter Montard, in his high-class tailored pinstripe suit, his button-down white shirt, the initials PM stitched over his heart, and on his feet—Wowee—a pair of hand-crafted imported Italian shoes anyone would die for. He was dressed to kill. Peter died within two blocks of the rare book, print, and letter seller that I had recommended where he would find the letter Jimi Hendrix had written—another black boy from Seattle. It was 4.27 in the afternoon. I had crossed Wooster Street with my plastic cup filled with ice and Coca-Cola. I had examined the King's College necktie worn by a dog named Parrot. About this same time, while I was downtown, kneeling beside this dog, taking a close look at the tie, Peter was walking his investment banker walk in midtown Manhattan with nothing more on his mind than pleasing Saint Anne. His path led him directly beneath a major office complex construction site.

There are many of these giant steel-framed structures scattered throughout the city. They are such a common feature that no one ever notices that they should be looking up rather than down and shouldn't be on the sidewalk period. But people take them as a normal part of big city life, forgetting that in a big city there ain't anything that a man or woman with a brain could call normal. Like most things in New York, you have to stop and actually think about what you are looking at although the people building on these sites leave clues. They write their warnings out in black and white for anyone to see; they have lawyers who tell them what to write, how big the writing has got to be, and what kind of scary pictures you have to include for people who can't read. Most of the time the danger is not obvious. Temporary walls screen off most of the action from sidewalk level.

For the most part, the activity is much the same at every construction location. Cement trucks are stacked up like planes over JFK Airport, these trucks have enormous rotating cylinders, and make a grinding noise as they wait on line to pour out a load of wet cement. Steel girders rise skyward. Piles of lumber and steel are stacked at the foot of cranes. Scores of men in hard-hats, sweat-soaked T-shirts, dirty jeans, and combat boots walk around the construction site, carrying tools, pieces of metal, wood, smoking cigarettes, stopping to scratch or to sniff the faint scent of perfumed air filtering from invisible women scampering under the scaffolding. These men are occupied behind the boarded-up spaces in the city, and the outsider would never know they were inside unless he stopped and looked through a hole in the wall. Sometimes they appear in entry holes where the trucks pass through. Or around quitting time, like coal miners, they appear in large packs, faces covered with a fine layer of filmy grime and dust. The metronome of hydraulic jackhammers follows them into the still of the night.

Peter was on the sidewalk, walking alone. And out of nowhere, without any warning, a wooden beam fell from about the thirtieth floor; it had been dislodged (I've tried to find a neutral word), beginning a descent to the street. Mathematically, the chances of that beam, a large piece of wood, hitting anyone at that time of day in midtown New York works out according to Jack to be about 1 in 32,876. The chance of it killing the person it hits is 1 in 114,962, give or take a couple of points. About the same chance of buying some obscure company stock in Microsoft and finding it ends up larger than IBM. In other words, the chances were small. Add one more variable. The chances of that beam decapitating, or, if you prefer, beheading, the person it hit is about 1 in ten million. The chances of getting AIDS, mugged, getting rich in the stock market, or run over by a taxi are much higher. But if you throw the variable of being beheaded in midtown New York on July 14th, on the French holiday, Bastille Day, then the probability is on the order of 1 in 100 billion. Less than the annual national debt, but nonetheless an impressive figure. Jack says that was destiny and there is no other way—even if you're not Chinese—to explain those odds coming in, and that's why he played the lottery with Peter's age, address, phone number, the address of the building site, and, of course, as I've already said, the needle number required to sew Peter's head back onto Peter's neck.

Peter Montard managed to get himself beheaded on West 58th Street in New York City. The law of probability personally caught up with him. Just as the probability of a major revolution finally pulled alongside the French aristocratic class. Peter's death, like his heritage, was very French in execution. The style, of course, was very American. Sudden, in public, and in New York. The only thing missing was a black teenager with a gun.

The French, who are great believers in the guillotine, maintain that a sharp blade cutting through the neck, skin, muscle, and bone is among the most humane ways to kill a person. No suffering results from the actual falling of the blade. Pressing the point, they might concede that there is a fraction of a second when the cold blade touches the skin of the neck. But is that suffering? Is that anything we could attach the label pain to? Or is it more like an ordinary flu shot? To be guillotined, they say, can be nothing more than a pinprick of sensation, followed by nothingness. There were French doctors who used to fish the heads out of the baskets and scream into the ear, "Can you hear me?" That was a scientific test about hearing, spinal columns, brain function, and some pretty strange notions of testing. The French are notorious chauvinists about their culture, language, wine, art; so there's little reason to believe anything they say about their custom of executing people. Common sense suggests that, at least for the living, it is substantially more gruesome than, say, the lethal injection preferred in many southern states.

In any event, Peter was spared what must undoubtedly rank among the worst aspects of being decapitated—the anticipation of placing one's neck in the wooden collar beneath the blade, and staring blankly down at the bottom of a wicker basket where what was staring would soon be stared at.

There was a downside, of course, to the absence of a container to catch Peter's head once the wood beam severed it from Peter's body. His head bounced, skipped, and rolled twenty feet away from Peter's body. The center of gravity of the head appears to be the neck because that is the only image that most of us have of the head; connected by the neck to the middle of the shoulders. Removed from this anchor of bone, muscle, ligament, cartilage, and skin, the head topples over onto its side. It is not very stable by itself.

Peter's head came to rest on two points: his right cheekbone and his chin, so that he looked downtown where his body lay in all that expensively tailored gear. The beam's rough, irregular cut made his neck area soft and boggy. His lips were slightly parted. The top row of his teeth, white as freshly picked cotton, were visible. He had the expression of someone about to hail a taxi. Intense and concentrated, his right eyebrow slightly arched. A slight stubble of a beard about thirty minutes away from a five o'clock shadow. Had any final thought flickered through his mind for a few seconds? Or does the engine shut down at once? With the chemicals and nerves still warm, if there were a chance of an image receding into Peter's nothingness, it must've been of a wind-surfer, the sail catching wind and heading seaward. But there was no one to pick up the head and scream into his ear, "Can you hear me? What are you thinking about?"

Peter's head didn't stay alone for long on the midtown pavement. Secretaries in short-sleeved dresses, office clerks in summer weight suits, actors, lawyers, agents, businessmen, flight attendants, tourists, and criminals were all in the immediate vicinity. Those who lived in the nether world of New York City started scanning for the camera crews, thinking Peter's head was a prop for a television series. Or maybe a commercial for an insurance company or a Stephen King kind of horror film. An exploitation film for fourteen-year-olds was invariably shooting somewhere in the city. There were those in the crowd who would've bet that the head wasn't real. That the body was a studio prop made in some FX lab according to specs given by a director from Europe. That the whole thing had the earmarks—no pun intended—of a special effect which was going to get broadcast on television because the entire world now thinks that there is no real violent death, seeing such things only on the tube when they are stuffing their mouth with take-out pizza or popcorn.

The New Yorker's reaction time before he or she recovers to non-television reality is normally two or three minutes. There is pride in that number. During that time dozens of people, keeping to themselves, avoiding eye contact with anyone on the street, walked around Peter. A man in his late sixties, a visitor from Iowa, knelt down beside Peter's head, then looked up at a small crowd which had collected around him.

"Someone had better call an ambulance," he said.

That's how they teach you to do it in Iowa City. Soon a couple of women in the crowd became emotional, started crying, "Oh, my God." One fainted. Another threw up between the sidewalk and the gutter. Finally, a young black courier stepped forward and put the shirt from his back over Peter's head. Leave it to a black kid to do the right thing and for the cameras to be filming something else.

The NYPD rolled in a few minutes later, then an ambulance, and the crowd was ordered to move along. The drama was all over. No more wind-surfing for this one.

You begin to understand why Jack was so hung up on playing around with the mortician's needle, B/6545. That needle had a precision hook; a loop of iron, more than what anyone would normally think should be engineered into a needle. A big thread hole for strong, durable cotton thread. Even so, it was risky business sewing the pieces of irregular neck back to the body. A study of French methods of execution, in the days before they abolished capital punishment, pointed out the difficulty of putting the severed head back on the victim. The flaps of skin turned purplish, and connecting everything back was a puzzle with some of the clues usually missing, left behind in the basket. One French expert from the eighteenth century said—and he was a doctor, or what passed for a doctor in those days—that the operation was like trying to get a champagne cork back into the bottle. It seemed like such a French way of thinking about the problem. "Hello, does this fit or not? Can you hear me? What are you thinking? Wink if you can hear me." I think Peter would've liked this turn of phrase.

I thought of Peter's departure in slightly different terms. I had known him for a couple of years, but not really known him if you know what I mean. He was one of those people you associate with, even have dinner and drinks with, and because he was doing business in Hong Kong with Jack, I would hear their frequent phone calls, but I didn't really know him. All I knew was that this guy had one great passion in life: wind-surfing. A passion that had about as much appeal to me personally as watching the fruit dry on the objects carted by clients into my studio. This yearning to ride a board back and forth across the Bay opposite Dune Road seemed a particularly lonely, solitary avocation. A means of putting distance between himself and companions. In ancient times, maybe Peter would've been a mariner. Maybe he would have stood shoulder to shoulder with Drake and watched him deliver the defiance to the Admiral of the Spanish Navy. Maybe. But I don't think Peter had any black blood.

What Peter's death made me understand was something about my own termination. Everyone's termination. It's rarely foreseeable but always inevitable. And the way Peter died, or to use Jack's creepy expression—the way he got his latch lifted—had a kind of cosmic fingerprint on it. What death really is, its shape and form, is the separation of the mind from the shell which imagines. What was inside might be like a silhouette without any point of view. I said to Jack, whatever you do about this don't go buying up cages of birds so Peter can get himself reborn into a better life. Peter had about the best life you can get born into and it didn't make any damn difference. Jack went kind of quiet and, in the end, he didn't buy birds, burn incense, pay for monks to chant in the loft. He just left it alone like all those deaths you see on television.

Alas, Peter Montard, as Saint Anne said after the funeral. It was one of Father's words she had never used before. It didn't sound right coming out of her mouth. But she recovered real well.

"He wasn't hit by a fucking meteorite. That beam came from fucking somewhere." That was more like Saint Anne.

Saint Anne was convinced beyond a lawyer's reasonable doubt that I would find the kicker. The construction worker who kicked off that beam from the thirtieth floor of the office building complex. In our family tag game, I was "it." And, of course, that meant going along with her and Frank Cora, finding the kicker and making him pay for dimming Saint Anne's prospect of basking in the limelight. Frank was the perfect person to find the kicker—he was one of those footnote-type entries in Saint Anne's professional life as a nightclub singer. She didn't need any professional hitman to wrap up this case. She had Frank—and Frank had me tagged from day one as his own private death squad.

IN New York City nothing gets built without the cooperation of the unions. Part of the cost of doing business is for the developer to make peace with the unions. And that means seeing to it that the presidents of the local branches of the various construction and trade unions are peacemakers. Think of these guys as modern-day warlords who keep the lawlessness in check inside their turf. That's what they do, what they sell and you know that without them life inside their territory isn't gonna be worth a damn. The last thing a fifty-million-dollar development needs is a walkout; a wildcat strike; a slowdown, or workers who don't know how to take orders, do what they're told, and keep their mouths shut. Unions, in turn, are a kind of business for the people who run and control them; cash cows, the coffers kept filled with not only dues, fees, fines, but all those pension payments the boss pays to the union to keep the workers from living as ticketmen in the Bowery once they reach old age.

People running the unions are smart enough to know that guys like Frank Cora are worth their weight in gold. Without Frank Cora watching the boundaries any hotshot can come inside and cause trouble. And when you are building a high-rise the last thing you want is trouble. Paying a lot of money up front to the unions is a guarantee against problems. Saint Anne had Frank Cora in her pocket; he was like the judge Arnold Keene kept in his pocket and got us adopted into a really good white middle-class family. Perhaps her real talent—not that the girl couldn't sing—was her ability to make guys like Frank Cora feel like they were falling in love for the first time. Jack jokingly called our sister a "Mob singer." Of course, she wasn't a Mob singer. She was a professional singer who had played in Tokyo, Singapore, Hong Kong and Bangkok. The crowds in Asia loved her because they could see something of themselves in her. She danced, showed some leg, and sang her heart out. Saint Anne had paid her dues. Only show business ain't a union and paying your dues don't necessarily mean you get your card punched into the hall of fame of the greats.

Saint Anne knew nothing of the movements of her nightclub customers although she had an idea that they might have some backroom world she didn't want to know about. The Thai-Chinese in Bangkok were crazy for her, competed for her, would have paid any price to have her; but she declined all offers, she was going to be a star. An American star. She didn't need their drug money or their gold chains. She had plugged fate into an audition for a spot in that exclusive symphony of fame. She never doubted for a moment that she would win her spot. It is strange how much you can see of the world and still have no idea how it works.

Saint Anne believed Frank Cora when he told her that his gun was loaded with rubber bullets and he wore it in the shower. From a rough-and-tumble neighborhood in Brooklyn, Frank had come up in the world, or at least his world, of street gangs, Coney Island hot dogs, sneaking into Dodgers games, robbing newsstands. He told Saint Anne that his uncle had persuaded him to join the police force. He helped out the right people; he got noticed by the higher-ups in the department, and in turn, was promoted and decorated. When he finally retired, the mayor and police chief attended his retirement dinner and called Frank Cora a genuine New York hero.

The afternoon I met Frank Cora in a Chinese restaurant on Mott Street, a stone's throw from the precinct house in Chinatown, he complained of a muscle spasm in his neck.

"Every time I think of that guy, I get this goddamn kink in my neck. Know what I mean?" Frank rubbed the back of his neck with one of those large fleshy hands, the kind with fingers with enormous creases over the knuckles.

"Yeah, it makes you think," I said, my elbows on the table with my head resting atop my folded hands.

"A hell'va way to get your ass canned," he said.

And that was coming from a guy who had a fair amount of experience with the way people died in the city. He looked a little seasick as he stuffed noodles into his mouth. Frank eyeballed me closely as he sucked the noodles. Sizing me. I could almost hear him thinking. So this is Saint Anne's brother. A big, rangy guy about six three or four. Kind of hippie-looking, black kinky hair pulled back into a small ponytail, tied with a rubber band. Full beard hiding those lips which look exactly like the ones on his sister's mouth. A downtown type with a pinched expression, like he'd eaten too much low-calorie health food and couldn't take a proper shit.

"You do drugs?" Frank asked me.

"Not even wine," I replied. That seemed to appease his uneasy feeling that I might have been a druggie. Someone who sold cocaine would've caused him personal grief with the people he took orders from. But I knew he was thinking of something else.

"You look black, know what I mean? I mean not really black. But there's something about you that makes me think black. I could be wrong. But why is this on my mind?"

"I've got some black blood," I said.

"I fucking knew it."

"What are you saying, Frank?"

"I ain't saying anything. Only I had this feeling."

"What kind of feeling?" I asked him point blank.

"That you were."

"Black."

"That's it."

Frank wasn't your average-looking noncommissioned officer in the private armies of Brooklyn. With the exception of the meat hooks he had for hands, he looked almost meek; nothing frightening in his watery eyes, which were too close together. He wore his hair short. Fifties army-recruit style. And he had Vulcan ears which gave his face a sharp, ferretlike quality. His head was out of proportion. Unlike Father and Jack, who had bulbous foreheads, Frank's upper skull had an oblong appearance, and his skin was yellowish and doughy. With the right make-up, Frank Cora could've passed for a Mexican priest.

"And you hate black, right?" I asked him.

His eyes, moist and motionless, stared straight through me.

"Saint Anne, is she black?"

I shook my head. "We are adopted. My brother Jack, too."

He seemed relieved. "I'd do anything in the world for your sister. She's got a million dollar voice that never stops making music in my head. But, between you and me, she needs some help to make it in the big time. She showed me the picture of Jack and you when you were on the road in Asia. You opened for Ray Charles. That's something. That's big time. Know what I mean?"

"Can you find the guy who did it?" I asked, using my chopsticks to play with my rice.

He looked at me cold, like some medical examiner. "You don't look black in your picture. That's why it was a surprise. Don't take any offense by what I said. One more thing. Why don't you just leave it to the police? That's what they're there for. I can tell you. I was a cop. A good one, too."

I snapped my pair of chopsticks in two and dropped them on the table. "Because the police don't give a shit. They got better things to do. Besides, they think it was an accident."

"And what do you think?"

"That Saint Anne's family has a right to take care of that asshole ourselves. Either you can help us or you can't." By now my lungs were heaving in and out, and I could feel my face get red as I clenched my teeth.

"You move ahead on this. We find the character. Before you know it, you've got yourself in real deep. Know what I mean? It ain't so easy to stop once you start. It's like a case of diarrhea, you just gotta keep on going. Know what I mean?" As he leaned back I could see the butt of his Smith & Wesson 38-caliber handgun. He was rubbing the back of his neck again, twisting his head from side to side, working out the kinks, as he called them.

"Yeah, I know exactly what you mean."

I would give anything to photograph Frank Cora's head. That was a real work of art. And Frank would know what doors to knock on to find the whereabouts of the kicker.

8

Men like Frank Cora travel around town with heavy-duty protection so that when they walk into a nightclub they are noticed right away and given a special table that goes with their status as someone who has enemies. The requirements of the back-up security job are straightforward—a foot soldier, preferably with commando experience, who is skilled in moving across open rooms quickly, who constantly searches the room for trouble and who is able to intimidate other people with a glance. The guy who followed Frank Cora around had this way of standing in the shadows with his hand half inside his suit pocket as if he were touching a gun. He never cracked a joke or a smile and didn't talk unless Frank asked him something profound like if he had an extra cigarette. He also had good posture and was two inches shorter than Frank. Chute, Frank's man, had a quiet ability to instill fear. It wasn't that he looked particularly mean; in fact he looked more like a school teacher than an enforcer, but he made people fearful because he appeared to have none of the human emotions that constrained most people from an act of violence. Chute chewed gum, listened to the radio, yawned, then looked out the window of a building, aimed his rifle and picked off children, women and old cripples in city streets or on jungle roads.

Frank, alone, would've been a small-time player, but with Chute on his team Frank intended to send a clear message—no one was to mess with him. Anyone who did what Frank said he should not do was likely to end up in a garbage dumpster. From what Saint Anne said, Chute was listed on the union payroll as a personal assistant to the president. She said Chute even had a name card with a title on it. But I found it difficult to think of people like Chute as someone's employee and I sure never saw a gangster in the movies handing someone his name card. Chute was a fast-draw bodyguard, getting a regular paycheck from the brotherhood of construction workers as if he were a real worker. But this was the kind of thing which made New York City a special place. And from the mayor's office all the way through the police department everyone just accepted that this was the way that buildings got built and torn down in the city. You didn't need an MBA from Harvard to know that the internal system wasn't based on logic, or even the most efficient means of supplying men and materials. It was based on a higher law—the mob system economics which is a dollar-with-muscle methodology no one teaches you when you are in school. They understood Tiananmen Square with no problem: people challenge you, show you disrespect, you have to teach them who is in control, hurt some people, kill some if that is what it takes.

What was Chute's career going to be? Was he going to stay behind the wheel of a limo, driving Frank around for years and years, and then one day, when he was an old man, the union would hold a retirement party for Chute? I tried to imagine some executive trembling with fear as he handed Chute a gold watch dangling on a gold-link chain. Would he draw a small pension, and follow the stock market with other old-timers huddled on benches at Battery Park? A slight palsy in his trigger finger each time he saw a market slump?

Frank Cora's system of doing business was closed to outsiders and the first rule was to secure the perimeter, check for bugged phones and bugs in the room, and to keep out journalists, union rank-and-file members, and anyone who might try to cause him trouble. Only a few exceptions like Saint Anne had an inside look at Frank Cora and that was because he was interested in her personally. And what about a Gideon Harvey, art photographer, who might be loaded down with concealed electronic devices? In theory they shouldn't touch me with a ten-foot pole. I was the kind of potential trouble they avoided and if I got in their face then Chute would take his hand out of his suit pocket clutching a knife and calmly slit my throat.

I had been a little uneasy when Frank Cora insisted that he needed me to accompany him on a couple of his rounds. One thing I promised myself was to act as if everything done by Frank or Chute was normal behavior for people who are doing a job. The last thing I wanted was to show surprise, or worse, appear furtive or inquisitive.

Two days after our Chinese lunch in Manhattan, I saw Chute up close as we made our way to Brooklyn. His head was filled with the twisted wiseguy stuff that psychoanalysis has never been able to figure out. Chute was behind the wheel of Frank's limo when I found out that he was an ex-army man. His nickname was derived from parachute. He had made over two hundred jumps. Chute had been dishonorably discharged from the army for black-market violations. Distributing hallucinogens on a small-time scale amongst his unit in Vietnam. Two of his men jumped loaded on LSD and they hit the ground from five thousand feet without ever trying to pull their ripcords. There had been a court-martial but there wasn't enough evidence to pin the deaths on Chute; some said the two men had crossed him and Chute laced their breakfast cereal with LSD. Whether he murdered them or not, he got out of going to prison. Frank said he hired Chute after he saw him kick the shit out of three ghetto blacks. Frank watched my reaction to his piece of information, as if this were a threat I should take seriously in case I had any funny business in mind. Chute's skill needed little retooling for the job Frank had in mind for him in the union. Life outside the army picked up pretty much where Vietnam had left off. Only he no longer jumped out of airplanes. Chute slid back into civilian life without so much as having to change his weapons of choice.

I felt Chute's eyes in the rear-view mirror. Prying me open like a bivalve with a weak muscle. He had quick blue eyes. He had the eyes of a trapshooter at that crucial moment when the word "pull" pierces sharply in the cool, thin air. I huddled in the back beside Frank.

"The first time I saw your sister I thought she was maybe twenty, twenty-two. Just a kid, I thought. Maybe a new singer who was breaking into the business, know what I mean?"

Frank sat low in the seat. Looking over his head, I glimpsed the old factory buildings as we crossed the Brooklyn Bridge. Chute smoothly threaded the limo through the double-lane traffic.

"Saint Anne takes real good care of herself," I said.

"She's got the voice of an angel. Why she's not on television shows, I don't know. These producers don't know shit. I could make her a star. I know people in the business."

"What business is that?" I asked. When I heard people who had never been on a stage before an audience say the business when they meant the entertainment business I got a cramp in my gut. Everyone in the world wanted to be an insider, trying to impress you that they are one of you when they don't know nothing about it except the bullshit they read in the newspapers and see on the television.

"Show business," replied Frank Cora. "You're not too bright, are you, Gideon?"

"No sir, I don't know nothing about nothing," I said.

He liked that even less than my question about what business he meant. But before he had a chance to work up an evil temper and throw his weight around we had a near collision. Ahead and to the right of us, a taxi ricocheted off a Dodge Dart, and Chute swiftly cut into the left lane.

"Did you see that?" asked Frank, leaning back lower in his seat. He had the attention span of a five-year-old, and at the moment that was good. He forgot that I had pissed him off and continued, "What kind of shit driving is that? This guy your sister was involved with. This Peter Montard. That's what happened to him. Some asshole, like in that Dodge Dart, just cuts him off. Assholes shouldn't be on the road. Was that some bitch from Jersey?" Now Frank leaned forward and talked directly to Chute. "Some bitch looking at her jewelry not watching where the fuck she was? I bet it was a Jersey shit."

"New York plates," said Chute carefully. "Some guy cleaning his teeth in his mirror. Figure that?"

Fifteen minutes later, Frank was laughing and slapping his legs. He'd had an uncle in Washington State who had hauled logs as a teenager. He drove one of those eighteen-wheel logging trucks with a ton of chains ratcheted down to keep the logs from falling off. Fully loaded, those trucks weighed as much as a train, and steered like a gondola. He told stories about how his uncle had scraped a deer off the front grille. The deer was a huge buck with big racks, too, but after the truck had hit it head-on you could have spooned it onto your plate like Spam. Frank had one of the road victim deers mounted on a wall in his basement den. Since we were raised in British Columbia, Frank had the idea that we came from a family of loggers and hunters and went to school in a dog-sled. And at midnight huge flocks of geese blocked out the sun, making us whiny and afraid. Frank knew as much about Canada as he did about show business. But his story about the uncle in Washington State got me to wonder if this was the same Cora that Saint Anne said had pull with the NYPD; someone who had heat with the major brass. This was exactly the kind of penetrating question I knew would make Frank nervous. "Why is that black guy asking me this?" I could hear him saying.

"Maybe you'll get a chance to show your stuff," Frank said, as Chute pulled into the driveway of a small frame house.

"What kind of stuff are we talking about?"

"Handling yourself under pressure," he said.

"What kind of pressure?"

He frowned. "You ask too many questions. I don't like a lot of questions."

How did I know that without even asking?

Frank was out of the car and knocking on the front door. Then the three of us were inside the small living room of the house, standing on a brown shag carpet, worn in spots. The walls were the color of lime oyster shells get on the outside after they start to rot and smell. Red and green lights flickered against the ceiling; the lights came from a Christmas tree that no one had bothered to take down even though it was months after Christmas. Homemade tin ornaments and tinsel drooped on the fake branches which I thought at first were covered in dust but when I got a closer look I saw that it was cigarette ash. This domestic neglect had crept in every part of that room giving it trashed out, desolate look. Beer cans were strewn on a table and the floor. A color television set in the corner was turned to MTV. In the entryway to the kitchen a thin woman, a can of beer in one hand, her other hand on her hip, watched us with bloodshot eyes, licking her thin, dry lips. She wore a pink robe which had mustard stains on the sleeve and toeless slippers. Taking a drink out of her beer, she booted a stuffed toy dog which rolled to a stop at the base of the Christmas tree.

"Honey, get Frank and his friends some beers," said a heavy-set man, his hair greasy and sticking up in the back like he had just got out of bed. Arching forward on his bare feet, he glanced at the woman in the kitchen. She disappeared and a moment later saucepans rattled against the sink. A glass, a bottle, something shattered on the floor.

"Fuck them," she called back. "They can get their own goddamn beer. I don't get beers for gangsters."

All the time Frank didn't say a word. He stood next to the Christmas tree, twirling a silver foil angel between his thumb and forefinger. Maybe he was thinking about the near miss on the Brooklyn Bridge but I doubted it. Chute leaned against the front door, cracking his knuckles one at a time, so they made that sickly crushing noise. I had seen a lot of grief and broken down dreams and gut retching despair, but until that third week of July, I had never seen the bloated corpse of a Christmas Day that had been dead a whole load of months. The house reeked of smells coming from directions you couldn't figure out; if someone had told me that someone had cut up a body and stuffed it inside the sofa, I would have believed them. The feeling of abuse, sorrow, and regret came from the people living there; it was as if they had moved into some stage beyond hate and debasement. I could imagine Chute coming from a house like this and from the way he hung around the door cracking his knuckles, giving no indication he saw anything wrong, I started to think I might have been right.

"Take your time, Gary," said Frank, as the man emerged from the kitchen with three open bottles of beer.

"My old lady's not feeling so good," he said. He handed out the beers. "She's got her period or something."

"I need a little favor, Gary," said Frank.

Gary lowered his beer slowly, letting the beer swell one cheek like a balloon and then shifting it over to the other side of his mouth. One of those buying-time tricks used by beer drinkers who used the same trick to rinse out their mouth so they wouldn't have to brush their teeth. Finally he swallowed hard and nodded. Frank, after all, had not bothered to knock, just walked straight into his house with a couple of strangers—although I had the feeling he knew Chute from around.

"A foreman like yourself hears things on the job. Know what I mean?" said Frank, carefully taking the angel off the Christmas tree.

"Sure, man. What's the problem? Did I fuck up or something?"

"Did I say you fucked up?"

"No but . . ."

"This ain't about you personally, Gary. Or at least I hope not."

"I don't want any trouble."

"Anyone you ever met that does?"

Frank looked at him hard after delivering his wiseguy answer. Could this heavy-set man with the thick neck, the white skinny legs, and greasy hair, have knocked the beam over the side and onto Peter Montard? Gary's knees looked as if they were about to buckle. He sat on the couch and took another long drink from his bottle.

"Let's don't fuck around with each other, Gary. All I wanna know is the guy who slipped the beam over the side on your building." Frank, with his thumbnail, flicked the angel's head off. It landed on the table in front of Gary.

"You think I saw it or something?"

From the kitchen the woman with bloodshot eyes shouted, "I don't have to put up with your shit. I can call the cops. You cocksucker. You're such a big man. Tell them how you punched me."

Frank smiled and with a slight nod of his head directed Chute over towards the kitchen like a shepherd giving signals for his sheepdog to control a member of the flock which was breaking free.

"You've got her real worked up, Gary. So you don't want to start up with us. Know what I mean?"

Gary stared long and hard at the angel's head. He knew what Frank meant, all right. It was one of those hopeless situations; the kind of moment that suggested that Jack was absolutely right to have opted out of real time. Gary's spirit buckled just like his legs had done a few minutes before. I had the feeling that Frank baited hooks like this one many times. Upstairs, almost above us, I heard a suffocated groan.

"He's a good shit. What are you going to do to him?"

"You protecting him?"

Gary didn't say anything.

"Okay, Gary. Have you talked to the cops?"

Gary smiled one of those half-drunk, half-fearful smiles. "You want to turn him into the cops?"

"Who said anything about the cops?"

"I just thought."

"Don't worry about it," said Frank.

The beginning of the end was this special pleading and everyone in the room knew it. Chute stepped back from the kitchen, which was now very quiet. Gary saw Chute standing with a satisfied grin on his face.

"You didn't hurt her?" he asked.

"He just asked her to go check on your kids. So, Gary. By the time she gets back, we'll be gone. Just one thing. The guy's name."

Gary blinked nervously like an animal frantic with the thought of escape.

"Teddy," he muttered. For the first time, I noticed that above the fake fireplace, Christmas cards with yellowing Scotch tape were hanging crooked and loose like dead skin peeling off the wall.

"Why you whispering?" asked Frank, standing very still, his hands clenched at his side.

"His name's Teddy Eliot. And it was an accident. No one's fault, Frank. It just happened."

"Is this Teddy Eliot colored?"

Gary looked confused like this was a trick question.

"I thought he was white."

Frank Cora smiled, looking over at me. "You can't always tell," he said.

As we left, I wondered which of the Christmas cards was from Frank.

FROM the glove compartment of the limo, Frank pulled out a large envelope with small photographs of men. Most of them were more like mug shots than photographs. Frank thumbed through them fast, he was a man in a hurry, racing against storm clouds forming on the horizon. The faces in the photos had a tight, suspicious look as if the lens had picked up friction between the one in the picture and the one taking it. We sat in Gary's driveway with the interior light on, as Frank thumbed through the 5 x 7 cards with the photo attached by a paper clip on the upper right-hand side.

"That's your boy," Frank said, pulling out some kind of union card with the photo of Teddy Eliot. So Teddy Eliot was the guy who had kicked off the beam. I'm not certain what I expected his face to look like but Teddy's face had an innocent, good-looking quality, an open, rawboned face, with a strong, firm jaw. A wiry mustache covered his upper lip. It was a weird feeling to see that Peter shared a similar type of mustache with the man who had killed him. The sort of mustache that thick cream soup sticks to and sours by the end of the meal. He didn't look like he had any black blood in him, I could hear Frank Cora thinking to himself.

Teddy smiled directly into the camera like a child in a playground. A comparatively young face—twenty-something, another member of the X-generation. A slight overbite made the light reflect off his front teeth. Teeth which, from the photo, seemed to grow out of facial hair. Wide, bright eyes, as if listening to a story, eyes that were shiny and carried a sense of movement on the surface, even in a photograph. This was the face of the man who had killed Peter Montard.

"Look at that dip-shit grin," Frank said, passing the photograph over to Chute, who took a look and then passed it back. "Aren't you gonna say something, Gideon?"

All I could think about was how Frank had decapitated the angel with his thumbnail as he stood talking with Gary and how Gary's eyes had stopped blinking as he started to watch what Frank was doing. And I was thinking about how Teddy had decapitated Peter. I had been the one who had told Peter about the rare bookseller who specialized in rare letters written by politicians, nobles, military leaders, authors, actors, and singers. A fine collection to choose from and, if he really wanted to surprise Saint Anne, then he should go to midtown, check out the inventory himself, and buy that Jimi Hendrix letter he wrote one week before killing himself at age twenty-seven. He never had to get as far as the booksellers in order to create a major surprise for my sister. And for me. And, I guessed, for Teddy Eliot.

"Now what are you planning to do, Frank?" I asked, clearing my throat. I slid over away from the direct gaze of Chute's eyes in the rear-view mirror, hugged the door, and leaned my cheek against the cold side window-pane.

I listened to the low roar of the air-conditioning blast through the front vents. Why hadn't Saint Anne been willing to leave well enough alone? It was like when we were on the road as the Harvey Trio, she had to have the last word. When she was on stage the audience had to be focused on her. If she found them watching the piano player too much then, Wowee, there was trouble after the show. But that thing was so deep in her that even she doesn't know where it comes from. The guy in the photograph had done more than upstage her; he had taken her off People magazine and no one at MTV was returning her calls. I had a dream that taking home the photograph, making a dupe copy, blowing it up, pinning it to a punching bag and letting Saint Anne wear herself out as her tiny little fist landed on those buck teeth was not going to satisfy her blood lust.

"Now we pick him up. We've got his address. Like you guys up in Canada, we get our man. He'll have left footprints all over his neighbor. We just follow them around the block. Know what I mean?"

Chute shifted gear into reverse, a sharp turn. He gunned the engine and the houses blurred into the night. "Why don't we turn Teddy Eliot over to the police?" I said, as we stopped at the first traffic light. Frank reached over and grabbed my knee with his hand and squeezed it hard.

"That's what I said the first time we had a little talk. And I said once you start something you can't stop. We've started something. So what are the cops going to do for us now? Write him a ticket for dropping logs? Shit, I thought you wanted this guy in your pocket for your sister. Or did I just let the wrong information sink in?" He released my knee from his grip.

I wanted to say it was a judge in a lawyer's pocket who got me in the fix I was in at that precise moment.

"Okay, we'll let Saint Anne decide what to do with him. It's her call. She gets to play judge," I said.

"Judge," he said to himself. "She'll have his balls. Have you ever seen your sister in operation?"

I had seen her kick a Chinese guy in the balls who was drunk and groped her on the stage in a nightclub in Hong Kong. Yeah, I knew her stuff.

"She's more than just another singer. She's smart and tough. And she's gonna be real big one day. She will be able to turn down million dollar contracts for sponsoring shit like perfume."

Frank had her career path all figured out and no doubt his role was laid down in his mind as well. I thought twice about telling Frank that Mother used to tie her up to an oak tree in the backyard of our house and how her real mother was a nightclub singer in Saigon before she became a hooker in Seattle and had drowned in Peugeot Sound with two other working girls including my mother. But I decided there was plenty of time down the road. Frank was on a roll. Here was a man who had spent time studying my sister, figuring her out, and little by little, I had this cold-blooded feeling that Frank was thinking about Teddy Eliot the way he thought about that deer which had cratered into the front of his uncle's eighteen-wheel logging truck.

9

Teddy Eliot lived with his mother in one of those depressed neighborhoods where yellow cab drivers were afraid to take passengers. The house was on the edge of the Howard Beach section of Queens where there were boarded-up shops, broken windows, and teenagers standing around in the street with their hands in their jacket pockets. If someone had said a couple of mortar rounds had landed nearby an hour ago you would not say they were lying. Mostly what I was thinking was why a man of Teddy Eliot's age was still living at home with his mother to do his cooking and laundry. With not enough jobs around, parents were getting the shock of their lives finding that children they had raised and sent into the world were coming back in their twenties with the clothes on their back, no job, no prospect of a job, and asking to have their old room back. Given Eliot's neighborhood he had to be desperate, down to his last quarter, to have come back to this situation. An area populated with people standing around street corners, walking on broken glass, knowing they didn't have any future, and wondering what you were doing in their neighborhood. Frank Cora's limo immediately bred a mixture of fear, respect, jealousy and dark suspicions. You could see in their eyes that they were running the numbers on the break-up value of the limo.

Chute stopped the limo in front of a squat house; a cement porch and cast-iron railings painted black had been added on as a kind of afterthought. Drawn curtains split with a crack of light from the inside. That crack opened wider as we got out of the limo and slammed the doors. Frank stretched out, drumming his fingers on the limo roof for a moment as he surveyed the geography. His eyes moved in a clockwise motion. Chute stayed behind the wheel, breathing through his mouth as if there were germs in the neighborhood that might go up his nose, then he climbed out and slammed the door.

"Looks okay to me," Frank said, standing on the sidewalk. "What you think?"

"Piece of cake," said Chute.

I followed Frank and Chute to the steps leading to the concrete porch. Frank reached forward and rang the doorbell, his hand coming back to rest in a clenched fist at his side. Teddy's mother came to the door, opening it as far as the security chain would allow. She was tiny, standing shoeless as she looked Chute up and down, and not much liking what she found on her porch.

"What are you selling?" she asked.

"Hi, Mrs. Eliot," said Chute. "Teddy home?"

"Who wants to know?" she asked, looking past him at Frank and me.

"Vic is my name. Vic Berton. I am not selling anything. Teddy and me were in the army together. Just thought I'd look him up. Say hello," Chute said.

She closed the door and undid the security chain. "He should've stayed in the army. That's what I've always told him." The door opened directly into a tidy, sparse living room. Chute walked straight in and Frank and I followed behind him, as she kept complaining about her son. She had a roomful of strangers who were towering over her and she was looking like she had made one huge mistake ever taking that security chain off the door. Also her manner suggested that she had spent a good deal of life making excuses for Teddy, for others, and probably for herself as well.

"He's just not established himself."

Frank Cora glanced around the sitting room.

"Tell us about him."

Chute went back to breathing through his mouth and guarding the door.

She wore a starched night-shift uniform with one of those strange hairnets that waitresses in all-night diners wear. Her bottle-red hair didn't look like real hair under the netting. Her hair looked more like a deep water sea plant. The kind of tropical weed that grows on the bottom of the ocean floor and strangles and eats fish as they swim past. Like Gary's house this one had a closed-up attic smell; a subway tunnel air smell, stale, used, and damp, once inhaled into your lungs it makes you feel like you are going to pass out. The atmosphere was like that of a rain forest. Walking into that house you expected to find fungus growing on the walls and people with web feet walking, muttering to themselves, and sponging themselves around the neck with a damp cloth.

"He's quit his new job. Two months ago he got fired from the service station. Teddy can't hold down a job. I don't think he's put enough effort into it. He's got people to give him a chance but he don't last. Vic, could you talk to him?" she said, scrunching her eyebrows together.

"I'd be pleased to talk with him, Mrs. Eliot," said Frank.

"Were you in the army with my son, too?" she asked.

Chute piped up. "We all were, Mrs. Eliot."

"I'm so glad. And that you're friends." She paused, looking at the right-pocket bulge in the outline of a Smith and Wesson 38-caliber.

"He carries it for protection," I said.

"It is so dangerous now in the city. I hate going out." She now looked a little alarmed as her eyes remained glued to the bulge.

"With all those blacks, illegal foreigners, you know what I mean?" Frank raised an eyebrow, opening his hands in the studied manner of a television preacher.

"Teddy's not in some kind of trouble?" The alarm took a sudden turn towards panic. She cupped her hands over her mouth. The bluish veins connected like roots to her fingers swelled in the heat.

"No trouble, Mrs. Eliot," said Chute. "But maybe you could tell us where we can find him."

"I knew that he shouldn't have opened his big mouth. That fire wasn't his business. Now all he gets are documents and calls from lawyers. God, oh God, I wish he'd stayed in the army."

"Yeah, like I told him in the army, you can't play with fire, Ted," said Chute.

"How I wish he had listened to you," said Mrs. Eliot.

❖

A Japanese sushi chef sliced off reddish pieces of raw tuna. As the three of us entered the restaurant, he glanced up and I locked eyes with him for a split second. He showed no emotion or recognition. The knife flashed white and sliced off a perfectly tapered piece. A Japanese woman in her early twenties, dressed in a black shirt and skirt, greeted us with a small bow. An image of Jack bowing to Father flashed through my mind.

"You see this guy?" asked Frank, showing her the picture of Teddy Eliot. Then he shoved his old police badge in her face.

She pointed at a pair of worn Reeboks on a wood ledge at the far end of restaurant. Teddy had his own koji-screened booth. And he was dining alone. Frank arched an eyebrow at Chute and smiled. They seemed so casual about it, while my blood pounded in my ears and throat. It was one of those moments when you really understand how differently members of our species were wired.

Jack, Saint Anne, and I played some rough nightclubs. We had been on the fringes of violent people, drug addicts, drunks, pushers, criminals and grifters who passed through nightclubs, leaving a dollar trail like they were famous. We were like the support and supply side of an army; we knew that out on the front lines there were guys like Frank and Chute who highly valued danger, who hurt people, sometimes killed people, but we never saw muscle in action, inflicting injury and pain. The tension in the air as they walked ahead made them appear stronger, focused, and assured. These guys thrived like junkies on the speed running through their blood, like members of a tribe whose genes had wired them to find excitement and pleasure in fracturing skulls. They made me nervous, and profoundly cautious. Jack, had he been present, would have been distracted by the sushi chef, lost in questions about whether the art was sacramental, and would have spent several hours explaining the Chinese views of food. Saint Anne would have asked them about yellow cabs picking up local customers for some wild times on the town.

I was representing Saint Anne's injured interest. I followed behind, as if I were one of them, thinking this is crazy, man. Wowee, these guys are going to hurt someone and what are the police going to do? They are going to arrest the guy who they find out has some black blood and let Frank and Chute go home as if they were bystanders. But I was into it; I couldn't back away, and say, "Hey, guys, why don't I wait for you in the limo?" Frank took the point, then, with Chute one step behind, they were holding their shoes in their hands as they walked back to join Teddy for dinner.

"Teddy, great to see you," said Frank, sliding over the bamboo mat, and folding his legs beneath him. He sat directly opposite from Teddy so that he could lead forward and get his face close to Teddy's. Chute and I stayed outside, sitting on the wooden ledge next to Teddy's shoes.

"Do I know you?" said Teddy.

"Look what I have here," said Frank, reaching into his pocket. He pulled out a jar of jam. "Homemade blueberry jam. A present from your mother. What a nice mom you have there. She's real proud of you, Teddy. But . . . just a little concerned. She says you've got real trouble holding down a job. That's the way she says it. We all go through some bad times, know what I mean?"

"Hey, look, I don't want any trouble, guys," said Teddy, dropping his chopsticks on the table. His hands began to shake slightly as the color drained from his face. Here was a man who disliked confrontations with anyone, and most of all with strangers.

"There's that word again. Trouble," said Frank. "Did Gary teach you that word? He doesn't like trouble."

The reason men like Frank Cora made a living, a really good living was that simple desire on the part of businessmen, bankers, politicians, the police, restaurant owners, barkeepers, prostitutes, drug pushers, number runners—none of them ever wanted any trouble. They wanted to be left alone. Frank Cora promised that he would keep them out of trouble; and there was enough comfort in that promise, despite knowing what it meant, for them to pay him a lot of money.

"You hear that, Chute? Our favorite word is being used by Mr. Eliot. And that's why we have come here tonight. Because I hate trouble, and so does my friend here, Gideon."

Frank sat with his legs folded Asian style underneath him. As he was leaning forward, talking about "trouble," his jacket brushed open and exposed the fact that he was packing a gun. Teddy's eyes got as big as saucers as he saw the gun. Frank reached over and with his fingers picked up a piece of sushi from Teddy's plate.

"With people starving in the world, you shouldn't waste food."

Teddy seemed to stop breathing as Frank Cora rotated the sushi between his finger and thumb like a short, green cigar. From the corner of my eye, I saw Chute disappear back towards the front of the restaurant.

"You really like this raw fish?" he asked, and not waiting for an answer, continued, "It smells like bait. Know what I mean?"

Teddy, looking like a trapped rabbit, shrugged his shoulders. "I kind of like sushi, if that's all right with you."

"I read somewhere raw fish is bad for your health," said Frank. "It can give you worms that eat your heart or your eyeballs from the inside. That's why the Japs have bad eyes. And that's why they keel over at their desk, clutching their chest. Worms."

That was one advantage to fish-sounds, I thought: no worms; and I thought back to that night in the Hong Kong restaurant when Tiananmen Square changed my life.

Teddy looked paler, taller, and thinner than his photograph. And, of course, in the photograph he had not been looking back at Frank with a gun strapped inside his jacket and playing with his food. I wasn't certain what role I was expected to play but standing in the door and watching Frank Cora slowly drive Teddy Eliot insane was more than I had bargained for. Why not confront him with the evidence we had that he had killed Peter? Then tell him what were the consequences for kicking that log off the construction site and decapitating Peter Montard before he could make my sister rich and famous, deliver her what she had wanted her entire life, the Great American Dream.

"I like sushi, too," I said, filling in the void of silence.

Teddy pushed the tray of half-eaten sushi across the table towards me. He must have thought I was trying to shake him down for his sushi. Before I could explain, Frank cleared his throat.

"The thing is, Teddy, when you kill a man, even if it's an accident, you can't just expect people to forget about it. Walk into a Jap restaurant, stuff your face with hunks of raw fish, and pretend you didn't kill a man, leave him dead on the street. The man you chopped up like Jap food had influential friends. And he had connections that don't like one little bit what you did. What I am saying is, that what you have done has upset some people. And when people get upset they can cause trouble. Know what I mean? And we would like to invite you to explain a few things to a woman who is feeling the loss of the man you killed. Do you think that you could do that for us?"

"Do I have a choice?" asked Teddy, his eyes on Frank's gun.

"Life's full of choices, Teddy. But in this case, the answer is no. You ain't got a choice."

Teddy's head dropped for a second. I dipped a piece of sushi in the soy sauce, and had brought it back towards my mouth, when the table up-ended. Glasses, dishes, sauces, and food flew towards Frank, tipping him over to the side as he tried to avoid the objects. Teddy bolted to his left. The koji screens were made from thin rice paper with wooden struts the strength of match sticks. The first screen ripped apart as Teddy smashed through it, and then ripped through another. Shredded walls. People who were eating in the private compartments screamed as Teddy ran over their tables, his feet knocking hot soup and raw fish in every direction. The crash of glass echoed across the narrow room. In one desperate, frantic movement, Teddy had done as much damage as a freak storm, twisting the decoration and rice-paper walls into a loose ball of shredded wreckage. All those sitting people with only partial walls separating them. Flakes of paper lining the air and falling like a fine mist over their food and hair.

I was half relieved thinking that Teddy had made his escape. Frank simply pushed the table back with a crash, found a napkin and wiped the soya sauce off his jacket. Soya sauce had soiled his shirt sleeve. Instinctively, he touched the butt of his handgun, his bottom lip flared out in irritation. The way this gesture disfigured his face made him look coarse and mean.

"I thought he might try something insane like that," he said.

He twisted around, swinging his feet back on the ledge.

"Guess that's that," I said.

"Those damp walls are like candy wrappers. How the building inspector ever passes this shit is beyond me. Unless he's on the take from the Japs," said Frank. He looked back at me. "Well, let's don't waste any more time. It's time Teddy had that little talk with your sister."

Chute must have been Teddy's worst nightmare come true as he bolted through that last rice-paper wall to the door and freedom.

In his mind, Teddy crossed through enemy lines without a scratch. But he had a surprise waiting for him as he ran straight into a guy who had two hundred jumps under his belt. In the oily light of night, fish smells in the air, Teddy's feet stopped moving. His mind floated away. The fear slipped away in that instant when the surface of things disappeared and silence channeled smooth and flat across his brain.

A single blow had knocked him out cold and the sushi chef, his staff and the clientele watched as Teddy fell backwards through the entrance and hit his head on the floor with a dull, sickening thud. Chute appeared in the doorway, cracking his knuckles. Chute leaned down, picked up the unconscious body, and hoisted him over his shoulders like a slain deer and carried him out to the limo, opened the front passenger door and dumped him in the front seat like a hundred kilos of rice. Then Chute opened the glove box and removed a first-aid kit; the kind with a red cross on the top of the metal box. Inside the box was a syringe and needle. As Frank swung open the back door, Chute leaned over Teddy, slumped down on the front-seat passenger's side. His shirtsleeve was ripped open, and Chute had an injection needle stuck in the fleshy part of Teddy's right arm. The overhead light illuminated a dense tattoo with faded blue ink over the flaccid muscle. I tried to make out the pattern in the shadows.

"Got that sucker right between the eyes," said Chute, pulling out the syringe.

What Chute had just jabbed between the eyes looked like a tattoo which was monkey faced, had a bushy raccoonlike tail, a bearlike chest, and long pads on the feet with sharp toenails. I thought of Gary's wife's toes in her soiled slippers. One of the animal's legs was raised in a half dance step. The face was that of a primate with thick, hairy eyebrows. Chute had sunk the needle between those brows. I figured the tattoo represented some rite of passage in the military, and made a note to ask Jack about it. No doubt Jack would be able to precisely guess the type of needle used by the tattoo artist on Teddy's arm.

"That should calm him down," said Frank, as he slid into the back seat. "Calm his nerves, know what I mean?"

I was beginning to understand what Frank meant.

10

Teddy was in a drooling state of unconsciousness as Chute carried him into our building and down the basement stairs. Slowly climbing down the stairs, he had Teddy slung over his shoulder. Frank Cora walked behind him. Chute grunted a couple of times under his load like he was back in basic training and a sergeant had given him orders to demonstrate a rescue operation. His name card said he was a personal assistant to the president of the union; his performance at the Japanese restaurant indicated his employment hadn't much to do with his record of scholarship or his commitment to collective bargaining on behalf of the working class who were members of the union. But he was real good at heavy lifting. Reaching the bottom of the stairs, Chute followed as I led the way.

"Put him over there," I said, pointing at the wall.

Chute lowered Teddy against an empty wall near where I had my darkroom.

He squatted down beside Teddy, pressing a thumb against one eyelid and then the other.

"Is he gonna be all right?" asked Frank Cora.

"Another couple of hours and he should be okay." Chute brushed the sweat off his forehead with the back of his hairy hand and then cracked his knuckles. He was staring at the wall.

"What are you gonna do?" I asked.

"I got an idea," said Chute.

I knew that any time someone like him had an idea, there was an element of danger. I thought that Frank Cora was the idea man. But Frank was looking up and nodding with a big grin on his face.

"I like it," said Frank.

I saw what they were looking at and it confirmed what I had already figured out about Frank and Chute—that we didn't come close to liking the same things. And I was thinking that Saint Anne should have been here to see what these people enjoyed besides her singing.

Teddy, still passed out from the injection, was slumped against the wall, his head propped against a filing cabinet. Chute was looking at two large iron rings anchored in the wall, red with rust, and he looked happy as he stared at the iron rings.

"Don't do that, man," I said, but no one was listening.

"He's making things easier for you," said Frank Cora.

Chute used each iron ring to connect Teddy's handcuffed wrists to a solid structure. By the time Chute had finished, Teddy was spread-eagled, his back to the wall and his arms stretched out between the two iron rings.

Teddy's face was bruised, scuffed from meeting Chute's knuckles at high velocity, and his lower lip swollen, ugly and deformed. He had a flushed, overheated, broken look. The man showed at a glance the lifetime of bad karma his momma had told us about; he was a man who had been defined by negligence, poverty, fear and worry. Here was a man who had been on the run all his life and ran back to his momma only to find out that was just one more mistake in judgment. He was breathing softly as if he were sleeping and he had found peace of mind. With his gashed cheeks and bloodied mouth, Teddy looked like another victim in some fly-blown village where rebels and government forces had collided; one of those nameless places to which television stations send their crews to come back with broken bodies to fill a twenty-four-hour broadcast schedule. People were held in cells throughout South America, Asia, Africa. And now in SoHo, the Harvey Trio had acquired a live, flesh and blood victim. Teddy Eliot was a prisoner in a windowless cell.

The grease spot left by the soya sauce still annoyed Frank as he crowded in next to Teddy. He was half hoping that Teddy would wake up so that he could show him exactly the damage done to his expensively tailored clothes. Frank Cora and Chute stood in front of Teddy like they were in an art gallery looking at a piece of modern art. I had photographed some strange pieces in my day but Teddy Eliot hanging on my basement wall was the strangest. I stood next to Frank Cora, thinking that even with all the illegals we had hidden in the basement nothing this weird had ever happened before.

"He don't look well," I said.

Frank Cora just laughed.

There wasn't a flicker of light from Teddy's eyes, as Frank pulled up the lid of each. The eyeballs were rolled back. They looked like sluggish, empty lacquered-over openings. Frank had no luck confronting Teddy with the soya stain. Two steps back, Chute, arching his neck—it had to be a little sore by that stage—stood looking at Teddy and then over at me.

"He's all yours. When you're finished messing him up, let me know. We'll be outside," he said, reaching out to shake my hand.

So that was the deal. I was delegated to be the agent of Saint Anne's revenge.

"Why don't we let him go? I can't see what else Saint Anne would want," I said.

"She wants a lot more. Use your imagination, Gideon." He didn't look like he was kidding and that worried me a lot, thinking Saint Anne had been talking to him, this gangster outsider, and she hadn't been talking to me, her brother. That wasn't the way we were raised.

"We are going over to the club," said Frank Cora.

After they left I phoned the club and the bar manager said that Saint Anne was singing and that was true enough because I could hear her voice in the background; she was singing Feel no Pain, that song Sade made popular. I said I would wait until she finished the song but there was a family emergency, it was life and death, and unless she came to the telephone, I could not be responsible for what might get into the newspapers. That usually did the trick. Jack would fire the bar manager if he screwed up and brought down bad publicity on the nightclub. He was running a real low key affair with just enough heat to keep Saint Anne happy. Saint Anne was on the phone and after I told her what had happened there was no need to tell her to get the hell out of there and come straight home before Frank Cora showed up.

❖

SAINT Anne was still in her stage make-up, a huge black velvet bow was tied on top of her hair and she wore a low-cut, slinky black dress slit up to her thigh as she paced a few feet away from Teddy. All right, now what? It was one thing in the heat of passion to want revenge, to demand action, and then it was something else to walk on a basement floor as some drugged guy was hanging on the wall. This was the kicker. His chin rested on his chest; his eyes were closed and he was hanging from the wrists. For fifteen minutes she paced in a semicircle. At first she didn't talk at all. Her audience was asleep. She examined every detail about him. His shoeless feet. His faded blue jeans. The flecks of rice paper in his reddish-brown mustache and on his shirt. Bits of wood in his hair. Teddy looked like he had checked off the night shift at a paper mill. In British Columbia, we grew up seeing at a distance the men with eighth-grade education who made a living with their backs and hands. Father would slow down the car as we cruised past rundown bars on Granville Street near the Bridge, pointing them out and threatening that unless we had a good education we would end up just like them. A lifetime of fist fights, knives, and drinking Molson's beer direct from the bottle. All three of us had a good education, and rather than ending up like one of those men, we had one mounted like a trophy on our basement wall.

Teddy's battered condition shocked Saint Anne. The basement had been a refuge for those who had escaped violence but not one of the illegals had ever been hurt during our watch. I could see it in her eyes; she hated violence and blood, and could never understand how it never seemed to touch Jack. Also she was expecting Frank to deliver someone, well, how can one put it, someone of a different type. The man in her custody was not good enough, strong enough, wise enough about life, worldly affairs, trends to have the right to take Peter's life; he looked like some regular Joe Lunchbucket whose sketch of life was about as sophisticated as one of the red-crayon trees Lucy had drawn at age three. And all Saint Anne could make out about Teddy was his abnormal desire to sleep chained to the basement wall. Teddy, a lumberjack type, chained to the basement, startled her. It was like a flashback to sitting in the back of Father's car in Vancouver, only we were much closer.

What had she expected? Saint Anne had a definite image of the person responsible for Peter's death. But when Teddy didn't fit the bill, she felt cheated of something that she couldn't put her finger on. The kicker, I guess, had become someone bigger than life; well-dressed, someone off the pages of GQ, someone with the power and force to send every emotion into white-hot fear. After all, having your head chopped off in midtown was not a common everyday-life experience.

"Chute said that he'll be okay in another hour or so," I said.

"It'll never be okay," she said softly.

"So what do you want to do now?" I asked innocently. "Go back to the club?"

"Peter was killed by a . . . ," she paused, " . . . by a logger!"

Saint Anne's body trembled as the frequency of her emotion struck the top end of her disturbance scale. What she said and what she meant were two different things; "My musical career was killed by a logger," was what she was really saying. "My MTV contract has been canceled because of a lumberjack." If Saint Anne could have converted that emotion into a radio signal, Alex could have tuned in to our basement from Paris and, so could Elizabeth from London.

A strained, sad, lonely expression settled in her eyes and mouth, giving her a middle-distance gaze, a half-focused, deserted look of lonely desperation. As if she wanted to let go of something bottled deep inside but couldn't find the right valve to twist open. The cadence of her breathing increased wildly. Saint Anne started to hyperventilate, clenching her teeth and grinding her jaw. The suffering collected and was about to bubble over in some physical act. All her words were frozen in rage; all that remained was violence.

THE night of Bastille Day, she had increased her daily dose of drugs. Medication that programmed new tunes for her mind to play as she slept. She tossed two more pills on the back of her tongue as chasers, swallowing hard, then smiled at herself in the mirror, saying, "You're going to make it, baby." This was Saint Anne wind-surfing over her mind, trying to survive, trying to understand how she could hold it altogether. And the tears appeared in the corners of her eyes and she started singing to herself, a soft whisper of a song, Stardust. Maybe that's what she'd seen in Peter that the rest of us had missed. Stardust. Or what she had seen beneath the surface was something she saw in herself, a quality of dealing with affliction and torment without showing that it hurt. It was this personal quality that got Saint Anne through the gray days and poisonous nights when we were on the road in Asia. The same quality helped Jack, through his Triad connections in Vancouver and Hong Kong (which finally merged into one place) to get us booking in five-star hotels and upscale clubs—the kind of bookings that make the good feel like they are great. Of course, I could have been completely off base about the reasons Saint Anne was eating Lithium; those little pills sent like torpedoes to destroy demons which roam the pathways of our mind and lay in ambush for us. By the time we had buried Peter, the pills had stopped her from waking up in the middle of the night and seeing Peter's head rolling like a bowling ball down 58th Street.

Jack thought that psychotropic drugs gave self-control to the kind of people who pulled handguns in crowded subway cars. In Asia the old people had smoked opium to calm their nerves, to make the world slow down, and to keep the lack of purpose, the injustice, the pain of defeat in their lives from driving them to throw themselves in front of trains. He knew a lot about opium and had been involved in the import-export business for a number of years. Another of those reasons the Harvey Trio ended up living in New York a stone's throw away from Chinatown. Legal drugs, illegal drugs, most of the time they were the same thing, going to the same people; often sold by the same people, too. The legal wonder-drugs in America were for people like Saint Anne who had been tied to large oak trees by their golf-playing mothers during a crucial stage of their development. They gave her wings, said my brother Jack. Wings that allowed her to flap away from the tree, circle over the golf course, find Mother, dive down and cuddle. Or buzz Mother midway through her back swing. The illegal drugs were for those in the ghetto, the projects, the streets, who had never seen a golf club, giving them the ability to live with their rage and cover up their pain.

Jack said the Lithium leveled Saint Anne's highest highs and propped her up during her lowest lows. Those pills performed a chemical reconstruction of her personality which broke down the extremes and kept her caged like a wild cat in the middle. Saint Anne had wanted to keep her drugs a secret from Alex. She was afraid of the mental picture he would have of her, seeing her on the stage of the club made to perk along like a China doll, singing her heart out, all the time powered by a chemical elastic band inside her skull.

TEDDY'S eyes blinked and he slowly raised his head. He yanked hard against his handcuffs, clenched his teeth hard as he rolled his head from one side to the other. For the first time he saw how the cuffs were attached to the iron rings. He shrugged off the drug. But the vision grew more intense with each passing moment. The last thing he remembered was eating sushi in a Japanese restaurant when Frank started picking food out of his plate.

"Shit, where am I? " he moaned.

Saint Anne didn't say anything, and neither did I. We just looked at him.

"What are you doing to me?"

He glanced at me, then over at Saint Anne.

"I hate you," Saint Anne said in a low, throaty growl, as if that explained everything. A voice I'd never heard come from her mouth before. "I hate your fucking guts. Why did you do it? You don't care, do you? Why did you do this to me? Why me?"

Of course he didn't have any idea what she was talking about, what had happened or even where he was.

She lurched forward and spit in his face. He cringed, closed his eyes, her warm spittle on his nose and mustache, dripping across a patch of dried blood. But with his hands chained against the wall he could not wipe it away. Saint Anne was out of con-trol. She drew away from Teddy. The muscles in her jaw flexed sharp, and her eyes coiled around the stacks of old boxes tossed to one side. Admist the piles of wrapping and dust where the illegals usually squatted, she spotted some of the stuff Alex had brought to New York from California and stored in the basement. Alex's stuff looked like it had been used by the illegals to build a nest. Her mind went vacant for a second, as she turned, and walked sideways through a small aisle. She recognized one of the boxes.

"Hey, lady, what are you doing with that?" asked Teddy, shifting as best he could to pick her out among the shadows.

Saint Anne brushed the dust off the ridge of one broken box. Inside it, Alex's football equipment tumbled onto the damp, uneven basement floor. She grabbed Alex's old Oakland Raiders helmet by the leather strap. A couple of roaches scuttled away under some boxes. Her knuckles turned white as she tightly clutched the strap. As she turned, her face was crimson, her breathing short and fast. She rushed Teddy from the darkness, swinging the helmet and catching him along the jaw with a loud crack. The whack grazed his jaw and blood trickled out of the earlier wound and dripped off his chin. This attractive woman in sexy gear and make-up had tried to inflict a major injury on him, and failed because she wasn't any good at swinging a helmet and not from want of trying. A spasm of terror swept through his face, as Teddy braced himself for another attack.

"Hey, lady," he shouted. "You're gonna hurt me bad."

"I'm going to fucking kill you," she said through clenched teeth.

I pulled Saint Anne back, wrapping my arms around her waist and lifting her off the cement floor. She wasn't in the mood to co-operate; she struggled and kicked, losing one of her high-heels in the process. Alex's helmet fell with a thud onto the floor and rolled a few feet away. That had been the first action it had seen in years. At that precise moment she might well have killed Teddy Eliot, when in her heart she really wanted to squash Alex like a piece of equipment from his own game.

"Calm down, Saint Anne. You are going to get yourself in serious trouble trying to hurt this man."

"You call her a saint?" asked Teddy, spitting his own blood through teeth turned liquid red.

"Hurt him? Hah! I want to kill him. See how he likes it. Let me go. You've got no right."

"You ain't gonna kill anyone."

"After what he did?"

"Jack's working on MTV. He can make it right."

"Jack doesn't give a goddamn about my career! He never has. Peter cared. The first man in my life who ever did. And what did this shithead do? He killed Peter."

Saint Anne sunk her teeth into my forearm, drawing beads of blood in the teeth marks which broke through the sweat and hair of my skin. Her face turned into this large, black hole as her mouth formed an unchecked wail, and she went limp. I lowered her real gently until she sat on the floor which was as cold as a switchblade knife, and with my blood on her lips and cheeks, Saint Anne wept into her hands like she used to do as a child when Mother would not take her to the golf course. She sat at Teddy's feet, sobbing and choking back her grief, while he stared down, wondering exactly what kind of a fix he had got himself into.

JACK'S first question as he looked at the bloodied kicker was simple.

"Where are his shoes?"

"In a Japanese restaurant," I said.

"He knows something about Asian culture," said Jack.

"Is that all you can say?" asked Saint Anne, fumbling to light a cigarette. But her hands shook so much that Jack had to strike the match and hold the flame to ignite it.

"Dear, dear Saint Anne. God knows I love you. We all do. But we can't have a guest in our basement without something on his feet. He might come down with pneumonia and we could be legally liable," said Jack, a slight frown knitting his eyebrows together. This statement was coming from a man who had violated the laws of a dozen countries.

"Guest? Are you insane? He killed Peter. God, I can't believe you. Whose side are you on?" Saint Anne had kicked off her other high-heel and walked about in her nylon stockings.

"I didn't know we had to choose sides. Is this some kind of game?" Jack, not having any reply from Saint Anne, walked over to within a couple of feet of Teddy.

"Do you ever eat Chinese food?"

Teddy wasn't sure if this was a trick question.

"I like chow mein," said Teddy.

Jack thought about this reply; he had often said that chow mein wasn't Chinese, but some bastardized American food product that clever Chinese passed off on Americans who thought they were eating something exotic.

"Tell me, what size shoe do you wear?"

Teddy didn't look too sure whether he should take Jack seriously. That was to be expected. After all, he'd only met part of the family, and under very unusual circumstances.

"A ten?" asked Jack. Teddy shook his head. "Nine and a half."

"Good. I thought you might be a nine and a half. That's my size." He stooped down and removed the Chinese beaded slippers from his own feet and slipped them on Teddy's stockinged feet one at a time.

"Those aren't too tight, are they?" asked Jack. "They're actually a nine, but I find them to be very comfortable. I do hope you agree. Otherwise, I can go upstairs and find another pair."

There was a long silence. "They're okay, I guess," said Teddy, after a moment, wriggling his toes.

Heather suddenly appeared and said, "Gideon, you photographing that or what?" She looked up at Teddy and then over at me, trying to understand the situation.

"It's not one of my jobs. This is Saint Anne's project," I said.

"It's a misunderstanding," said Jack.

"Freaky slippers," she said.

"They were a gift from me," said Jack.

"Hey, I thought I had seen them before."

She had come down from the roof of our building without changing out of her workout gear. A sweatband pulled her hair back and wrapped around her ears. The gray sweatshirt and matching pants, damp from sweat, gave Heather the kind of color coordination she loved to achieve with her environment. We stood around Teddy in a little clump like people at the Bronx Zoo monkey cage. Except even the zoo didn't handcuff their monkeys to the wall.

"I think we should talk to him. I know you're pissed off. Scream at him. Get it out of your system. Then we'll let him go. We can't keep him here indefinitely," I said. But Saint Anne avoided eye contact with me.

"A wonderful suggestion, as always, little brother."

"Come on, Saint Anne, talk to me, baby," I coaxed.

Heather saw that Saint Anne's face was all bloody from biting me and her eyes red from crying.

"Something happened to you at the club tonight?"

Saint Anne shifted her weight, inhaling on her cigarette. She ignored Heather's question and blew out smoke, one arm folded over the other.

"Freaky," said Heather. "You wanted to murder him?" She was looking at Teddy with renewed interest.

What followed was what Jack called "a long Saint Anne silence." One of those awkward silences which could drag on and on, as happened once when we were ready to start a set in a club in Bangkok and Jack was running late, and he arrived and picked up his violin and Saint Anne refused to sing. She stood on the stage glaring at Jack, then at the audience. Someone started to boo, then threw a bun or something but nothing could break that silence once she made up her mind to punish someone. We had lost a number of jobs because of that silence. Waiting for Saint Anne to play out the Hamletlike choices in her mind was something we were used to. Any attempt to hurry the process inevitably failed. Of course, an outsider such as Teddy Eliot would have no way of knowing that. For a stranger, Saint Anne's peculiar reaction created a sense of suspense, of tension, of anticipation, and finally boiling over anger. The temptation, always, was to find a metaphysical plunger to force-pump an answer out of her. Alex had been the only one who ever succeeded. Peter laughed it off after his initial failure. Jack and I had never known any difference.

"Don't I get some say in this?" asked Teddy. That, of course, was the hydraulic ram that drove deep into that small withdrawn place where Saint Anne buried herself before making a decision.

She stood upright, stiff and rigid. "No," she screamed. "Why should you get a chance? Did you give Peter a chance? Did you shout a warning from the building? Did you go over the edge to try and stop the beam from falling? No. You didn't do shit. You just kicked it over the side. You didn't care. You probably laughed with your buddies. A big macho guy, right? And we are going to teach you the meaning of pain. Not show business misery but the real life misery of feeling fire burning in every part of your body."

There were two words I didn't like—"we" and "pain"—and I didn't want any part of this we business and pain was one of those words, like trouble, from which you turned on your heels and headed for the first exit.

11

Heather picked up the scuffed football helmet, looking at the smudge of fresh blood glistening on the plastic. She turned it over and smelled inside, taking a long whiff as if past glory was a scent you could smell, one that could never escape the gravity of the plastic interior. As her head emerged from the helmet, a filmy sheet of cobwebs stuck to her face like a mustache.

"Can you believe that?" she asked with a small laugh. "There are spiders' nests inside Alex's helmet." Her hand brushed across the bridge of her nose, she looked at the web, and wiped it on a cardboard box. "Look at this," she said, handing me the helmet.

I took the helmet, Heather grabbed the chin strap and stared at my forearm.

"What did this?" She stared at the bite marks made by Saint Anne.

"A fuzzy spider with an evil temper," I replied.

Saint Anne's eyes rested on my arm. "I did it," she said.

"It was an accident," I said.

"Hey, up here, could I ask when I can go home?" Everyone looked up at Teddy but no one had the answer. We just weren't ready for him; it wasn't his turn. He was a stranger and our basement had known many a stranger and all that, but we had some serious family business which had to be dealt with first.

Saint Anne stood by herself, nursing her grudge, frozen in the shadows, watching Teddy the way a spider watches a fly hovering near the web. Whatever she was thinking she was keeping her thoughts to herself.

Heather touched the small patch of caked blood turned dark on my forearm.

"It ain't nothing," I said.

"It could do with a couple of stitches," said Heather.

I pulled my arm back and walked over to where Frank Cora had left Teddy hanging on the wall like he was waiting for a subway to hell. Some time passed, I don't know how long, but no one said anything. Everyone was thinking to themselves, their thoughts staying inside, just flies buzzing in the humid air. An achy, troubled lull filled the void. I looked at Teddy, seeing he was a mess, his hair, his clothes, his face, and I licked my finger, reached up and cleaned the brown blood stain off his chin. He squirmed a little but he made no real effort to turn away. There was the sour smell of fish, and I was thinking it was probably all that raw tuna undigested in his stomach, the blood had raced just everywhere else once he was under attack, leaving the sushi to rot in his gut.

Heather tipped forward on her toes, did a deep-knee bend squat, stretched down, touched the floor, came back up, then down again, doing her exercises as if the exertion of muscle might clear the air of the fishy smell Teddy had brought into the basement.

"Bet Alex forgot all about that helmet," she said. "You don't just leave something like this behind. People in Paris might get off on it."

"Alex did play football," said Jack. Sometimes his memory surprised him.

"So what's the deal with the helmet?" Heather asked Saint Anne.

But Teddy chimed in first. The disturbing memories of the night hanging heavily on his brow. "She tried to kill me with it."

"I did not," Saint Anne said in an ultra-defensive tone. She fumbled around in her handbag for another cigarette. Her hands searched the side pockets for the pack but all she came up with was an empty pack. She balled it up and threw it on the floor. Saint Anne pulled on her shoes and ran up the stairs. "I hate your guts," she shouted back, then the sound of her high-heels filled the silence with the tempo of fashionable retreat.

There was something of Old Testament fury registered in Saint Anne's words. She had screamed the words in Teddy's direction.

She fled the stage, as it were, with the remaining players, looking among themselves as if to find out how to carry on. Was Teddy the sole object of her hatred? I doubted that her anger had centered only on him; she had other fish-sounds to fry. Peter, who had left her under unforeseeable circumstances. Alex who had constructed the circumstances of his departure. The man who had drowned her mother.

"Did I say something wrong? I know Alex still sets her off. But a football helmet. Man, that's wild," said Heather.

I shrugged and crossed over to shove back the mess made by Saint Anne's efforts to dislodge Alex's old football gear.

"I played football in high school," said Teddy.

"Yeah?" asked Heather. "You were a jock?"

Jack, standing in his stockinged feet, kept his hands in his pockets. He didn't say anything right away. He stood a few feet away from packing crates stacked to the ceiling. He took a fist of packing paper and went back to Teddy, stooped down and stuffed the paper inside the Chinese slippers.

"There," he said. "Now they fit perfectly."

"Jack, what are you doing?" asked his wife.

He rose up from the floor, wiping his hands off. Jack had been confident that Teddy's real size was a nine, and not a nine and a half. Twisting to his side, he playfully pinched Heather's cheeks and brushed his lips against hers.

"Isn't she beautiful?" he said. Then he pivoted around to Teddy with an attitude of inspired confidence. "Heather was a divine athlete. She is pure muscle. A full-blooded white woman, who is full of great strength. And firm from all that exercise."

"I was pretty good at sports," said Heather.

EVERYONE liked one aspect of Heather's character—the American part, which made her direct, honest and open; she said what she thought without reflection and without any thought someone was going to punish her for speaking her mind. What made her an original was her total absence of deception or guile. She came custom-made without the usual emotional instruments needed to screen words, thoughts, and ideas before they entered the gravitational field of conversation. No one thought her conceited or affected for such statements. Because Heather, unlike the rest of our family, had a natural aptitude for telling the truth. She had no secrets. If it wasn't on the surface, it wasn't on the interior. This was a quality that she shared with my wife Elizabeth. And for that matter, it was stamped deeply on Alex's personality. The Harvey children had fitted their private living quarters with partners who could never become strangers.

Heather was one of those people who peaked in high school; her most significant accomplishments occurred while she was a junior and senior. After that, she coasted, mainly downhill. Her achievements on the basketball court had made her a minor legend. The full weight of what Heather had to give to the world had been exhausted by the time she was eighteen. And she was anchored to the greatness of a girls' basketball court in the Bronx. This state of being, where she had experienced one intense, vivid accomplishment and then nothing but years of obscurity, was a condition, which in her mind, she shared with Alex. They were two old, indestructible jocks condemned by their individual excellence of their youths to an adulthood of living in the past. There was no way they would have such a high again. It was like in the music business. There were performers who hit it big for a couple of years and then you only heard their songs in elevators in third world countries and you never read about them, heard about them again. They simply vanished from the face of the earth, living off their royalties and past glories. There had to be a club where people who were addicted to the wild applause met one another, talked over old times, laughed, and cried over their fate.

Heather never found that club. Instead she brought back the feelings of those early victories with cocaine, and Alex, well, Alex reckoned that in a land of Monet, Balzac, and the Sun King, he might have another shot at reaching the summit. That region where the stars seemed brighter and closer, so close you could stand on your toes on a clear night and touch them.

Jack had known Heather for six months when she told him about her past athletic splendor. Of course, my brother had no use for anything concerning sport, except for golf, and even with golf he had specialized himself to a nine-iron and a putter. In a cursory fashion, Heather and Jack had shared a common bond that comes with a slight brush with that brother everyone wants on their side—early fame. This bond was Heather's initial attraction to Jack. On their sixth-month anniversary, Heather poured a bottle of Bollinger's down Jack and drove him to the Bronx. She knew the neighborhood of her old school as if she had attended classes the previous week.

Heather knew the bottom of each hill, the curves, and the crawl spaces between buildings where kids used to play before dope dealers moved in. She didn't miss a turn or a street. She parked her BMW behind the school. Jack got out of the car, stretched, and threw up his portion of the champagne on the grass verge beside the faculty parking lot. A combination of the weather and Heather's apparent lack of control on the sharp turning of corners had worked their effect. He rubbed his neck. I thought of Jack cursing in Chinese and suffering in English, thinking how growing up in Canada we never had any neighborhoods which were remotely like this.

Heather grabbed him by the hand and dragged him back around the school. She paused halfway down a row of hedges that had been trimmed level with the windows. No lights were on around the back. In the pitch dark, Heather showed Jack the secret entrance into the school that she had used years before, and to her amazement it was still there. It was a rear side window which had never properly locked. Jack crawled through the window. Still a little dizzy and off-balance from too much to drink, he needed her help to get in. She pulled him by his belt buckle onto the floor.

Jack propped himself on his outstretched hands, looked around a small room, wondering exactly where he was. One corner of the room had a dripping sink. Smelly towels were hanging on a rack underneath. Janitor supplies were piled on a shelf on the opposite wall. Heather opened the cold water tap. Jack lowered his head underneath this for several minutes, trying to sober up. The water, he said, smelled dank, like an old wig scooped out of Hong Kong harbor. The coldness stung his skin at first. Then he felt a numbness, and finally his scalp began to tingle. He lifted his head, his eyes half-lidded, and turned around to find a worn towel dabbing his face. With his face dry, Jack glanced up to find Heather leaning in the doorway and staring down the hallway.

"It's incredible," she said. "I haven't been inside here for years. It's exactly the same. This blows me away. Down there is the gymnasium. I used to be pretty good on the balance beam. But basketball was my game. I was the best."

"Basketball," Jack said. "Yes, I can see you as a splendid player. No, let me take that back. Not simply splendid. But the best."

She looked back at Jack, her eyes on his forehead. He draped a towel over his shoulder, making him look like the dishwasher in a Chinese take-out.

"Oh, yeah," Heather said. "Wanna see me do a lay-up?"

"Someone might call the cops," said Jack, pulling his eyeglasses down over his nose and looking back at the window.

"No big deal. So are you gonna come or not?"

The polished gymnasium floors reflected the glint of light from the doors. Jack stood there in the dimly lit entrance waiting for Heather to find the lights. Refreshed by the cold water, Jack tried to focus in the darkness. Then Heather hit the light switch. From the far end of the gym, the overhead lights came on in a single, blinding flash, and Heather appeared on the floor dressed in uniform number 26. She was bouncing a basketball and grinning, looking over her shoulder at the empty bleachers, as if she could see an audience with their eyes on her charging the hoop.

Heather dribbled down the full length of the court, swinging in and out with the basketball, changing hands, stopping, staring, challenging an old ghost, then jumped under the basket for an easy lay-up. Jack applauded wildly as if released from his daydream. She had executed the basket perfectly. She grabbed the ball, dribbled behind her back, passed the ball between her legs, over her shoulders, then took off towards the opposite court, and made another lay-up.

"Bravo," shouted Jack. "Well done," he yelled through cupped hands.

In the empty gymnasium, Heather persuaded Jack to take off his shoes and pulled him to center court. They played one-on-one until four in the morning. As they were about to leave, she took Jack by the hand to the top row of bleachers. On the wall were a series of bronze plaques with names on them, dates, and the magic word Senior Captain beneath. She stopped in front of her plaque, reached out, and touched the letters.

"I earned this, Jack. The only thing I've really ever been good at. Ever really earned. I guess it is the only thing I've ever been proud of."

She had been good but she had never been great. Sometimes, however, being good is enough; you can live with good. Most people never get close to good, that's the truth. In basketball or on the stage. Almost all you ever see is the really good ones making a living for a while, before they go on to something else, maybe looking for that club where people go who had made it for a while and then had to leave it for others to do.

12

Saint Anne was singing along to All by Myself, her feet propped on a stack of decorator pillows, the CD playing on the table. She sang with heart-felt emotion as if the words had been written for her. There was a piano at this end of her loft, and I sat down and touched the keys, picking up the melody of the music. She nodded and kept on singing until the song ended. Using her toe she switched off the CD player, lit a cigarette and, blowing smoke rings, stared at the ceiling. She had sunk deep inside herself. Her face had softened only a little. The lines of anger were still etched along her eyes. She pressed the remote and turned on a 50-inch Sony, where an old Raiders-Jets game came to life. She watched with the volume turned off. This was one of Alex's videos. More relics he didn't take to Paris. I played some Herbie Hancock on the piano—Just Enough. This was the way in our family of talking without having to talk; we communicated through our music and the others understood what was on our mind. Playing Herbie Hancock was putting fish-sound in the soup of the day, and you just sat back, your finger going over the keyboard, waiting for that soup to come to a boil. We were born on the outside; we never knew an inside to which we belonged. That was just the way it was and we accepted that we were different, except for Saint Anne. The desire to be famous is the desire to come inside where everyone loves and admires you. Jack and I, we never had that urge.

We watched the rerun of Alex's glory days with the Raiders.

No one had played any of the tapes of Alex's football career (university as well as pro) since he had fled the scene for Paris. On the big screen was his famous helmet with which Saint Anne had belted Teddy. Darting down field, the football tucked under his right hand. Then the bruising tackle, and Alex rolled into a crumpled ball and lay silently on the Astroturf. Saint Anne pressed the replay button, and like a collapsed puppet Alex came back to life, running backwards. She allowed the tape to play again, this time stopping the play at the exact moment of impact. The shoulder and helmet of the Jet defensive back appeared to cut Alex in half.

"I like watching the bastard get hit," she said.

I turned away from the piano and looked at her, smoking her cigarette.

"He's still under your skin."

"He didn't have to go," she whispered.

She touched the pause button, turned on the sound, and activated Alex's bone-crunching hit once again. A bottomless thud which bounced and twisted him. It was true that the reason for his leaving was a matter of personal honor, or at least that was how Alex saw it. Saint Anne said she was more important than his personal honor and that going to Paris because of a silly, wrongheaded bet had made him an asshole. That was one of the strange things about life; how a man's action made him a hero to some and an asshole to others, because when you are growing up you have this feeling that adults have a consensus on this sort of thing and maturity means you realize there ain't no consensus.

No one had put a gun to Alex's head to get his bone marrow realigned on the football field for Oakland. That had been his decision. But Alex had a sense of honor that made him hold positions others would have had abandoned. Saint Anne's worst fear came true the day he had to choose between her and his sense of honor. And she realized that she had not been picked. For Saint Anne this was like having a nightclub manager who had hung around listening to every set she sang, believing in her, supporting her career, calling her into his office and saying that he was canceling her contract because he suddenly got religion and thought singing, playing cards and drinking was evil and he was a messenger of God, going out to do God's work. I never heard of that happening, but it might have happened. Then again I never heard of a man throwing away his job and family to manage a fledgling American-style football team in Paris, a team financed by Peter Montard's uncle.

"I think we should phone Frank and have him come around for Teddy." All the time I wondered whether Saint Anne was thinking about Peter at all.

"No way am I going to do that."

"What are you gonna do with him?"

"I don't know. But I'm thinking about it."

"Jack's already befriended the guy. Turns out he's a Capricorn just like Jack. And Jack's doing his chart. But we got a shipment of illegals coming in two days, he can't stay down there much longer," I said, taking the remote control and pushing the power-off button.

"Tell Jack to keep his hands off him."

"You know how Jack is. He's gonna do what he wants."

She knew that anyway. Jack had made the money which financed the family. Without Jack we would have never had the money for our building, the piano, the darkroom and camera equipment. Not that he went around throwing this in our faces. Jack wasn't like that. I turned around to the piano and started playing. Some Ray Charles stuff that was going through my mind.

Saint Anne listened to me playing, then said, "I just want to get the best once. Can't I win just one time? Come out ahead without getting knocked down? You see anything wrong in that?" The tears welled up, spilling down her cheeks.

I just kept on playing the piano. She had fired a lot of questions which didn't have any answer; the kind of questions which she could only answer herself. But it was starting to make sense now. Teddy was paying a price not merely for beheading Peter, but for all the accumulated wrong turns, broken dreams and deadends in Saint Anne's singing career. The bill had come due and Teddy was the guy who she decided was going to pay.

She tried to light another cigarette. Her hands were shaking badly. She dropped three matches before lighting the tobacco. Throwing back her head, she exhaled.

"You think I'm crazy," she said. "That it was an accident."

"That's what I'm thinking. It was an accident," I said.

"Gideon, you think I can still have a shot at it?"

I knew what "it" was—her face on magazine covers, T-shirts, posters and her name in neon lights so that when she walked down the street people would run after her, asking her for an autograph.

"Of course you can."

"Why is it so hard?"

"It's the nature of the business. Everyone wanting to be famous at the same time and there's only enough fame for a few people at any time," I said.

"It never mattered to you," she said.

I smiled, and ran a finger over the keys on the piano.

"Gideon?"

"Yeah?"

"There's something else."

"Always is," I said.

"The producer, you know that guy Sam who was Peter's friend, who was doing the storyboard for the video. He's dropped out. He said an old client called him and needed a favor. He said he would send me everything he had done. It was the kiss-off, Gideon. Like fuck you, babe. Peter's dead. I don't what to hear from you. Don't call me, I'll call you. And this was the guy who was saying how big I was going to be. How the video was going to knock people out."

"I figured that fame was like a cheating lover. You never really have her. You think you do, but deep down you know sooner or later you're gonna lose her. She's fickle and don't care nothing for you. That kind of lover just makes you hurt until you want to die. Or hurt someone else."

"But excitement in bed with someone who is really hot makes you forget about what comes next. Makes you feel like you are standing on top of the world."

Forgetting could work magic but it is also a dangerous illness. She didn't want to hear that her dream of standing on top of the world was a trick she was playing in her own mind; that if fame could live without her, then she could learn to live without fame.

"You know what made me think about Alex?" she asked, bringing her head forward, her eyes focused on the empty television screen.

117

"His Raiders helmet," I said.

A half grin passed over her full lips as she nodded her lips. "No, not the helmet. The Aramis cologne."

"Teddy?"

"He's wearing Aramis. You never had a sense of smell. Alex," she nearly choked on his name. "That bastard. I'll never forgive him for that time in Bloomingdale's."

SIX months before Alex left New York, he and Saint Anne had gone shopping at Bloomingdale's. On the ground floor were all those young women all looking like movie actresses with their made-up faces, tight dresses, and pouting red lips holding up their samples of perfume for Alex to smell. As Saint Anne and Alex reached the Aramis counter in the far end of the store, Alex had been sprayed on both hands, his forearms, his elbows, and both sides of his neck. He had the salesgirls giggling and flirting with their eyes and mouths. Saint Anne had reached the Aramis counter first.

Saint Anne requested some new shaving soap for Alex. By the time Alex nudged in next to her, he smelled as if he'd been dipped between the legs of a thousand whores. The salesgirl behind the counter gave Saint Anne the American Express bill to sign. Alex leaned over the bill and spelled out each letter of Saint Anne's name as she wrote it on the signature line.

"You don't get a lot of saints in New York," Alex had said to the salesgirl in his Jack Nicholson voice. "This saint is a famous singer. Aren't you, darling?"

The salesgirl looked at the signature.

"If she's so famous how come I never heard of her?"

The salesgirl began to laugh, one of those nervous, you are putting me on laughs that Saint Anne had heard a million times before. And Saint Anne listened to this salesgirl laughing in her face, and did a slow burn.

"Maybe you're not into music," said Alex, trying to head off trouble.

But he was too late.

"I love music," she said. "Like what have you done on MTV?"

"My people are in negotiations with MTV," said Saint Anne.

The salesgirl gave her one of those smug, sure-you-are looks.

"Look, bitch, I don't need this."

She stormed off but not before knocking off a couple of bottles of perfume, smashing them on the floor. The sound of broken glass made her feel good.

"Hey, lady, I'm calling security."

Alex unfolded a wad of twenty dollar bills from a gold clip, glanced at the price tag on the bottle of perfume, and started slapping them down on the counter.

"How much is the damage?"

"What's with her?" Her mouth hung open as she looked at Saint Anne.

He stopped counting twenties, smiled with his perfect set of white teeth and then pushed the money at the salesgirl. "It's called Obsession. That scent makes her go crazy. But she gets over it."

"I think it's pretty weird."

Alex leaned over the counter and watched Saint Anne disappearing into the crowd of shoppers.

"She really can sing the blues."

"I'd say that lady has got the blues," said the salesgirl.

That was the thing about strangers; they could see things, put a name to it that no one in the family could if their life depended on it. Alex thought about this, "Yeah, that Saint Anne. The girl's got the blues and she's been trying for a lifetime to break free," he had said. I had thought so, too.

JACK dragged a chair across the concrete floor.

"You're a fine fellow," he said, as Saint Anne and I returned to the basement. "You know, Teddy agrees with me. At a stage in one's life, you have to start giving up things. I've given up the ballet. No time. Basketball. And now football. I'm not starting any new books. Only rereading old classics. I'd rather know 2,000 books inside out. Every character. Every detail of nuance, scenery, dress, and expression. Rather than 20,000 that are just a blur. I want to glean their essence.

As a Capricorn, I'm certain you understand everything I'm saying. I know that I don't have to explain these things to you."

Saint Anne pushed in close to Jack, reached down and wrapped her hands around his mouth. "Shut up for two minutes. I want to ask him something." Teddy watched her intently, this petite, reduced-to-scale, small childlike creature with deep blue painted lines under both eyes and a cigarette dangling from the corner of her mouth.

"Why did you do it?" she asked him.

"That's like asking a guy when he stopped beating his wife." Teddy pulled his handcuffs tight against the thick iron rings. "I didn't wake up one morning and decide to kill someone. I didn't know the guy. Never heard of him, if you want to know the truth."

"You're maneuvering," she shot back.

"Hey, that's something I did in the army. But there's no maneuvering in the construction trade. Not when you are working thirty stories above the street."

"He's got a point," said Jack, lowering Saint Anne's hand from his mouth.

Teddy's body went limp against his handcuffs, his hip slumped against the concrete wall. Within this limited sphere of movement, his strength was all exhausted. He'd stopped fighting long before we had come back downstairs. The splintered pieces of bamboo and rice paper were like feathers stuck on his work clothes, the debris added desolation to his wrecked, defeated look. Perspiration stains spread out from his armpits. His right jaw was swollen from the punch inflicted by Chute, and then the punch from Alex's helmet. He looked pretty beat up and wretched as he licked his swollen lips with his tongue, eyeing Saint Anne.

"If you're smart, then you'll help us," Saint Anne said. "But if I so much as think you're lying you are gonna be real sorry."

Jack sensed a renewed attack by our sister. He scooped up the Raiders football helmet and quickly slipped it onto Teddy's head. One moment Teddy Eliot had been minding his own business, eating sushi in Queens, and a few hours later he was chained to a basement wall in SoHo, Chinese slippers on his feet and an Oakland Raiders football helmet on his head.

"Hey, the helmet fits," said Heather.

"Saint Anne, I hate it when you become angry. Why not let the man tell his story. Why not listen to what he has to say?" asked Jack, trundling back to the side, where Heather had lit a thick joint. The blue smoke seemed heavier than air, creating layers of pollution. It was part of her workout routine. The pot made her relax; come down after a hundred setups. Her Walkman was tuned to U-2. With a set of padded headphones covering her ears, she leaned against one of the old machines that made needles.

"Go on, Teddy. It's okay, man. Tell us what happened. Then we pack it in, call it a night, and you can go home. Okay?" I pulled out flecks of rice paper from his shirt, beading them up between my fingers and dropping them on the concrete floor.

"You're safe now," shouted Jack from the other side. "Tomorrow we'll all be laughing about this over a drink at the club."

"Shut up about the club. I don't want this asshole to know where I work," said Saint Anne.

And she would not want him to know that Jack owned the club.

She had a contract to sing as long as she wanted; a contract no one was going to take away from her, only that wasn't enough for her. Saint Anne wanted more; she wanted it on her own, because of her talent and she lived for the day she could deliver herself.

Teddy raised his head, his face a deep shadow within the football helmet. Behind the face guard, a view of the world Alex must've seen a couple of thousand times, Teddy coughed out a series of short, flat laughs. He turned his head toward Saint Anne, flipped the helmet back, thumping it lightly against the concrete block wall. All jutting bearded chin and throat, Teddy eyeballed the ceiling. For a second he didn't say anything. Then he whispered something inside the helmet. And soon the sound of the whisper sharpened, his mind was working itself back to the construction site. Teddy was ready to take us thirty stories above Manhattan on Bastille Day.

13

Teddy Eliot shifted his weight as best as he could. His right leg had the eerie feeling of going numb; between his thigh and knee, the muscles tingled, then twitched, his foot kicking like a doctor had hit his knee with one of those rubber hammers.

"My leg's fallin' asleep," he said to Lloyd, whose olive-drab shirt smelled of sawdust and sweat.

"Shake it a little. That brings the blood back," Lloyd suggested.

"I hate that feeling, you know, all jammed up. Like your leg isn't there." Teddy pounded the deadened flesh with his fist. His brow furrowed in a worried expression, then Lloyd knelt down, humming to himself, used his large hands to work the knot out of Teddy's leg. The leg, twitching like a wind-up toy wound too hard, snapped back after a couple of minutes.

"Thanks, man," said Teddy, stretching out. An attack of muscle cramps was an affliction brought on by the heavy work, the heat, humidity, and long periods of working in a single position. Cramps that high off the ground caused some panic; the man lost the use of his leg, and this made him feel vulnerable, giving him an undercurrent of desperation. The unpleasant reality of looking over the edge at the cars and people as small as ants crawling around a disturbed nest and knowing if your body locks up, and they have to carry you down, then that's the end. No one said it to a guy's face, but a guy who couldn't hack the work was finished as a man. There were no second chances, even on union jobs like this one. Teddy was still on probation and getting rid of him was no big deal. All the foreman had to say was that he was a fuckin' wimp.

These thoughts raced through Teddy's mind, as he squatted next to Lloyd on a makeshift platform which had been slung between a grid of steel beams, glistening with fresh bolts as big as grenades. A spiderweb of corrugated steel thirty stories above the traffic signals, which on a clear day, you could watch changing twenty blocks away.

Fortunately his leg cramp hit during the mid-afternoon break. It had gone unnoticed like a minor wheeze a performer might make offstage. Bastille Day was dead still, hot, steamy. A gray haze clung in the airless sky. That morning, a worker down on twenty-eight, a guy with grizzled red hair, and a nose smashed from bar room fighting, had fallen back on his tail. Passed out like a front-row true believer at a revival meeting. His legs had buckled in the heat, and two guys had to hold him down because old Red was shivering so much he could've rolled off the edge. A line of yellow-green drool fell down his chin. In that intense heat, Red's face was the color of a boiled white turnip. He thrashed around as if something heavy was on his chest, pulverizing him with a heavy iron weight. The supervisors had some men carry him down to an ambulance. Teddy listened to the fear in the voices of the other men. He looked down and saw the tiny red flashing light as the bug-sized ambulance moved slowly through the ant colony.

After Red had been carted away, most of the guys started feeling pains in their bowels, heads, arms. It was a liquid achy feeling that unnerved more than it hurt. All the guys had begun moving in slow motion, conserving their strength. With a crew of wobbly legs and heat-fogged brains, one of the foremen passed the word down that the men could have a beer and take an extra ten minutes. A helluva way to build a high-rise in midtown Manhattan. Someone else's dream was always in a rush. Forget the heat. Forget the danger. Forget the physical exhaustion. And above all, forget the constant pushing to keep things moving. Overload. Overlook. Overhead. The three "overs" in the construction trade.

"Sure is fucking hot today," said Lloyd.

Teddy pulled off his hard hat and slid it between his feet. The heavy rubber soles of his boots pressed down on the outer rim. The trick was making sure that the hard hat didn't get "legs" and walk away. Or crash into the crowded street. Lloyd had nearly lost his hat before noon. Not watching where he was going; he nearly got blind sided by a freshly placed beam. One that hadn't been in that space a day ago. It happened twenty minutes after they took Red down. Just at the moment when everyone's concentration was off. The moment when guys start thinking of grievances instead of hazards. That's the most dangerous time on a site. Nothing's more treacherous for the street level world than hard feelings filling the heads of those thirty stories above.

The landscape in the sky above Manhattan was constantly changing, and each step had to be adapted for the previous day's cluster of new crisscrossed bars, beams, angles, fine wires. The scenery was always in flux, and cluttered. In the heat, you never knew where you were. And you couldn't find your bearings like at home where the sofa and chairs always stay in the same place. Nothing weird or crazy sticking out of a left corner you never saw before.

"It's hotter up here than my mom's oven," said Teddy.

He drank long and hard from a can of beer, then wiped his forearm across his lips. A tiny streak of wet beer matted down the hair on his forearm, leaving a clean mark zigzagging and exposing the white flesh behind the sweat, dirt, and grime.

"Not as hot as your trial is gonna be," said Lloyd, the pink gums sucking a laugh into the back of his throat.

"It's not my trial."

"That's not the way I see it."

"What else could I do?" Teddy glanced down at the cars on the street below. Mostly a stream of little yellow bugs creeping down narrow paths, swallowing and disgorging one or two ants at a time.

"You could've minded your own business, man."

Yeah, thought Teddy. His mother had said the very same words. More than once. Why puff yourself up with other people's problems when we have enough of our own? Was it self-importance? What was he trying to pull off? Prove that he was better than anybody else? The abrasiveness of life soon took the polish off. Why hurry the whole damn process along? A lot of questions that Teddy had slept through for over eight and a half months. Things always looked different afterwards. After the second guessers. The Monday morning quarterbacks. Where were they the night of the fire?

Teddy Eliot had been back from California for almost a year. He took odd jobs, getting his feet firmly planted back on home turf. But New York was cut in a different groove than California and as far as he could see almost no one had their feet planted on anything approaching firm ground. And living back at home had a different emotional circuit system than he remembered from living in prison. Two years inside the deep shade, as one of his cell mates called it, was a long time. The fine coil of terror remained drawn tight, and as sharp as an ax blade, for months after Teddy got out. Outside life looped a rope over him and yanked him in two directions at once. Confused, distressed, and a little afraid, Teddy made a straight line for Queens and his mother's house where his room was still the way he'd left it years before.

With sustained effort, Teddy stopped hearing the prison bullhorn in his sleep. The sullen moods no longer washed over him like breaking waves. Then he had a stroke of luck. The owner of the Philip's station took a chance on him. He believed, or so he said, in second chances. People had a streak of bad luck. Things went wrong, not because the person was bad, but because there were evil and dark forces stalking the world. America had invented a blame machine, and when something went wrong, they threw in a victim, the machine chewed that victim up and that made everyone feel happy, secure. The thing was, though, this blame machine was always hungry for fresh victims. If this constant feeding binge stopped then people got real nervous, all of this was according to his new boss, so that someone had to be held responsible and fed to the beast. And Teddy Eliot got the nod and the blame and the prison time. That meant that he was now immune. Of course, the boss said, Teddy had learned his lesson. As soon as Teddy was in touch with the higher energy levels, and understood their true nature, then the universe would no longer treat him like a pronoun, a fraction, but rather as a whole, specific person.

This boss called himself a member of the New Enlightened People's Association, Manhattan Chapter. He talked about seeing a tunnel of light, hearing waves breaking on the beach. Teddy only wanted a job.

After several months at the service station Teddy hadn't been late once. Never phoned in sick. Never slacked off on the job. He stood toe to toe with a robber, and held him for the cops. He passed the test of time. But the beast hadn't forgotten Teddy. What his boss had said wasn't true; when that beast got you once, he kept coming back, and back until there was nothing left of you. This time the beast showed up on a Wednesday evening shift, his jaws open, hungry and happy to see Teddy wasn't expecting him. Teddy had been distracted, and as the beast crept nearer, he turned his back. Across the street, a factory had caught on fire. Tongues of flame shot through window-panes which burst into glass showers, showering pellets of silvery comets over the parking lot. Before the fire, Teddy had had a chance. He had no warning that something dangerous was panting heavily at the hollow of his knee, nipping at his heels, waiting to drag him back to the deep shadows.

The hammer cocked at ten that evening. Teddy pumped gas into a dirty, beat-up Olds with Jersey plates. The radio blaring Latino music. In broken English the driver complained about his left front tire being low on air.

"Yeah, yeah," Teddy shouted over the music.

"You gonna fuckin' fill it up or stand around all night?"

"Air pump's broke," said Teddy.

The young Spanish driver with a golden front tooth lowered the volume of his radio. "What'd you say?"

"Neighborhood kids broke the goddamn pump." Teddy had seen that kind of face in prison lots of time. Cocky, angry, eyes full of other people's bright objects. That three-day unshaved look, the long shaft of a jaw, and the drug-yellow eyes that looked like they'd been transplanted from a long-dead ancestor.

"Shit." The Spanish man slapped his dashboard with the flat part of his hand. He stuck his head out the window, and looked back at Teddy. "What time you got, man?"

"Just about ten." Teddy glanced across the street. His eyes rested on a new, shiny red BMW with New York plates. He thought at the time that one day he'd have a fancy red sports car with AM/FM radio. The gas nozzle overflowed, spewing gas out of the rusty hole in the old Jersey car and running onto the pavement. Teddy wiped his hands on a paper towel, walked around to the driver's side. The driver handed him a credit card. Teddy thought at the time, "What a world." This young punk behind the wheel was no more than his own age—maybe twenty-five or so—and had paid with a gold American Express card. He looked the guy over, then went inside and phoned American Express to check it out even though it had a Spanish name on it. He got back a confirmation number. Teddy filled out the slip and crossed back through the pumps. He glanced across the street. The red BMW was gone. BAR-483. The New York license plate stayed in his head. He repeated it to himself.

He didn't think much of it. Until thirty or forty minutes later, he was checking the oil on a Chevy van. Across the street he saw smoke billowing in large black clouds out of a factory window. Then smoke poured out of a number of other windows. Teddy ran back into the station and dialed emergency services. Soon hook and ladder trucks filled the street. Firemen rushing around with axes and gas masks, and the sky alight with an orange glow that could be seen all the way to the East River. Six in the morning the firemen had left and across the street the factory smoldered and a black ash hung in the air. Tiny particles of soot smudged Teddy's clothes, face, and hands.

He remembered those plates—BAR-483 danced in his mind's eye. The beast had sent transportation to carry Teddy back to the blame machine. The cocked hammer was about to fall, and even then escape had been possible. But Teddy couldn't help himself. He couldn't have stopped himself from putting his own neck on the striking surface. A month later when the insurance company lawyer came around to the station, Teddy remembered the red BMW and the license plate. That day his life changed, or maybe it just went back to being what it had always been. Because the car belonged to the owner of the factory; the man who had claimed against the insurance company, and gasoline cans had been found inside in four separate parts of the factory.

The lawyer had said to Teddy, "If that isn't arson, then hell's walls are made of ice cream." A funny thing to say, Teddy remembered thinking at the time.

It never occurred to him that Mr. Garson, the station owner, would be anything but proud of his truth-telling. Early on, within the first couple weeks of work, Mr. Garson had explained his philosophy of life. The New Enlightened People's Association in a nutshell. He'd told Teddy that the quality-control test of a man's character was whether he could be relied upon to tell the truth. Teddy would be in charge of the service station and unless Mr. Garson had absolute confidence in his honesty—and his criminal record in California had nothing to do with dishonesty or fraud, in fact was the result of honesty to the extreme degree—then the toxic waste of doubt would make them both suffer. All lies had to be surgically removed. And once the structure of the relationship was freed from deception, then there could be a real basis for love. Not sexual stuff, Mr. Garson had explained. But brotherly love and trust. That's what kept the beast at bay, said Mr. Garson. And Teddy had started to believe there might be something to what Garson had been telling him.

Only it hadn't dawned on Teddy that Mr. Garson wouldn't have expressed his worldview to the owner of the burned-down factory or that this owner could put so much pressure on him that the question of brotherly love became a troublesome, an entirely awkward construct, and something to stay away from when Mr. Garson, the Garson wife, and the little Garson children were threatened with extinction. Mr. Garson changed his mind about the meaning of life at the first sight of a sharkfin slanting towards him. Where did that leave Teddy? The beast was starving again.

"You see, we have a problem," he'd said to Teddy.

Mr. Garson said, a year after employing Teddy, that his insurance company, the one that insured his business, his home, his life, and his health, had informed him that an ex-con on the payroll meant cancellation of all these policies. Teddy was an extraordinary risk.

"Not that I agree with them," Mr. Garson said. "But I can't run my business without insurance."

Insurance companies seemed determined to turn Teddy's life inside out. Truth became this thing which passed through a smoked glass and came out the other side a different color altogether.

"Is it possible," Mr. Garson stumbled on his words, his tongue lolling inside his mouth, "At least a maybe, you might've been wrong about that red BMW? Hey, I make mistakes all the time. If I think about a lot of things I see, I have to admit that sometimes I forget. It's not clear. So if someone asks me, I just say, I can't remember. Or something like that."

"I'm not lying, Mr. Garson. It was red. I know my cars. It was definitely a BMW. And the license plate. BAR struck me as funny. I like numbers. I was always good at numbers in school. They just stuck in my head. BAR-483," said Teddy.

So Mr. Garson fired Teddy for telling the truth. And Teddy was already into the case too deep to suddenly pretend that he hadn't seen the red BMW which just so happened to be registered in the factory owner's name; the same person who claimed that he was at home watching television with his wife the entire night of the fire. When the insurance company lawyer found out that Teddy had lost his job over fingering the factory owner, he drove all the way in from Westchester County, parked in front of Teddy's apartment—from which he would soon be evicted—and told Teddy that there was something called the Insurance Institute of America which gave plaques and medals to people like Teddy for telling the truth about insurance fraud.

He presented Teddy with a small wooden plaque with a fake gold scroll glued to it. Teddy Eliot's name was inscribed in beautiful writing. So Teddy felt all the more certain that his neck was safe and sound. That glossy finish glittered in the reflected sunlight, evaporating any nagging thoughts about doing the right thing.

TEDDY finished his beer and rose to his feet, his hard hat still between his toes, as Lloyd just shook his head. "And I told that guy, 'I don't need a medal for doing what's right.'"

"Tell me straight, man," said Lloyd. "You mean to tell me you would've told the cops about Mr. Red BMW if you knew all this shit was coming down?"

The question made him smile and he squinted at the sun. Then he looked over at Lloyd, shrugging his shoulders. "What should I've done? Stepped back from it all?" And to illustrate his point, Teddy stepped backwards without looking first and hooked the heel of his boot on a loose beam which someone had fucked up and left where it should not have been left. With old Red having convulsions, a sediment of rumble collected, here and there, like weeds growing out of cracks in the sidewalk. If Red had stayed in bed that morning, if it hadn't been so hot that it oxidized a man's breath in his nose, if Teddy hadn't been seized with a leg cramp and a strong desire to talk about the insurance trial, then, of course, Peter Montard would've crossed West 58th Street, turned left and looked at a large collection of rare letters, maps, and prints, thinking that a Jimi Hendrix letter would make one member of the Harvey family real happy.

The "ifs" could have been stacked all the way to the moon, but a member of the ant colony was destined to lose his head. Someone hadn't tied the wooden beam down; moved it away from the edge. Teddy could see from the expression of horror on Lloyd's face but it was too late. The beam knocked him forward onto the concrete floor and then began a high velocity descent like a missile launched to the street below. Teddy lay on the concrete, his eyes squeezed shut, praying hard, as Peter Montard strolled down the street.

TEDDY was beginning to believe that he was one of those people born with the knack of always being exactly at the wrong place at the wrong time. He was a white man destined to spend his life pinned like a butterfly by the misfortunes caused to others who stumbled into his path; he was someone who no longer had the ability to avoid the blame machine.

How had it all started? Why, simple enough, in the service of truth. He had been set up and ambushed by defending his commitment to the truth. Teddy Eliot was a casualty of veracity.

Father said that "man is finished when he becomes altruistic." Jack reminded me that Father had said this a few weeks after he broke the news that our mothers had been murdered years ago in Seattle, and how less than a year later the whole family had moved to Canada. Jack said, "You can't condemn a man for quoting the classics."

From the expression in Jack's eyes, I felt the presence of Father in the basement of our building; standing among us in that old needle factory, listening carefully as Teddy finished explaining every detail of what had taken place at the hour of Peter's death on Bastille Day. Witnessing, along with his children, the painful tragedy of Teddy Eliot. A moment loaded with a feeling of sorrow that a man of courage should've lost his foothold on that beam and severed Peter's head. So there it was.

"A remarkable story," said Jack. He was the first to say a word after Teddy finished. "Absolutely remarkable. Though it doesn't surprise me in the least. You seem, Mr. Teddy Eliot, a sublime creature. A real American, a wonderful example of a Capricorn. Yes, yes."

"How do we know you're not lying?" asked Saint Anne, her mouth more relaxed. Then her fists clenched at her side. She cocked her head, her eyes resting on the handcuffs which bound Teddy to the basement wall. "Are you?" shouted Saint Anne, her face flushed.

She was looking for weakness, ambiguity, and the small, telling inconsistency. Saint Anne's mind demanded not so much proof as emotional satisfaction. She knew when someone missed a note, when the tempo was wrong. That was her strength; she knew, no, that's not it, she felt music in the way other people can touch silk and know the grade and quality.

Before Teddy could answer her question, the old black Ma Bell phone rang inside my darkroom. It startled Saint Anne. I ducked inside and picked up the receiver on the second ring.

"I went to the club and they said she had gone home," said Frank Cora.

"Yeah, she has a headache," I said.

There was a long pause.

"Have you done it yet? Know what I mean?" asked Frank in a clear and distinctive voice.

"Done what?" I replied.

"Don't play games with me. Did you do the right thing?" His voice suddenly became angry and tense. When he found out Teddy was still alive, Frank screamed into the phone. "You fucken candyass. I should've known. Anyone with a little black blood and the name, Gideon. Shit. Well, I'm tellin' you now. Either get it over with. Or give that asshole back to me. You understand what I'm saying? Am I making myself clear?"

"I think you ought to speak to Saint Anne," I shouted back.

I cupped my hand over the receiver, dragged the phone by a long coiled cord out of my darkroom and into the corner where everyone watched me in silence. I motioned Saint Anne with the phone. Jack rolled his eyes, and immediately interrupted.

"No, no. My good brother. Tell whoever it is that Saint Anne can't possibly take a call now. You can't expect her to talk when we have an innocent man chained to our wall. Here, give me that," he said, approaching the phone. I held the receiver away from Jack, and nodded to Saint Anne.

"It's your fan, Frank. The one who is going to make you famous,," I said to Saint Anne. "He's asking same weird shit questions. I think you'd better talk to him. Now."

Saint Anne stepped over and taking the phone, half turned, twisting the long cord around her waist. She kept eye contact with Teddy as she said hello into the phone. Jack traveled back to his corner beside Teddy, shaking his head.

"This is wild," said Heather. "Really out of control. I'm headin' out."

Saint Anne shot Heather a glance that froze her on the spot. She covered the phone. "Wait. We've all got to talk about him. And decide what we are going to do as a family. That's the way we've always lived."

Saint Anne cradled the phone between her neck and shoulder. From her end of the conversation, it was clear that Frank had gone on the offensive with her as well. A series of but's echoed in the basement as she tried to interrupt Frank. Finally, she got to say something other than but.

"You believe in my talent, Frank?"

She paused.

"That's not believing in my talent, Frank. You gotta go with me on this. Let me make the decision."

Then she listened again, rolling her eyes, her lips pouting.

"What did I ever do to make you think that?" she said, her voice breaking. "I never said any such thing. I've never thought of you that way. Not ever. And I resent you saying these things. Of course, I won't marry you. I don't care if you've told your wife. Divorce her for me? You're making yourself crazy," she said. Then there was a long silence, and her eyes met Teddy's eyes, her head shaking as she stared at him.

"Don't threaten me," she said into the phone. "Or him. No, it wasn't a loan. No, you can't have him back. Not after what you said. You think I'm getting involved in something like that? Not on your life. Not on your goddamn life." She slammed down the phone.

Saint Anne didn't say anything.

"Why don't I make a call to Chinatown?" asked Jack, real casually.

We all knew what that meant.

"I want to handle this one, Jack. If I need your help, I'll ask. But this is my business. I am in control."

She didn't look in control. Jack and I exchanged glances with Teddy hanging on the wall, listening and watching to the Harvey Trio performing one of our usual gigs—a disharmony special.

"Frank wants to marry me," said Saint Anne, looking deathly pale. "But I never did anything."

"What about Teddy?" I asked. I looked over my shoulder and Teddy seemed relieved that someone was paying attention to him.

"Frank wants him," she said, but her voice trailed off.

"Wants him dead," I said.

A frightened animal sound came from the wall.

She nodded her head away from us, and began crying. She kicked the filing cabinet. The blow dislodged the phone, sending it crashing onto the floor. Plastic bits of the shattered base flew across the room.

"What do we do?" she asked.

"I will phone my friends,," said Jack.

"That won't solve anything. It will only make it worse," said Saint Anne.

I could see the Italians and the Chinese squaring off on Canal Street and blood letting on both sides.

"Forget it, Jack," I said.

"Of course, that's the right thing to do. Not that anyone in this family ever does the right thing. Or wishes to listen to me. But why not try? This one time. Is anyone listening to me?" A question which made me think of Elizabeth's father doing one of his little song-and-dance routines up north. Like Jack, the old man arched his back, bit his lip at a disorderly audience, and cried out at them, as he began juggling oranges.

"Not cool," said Heather. "We're kidnappers. We got a guy hand-cuffed to the wall. And you want to phone the Triad? You want to get us all killed?"

"What else did Frank say?" I asked.

"That unless we sent Teddy out in thirty minutes, he was coming in to get him," she said.

Teddy pulled against his cuffs. "I guess I'm in trouble."

"Major trouble," I said to Teddy. "The kind that can't get any worse."

And I remember Frank Cora asking Teddy's foreman in that hellhole of a house if he had ever met anyone who was looking for trouble and the foreman admitted that he hadn't.

14

Jack sat cross-legged on the basement floor, his violin held under his chin, playing Vivaldi's The Four Seasons. Heather hated classical music. She fixed her Walkman earphones over her head, turned up the volume on Eric Clapton and went upstairs to where Saint Anne and I were hanging out. Shaking her head, she walked on past without saying anything. What was there to say? Either you liked Jack's playing or you turned and ran as far away as you could. Teddy was the only one who couldn't flee from Jack's Vivaldi concert. I could see him looking down at Jack, squatting Asian style on the basement floor, playing the violin, his eyes half-closed in pleasure.

"If you are going to kill me, just get it over with," Teddy had said.

That's what Jack reported he said; and Jack did what you would expect Jack to do, he ignored him and played on.

Saint Anne walked around my studio in circles, her eyes slanted at the eighteen foot ceiling. Heather, her ankles hooked, sat on a stuffed chair, smoking a joint and into her music trip. She moved her head to the beat and flicked ash on the floor.

One of those long silences followed. From the basement we heard the violin. Jack had a talent for the violin, a fine, soft touch. He had everyone lost in thought, trawling like a fishing boat through the night, searching for three young women trying to keep their heads above water in Peugeot Sound, waiting for the boat that never came. Saint Anne's MTV video was shot on a sailing boat. They had her singing above the water with three beautiful women swimming in the background. It wasn't clear if this was a music video or a Red Cross lifesaving commercial; but it was Saint Anne's dream, and Peter had let her get her way.

At the far end of the studio, I straddled one of the chairs and rocked forward, and after the music stopped Jack emerged from the basement and wandered around the cameras and lighting equipment, turning lights off and on, looking through the camera viewfinder; opening a few cupboards, taking out a box of needle samples, he looked happy. He had bought all the equipment I used and had no idea how any of it worked. It didn't matter to Jack so long as I was happy. So long as Saint Anne was happy. She had a place to sing; I had a place to take photographs. Why complicate life and want something more? That was Jack's view of the world, one I thought made a lot of sense. He went over and kissed Heather, she looked up, smiling and bobbing her head to Eric Clapton. Saint Anne was too upset to sit, and instead she smoked, paced, her hands shaking and her heart racing.

"Teddy likes Vivaldi," said Jack.

"Did he have a choice?" asked Saint Anne.

"That's rather cruel," he replied. He carefully put his violin in the case, put the case in the cupboard and pulled out a box of needles.

"Jack, would you put away those goddamn needles," shouted Saint Anne. He emptied a dusty, faded red sample flip-book onto the table.

"Did you see the tattoo on Teddy's arm? That's a Triad tattoo but he doesn't know it," he said with a chuckle. "I am certain that we have tattoo needles in one of these boxes. One of those best quality elliptic gold-eye needles," said Jack.

"What's the tattoo mean?" I asked.

He put a finger to his lips. "I can't tell you, Gideon. But let's say it grants him protection."

"It doesn't seem to be working all that well," I said.

Jack sighed, twisting his head around to look at Saint Anne who was pacing behind his back. He watched her smoking a cigarette, her face filled with anxiety.

Saint Anne inhaled deeply on her cigarette. "Don't you understand how dangerous Frank Cora is? He can have all of us killed and no one could stop him. Not your Chinese Triad friends, not anyone."

"I wouldn't be too sure about that," said Jack.

In reality, Jack had been bottom-fishing in the needle sample books for a particular reason. He had in the loose folds of his mind a Chinese notion that selecting precisely the right needles might enable him to divine the right answer. Needles could be used as yarrow sticks, overlooking the fact that the needles had a single eyelet in one end. And the I Ching wasn't merely about throwing the yarrow sticks; it had to do with acuteness in finding them. The mortician's needle, number B/6545, the one Jack had carried around in his shirt pocket since Peter's funeral.

"You make me crazy with your Chinese superstition," snapped Saint Anne.

"Would we have done better to follow American superstition?" he said.

No one in the family could say he didn't have a point. He had become rich and we had become his tax shelters in an alliance between superstition, fortune-telling, Asian stock exchanges, and a battery of lawyers and accountants who protected him against attacks launched by the American Internal Revenue Service.

"I have some right in this, Jack," said Saint Anne.

"Of course you do. This is your show. We are just the back-up players like in the old days. We need a little more time," said Jack.

"It's not Teddy. But Saint Anne's boyfriend, Frank. That's our major worry," I said.

Jack looked up from the needle book. "Boyfriend? I didn't know that."

"He's not my boyfriend and don't ever say that he is again."

"Doesn't he want to marry you?" I asked.

Heather kicked away from the wall, shaking her head. "Wow, you're incredible. You want to marry every man with money who comes into the club."

"That's ridiculous. Sick." Saint Anne spun around, and leaned over the table, lighting a new cigarette with the old one. "You do believe me, don't you, Gideon?"

I wasn't so sure that Heather was wrong; Saint Anne was in a comfortable position, but she lived in a gilded cage, and she wasn't certain whether she could live without Jack's support. About the only way out was for her to find someone who would take care of her, give her career a chance. Jack had given her a club. That had been enough at the time and she was grateful. But when that bitch fame failed to come into the club, one year turning into the next, she got concerned, then worried, then angry and a little bitter.

At the other end of the table, Heather slumped over the edge. She had put out her joint and inhaled a long hit from her plastic bullet loaded with coke. She sneezed once. The second sneeze snapped her neck back. All this distraction permitted Jack to continue what he'd wanted to do anyway which was to find the sample of tattoo needles. Heather's eyes shone brighter, like a batter watching the curve ball coming inside and high.

"What's this guy to us?" The slack had gone out of her face.

The question, the obvious one, had us all thinking hard, including Jack.

"You mean Frank?" I asked.

"Naw. I mean the freak we got chained downstairs. Hey, maybe it wasn't his fault about Peter. But who cares whether it was an accident or he took aim and threw the fucking beam? He killed Peter. Am I right or what? So do we give a shit what happens to him?" Cocaine gave Heather the urge to talk. Three hours of Heather's thoughts were compressed in a few sentences.

"Heather," began Jack. "You're so . . . so, so much a Pisces sometimes. That dear boy opened his heart to us. He didn't have to tell us his life story. And you want to throw him to a criminal like Frank Cora who is making Saint Anne think that he can go around murdering an entire family and nothing can be done to stop him? Why, Heather, I'm so very disappointed in you."

What Jack meant was that he was disappointed in Saint Anne for thinking a third-rate gangster was more powerful than her brother.

Saint Anne caught my eye, as if to ask where I stood. "Frank isn't someone to fool around with. But should we hand Teddy over to him? I don't think so. Jack's right, he can take care of Frank," I said, as the conversation began to accumulate thermal heat.

"It's Saint Anne's call," said Heather, then a big grin broke over her face. One of those drug-induced smiles from some inner space of blackness. "The bastard cut off Peter's head. That was a bad thing. I don't like it at all."

The phone rang at the opposite end of the studio. Saint Anne and Heather simultaneously glanced at their watches. It could've been a wrong number.

I sat back on the rear two legs of a wooden chair, watching the lights cast shadows on the oak floor and letting the phone ring.

"Aren't you going to answer it?" asked Jack, pulling out a long needle from a sample case. "Or are we out?"

When I finally picked up the phone Frank sounded normal. I could hear Chute cracking his knuckles in the background. Frank made a couple of wisecracks about how he was blowing off steam the last time he had phoned and he hadn't meant anything by it. He knew that I knew how sentimental he was about my sister. Perhaps I might reason with her. Tell her what a splendid fellow he really was, how he stage-managed the whole union like a genius, and why she should let him rescue her singing career before it was too late, after all there was always new talent coming out every year. He saved Teddy Eliot for last. After all, this wasn't just a little lover's quarrel. And hadn't I told him that day he took me to the Chinese restaurant that we were going to do the right thing once we got our confession out of Teddy? Now, what was all this I don't know bullshit? What did it mean? Why hadn't we warned him that we might have some minor aesthetic problems with applying the old eye for an eye, tooth for a tooth principle? He was starting to sound at the fringe a little like one of those TV preachers who tell their audience—you reap what you sow. What goes around comes around.

Chute could save us all a great deal of trouble, and a lot of other people from a case of the bottom-line blues. If I knew what he meant. This time he didn't ask to speak to Saint Anne. But before I put down the receiver, he reminded me that if, just if, I was pulling his leg about thinking of Teddy as a target rather than a person, then he had a surprise for us. Something nasty. Something none of us wanted to even think about. Not for a minute; not for a second.

"What did he want?" asked Saint Anne, sliding into a chair.

"He wanted to know if the engagement was still on," I said.

"Oh, my God," said Saint Anne.

"He sounds nuts," said Heather, refilling the plastic bullet. "Like all fucked up. It's crazy. A dangerous groupie. Just think what hell your life would be if like you got famous. It would be a living hell."

"What did you tell him, Gideon?" asked Saint Anne.

I looked at her, thinking of our target pinned to the basement wall below. "I said, 'yeah.' Hey, what'd you want me to say? Besides, he was more interested in Teddy. He wants us to kill him." Even Jack dropped the tattoo needles and looked up.

"Don't be absurd, Gideon. We aren't going to kill anyone in our own building. Least of all a most interesting working-class lad like Teddy with a powerful tattoo. Why, it would be shameful. Surely, you can reason with this Frank?"

Saint Anne cut him off. "What did you tell him?" Her voice choked up, she reeled forward and grabbed my arm just above her own teeth marks.

"That we'd do the job," I said, trying to think of Teddy as a crime statistic for the Borough of Manhattan. "Of course, I lied." I waited for Saint Anne, who looked like a drunk sobered up after causing a fatal driving accident, to break into a smile. Breaking her grip, she slowly released my arm and sighed.

"I'm not so sure," said Saint Anne, rising from the chair, wrapping her arms around herself. She walked over and stood behind Jack. She placed both hands on his shoulders.

"Of what?" asked Jack.

"Whether we should kill him," said Saint Anne.

"You got my vote," said Heather. "I've got a baseball game to watch tonight. So we should do it before the game starts. I hate missing the opening pitch."

"How much you put on the Mets?" asked Jack.

"Two hundred."

Jack loved to gamble, said it was his Chinese blood that made him want to take risks, place bets on events, people, and things which had no certain chance of winning. Saint Anne's singing career was a gamble. So was my photo studio, and that gamble had started to pay off and deliver a return which made me feel proud that Jack's faith in me hadn't been misplaced.

"That's a tidy sum," said Jack. "But two hundred's not quite enough to justify killing someone unless you are in Bangkok or Phnom

Penh," said Jack. As he finished, Jack flipped open what proved to be the first page of the tattoo needle book he'd been looking for. He clapped his hands. "Wonderful," he shouted.

"Excuse me," I said to Saint Anne. "Did you say kill?"

She did not reply. I had no way of knowing whether Saint Anne was saying something because she wanted to shock us, whether it was a fainthearted attempt at irony, or whether she really would do it. Her Hamletlike quality caused a number of such mistakes about her motives.

"But you're not sure," I said.

"I want to know whether Teddy has a good character. Why he was in prison. Even in California, they don't just throw you in prison for double-parking on Mulholland Drive," said Saint Anne, blowing cigarette smoke across the table.

Heather half-laughed to herself. "California was good to Alex. I wish he were here now. He'd know how to handle this joker."

Saint Anne nearly broke both of Jack's collarbones with her bare hands. He moaned and shrugged his shoulders until they touched his neck. Everything was happening fast. Crosscurrent reacting on crosscurrent through the studio.

"So how you gonna find out about Teddy's character?" I asked what I thought was the logical question.

She looked directly at Heather. "That's simple. We'll ask him about his felony conviction. Then I'll know what we should do. His character. That's all that matters. That's all that should ever matter to anyone."

And therein lay Saint Anne's moral fingerprint. One she smudged on Alex. Each time he looked the wrong way, his good character was the victim of a slow-motion homicide. And so it was with Peter. Bad character to Saint Anne's way of thinking could never be blotted out; it had to be put in leg-irons, then extinguished.

Jack held up the mortician's needle and two tattoo needles in the palm of his hand and slowly swept his upturned hand around the table.

"That's it."

"That's what?" I asked.

"Friends will be found in the remote countryside," said Jack, reading the position of the needles in his hand. Every time Jack pulled his I Ching stunt I felt like I'd shrunk; that my life had coiled down so far that I'd dropped out of view, and details of life exploded in size. What hung suspended on that huge slab of reality were giant images of Frank and Chute shooting at shadows stealing down the street like a sudden case of bad weather.

15

Teddy's criminal exploits occurred in Northern California where the large houses with bougainvillea-covered decks were owned by computer people. He confessed to his criminal record straight away without any elaborate excuses either. In a place like California where earthquakes, race riots, looting, fires, floods, mud slides and disease destroyed people and property as efficiently as in any third world country, Teddy's crime wasn't any big deal in the larger scale of disorder. He said he had been a victim of circumstance. A lot of criminals say that, to find someone or something else to blame. In our basement, Teddy had slipped back into the insanity of California, only this time there was no Constitution of the United States, no Bill of Rights to protect him. He was facing the Harvey Trio. We had been pretty good as a trio. The question was whether we were any good at handing out justice. We had to face the facts that we had about as much choice as a member of a firing squad ordered to excuse a prisoner. Outside our building organized criminal elements, a small detachment, sat in a big black limo waiting for us to dismember Teddy and hand the pieces back in a half-dozen plastic bags.

The Frank Coras ate on Mulberry Street and lived in Italian neighborhoods in Queens, Brooklyn and Staten Island. Or in houses in New Jersey, where they played cards, planned extortion, kickbacks, bribery, and other old-fashioned ways to make money out of the barrel of a gun. I thought of Chute's eyes in the rear-view mirror. Cold as the seat of an outdoor toilet.

"What you gonna do to me?" asked Teddy, as we assembled around him in a semicircle. I pulled Alex's helmet off his head. Teddy's hair, moist and matted, stuck to his head as if he'd come out of the shower.

"That depends," said Saint Anne.

"Depends on what?" he asked, thinking this was a trick of some kind.

"On your character," added Saint Anne. "If we're to go out on the rope for you we must know whether you're worth saving."

"Of course, I think you should know, as one Capricorn to another, that you have my vote," said Jack.

"Are you members of the New Enlightened People's Association?" asked Teddy, a goofy smile appearing under his mustache. He thought we were like his old boss, Mr. Garson, with all this talk about character.

"We don't belong to Associations," said Jack.

"Why were you sent to prison?" asked Saint Anne.

That question got Teddy's pistons moving. The basement took on the appearance of an Asian detention center (which in a fashion it was), one of those places with lots of laws or regulations, and enforcement was discretionary, no questions asked, no answers given. We were like government officials in most places of the world, doing what people in uniform do best: terrifying and threatening a captive for an offense yet to be determined. But Teddy was no fool. Though we had no real authority, and seemed to have just enough inbred decency not to knock off his block with a loose beam, Teddy saw one important thing. Saint Anne had reached the outer limits of what passed for reason. She had spread herself thin from the start, and it made her appear slightly out of control. Hands shaking, chain-smoking, her face going flushed as she screamed and demanded and raged about good character. So Teddy, knowing he didn't stand much of a chance trying to outsmart Saint Anne, he did what Teddy always seemed to do best, he told the truth.

AFTER Teddy had mustered out of the army in San Francisco, he had received an honorable discharge and had saved nearly six hundred dollars as a nest egg for civilian life. An army buddy found Teddy a cheap studio apartment in Chinatown. Two weeks later, Teddy was hired to work on a construction crew. His military background impressed Mr. Duncan, the construction company owner, and he made Teddy a foreman a month later. There was goodness in the world. A hard worker could get ahead in this life. The American dream Teddy had served to protect was rolling like the Bay fog right into his life. A soft, warm blanket of satisfaction settled over him. Not long after getting his promotion to foreman, he began dating Holly Wong. Holly, a Chinese girl, had long, flowing black hair which cascaded to her hips; a small delicate porcelain-doll face and tiny hands which worked chopsticks like surgical instruments. Although Holly spoke some Chinese, she was totally Americanized and sometimes he would forget she was Chinese. Teddy was liked and trusted by his boss, his landlord, his friends and his girlfriend.

Teddy might have gone on courting Holly. He had planned to ask her to move in and set up a real domestic household. His boss, Mr. Duncan, took him aside one day and told him that he had plans for Teddy in the business. That he wanted to pay for Teddy to go back to school at night and study business management and computer science. Unfortunately the cables that fastened people to the good life sometimes snapped and what they were holding fell into a vast, empty void.

The job had been an ordinary one; nothing in the job suggested that his life was about to change forever. The morning began pleasantly enough. Mr. Duncan was in a good mood since he had won a hundred dollars on the Giants' baseball game the night before. He slapped Teddy on the back, and offered to buy him a beer after work. But Teddy never got a chance to taste that free beer or to send in his application form to the local junior college. The trouble with Teddy was his innocent belief in the value of work, his faith in the satisfaction and glory of doing a good job. He never anticipated that doing the right thing could throw him against a hard edge of fate.

Mr. Duncan had contracted to supply the insulation to a house up in the hills near Palo Alto. The job was at the Pink Horse Ranch. Teddy loved this part of the world which clung to the names of the old ranches, with the cattle and cowboys long displaced by lavish houses, circular driveways, and heart-shaped swimming pools with diving boards. The air clean and crisp on the face. A sky so blue that the ocean looked inky black around the bay. And up in the hills were all those lean, tanned people with perfect teeth and easy smiles. No wonder Mr. Duncan liked doing business with the developers who worked in the hills putting up houses. There was a minor hitch. Teddy was to deliver the insulation materials to the Pink Horse Ranch and supervise the installation. The open-bed Ford truck, no matter how much rearranging, wouldn't hold the entire load. About six or seven large sheets of insulation were left over. That meant, of course, making two trips, or adding another two hours to the job. Mr. Duncan in one of his jolly public displays of good humor just smiled at Teddy's dilemma and then called him into his office.

"Goddamn, Ted. I don't care how you do it. You make it one load. I bid this job close. And you start farting around with another trip, and then where am I? You see my point?"

Teddy saw everyone's point, and that was part of his trouble, because by seeing everyone else's point he forgot about standing up for his own. Mr. Duncan was like a father to him. He admired him. But he knew that he was wrong to overload the truck. He should've had the courage to flat out tell Mr. Duncan, "Mr. Duncan, overloading that truck is dangerous. I don't think we oughtta be taking a chance. The cops patrol that freeway real good."

Here was the overly generous man who had promised to pay his way through business school. Teddy crumpled under the weight of Mr. Duncan's small request. "Sure thing, Mr. Duncan." That's all Teddy said, like some dumb ranch hand who'd been told to go out and brand the neighbor's cocker spaniel.

The last six or seven pieces of insulation were wedged in on the sides, and a couple of pieces laid over the top, with rope tying down the load. They were running late already. Teddy gave the load a quick glance as he ordered the two laborers into the truck. Those thick panels of insulation were the size of a man. Inside the truck, Teddy slammed the door and switched on the ignition.

"Remember that beer tonight," shouted Mr. Duncan, as Teddy popped the clutch and shot out of the driveway.

Teddy waved his arm out of the window. And as he looked in the rear-view mirror, he saw Mr. Duncan give him the thumbs-up sign.

He switched on the radio and his two-man crew began tapping out time to the sound of The Charlie Daniels Band. Stomping their boots on the floor of the truck. Teddy started to relax and sing along with the men. Twenty minutes out of San Francisco, he'd forgotten he was behind the wheel of an overloaded truck. Not too far from the Joan Baez estate, and where Steve Jobs lived in a mansion, Teddy was brought back to reality. The parched hills with their dandelions, thistles, and ragweed were the backdrop to Teddy's headlong collision into the world where things that aren't tied down tight shake loose and enter the lower cavity of the atmosphere as if propelled by their own free will. Though things by their very nature don't have free will, one insulation panel from Teddy's truck did its very best to disprove this conventional wisdom.

He saw the random sheet of insulation in his side mirror. Hanging in the sky for a moment like a child's watercolor painting of rain clouds. A dull gray cloud with perfectly cut edges had flown off the truck. He watched the insulation bounce off the windshield of several cars behind him. It could have been a Hitchcock film, Attack of the Cloud. It smashed against the window of a new Porsche, lifted up like a tumbleweed into the air, rolled across the roof like a piece of loose fuzz, two cars back, struck the windshield of a Rolls Royce. The startled driver's jaw dropped down, hitting his cellular telephone. But the impacts left no mark. Pillow-fight blows. No damage of any value had been caused as the piece of insulation sailed downwind. Then the law of averages stepped in. Not every woman passes her Pap test. Not every loose piece of insulation just harmlessly blows off the freeway and wedges in a fence. That would have been a second chance. The ancient strings playing that day dictated another use for that loose piece of insulation.

A two-year old Lincoln Continental with two couples inside drove over the slab of insulation. Two inches either side and the Lincoln would have run over it like a prairie dog. No such luck. Rather than the panel coming out the end, it stuck to the undercarriage of the car. This single mattresslike piece of insulation bonded itself as if it were a factory-installed extra device. Teddy watched with horror out of his truck window, as the Lincoln shot past doing about eighty or so. The driver smiling, his head half turned, talking with the other couple in the back seat. One of the workmen commented on the large hood ornament on the front. A fierce, raging mustang horse, rearing back on its hindlegs, nostrils flared, kicked at the fast-moving sky with its front hooves. The driver failed to acknowledge Teddy or his laborers. His silver horse clawed the open spaces. And the owner, his hands grasping a pale green snakeskin-covered wheel, was lost in conversation with the other occupants.

The body contour of the Lincoln was such that Teddy couldn't see even a speck of light between the freeway surface and the underbelly of the car. The Lincoln, a car engineered to get drunk on gas, disappeared as a small dot on the horizon, dragging a chunk of disaster beneath. A second choice presented itself to Teddy. Just get off the freeway at the next exit and go back to the shop. Call it a day. At that moment it was reasonably clear to Teddy that the interconnected parts of that Lincoln's undercarriage had never tested to ride long distances over a large section of highway covered with insulation material. Silver mustang or no silver mustang, the heat and sparks flying left no doubt that black flames would appear.

Six miles up the road the Lincoln had pulled over onto the shoulder of the freeway. Teddy had passed an exit and just kept on driving until he saw the disabled Lincoln. He pulled over and stopped his truck twenty feet or so behind the Lincoln, and told his men to stay in the truck. He was the boss, wasn't he? He left the radio on, got out and slammed the door. The two men he'd seen a few minutes earlier inside the Lincoln were now standing outside the car, leaning over the engine. The hood was wide open, the mustang now reared upside down, and steam poured out of the car. At first blush it looked like the radiator hose had burst. Clouds of steam rolled out over the freeway. Cars slowed down for a gawk, their windshield wipers swishing clouds of fine white mist that rolled across the freeway. Teddy stood no more than a couple of feet away, his hands dug in his jeans pockets, shuffling his boots on the loose gravel. He saw the little orange color of fire starting under the Lincoln.

"Anything I can do to help?" Teddy asked. He tried not to look at it. He wanted to say, hey mister, your car's on fire. Get the women out of the car. But he couldn't find the words. If he ignored the fire it might just go out.

The driver of the car pulled down his sunglasses and looked at Teddy. "Damn thing's overheated. You know anything about engines?"

"A little," said Teddy, glancing at the woman in the front seat, twisted to one side, and talking to the woman in the back. Both wore lots of jewelry, and cotton sleeveless shirts and shorts. They looked to be in their early twenties, cute, and sexy. The guys were a good fifteen years or more older than the women.

"You wanna have a look?" asked the driver. "I can't see a fucken thing. And neither can Sam."

Sam used a finger to close one of his nostrils and shot a line of snot along the side of the freeway. "This shit doesn't smell right. Kicks up my allergies. It doesn't smell like anything I ever smelled coming from a car. Smell that shit." Sam emptied his other nostril and stepped back from the car.

"It's the insulation," said Teddy at last.

"Say what?" The driver spit on the road.

"Under your car. It's burning."

They had just pulled the women out of the car when the gas tank on the Lincoln blew, lifting the rear end of the car into the air and sending debris and black smoke across the freeway. One of the young women suffered burns over twenty percent of her body, but none on her face. It was the other woman. The one who'd been in the back seat. The right side of her face had sloughed off from the intense heat. Teddy suffered burns on his face dragging her out. Later, in prison, he started the mustache to cover his upper lip; the lip that he'd smelled burning, his own flesh roasting under his own nose the day of the accident.

At Teddy's trial for reckless endangerment, the legal aid lawyer had Mr. Duncan testify about what a hard worker Teddy had been. All the jury and judge could see was the awful, evil-looking tattoo on Teddy's arm. The same tattoo he got in a seventy-two hour layover in Hong Kong. It's doubtful they ever heard a word of Mr. Duncan's character reference.

"The boy's of good character," Mr. Duncan testified. "His only flaw," Mr. Duncan paused and looked Teddy straight in the eye as he sat at the defense table, "Only one real flaw. He can be careless. Cut corners. Something I warned him about several times."

The injured girls filed large lawsuits against Mr. Duncan. This wasn't a case of fake whiplash. Serious personal injury had been done. Duncan and his insurance company were on the hook for enough potential damages to support a small country. Teddy suddenly had become an orphan. Someone from the lowest deck of the ship who had been volunteered by his commanding officer to walk the plank. It had been hard, though. Mr. Duncan had been like his father, and fathers don't answer questions in such a way as to guarantee that their son will be put away like a dangerous virus. But he had valid economic reasons. Mr. Duncan stood to lose his entire business. His insurance didn't cover the full liability. But his lawyer came up with an attractive theory: an employer isn't liable for the criminal acts of his employees. And Mr. Duncan decided he liked being an employer a whole lot more than being Teddy's father.

Teddy's progression from foreman to convict moved as smoothly as if he had been carried on an airfoil. Four years became two years actually served with time off for good behavior. Teddy, of course, had been a model prisoner. Holly married midway through his second year in prison. Teddy sent a card and flowers to the place that the newspaper said Miss Holly Wong was to be married. But the flowers, all wilted, and the card, which had been folded, were returned to the state prison. He found out later that Holly had met her husband shopping at Safeway. He was an assistant manager at the Safeway out where the park joins the sea. They met on a singles night at the supermarket. Wednesday nights had been set up to bring in shoppers who scooted their carts down the aisle looking for more than food.

California hadn't been the answer for Teddy. After he had fought his way up the ladder, two steps from the top, he'd fallen and lost a life decorated with good credit, honor, and a lover who said she believed in him. After Teddy's parole came through, he went around to see Mr. Duncan. But a secretary stopped Teddy from going inside his office. He was in conference. But if Teddy would like to make an appointment sometime next week, then maybe.

Teddy Eliot went back to Howard Beach in Queens by Greyhound bus with one suitcase and one hundred and fifty-five dollars, and a genuine desire to put California behind him and start afresh.

"Howard Beach? Man, that's where they have killer gangs," said the middle-aged man who sat next to him. The man had climbed into the seat next to Teddy somewhere in Missouri.

"What are you talking about?"

"Where you been? Don't read the papers, huh?"

"I've been in prison," said Teddy. A few minutes later, the stranger shifted out of his seat, eyeing Teddy closely, and walked back to another seat.

There was a pattern to Teddy's life. A kind of personal archaeology had begun to emerge for him: No matter where and when you asked him to dig down into his past for an explanation of the present he always brought up basically the same type of bones. At the bottom of each grave was the finger of some insurance executive pointing skyward like a broken shard of clay pottery. The only difference this time was that the finger had turned into a fist, and this time the freshly dug grave bore Teddy's name.

16

Without exchanging a word between ourselves, a clear consensus had formed that, if anything, Teddy's character was better than ours. Saint Anne's reverential whisper for Jack to cut off the left handcuff sealed Teddy's fate.

The needlemakers' hacksaw—another tool they had abandoned—sliced the handcuffs and Teddy, his arms at his sides, rubbed his wrists, and slowly turned his neck from side to side. He looked like a half-drowned man who had been pulled to shore. On our way through the piles of boxes, rubbish, lumber, and old equipment, we quickly moved towards the stairs. The shock was already wearing off Teddy. He complained about his shoulder blades aching, where the muscles had been pulled. His jaw throbbed. The full weight of his inflictions, some made upon his body by us, flooded over Teddy with each breath, with each step, and he suspected secretly, I believe, that we might have same shabby purpose yet in store for him.

In the dank shadows, Jack walked alongside Teddy, one hand resting on his shoulder, like he was a coach, sending a player onto the field with instructions for the next play. Jack was talking about Holly Wong, the girl Teddy had lost while he was sitting out his sentence in prison.

"Your girlfriend sounds very much like my first wife. Did she speak any Chinese?" he asked.

"She spoke some with her mother," said Teddy. "But I don't think she was fluent."

"My ex-wife once knew Chinese. But she forgot most of it. That's a pity. But it's the cost of assimilation. The melting pot.

We never melted in Canada," said Jack, putting his arm around Teddy's shoulder.

"What's Canada got to do with Holly?" asked Teddy.

Jack stopped and wiped the dust as thick as congealed frost off one of the split cartons, and pushed it back against an unopened second. He carefully unpacked a box of blues from a long row, turned and held it up like a prize.

"Why nothing, of course not. It has do with us. My brother and sister. We were raised in Vancouver. A beautiful, wonderful city. Perhaps you've been there? That's where we got our start in show business. We were billed as the Harvey Trio. Maybe you heard of us?"

"Is that some kind of a trick question?" asked Teddy, looking around at all the boxes in the basement.

"No, of course not. We worked mostly the Asia circuit. But that was a long time ago."

WE divided the building into three living lofts, my photography studio and the basement, where my darkroom occupied one corner, the remainder set aside by Jack for the illegals who in their escape from China had gone from the hold in a ship to the cramped, dark basement. Our world was different. We each lived in a loft and each one had a different feel. Jack's was all modern columns, Chinese screens and silk-screen prints, and Heather had gone through the modular furniture stage. Their apartment was split into different levels and the surfaces, all polished red and gold, glistening under the skylights and an overhead lighting system. Access to the roof was through the bedroom window of Jack's loft.

Saint Anne's loft, directly below Jack's, bore the relics of the former professional football player to whom she was married. After Alex's departure to Paris, she left everything the way it was on the day he left, thinking he would change his mind and come back; she wanted the loft to look like he had never gone. He packed two carry-on bags of clothes and football books and manuals. Not long after Peter Montard distracted her from worrying about Alex, they started meeting in the loft to go over the latest plans for her singing career. He would show up with someone in public relations, or from the music industry press and they would meet and plan to meet again. Things were starting to come together when Peter lost his head. Only after Peter's death did the full weight of Alex's presence turn up in every corner of her loft.

The furniture looked as if it belonged in locker rooms and bars rather than inside a Manhattan loft. Overstuffed chairs, some with wicker backs, an imitation leather sofa, a couple of empty trophy cases filled with old copies of the New York Times, and a canopy bed at the far end with a few beach chairs at the foot of the bed. At one end she had an elevated stage, professional lighting and video equipment. She had dozens of demo tapes which she had sent out to every record label and agent in New York.

Elizabeth and Lucy transformed our loft, directly below Saint Anne's, into a playland with domesticated jungle plants and stuffed toys. It was messy, like the underfur on the old overstuffed bear Lucy kept next to her bed. Each summer Elizabeth found something at a country auction in England and shipped it back to New York, so that we found ourselves guardians for the estates of many a deceased old lady. Edwardian furniture with missing clawfeet. A dining table reputedly used for a century in a Franciscan monastery with pious graffiti carved along one side. Graceful, elegant chairs with the springs spilling out of the top or bottom. Tables so weak with history they could no longer hold a magazine without collapsing into dust.

Over the years, with our apartments all connected by a spiral staircase, various exchanges and borrowing had resulted in an overlap of taste, interest, and each other's junk. Although our lofts were different, those who knew all three of us saw a common thread. A framed photograph of the three of us as kids in Seattle. In the far corner you could see Mr. Hedgecock's vegetable garden, and Saint Anne's bicycle on the ground. All three of us had that photograph on the wall somewhere in our loft. Also Saint Anne displayed several photographs from our days as the Harvey Trio; her favorite was of Jack and me dressed in dinner jackets and her wearing maybe the most sensual national costume in the world—a silky-white transparent Vietnamese *ao dai* with black bra and panties outlined underneath. It had an awards night look; like we had won an Oscar when in fact we had been hired by a wealthy Chinese businessman to sing at his daughter's wedding reception at the Oriental Hotel in Bangkok.

Ten minutes inside Saint Anne's loft, Heather was in the back watching the Mets game in one of the beach chairs, and sniffing more cocaine. Jack plugged himself into a Sony radio which was tuned to the BBC News so that he could pick up the latest financial information from the Asian stock markets. He'd spread out on the end of Saint Anne's bed, resting on his elbows, watching the Mets less than a foot away from Heather, and trying to figure out how much money he had made while Teddy had been chained to our wall. He threw the mortician's needle, B/6545, along with the tattoo needles, a couple of times, but absent-mindedly, as he grinned.

"Hong Kong's up three percent," he shouted.

Saint Anne led Teddy and me to the opposite end of the loft. The four windows overlooked Wooster Street, the parking lot enclosed by the kind of steel and barbed wire fences used for minimum security prisons, and a vacant lot beyond which was patrolled by Dobermans. On the street was a black limo. Chute, one foot hooked over the other, stood outside, leaning against the door, watching a girl in a miniskirt walk towards Canal Street. I pulled Teddy away from the window.

"Keep away from the windows. Frank's outside watching the street," I said.

He needed no further explanation as to why Frank should be kept at the shallow end of the pool, so to speak, for as long as possible. Saint Anne stood a few inches away from Teddy. Tears welled in her eyes and her lower lip quivered slightly.

"You're a wonderful person," she said in a half whisper. "I mean that. I'm not someone impressed by just anyone. Ask my brothers. They'll tell you." Saint Anne seemed about to kiss Teddy on the cheek; more of a peck than a true kiss. She had a second thought, and that storm cloud passed through her face again. "Would you like to hear me sing?" she asked him as Heather shouted, "All right" from the back room as the Mets scored in the bottom of the fifth.

"Sing? Yeah, why not, if you want to," said Teddy, looking confused. "And I want you to know that I'm real sorry about what happened to Mr. Montard." Teddy pulled his hands free from his pockets, his eyes gliding over the couple of thousand feet of open space.

"It was an accident," said Saint Anne.

"Still, it was a rotten thing," said Teddy, rubbing his wrists. His eyes bulged out. Clearly Teddy Eliot had never seen so much space. "All this for one person," he said after a moment. "My mother would never believe this. Hey, I'm sorry. For everything. That beam just slipped over the edge. And I was trying to be so careful."

"Do you have a favorite song?" Saint Anne asked.

It was funny how that question tripped up a lot of people. They had a favorite song but they could never remember the title of it. Teddy had that pained look of someone who was trying to remember a song but it wouldn't come into his mind.

"What about a favorite singer?" she asked.

He smiled. "Whitney Houston is pretty good."

I saw it coming, he was going to ask for a song that was like a bad cold virus, it made you sick, you could never quite shake it off, everyone else had it, and there was no escape from the queasy feeling it gave you. That's how I felt about Whitney Houston's tune which was the theme song to a movie called The Bodyguard. And Saint Anne started humming, and gestured for me to go over to the piano. Man, I hated playing that song but I went over and sat down on the stool and started playing I'll Always Love You, wondering why there wasn't some international law that prevented such sentimental trash from being inflicted on others.

Saint Anne sang the song. A solo performance dedicated to Mr. Teddy Eliot. I seemed to recall it was a song that she had sung for Peter Montard, and if my memory served me right, Alex Walker had been in the audience at the club one night when she came over to his table and sang that song.

Wowee, she had wanted to kill this guy a few hours ago and now she was singing him a love song. Freakish might have been a better word for what had happened to Peter Montard. But what was happening now made his death ordinary. The reason Teddy had been delivered to our basement had been premised on Saint Anne's desperate need for seeking justice for the man who had wrecked her singing career. Frank hadn't merely knocked on our door out of the blue and handed the kicker over. We pulled out all the stops to abduct him. It's not rare that people have a change of heart. It happens all the time, especially in the music business where nothing is ever constant. Her instinct for revenge which had seemed so solid immediately after Peter's death was more like an ice cream cone in the sun.

Heather shouted at her from the other end of the loft, "I'm trying to watch this game. I've got money on this game. Can't you sing some other time?"

Saint Anne ignored her the way you ignore a heckler in the audience.

If anything, Heather's outburst convinced Saint Anne that she must sing the lyrics one more time. I kept on playing the piano, thinking about the beam as it had plunged thirty stories to the hard, asphalt pavement. Its journey to earth had been caused by a careless gesture. He had given it a push, not a shove. A stumble, not a kick. The lyrics to I'll Always Love You was another careless gesture.

Peter's Bastille Day decapitation in midtown New York was nothing more than a miserable piece of bad luck. A scrap of insulation caught between the wheels of life. The fluid movement of our emotions now turned to the peculiar circumstances of the Harveys who'd backed themselves into a trap. And in weighing good against bad, Saint Anne at that moment decided she cared very much if Teddy thought she had talent. What was he going to say? "Hey, sweetheart, don't quit your day job?" Saint Anne didn't have a day job.

When Saint Anne's private phone rang, she stopped singing, walked over and picked up the receiver. Teddy was clapping, and Saint Anne gave a little bow. She didn't put the phone to her ear. Instead she slammed it down. A moment later it rang again.

"Frank's got your unlisted number?" I said, reaching for the phone myself. My lower jaw dropped. I couldn't believe it. Saint Anne only gave out her number to presidents of record companies, Jack, Peter, and me. She stressed that private meant exactly that; anyone other than family and VIPs in the music business shouldn't be interrupting her private life. Frank certainly wasn't family and it was very unlikely that he was the president of a major record label. He was a fan, plain and simple.

Saint Anne twisted the cord around her forearms and yanked it out of the wall in one motion. "I don't want to talk to him. Not ever."

"But he's a fan," I said, as she reeled in the limp black telephone cord like a fishing line. "And you gave him your unlisted number. I think you ought to tell me why."

"He's Mafia," said Teddy.

"I know," said Saint Anne, ignoring me. She dropped the cord and walked over to Teddy. "All right. I didn't tell you the whole truth. But I didn't lie. Understand that. You do believe me?" I wasn't certain at first whether her question was directed at Teddy or me, or perhaps at both of us. Since Saint Anne had this thing about good character, any suggestion, however slight, that she might have done or not done something bad made her insecure. When she asked such a question, there was little choice. One had to assume she acted honorably or, at the least, out of weakness. She might be confused or perplexed; that she would admit because it left her character intact.

"Of course, we do," I said. "Now, I think you better level with us about Frank." Teddy had suddenly become part of us. Saint Anne looked back and forth between us as her mind worked over the unfairness of being caught out like this. That if only we'd gone up one more flight to Jack's, or stopped one flight below and gone into my place, then none of this would have had to come out.

"It unfair," she said.

"You have to tell us, Saint Anne," I said, reaching down and squeezing her hand.

"No," she said, her lower lip quivering again. In the silence that followed, Heather erupted from the Greene Street end with a muffled, "Hot bat, man. You see that, Jack? What a hit. Did I tell you, I've got two hundred on this game?"

"Come on, Saint Anne. It's important," I said quietly. A distant barking and loud voices filtered up from Wooster Street. A low, throaty yapping of old Parrot. A bark from a scratchy, tired old dog going through the motions of anger. Then a loud yelp, and finally, the crushing weight of completed silence.

17

Heather flapped her arms like a large African bird doing a mating dance as the final strike at the top of the ninth inning ended the game, with the Mets defeating the Cardinals 5 to 2. She celebrated the victory which brought her two hundred dollars by running up and down the loft, shouting one of those victory screams that I could imagine her doing in high school after her team won. It wasn't the money she had won, it was that she had won at sports again, her team had come through. I played some John Wayne cowboy movie music on the piano as she ran around making ear-piercing noises that careened like a wild pitch through the loft. When she was finally out of breath, she dropped to her knees and drummed her fists on the floor. Heather swung around onto her back, her knees pumping up and down, glanced back at her husband who lay on the floor behind her. Jack's head rose slowly, as if pulled by a string, from his spot on the floor. It made me wonder what the reaction would be if she had won a thousand dollars. She had a white cocaine mustache and a happy grin.

"The Mets won," Heather shouted. "Wow, what a game. And, hey, what about that pitching?" Then her voice shifted tone, fell off as she was distracted. She stopped kicking and sat up, her hands grabbing her ankles.

"Jack, you're going to get dirty on the floor. What are you doing there? Did the market drop again in Hong Kong?"

Her voice had a wired sense of concern. She wiped off her white mustache and sneezed into her hand.

"Hong Kong is fine. I am calling on the gods of luck." Jack was stroking an object cradled between his outstretched legs: a killer whale carved of soapstone. The Eskimo carver marooned the tar-black whale on a base of gray rock. The head drooped over one end; and the tail over the other. He sat the carving on the floor between his legs like a stone doll.

"Man, I just won two hundred big ones. How's that for luck?" Heather was again childlike in a surge of happiness.

"In Canada, the native Indians believe that rubbing a carving like this one makes one immensely lucky. Of course, we are lucky, aren't we, Heather? Just think of it. All this space. The whole building. A wonderful life. We are rich, safe, protected. Then why do I feel a threat?" Jack puckered his lips and bent forward, kissing the whale's drooped-over head and looking over at Teddy Eliot. I knew what was going through Jack's mind—he had a contract for a load of illegals and he was starting to worry that Frank Cora, Teddy Eliot and Chute—playmates of distraction for the moment—would still be hanging around when thirty Chinese peasants were living downstairs.

As Heather switched off the TV, an object blasted through the window, showering glass fragments, and bounced off the keyboard of the piano with a thud. I ducked to the side, wondering if there was someone in the neighborhood who hated Whitney Houston's *I'll Always Love You* as much as I did. This thing left a trail of slobber all the way down to Saint Anne, where it rolled to a stop at her feet. She was lighting a cigarette when she saw it. The fleshy, warm head had bounced, ears flapping, making a liquid, sucking noise. Now it had stopped.

Jack looked over the sandstone whale, his eyes as big as saucers, his mouth opened in the shape of a giant "O" ring like one of those female condoms had been shoved down his throat.

"What the fuck was that?" asked Heather, rolling to one side in the beach chair.

"Don't look. You don't need to know," I said, looking at the mess on the piano, and thinking, Wowee, what a fucking fix we're in, and remembering the Godfather movie and the horse's head. But this wasn't any horse. And Frank Cora wasn't Marlon Brando. Jack dropped the whale and screamed. He hadn't done that since I was a kid and it made the hair on the back of my neck stand on end. There was general panic in the loft. From the window a trail of splattered blood ended with a large wet puddle forming at Saint Anne's foot.

I got off the floor beside the piano and went over, taking off my shirt as I walked.

"Just don't look, that's all," I said.

Saint Anne was shaking, hardly able to hold the cigarette. But Teddy, he was looking, the color had gone out of his face. He didn't say a word but I thought he was going to keel over. He was probably wishing he were back on the wall.

Jack, who had moved quickly across the floor, sat glued to the floor, the whale at his feet, examining the severed dog's head with his free hand. Parrot's fogged eyes stared lifelessly back at Jack. The neck area, ragged and torn, was saturated in half-dried blood. The mangled fur leaked from old Parrot's injury.

"Vietnamese eat dogs. Cambodian eat dogs," said Jack.

"And the Chinese eat anything," I said.

He glanced up at me with no expression on his face.

"Like Africans," he said.

"Like the last lot of your illegals, Jack," I said, forgetting that Teddy was listening.

Jack shot me a hard look.

Saint Anne was crying and throwing up at the same time.

"My luck, as always, has held. Thanks to this baby," Jack said, scooping up his sandstone whale. "You protected your Jack, didn't you?" I hated it when Jack, my older brother, spoke baby-talk to the soapstone whale.

"Man, this is fucking sick. We gotta do something," said Heather, as she crawled along the floor, avoiding the large pieces of broken glass and the pools of blood that spread like moon rays from the window.

"Frank Cora."

"He's a sick puppy," said Teddy.

That was one of those unfortunate metaphors.

I draped my shirt over Parrot's head. The dog had looked good in that King's College tied that Ali had slipped around his neck. Now he was dead. His head in our loft and his body somewhere out in the street.

Frank knew how to get us all worked up. How to throw us back to the nightmarish memory of Peter's death. Most of all, I think, Frank had delivered a personal message to Saint Anne so that she could see right up close what he was capable of doing. Saint Anne crept away from the head on tiptoes as if drifting in and out of a bad dream. Her knees collapsed. Teddy grabbed her before she fell and, his arms around her waist, lowered her slowly.

"Is it dead?"

That was one of those questions which comes from someone in a state of extreme shock. No one in their right mind ever asks if a severed head is dead or live. Parrot was dead.

"Cut around the throat," said Jack, looking under my shirt.

"It's Parrot. Ali's dog," I said.

"I thought I had seen that face before," said Jack.

"Man, how can you look at that?" asked Heather.

"Dead is dead. Funny expression on its face. It's smiling. Look, one of the teeth is chipped. It must have happened when the head hit the piano," said Jack.

He had the women freaking out. And Teddy didn't look all that stable on his feet.

The head had that awful attraction, you didn't want to look but you couldn't stop yourself.

"Where's the rest of Parrot?" asked Heather.

No one had an answer or if they had, they kept it to themselves; as I said, I thought it was in the street or a dumpster. My thoughts turned to Ali. Had harm come to him as well? But my worst fear was that nothing stood between us and Frank. Whatever sense of safety, reason, normality we might have had, dissolved when the window exploded with Parrot's head. Frank's timetable wasn't a joke. This was serious business and sitting around watching a Mets game and Saint Anne singing I'll Always Love You was living in a dream world. We were back to reality, sharp, evil and frightening.

"There's a message," said Jack, squinting at the base of Parrot's neck. Soggy from the blood, I could see a note. Jack unpinned the paper and held it up to catch the light. "Written in a rather boyish style. It says, 'Send out Teddy.' Funny thing to write. That's all it says, 'Send him out now or we will come inside and take him.'"

The message was pretty clear, Frank Cora had put us on notice that Teddy was his property, not ours. Either we passed him out—which meant we were on his side—or we ignored Frank which meant whatever Teddy had coming to him we could expect to get the same. Parrot's head was a bloody example of what might be expected if we elected the latter course of action. Looking at it kind of made your neck ache.

"He's spoiling my win," said Heather, squatting down beside Jack. At first she had been revolted, but after she did a couple more hits of coke, she composed herself and smiled. She poked at Parrot's bloated tongue. "He really fucked over this animal good." She took the note from Jack, walked over to the kitchen and opened the fridge door. She leaned forward between the milk and the cooked ham, and read the note by the inside light.

"You missed part of it, Jack. It says we got five minutes." She pulled her head out of the fridge, slammed the door, and leaned her head against it. "Imagine that. Five minutes," she added, her tongue licking up at her new white mustache.

"Frank Cora is a maniac," said Jack. "Obviously, dangerous."

"Obviously, a determined man who is not leaving until he gets what he wants," I replied.

"Why don't I just go?" asked Teddy Eliot. "None of this has anything to do with you. It's my fault."

That wasn't exactly right and everyone but Teddy knew that it wasn't right.

"Hang cool," I said. "It's not over yet."

A demand, a time restraint, and an implied threat was carried around the ragged edges of what had been Parrot's neck. Saint Anne and Teddy talked quickly to one another in muted tones. She was using her little angel's voice. The one she had sometimes used with Alex when she thought no one else was listening. It was the same voice I had overheard her use with Peter Montard a couple of times when we were staying in West Hampton. That fragile, little girl's voice, a variation of the voice Jack used to talk to the whale, the voice she'd used with our father until that day she found out that he had known about the boating accident which had killed all of our real mommas. After that she, at least in my presence, never used her angel's voice with Father ever again. She could prove nothing, none of us could, but we had that feeling . . .

TEDDY Eliot was not a stupid man. His life had been defined by a mother who was always on his back, by a lousy public school education in Howard Beach, by his experience in the Army, a construction job in San Francisco, a prison sentence, another job in New York, being a witness to arson, and a midtown construction worker. A Chinese girl who had abandoned him for someone she met at Safeway. Within the orbit of his universe, Teddy had patched through the coordinates and dimensions of a normal life and came out on the other end in an alien region beyond the experience and understanding of most people. Teddy had managed to puncture some invisible envelope, and bodies, hospitals, funerals, police, and courtroom had spilled out. And now a dog head which belonged to a neighborhood dog named Parrot, a dog, if I can go on record, I liked and thought liked me.

The one thing Teddy Eliot knew for certain after the beam severed Peter's head was to keep away from the job site the next day. Call in sick. Better yet, he had his mother call in sick for him. Because Mr. Duncan had provided Teddy with a true education in what happened to people who walked into that intersection containing all the bad things of life and where the traffic lights of right and wrong had gone on the blink. He had better run. Mr. Duncan had been a decent, West Coast man, someone who gave to charity, someone who had promised to help him go through night school at the local junior college. That seemed like a lifetime ago since he had returned to his home ground.

He knew one thing about New York. That beam might just as well have landed on his head. Because Mr. Duncan had taught him an important lesson about the nature of business insurance. No one was putting Teddy in the witness box to testify this time. Not with his prior conviction. Not with Peter Montard's relatives waiting in the wings to file a multimillion lawsuit.

Teddy pulled out his shirt. Underneath he wore a money belt, and inside he had a passport and a one-way ticket to San Francisco. "All

I ask is a chance of getting my plane," said Teddy. "When you came to the restaurant I was killing time until I went to La Guardia."

Saint Anne leaned over, stroked his hair as if he were a child. "And we owe you that much. Don't we, Gideon?" Saint Anne looked up in the dark loft, catching my eye in the street lights.

For a flash of a second I found myself being grateful to Frank. He had made me understand for the first time what had taken Alex to Paris. What had kept the spirit of Elizabeth's London relatives high during the Blitz. That when a predator tries to cart you off as a food product to its nest, stares at your flesh like it's a burger ready for the grill, you cave in and say, "Do it baby, eat me," or you find the strength to repeatedly and forcefully resist with all your energy, and if that sucker gets you, then it is not without a fight. All that personal selfishness which might, just might, have pried Teddy loose from our lives, so that we could tip him over the side like someone cleaning out a boat, had vanished. A low-grade wisp of doubt about Frank's intention—the very doubt that would have let us play into his hands—had been replaced with a resolute conviction of knowing what was the right thing to do. The only real course of action from the start, if we had taken any care to think of the evil Frank had thrown in our faces but we didn't want to see. He had promised to make Saint Anne famous, that had been enough. Evil was a small price to pay for fame. That had been before Teddy had told his story, and after that no one was thinking the pact Saint Anne had made with Frank Cora was worth MTV. The *New York Times Sunday Magazine, People* magazine, and Larry King Live rolled into a single week-long orgy of publicity. All we could think about was the fear we were feeling and the smell of the dead dog's head.

"Yeah, I think we can do it, man," I said. "Only one question that really matters. How do we get you to La Guardia?" Teddy smiled as if to say he was real glad to hear that he had some friends given what the stakes were. In that smile I saw Father's paper airplane sailing across the sky toward Teddy. Inside was Father's simple, senile message: "Is there danger?" A question to which Teddy knew the answer better than most.

❖

ONE of the reasons Alex uprooted himself from his comfortable life and moved out of San Francisco and into New York was the splendid gym on the garage roof abutting our building. We had access to one of those old-fashioned garages with two large lifts that moved cars from street level to the upper floor. A pimple-faced kid from Riverdale had inherited it from his father, and sold his inheritance to a limited partnership of lawyers, doctors, and investment bankers. He took their money and ran. We had always parked our cars in the garage. Both the old and new management installed by the limited partnership knew us by name. On occasion, feeling in an expansive mood, I had shared some of my tomatoes, grown from Mr. Hedgecock's seeds, with the Latino men who parked the cars, and spent long, hot summer afternoons, washing and polishing cars on the sidewalk.

The reason Alex liked the garage had nothing to do with these personal contacts. His eyes fed exclusively on the equipment and jogging track. Heather turned it into a first-rate gym. It had been written up a couple of times in weightlifter magazines. Photographs of shiny, well-polished, oiled equipment; seats covered in imported leather. Stationary bikes with all the modern electronic hookups. Racks of Olympic free weights and barbells stood next to a free-standing mirror measuring twelve by eight. One corner contained half of a basketball corner, on which Heather had painted a proper free-throw line. That would have been amazing enough. But Jack added his own touch. He installed a four-hole miniature golf course. As Heather lifted weights, or practiced foul shots with the basketball, Jack putted around the course. He taught Lucy the finer points of the game. And he expected her to pick up Chinese expressions along the way. He taught her that the characters used to write "crisis" in Chinese came from two other Chinese words—"danger" and "opportunity"—and when you put them together you had written "crisis" in Chinese and at the same time explained the current condition of America.

"Uncle Jack, you're strange," she'd say on those late spring mornings.

It was Elizabeth's idea to keep a table and chairs on the roof, and on those long, summer evenings when Elizabeth was back in England, I missed her and Lucy as I sat outside watching Heather mix a large pitcher of Bloody Marys. We would all sit on the roof and watch the sun disappear behind a horizon of brick buildings and tarpaper roofs, listening to the backed-up traffic on Canal Street. A chorus of horns playing the same angry, frustrated tune. Our roof, in contrast, was smaller; cut up by the five domed skylights which rose like dinosaur eggs over Jack and Heather's loft. The roof over the old needle factory sloped dramatically from the ends like an irrigation ditch. Sometimes, sitting out in the night air, we talked about fixing up the roof of the needle factory. But there was, of course, no incentive to do so. Sitting above the garage was just so much better.

What made the roof system work like clockwork was the proximity of the garage roof to Jack and Heather's master-bedroom window. The window was reinforced with steel shutters painted white; they locked from the inside by a dead-bolt, so as to make it nearly impossible for burglars to use the roof as an open invitation, if not hatch-door, to the interior of our building. But from within our building, or more particularly from the confines of Jack and Heather's master-bedroom, we could climb through the window and stand on a small balcony, and reach back inside and press a single button and a little bridge on a hydraulic system slowly advanced from the balcony until it touched the lip of the garage roof. With the bridge in place, four or five steps later, we bounded onto a roof larger than center court at Wimbledon. It was a major reason for buying the building; it came with a perfect route to ferry the illegals in and out without anyone knowing what we were doing. Looking south, the old AT&T building blotted out a large slice of sky. The traffic streamed up Church Street beside a huge red brick structure Saint Anne said had inspired George Orwell. That always brought a smile to Elizabeth's lips. The thought that we lived in the shadow of Big Brother's turf and his name was not George but Jack.

Saint Anne hated the roof, so she said, because she felt the eyes of dirty old men gawking at her from behind their scratched desks, lurking inside dingy offices, taking their minds off divestiture by watching her sunbathe seminude. To the north, the top twenty floors of the Empire State Building and 100 Avenue of the Americas—written in bold, black letters on the side on a cream colored building—defined our landscape as much as the moon and the stars. Only their position in our orbit never changed.

The real reason that Saint Anne stopped using the roof was that after Alex installed five nautilus machines, he started a regular workout routine, and Heather quickly joined in. Saint Anne felt left out. The eyes on the roof weren't those of bored AT&T workers; they were Saint Anne's eyes, staring at Alex, as she followed Jack around his golf course. After a couple of minutes, Saint Anne would begin crying, turn away, leaving Jack in mid-Chinese sentence, run over the little drawbridge, across the balcony, and jump into the master bedroom where she'd throw herself on the bed and bury her head, weeping, into Heather's pillow. It didn't take all that long for her to stop going out on the roof. In fact, she swore in a knockdown and drag out fight with Alex, not long after they moved in, that she would never, ever set foot on the roof again. Nothing and nobody would ever get her on the roof. Of course, at the time, she wasn't thinking of Frank Cora or Teddy Eliot, and that the roof one day might be the only way of escape.

The roof was the answer to Frank Cora. Our plan was extremely simple: we would climb the spiral staircase from Saint Anne's loft and come out near Jack's desk in his sitting room. No lights would be switched on. A little something I thought might throw Frank and Chute off our scent and possibly add a few more minutes to the five in the note.

After we were all assembled upstairs, Heather jogged ahead and turned a corner, stopping, next to the linen closets built in and pulled out drawers. Towels and pillows flew in all directions. She dug deep among the sheets, and emerged a moment later with two handguns.

"Just let them fuck with us," she said, sticking one of the Smith & Wesson 38-caliber guns in her handbag, and slapping the matching gun into the palm of my hand.

The touch of the cold metal against my skin gave me a little shiver. I cradled the gun, trying to give the impression I knew what I was doing and trying not to seem surprised that Heather had such an arsenal hidden away. She was a real American. In Canada no one we knew was raised around guns. We thought they were strange, dangerous objects and had nothing to do with them, Father warned that any man who kept a gun was a fool, looking for trouble. There

168

was that word that Frank had used, "trouble." I must've had a funny look on my face.

"Don't worry, it's loaded," Heather said.

"Let's go," I said, feeling weighed down by the gun.

"I wish I had just a few moments to show you my golf course," said Jack, ignoring the guns. He grabbed Teddy's arm at the elbow. "I'm quite a good golfer, you know. A little unconventional. But as one Capricorn to another, I think you'd appreciate my course. I designed it very carefully."

I grabbed Teddy's other arm. "Another time, Jack."

"Yes, yes, I do understand," said Jack.

Heather pressed the drawbridge button. "Man, Jack. You're something else. We got guys in the street who want to kill us. Throw a goddamn dog's head through the window. And what do you want to do? Play golf." The hydraulic system kicked in and the high-pitched pneumatic sound startled Teddy.

"I wanted to phone my friends but everyone said no. So what do you want from me now?" Jack replied.

Teddy ducked, doubling up on the floor. "It's them," he said in a loud whisper. Saint Anne bent down next to him, and gave him a kiss on the cheek.

"It's the bridge to freedom. We call it the Freedom Bridge," she whispered.

That was Jack's name for the bridge. We had Chinese illegals. We had Vietnamese and Haitian illegals. Over the years we 'd had hundreds and hundreds of illegals crossing that bridge. The first ones were from Tiananmen Square on the run for their lives, then boat people from Vietnam and more boat people from Haiti. All of them folks were hungry for work, for a shot at the great American dream. Maybe some of them were aiming to become famous. Most were happy just to live a life without getting shot at, or getting drowned in a boat because they wanted their babies.

Teddy, in the dark, tried to make out my face for some guidance. "Yeah," I heard him say. "But where's it go?"

"To San Francisco," said Saint Anne.

We had played some nightclubs in San Francisco. Saint Anne knew the scene. I was remembering that was where she had met Alex.

18

Alex had become a taboo subject since his departure to Paris. His name, his football, his trophies, his fame—above all his fame. After a couple of weeks when it was clear to everyone that he wasn't coming back, Alex ceased to exist; he became a non-person like the old-time Soviet leaders who fell from grace and all the photographs were doctored to eliminate their presence. I'll Always Love You, blah, blah. The fact that Alex had, so to speak, disappeared from our lives so suddenly made his passing feel more like death, like Peter's losing his head in midtown.

Sometimes a teaspoon of absence can weigh in as heavy as the sun. That's the legacy Alex left behind on each floor of the old needle factory situated on Wooster Street. His memory had been richly carved in each of our lives. One evening after the club had closed and we were all sitting around the table, Saint Anne stood in the spotlight on the stage, holding the microphone, staring at us. She gazed carefully around the table. She waited until Heather had returned from the washroom. We could tell from the bounce in Heather's step that she'd done a couple of lines. Elizabeth nudged me beneath the table as Heather sat down. We exchanged that flicker of a smile with which married people define reality in place of language.

Once Heather slid across the bench, rubbing up against Jack's arm, Saint Anne tapped the end of her fingernails on the side of her glass. It wasn't clear from her expression whether her intention was warlike, or an attempt to gain the floor.

"Any final requests?" asked Saint Anne.

Heather said something flip, "What was that song Alex liked so much? Evil Ways. You know, the old Santana song."

Saint Anne froze, a little shudder passed over her bare shoulders.

"I never want to hear his name again," she said softly. So softly she repeated her message, pressing the microphone to her lips, giving her words an eerie sound. "Never, never, never . . ." she said over and over.

No one knew what to say. Was she being serious or was this an act?

"I want you to promise me," she said.

"We promise," said Jack. "Now let's go home."

She looked thoughtful. "Yeah, Jack. I'm tired, let's go home," she said.

Later she said that she had been dead serious at the club and asked us not to refer to Alex in her presence. Not ever again. It was forbidden forever. I strongly believed then, as I still believe now, that her speech was intended primarily for Heather's ears. Alex and Heather, two ex-jocks, had that glory thing in common which Saint Anne had felt excluded her. Jack was easier to handle; he gleefully made the gesture of sealing his lips with a key and throwing it away. Saint Anne had each of us promise. Her gloom was oppressive, sparking with flashes of anger. We all felt her loss, her pain, so we promised. We ended by putting out our right hands and placed them one atop the other. My hand cupped over Elizabeth's, then Jack's, followed by Heather's. Lastly Saint Anne laid hers on top.

ON the roof, Teddy looked over all the gym equipment and the golf course. "You people live like rich communists," said Teddy.

"I'm afraid he has a valid point," said Jack. "I'm quite to the right myself. Very far right. And conservative enough to be appointed as a Chinese leader. Or at least a high official with diplomatic immunity. I could fix their economy. I could fix a lot of things."

"Then fix a way for me to get to the airport," said Teddy.

Jack smiled, "I'm working on it."

A soft glow of light spiraled from the galaxy of buildings surrounding us, throwing spikes of inky, narrow shadows over the chrome bars and frames of the equipment. It was dark on the roof, and the landscape was filled with metal surfaces. Teddy was disoriented from his beating by Chute and his time chained to the basement wall and stumbled into one of the nautilus machines. The leg-lift machine snagged his knee. The outer metal edge shadowed by the arm-curl machine seemed to almost reach out and tackle him knee high.

He howled in pain, pulling up his left knee into his hands, and hobbled forward before collapsing onto the flat surface.

"You okay?" I asked. But I was thinking this guy must be one of the most accident-prone men to walk the face of the earth.

Jack must have been reading my mind.

"Why couldn't that nautilus machine go over the edge and land on Frank?" Jack asked.

Heather stepped forward out of the shadows. "Alex could do thirty reps with a hundred and twenty-five. He didn't even break into a sweat. Alex was the best."

She was coked up and her nose was dripping and she was sniffing like she had a cold. Saint Anne had avoided the roof since Alex had left. Heather had broken her promise about Alex. But the combination of drugs, place, and time conspired, as it was bound to sooner or later, to make her forget that promise, to reach deep into the moment and to find Alex present. The surprising thing is that Heather hadn't blurted out about how great she thought Alex was, how he was the best, how famous he had been. The timing could not have been worse with a couple of criminals waiting in the street below to kill us.

Saint Anne stormed in front of Teddy and went straight toward Heather. I should have seen what she was intending and stopped her. But violence often happens so quickly that you can't intervene in time. Her punch caught Heather smack under the chin. And the force seemed to lift Heather off her feet and then she lost her balance and crashed into another machine. Saint Anne hovered above her, breathing hard, her jaw clenched.

"Get up, you son of a bitch," said Saint Anne.

"Hey, my mother wasn't a Saigon whore."

Jack ran between them.

"That's enough, girls."

Behind Heather, an enormous American flag billowed above the AT&T floodlights. The Stars and Stripes flapped in the wind as Heather reached into her purse, fumbled, then yanked out the 38-caliber Smith & Wesson. Holding the gun with both hands, the waves of rage shook her, made her, for a brief moment, appear she was doing arm curls.

"And who the fuck are you to hit me?" asked Heather, pointing the gun at Saint Anne. "You bitch. That's why he left you. And you don't even know what a fuck you are. Saint Anne, the bitch. The cunt. The fuck."

"You forgot gook," said Saint Anne.

Heather looked over at Jack. She had never used any racial hate words. Swallowing hard, her hands squeezed around the gun, she looked evil and deadly.

"Put away the gun, Heather, before you hurt someone," said Jack.

"Listen to him," I said.

"You promised," said Saint Anne. She held her ground as Heather waved the gun like a Bowery drunk.

"Give it to me," I said to Heather.

"Hey, what's this? Why are you siding with her? You know that she was in the wrong. She shouldn't have hit me. That was wrong, Gideon," Heather said, touching her jaw where Saint Anne had struck her. "You saw what she did."

"We'll settle it later," I said, reaching out to her.

"I want to settle it now. Here. Now."

"You always fight like this?" asked Teddy, standing by himself.

I think our family chaos made him feel better, more normal than he had felt in a long time. No one answered him.

I lost Heather's face in the shadows. A shaft of light streaked across her face, then disappeared. The last sledge of cocaine pounded in her temples, made her slightly clumsy. I kept my hand suspended. She jumbled her words as if an electrical current charge had been cranked high. Heather was in high speed, her thought a clutter of explosions and fire.

"Let's get Teddy out to the airport. Then we'll sort it out," I said, walking over towards Heather. She began to back up, the gun now pointed at my feet rather than Saint Anne's chest.

Saint Anne, with Heather retreating, regained her courage.

"It was because of you. Wasn't it? You're the one who told Alex to leave me. You told him I was a loser. That if Jack didn't have the nightclub, I would never work. And that I was never going to make it, didn't you?" Saint Anne pushed Jack aside as he tried to stroke her hair. "Just leave me alone," she said to him.

"Alex left because he lost his bet with Peter," said Jack. "And if that makes him a bastard, I guess he's a bastard."

Heather had moved over to the second putting green, shifting the gun from her left to her right hand.

"A bastard," said Heather, with a half-laugh. "What a joke. He didn't belong here. That's all. Alex was the best. Not second rate. But the best."

"Okay, Heather. If you insist, Alex was the best. Now give Gideon your gun. And let's stop this nonsense. Besides, you're ruining the second green. You're going to spoil all my work."

Jack walked straight up to her and took away the gun as if freeing a toy from a child's hand. He tossed it over to me. "Now, you're a naughty girl, pointing a gun at my sister and brother. It doesn't make them want to like you."

Teddy, who'd sat back on the nautilus bench, had forgotten about banging his knee. His arms folded, he had simply watched the scene unfold as if he had stumbled onto a street play midway, not really knowing why two characters wanted to kill each other. "Are we still going to the airport, or what?" he asked.

"We're on our way," I said, tucking the second gun into the waistband of my jeans.

"Just one question," said Teddy.

"I thought the guy I accidentally killed was named Peter."

"Yeah, that's right. Peter Montard," I assured him.

"Why are they trying to kill each over a man named Alex?"

There was no way I could explain—or wanted to explain—how murder was somehow in the air, floating above us, first it appeared to arise from Peter Montard's death, then from Alex's departure, and from the threats made by Frank Cora. I had this bad feeling that someone was going to get hurt before the night was over and before we got Teddy Eliot loaded on a plane and out of New York.

❖

WE walked quickly through the garage and got into Heather's new BMW. She always parked sideways, taking up two spaces in a far corner. This was her favorite parking spot on the top floor. Her small private shelf carved out in such a fashion that no other car could slide in beside her BMW and crash their doors' edges into her car. Indeed, for a number of reasons it was a perfect slot for Heather to dock the latest load of illegals. And she maintained the spot with a blue NYPD street barricade which she'd lifted from West 12th Street in the Village one Halloween at three in the morning after the club had closed.

Frank Cora would recognize Teddy, Saint Anne, and me so we had to stay out of sight, and Jack had never learned how to drive. But Frank had never laid eyes on Heather. Only her head would be visible as she drove out of the drive and turned into Wooster Street. I knelt in the footwell in front, bent over the passenger's seat, my head touching the silky smooth leather. Heather slipped a Bee Gee disk into the CD player and cranked up the sound, the back window speakers blaring, You Should Be Dancing. In the back seat, hunched over like Thanksgiving pilgrims at a prayer service, Jack, Teddy, and Saint Anne huddled shoulder to shoulder.

"I can't stand the Bee Gees," said Jack from the back seat.

"They're great," shouted Heather, thumping to the beat of the music against the steering wheel.

Jack groaned loudly. "Kitaro's Silk Road, Gideon. Please put it in. The second track, The Great Wall of China."

"Kitaro sucks," said Saint Anne. "Put on the Simon and Garfunkel album. The one with Baby Driver on it."

The only who hadn't made a request was our former hostage.

I shot Heather a blank look. It was news to her as well that Jack had smuggled some of his Kitaro CDs into the BMW. "No more fighting," I shouted back. My words hung in the night like one of Father's musical airplanes shrouded in the mist.

Did we have the slightest possibility of fooling Frank and Chute who were directly in front of our building? Did the English have a good chance to defeat the Spanish Armada before the actual battle?

In our praying position, with the Bee Gees' Stayin' Alive blaring in our ears, no one, after this brief exchange, was in the mood for denying this was a good theme song for the rest of the evening. A collective tension rolled over us like a fast-moving storm off English Bay. Parrot's severed head fouling Saint Anne's loft, the fight between Heather and Saint Anne on the roof, Heather's guns, the guilt of even thinking killing Teddy was an option, and all that built-up panicky hostility, swirled relentlessly around us, pinning us face down into the seats.

Heather slipped the BMW into gear, made a sharp right turn and stopped smoothly beside the elevator shaft. She opened the door, and, as a thousand times before, pushed the large, red service button. The meshing of gear teeth and chain blasted far away deep in the shaft below. Heather continued to drum her fingers to the sound of Too Much Heaven. The beat rose over the oily screech of the crackly old machinery of the elevator.

"I'm gonna smoke them bastards when I hit the street," she said, talking to herself. "You just watch me. They won't stand a chance. Not against this car. No way. Not in that limo. Are they kidding, or what?"

"I don't think these kind of men jest," said Jack from the back seat.

"I'll lose them. You can be sure of that." She reached over and turned up the volume. When Heather got this high there was no such thing as a defeat, or even a setback. She had the tendency to become imprisoned by her self-confidence. After all she had won two hundred bucks on the Mets game, she was juiced for victory, nothing could take away her win. But as she gunned the car forward onto the elevator platform, time stopped as I remembered the shock from two years ago when she told me that Jack was dead. And that it was her fault. Then, as now, chemicals she had put up her nose had dulled her, made her blur her words and thoughts like tired, exhausted gears full of slippage and on the edge of failing. She had said that Jack was dead at the bottom of the sea. In a disturbed moment of panic, the blood had drained from my face, I had gazed at the sea and, bleary-eyed, wept.

I had asked if it was the Triad.

She shook her head, crying.

"No, he did it himself," she had sobbed.

Of course, she had made a mistake about Jack's death. His boat had been lost but he turned up ten hours later, wet, alive and hungry. Like Teddy had made a mistake about the beam which killed Peter. There was no reason to believe the world itself was not some kind of a mistake.

19

The garage elevator slowly descended. Except for Heather, we huddled below the window level, so we felt the vibrations as the gears rumbled, and the motion of being lowered into a dark void. Heather kept beat to the music by hitting the flat of her hands against the steering wheel and singing. She couldn't carry a tune and she could not for her life recognize a musical note. She was tone deaf but like a lot of people it never stopped her from belting out songs at the top of her lungs. The groan and screech of the old machinery and Heather's off-key singing made me feel a little queasy.

"Heather?" called Saint Anne from the back seat.

"Yeah."

"Would you really have shot me?"

Heather turned down the volume of the CD player. From my position leaning over the passenger's seat, I could see Heather purse her lips together and knit her eyebrows. I took the opportunity to slip Monk's Moods, The Great Jazz Trio into the CD. Now there was something to listen to, something which was great. I loved that piano. Could the man ever play!

"I'm asking if you would have killed me on the roof," asked Saint Anne again.

"Are you kidding, or what?"

Saint Anne was silent for a moment. "I think for a moment you really hated me, and that you would have done it."

"You really think I could blow you away?" Heather rolled her head as if working out a tight muscle, her eyes half closed. "Hey, this stuff gets me exercised sometimes. That's all. You know, it makes me a little crazy."

"Can I ask you another question?" Saint Anne's little-girl voice filtered out of the back seat.

"I don't like the sound of this," said Jack.

"What?" I asked.

"Can't you hear those gears choking? Missing. Hitting against something. Full of rust and dirt and grease. All clogged with sweep-ings. We could die easily." Jack hated elevators and normally would meet Heather at the street level rather than ride down with her.

"They inspect them every six months," said Heather, reassuring him.

"And this limited partnership of doctors and lawyers pays off the inspector. You know that's true, Heather. This place is a death trap."

"Hold on to your ankles and take deep breaths," I said through the seat.

Saint Anne was temporarily deflected, and for the moment Heather was saved from answering whether she would have pulled the trigger and plugged Saint Anne full of hot lead. Sometimes she would forget things under the influence of coke and heavy emotions. Jack wanted her to tell him that he wasn't going to die in the garage elevator. I heard Saint Anne patting his back. Jack's whimpering faded into nothingness. For a guy who had traveled the world, walked into the office of Triad bosses without any fear, he had an irrational fear of heights. He said he never got close to the edge because he thought he might jump. He never wanted to hold a baby on a high building because he had an irrational fear he would throw the baby off, then jump himself.

Normally, Saint Anne would have allowed such an interruption to override her own concern. But not this time. She clung to the image of Heather's pointing the gun at her head. Jack's fear of death in the garage elevator hadn't erased Heather's squinted eye behind the gun. Saint Anne's single-minded need was to ask Heather one further question.

"Heather, I want to know something. And I want you to be perfectly honest with me. Because whatever you say, I want you to know I'll always love you. You are part of this family, and nothing will ever change that. Do you understand?"

Heather looked into the rear-view mirror at the empty space behind her where this voice had come from. The webbed feet split away from her eyes as she smiled. "Yeah, that's kinda heavy. But I get you."

"You knew Alex was going away, didn't you? Wait, let me finish. And you not only knew, you helped him. I know that you two were friendly. Maybe a little too friendly. I said that to you before. I said it to Alex. But for the life of me, I can't understand why you did that. Why you helped Alex. Do you really hate me that much?"

In the moment of silence that followed, I heard Teddy whisper to Saint Anne, asking her for a cigarette. His voice sounded as if he were under duress; the same tones which I first recall coming from his mouth when he woke up chained to the basement wall.

"I owed him a favor," said Heather.

"What did you owe me? I know Alex saved Jack that time at the beach. But this was my marriage. Didn't that mean anything to you? Besides, I think Alex and you were having an affair behind all our backs. That's what I really think."

Saint Anne's voice was moving into that emotionally unbalanced range. In most circumstances, Heather would've walked out of the room, slammed the door and gone over to Spring Street for a drink. This time she had no such option. She was stuck. We all were, on a sticky, hot, late July night. Saint Anne sensed that she had a captive audience and no matter how hard she hit, or how wild she swung, she was safe in the back seat and the object of these deep, sweeping blows was unarmed and, in effect, chained to the wall.

"Then you're not thinking too good," said Heather. "You really think I slept with Alex, don't you? Well, I didn't. And sure, I helped him out with a few names in Paris. But he was going anyway. Nothing could've held him back. He'd put his word on that bet with Peter. And that meant something to him. That should've meant something to you as well. And you know why, Saint Anne? I'll tell you. Alex kinda changed the way all of us looked at things. He certainly changed me around. I could've got pretty bummed out that night at the Rainbow Room. But I didn't. And you know why, because

Alex understood Jack better than I did. And when he explained it to me, you know what? Jack and I have never been stronger. You understand what I'm saying?"

"How do I know whether to believe you?" said Saint Anne.

"Because I wouldn't bullshit you. Not about Alex. That's why," said Heather. "And like your friend, Teddy, back there. I've got pretty good character."

"The best," said Jack, choking back his own fear.

20

From the Rainbow Room atop the RCA building it would be possible to look down midtown and pick out the construction site where Teddy Eliot's boot dislodged a heavy wooden beam. A block of timber, more likely than not cut from a Canadian forest in British Columbia or Alberta, which severed Peter Montard's head with the efficiency of a sword-wheeling Tokugawa shogun. But the night of Jack and Heather's tenth wedding anniversary, Peter was on the guest list; among those who freely mingled among the Hampton Beach crowd, the art world, the film, music, and a couple of sports personalities. Peter might have passed before the window and gazed directly across at the embryo of a building that would bury him.

A champagne reception had been scheduled for 7:30 pm. The men were dressed in black dinner jackets and the women in evening dresses. Heather, who lived in designer jogging suits, had slipped into a low-cut dress; from the waist, the dress billowed out, layer upon layer, like the kind favored by 50s prom queens. Saint Anne looked radiantly happy on Alex's arm as Peter Montard explained wind-surfing on the choppy, churning waters of the Columbia River in Oregon. Elizabeth leaned close to Saint Anne and whispered how perfectly glowing she looked that night.

"I'm pregnant," Saint Anne whispered back. "No one knows. I'm gonna tell Alex tonight."

Elizabeth looked real happy at the news. "I am so very pleased," she whispered excitedly.

JACK, of course, had not arrived. No one really gave much thought to his absence; even at 8:00 pm., Heather was still circulating among the crowd of thirty close friends without worrying very much about Jack. The first flutter of concern, well short of panic, yet it set the needle into the groove of a moody night, came around 8:30, when the maitre d' took Heather aside and asked her if it was her wish to keep the bar open. Soon another case of champagne—vintage Pol Roger—(it was, after all, ten years of marriage to a man who had been married and divorced once before and in a town where the champagne aged better than most marriages) and yet another round of toasts were exchanged. As best as I could, I stood in for Jack, raising my glass at Heather's side.

Saint Anne in her white *ao dai* had the spotlight on stage, singing Blue Velvet, but only a few people were listening, as the gathering had broken into small groups who were talking shop, doing deals, doing what the famous do, like smiling and drinking champagne. She looked like a million dollars but that was walking-around money for the tough audience she was playing to.

By nine the crowd had broken into smaller groups of two or three, whispering, and slightly drunk from so much champagne on an empty stomach. Meanwhile I'd phoned Jack's loft, and there was no reply. So we started dinner without him.

At ten o'clock, halfway through the meal, Jack walked into the Rainbow Room, wearing a dinner jacket, shaved, his hair looking as if he'd just climbed out of the bath. His arms extended, he walked, smiling and sighing, over to the head of the table, leaned over and kissed Heather on the cheek.

"Jack, do you know what time it is?" In the time I'd known Heather, I'd never seen her more upset. Of course, Jack didn't have the slightest idea about the time. He hadn't then, nor had he ever before or since, carried a watch.

"Yes, I know. I'm a little late. I had a long distance from Hong Kong, and then from Singapore. Well, please, everybody keep right on eating. I'm very glad you could all come," he said, addressing the crowd. "But I was sorting through the mail on my way out. And you know, I came across an envelope addressed to me from an old friend in Hong Kong. Actually, the cousin of a very dear, dear friend of mine, Mr. Ling. A great man, who unfortunately is now dead."

Heather angrily jerked her chair away from the table, tossed her crumpled napkin in her plate and stormed out of the room. She was crying, and doing very little to hide that fact from the assembled friends who had come to celebrate ten years of marriage.

"You see, every time I mention Mr. Ling's name, even my dear wife feels the sorrow of his death. Sad. Yes, very sad." Jack gestured with his hands. "Please, finish your meal. And thank you so much for coming tonight. It means so much to me and my lovely wife."

Not more than a minute after Heather ran out of the room, Alex discreetly bent over, whispered something in Saint Anne's ear. I could see Saint Anne tentatively nod her head, kiss Alex on the cheek, and he passed behind, stopping for a second to give me a squeeze on the shoulder. "I'll handle it, Gideon. Keep your sister occupied. I'll be back in a minute."

Alex went back to the ladies' washroom and barged through the door. He found Heather, mascara dripping onto her prom dress, crumpled in a chair. Alex chased two other women out of the washroom, then stood with his powerful Raiders back to the door; no one was getting in or out until he'd had his say. As an object calculated to arouse profound sympathy, Heather would've been difficult to match that evening. She had collapsed in the sitting area of the women's washroom of the Rainbow Room, crying in her prom dress.

"Any other night, I could take it," she sniffled.

"You didn't really expect him to be on time, did you?"

Heather looked up at Alex, her jaw clenched. "You're goddamn right I expected him. It's our tenth anniversary for Christ's sakes. All those people out there. You know the bar bill is over one grand? Why couldn't he just this one time, just once for a very special occasion, think about someone else? The fucking Asian stock markets could wait one day. Couldn't they, Alex?"

She could see the glint in Alex's eye in the mirror, as he stood behind her in his black dinner jacket; his weightlifter's shoulders and neck tensed, as muffled pounding filtered through from the other side of the door. Women slammed against the door, demanding in faint voices, pleading for the chance to take a pee.

"Jack gave you a pretty decent gift," said Alex.

Heather shook her head slowly. "Hey, I never thought you'd take his side. Why can't someone in this family take my side? Just once."

"If Jack had been on time tonight or any other night, do you know what that would've meant?"

"Yeah, that he gave a fuck about me," said Heather. "I'm no more than a chauffeur for the illegals."

"You've got it the wrong way around. Think about him showing up on time. Pretty scary thought, isn't it? Because then you know that he's capable of keeping an appointment. Capable of knowing how time works in everyday life. But then, that would mean that, since he's always running four hours late on New York time, he knows what he's doing. And he intends to do it. For effect. For attention. Out of malice. Whatever. That would be a thousand times worse, Heather. Then it would mean he's been playing some sick game. Or that Jack's a fucking monster. Or an insane criminal. He'd be as guilty as hell in either case. And he wouldn't give a good fuck about you. But Jack has Hong Kong time in his genes. He can't adjust to this time zone and never has. He does the best he can but it isn't all that good when you want him to be some place in New York. Like tonight. What he did tonight was just good old Jack being himself. Thank God, Jack, on this most special of nights, showed up when he did. If he had been on time, then I'd tell you to divorce him."

Heather raised her head, slowly dried her eyes and swung her feet around to the floor. A moment later, Alex was gone, and a surge of women poured through the small rest area and into the stalls. When Heather returned to the dining table, she no longer looked crushed or angry or hurt. Her eyes, still swollen a little, had been redone with fresh make-up. She shoved her chair next to Jack, reached over, filled his champagne glass, and then her own. Then she pulled Jack by the collar of his dinner jacket to his feet. He rose, his fists clasping his knife and fork, his mouth chewing a piece of lamb. Jack swallowed, picked up his glass. Heather touched her glass against the rim of his.

"To ten happy years," she said, tears springing from her eyes.

"And to another fifty," said Jack. Our crowd of friends applauded and the real party had begun.

21

Saint Anne silently twisted her body, squeezing herself between Teddy and Jack, and Jack was trying to pull her back down, fearing an attack on his wife. But she pushed him away, sitting up straight in a sudden movement right behind the driver's seat. Heather caught a look in the rear-view mirror, and made one of those gaaa noises. Saint Anne had flung her arms over the leather bucket seat, and wrapped them in a hammer-lock around Heather's throat.

"You're choking me," gasped Heather.

Saint Anne madly kissed her on the cheek, smudging lipstick all over her face. "I love you, Heather," she said, pulling slightly back, loosening her hold around Heather's neck. "I really do. Do you know that? How much I really care about you?"

As Heather was about to turn round to look at Saint Anne, we reached street level.

I heard the traffic outside and saw the light of the street lamps streaming through the car windows.

"Get down, Saint Anne," I said.

The elevator platform locked with a thud and a small bounce to the metal ramp which connected the garage to Wooster Street. Heather's body tensed as she leaned forward. Saint Anne looked out the window and saw someone in the street looking straight at her.

"You know that guy?"

"I know him," said Saint Anne.

Heather rolled down her window. "Hey, you're blocking my end. What is this?"

Slowly Saint Anne's arms came down from Heather's neck, and her fingers, forming a prayer cup, came to rest over her mouth. "It's Frank Cora."

"The gangster who's going to make you famous?" said Heather.

"He wants to kill me," said Teddy from the back. He was struggling to get out of the car and Jack was holding on to him and trying to lock the back door at the same time.

"Get down," I shouted to Saint Anne again.

But it was too late. Frank had seen her. "I just wanna talk to you," I heard Frank Cora's muffled voice, coming over the music. "Nothing heavy. You know what I mean?"

"Heather, just run over that evil man," Jack cried from the back seat, still doubled up on the floor.

"Shit," Teddy muttered. "He carries a gun. I know he's going to kill me."

Saint Anne reached up and opened her door. "No one's going to kill you, Teddy." She was out of the car, slamming the door, and then we were all sitting up and watching as she walked with Frank across the cobblestone street to the limo. Chute sat inside with the air-conditioning running. I was nervously checking both of Heather's handguns, thinking how did Gideon Harvey, whore's son from Seattle, ever find himself holding loaded guns, and faced with the real possibility of killing people? From where I sat, it looked like Frank was doing most of the talking. He gestured with his thick, hairy hands. A smile flickered across his face, then the happy face dissolved into a frown like he had drunk some acid. Saint Anne just nodded and her mouth wasn't moving. Then something strange happened. She was singing in the back of the limo. Then either she or Frank rolled down the window so we could hear her singing. Saint Anne was singing The Time of My Life. The theme song from Dirty Dancing which ranked alongside of I'll Always Love You. Why was it that gangsters liked the most sentimental songs filled with false emotion? She was singing it and he was singing with her. He had a mike and it was hooked to the speakers in the back seat and Wooster Street was filled with probably some of the worst singing ever heard in New York. Parrot's head could have been howling even though it was no longer attached to his body. Jack started to laugh, then Heather. How could you feel in mortal danger from a man who made that kind of sound when he sang?

After they stopped singing, Frank sat in the limo grinning at her, did a drum roll with his fists on the side of the limo in mock celebration.

Jack rolled down his window, stuck out his hands, and clapped. "Bravo," he shouted.

"If Frank starts singing again, we should hand over Teddy," I said.

Everyone went silent.

"Man, I was just joking," I said, holding onto the handguns.

Saint Anne reached out to Frank with both hands, he kissed each one. Even from across the street, I could see her hands tremble. Frank kissed her on the forehead. He pulled her closer and gave her a small embrace, she held her breath a second before she broke free and climbed out of the back of the limo.

Then she turned away from Frank, who couldn't keep his eyes off her. She walked back across the street to our BMW. It seemed to take forever as she crossed the no-man's land between Frank and us. Jack opened the back door and Saint Anne, looking pale , climbed inside, fumbling in her handbag for a cigarette. I had the idea that some new program had been accepted by Frank's camp. Alex had always said she was good at negotiating with what he called the "hairy hand" customers who came into the club and tried to paw her. Looking out into the empty street, Saint Anne glanced at the limo, lighting a cigarette.

"What's the deal?" I asked.

"He's taking Teddy to the airport," Saint Anne said. I caught her eye. "You trust him to do that?"

"I'll be going in the car with them. And you will all be coming too, just to make certain nothing weird happens."

"It's already too weird. I don't like it," said Teddy from beside her on the back seat.

"None of us like it, Teddy," said Saint Anne. "But what other choice do we have? Do you want my brother to walk across the street and pop them?"

"Gideon wouldn't hurt anyone," said Jack.

My hands were sweating as I held the guns. What if I really had to shoot that motherfucker and his sidekick? Could I do it?

"Why would Frank do this? Why not just let us take him out. Tell me what that's all about," said Heather.

Saint Anne shook her head, as she pulled the cigarette from her lips. She held the smoke deep in her lungs, not breathing for a second, then turned her head to the side and exhaled long and hard. "I've thought of that. No dice. He wants to talk to Teddy. It's important. He can't just let him get on the plane without making sure of a few things. Look, I think Frank's scared. But if he talks to Teddy, it'd make him feel better. What's he gonna do with me in the car? Shoot Teddy?"

"And the Dirty Dancing song. What was that about?" I asked.

Saint Anne looked ill. "Forget that."

"Why?" asked Jack.

"Okay, it's part of the deal. We're going to record it together. Just for a lark. He wants us to sing together. Okay?" said Saint Anne.

"That's weird," said Teddy.

"His friends say he has a voice like Sinatra."

"Gag me with a spoon," said Heather.

"He's not that bad," said Saint Anne.

There were groupies and then there were guys who thought Saint Anne could make them famous, thinking that because she was working a nightclub she had already made it. That was it, his hidden agenda finally coming out into the open. Frank Cora was thinking himself the new Francis Albert Sinatra, an Italian icon, whose picture alongside Jesus was in every Italian restaurant in Hoboken, New Jersey.

FRANK had the good fortune to find himself in exactly the right place at the right time. Saint Anne, her arms hugging Heather, had reached the peak of her reconciliation when the sheer force of forgiveness had blotted out the rest of the world. Even Frank Cora got a free ride, reaping what he had not sown. He cruised in on the tide of Saint Anne's emotional outpouring. Call it, if you like, a spillover effect. But a warm glow rushed through Saint Anne. Saint Anne had fully realized how badly she had misjudged Heather's intentions about Alex. This good feeling toward the victim of her misjudgment created an entirely new possibility; that Saint Anne had also been too harsh on Frank Cora, that cloud of violence particles swirling at every turn of his life. The upsetting phone calls and the head of Parrot smashed through her own window had been a child's cry for attention and recognition.

She was asking us to believe that Frank was a man haunted, driven by his dream, her dream as well. This was what they had seen in each other, the same hunger, desire and one was trying to use the other to hike up that mountain of success. Only that wasn't exactly my reading of Frank Cora. I think that Saint Anne's relationship with this gangster had colored her judgment. She should have known better than to get mixed up with him in the first place. He was one of those guys who rode an invisible wire between his public jobs and the back rooms where he conducted his private business. Frank Cora didn't like to think of people who were living and breathing beyond his control. He didn't come right out and say it, but he didn't have to. From the way he had been hunting Teddy Eliot it was clear what his business was. He had a contract to kill Teddy Eliot. All the signs were there for me to see that night in Gary's driveway. The envelope Chute pulled out from the glove compartment contained a number of photographs. But Teddy was marked. He'd gone straight to it. Frank and Chute had been told that Teddy had to go before I had come along. I was going to be the black guy who took the fall in case anything went wrong.

Frank must have thought his ship had come in when I approached him. It was almost too good to be true. An irony of fate. This nightclub singer had bought his story. Frank Sinatra. The man could be arrested for violating the peace and good order of the neighborhood, given the loud noise he had been making into the microphone.

Frank Cora, his chest puffed out, could saunter into the back room of the fishing and hunting club in Queens and tell everyone how his honey, a nightclub singer who was about to hit it big on MTV, a real little beauty, with the face of an angel, had a brother with some black blood and how he got that brother to kill Teddy

Eliot, and how he collected the money for the job. That would have got him some respect, a reputation as a man who made things happen and with the people who counted. Frank Cora was not just another piece of ham on the payroll. He was an operator. He had big connections in the entertainment business. At that vulnerable moment when Heather's white BMW reached street level, Frank Cora's good fortune star was shining overhead and he was thinking, "Hey, I gotta voice. Don't you think, Chute?" He was starting to believe his cover was reality. That was always a bad mistake, confusing what you know to be true with what you wish were true is always a recipe for an accident you inflict on yourself.

I knew the inner workings of Saint Anne's mind. For Saint Anne, the mere thought of Heather having fooled around with Alex behind her back had symmetry with the relationship between Frank and Teddy. Frank had simply misjudged Teddy Eliot and once she could explain to him the full story, the two men could shake hands warmly, maybe exchange an embrace and part as friends.

FATHER'S mind wrapped around reality looking for all the logical connections, trying to figure out how to fit together the loose ends. Perhaps his mind was closer to a dedicated computer; one that performed intellectual equivalency games. But this wasn't how Saint Anne's mind functioned. She had a singer's brain, which worked from one tune to the next. Her mind was shaped by growing up with Mother. Music is about a lot of things, but one of the things it isn't about is logic. Mother was the one who practiced a kind of moral and emotional equivalence; hers was a mind which had been troubled that what she heard in love songs never appeared outside of them.

Mother, then in her late sixties, decided that she didn't want to grow old in Vancouver. She was, by God, an American. She wanted to die on American soil. These reports were mostly second-hand since Mother never expressed her nationalism to Jack, who was more Chinese than American, or to Saint Anne, given what the Americans did to Vietnam, or to me, who had a lot of questions about all the slaves owned by the Founding Fathers and had Ray

Charles and Glover Washington, Jr. posters on my bedroom walls. And Mother decided she wasn't going to grow old with Father either. This desire was partly due to Father's lack of any capacity to age the way people normally do over time. Father just never matured and ripened. And his sheet music kept accumulating, spilling over into their bedroom. She knew the old man was lost. He was never going to figure out what had been behind Mozart or anyone else. He was a lost soul and always had been and she wasn't going to live out the rest of her life with someone who had gone over that edge. There was nothing left between them that mattered. So she left.

Like Jack, he lived according to his own time, inside his own reflections, moods, and these avalanches of youthful melancholy rolled over him, his children and his wife, who would have to pick their way free of the debris. Even as Father's hair grayed and thinned, his features grew larger, more coarse, and his lean, tall frame settled and his shoulders stooped, he climbed deeper into the kind of void where there is only room for one inhabitant.

Mother left him for a retired real estate agent in Seattle. A man who was several years younger than she. Donald Garrett, Mother's new husband, had two grown kids of his own. They lived in Seattle and he had grandchildren as well. We spent one Christmas in Seattle with Mother and her new family. They lived in a house five miles away from the whorehouse where the three of us had been conceived. The three of us managed to get Mother alone and she told us how it had all happened. She had met Donald Garrett on a Vancouver golf course. By that time, Mother had long given up the game, so long, in fact, that I think she had forgotten exactly why. She was out on the course photographing golfers for the sports page of the Vancouver Sun.

Every fact about Donald was normal and irresistible by virtue of its ordinariness. Donald, no question about it, was a normal guy, with normal kids and grandkids, a normal little house and no desire but to keep on living in this simple, uncomplicated fashion. Donald's normality swept Mother right off her feet. This bland widower from Seattle who had never heard of Nietzsche, the I Ching, the ying and the yang, did not have a single classical record in his house. He would have never adopted kids from a whorehouse lawyer. Later back in New York, we had arguments about what Mother had said, and what she knew and when she knew it.

"Donald never would have hired someone to murder three prostitutes because they wanted their babies back," said Saint Anne.

"You don't know he did that," I said.

"You think it was just an accident us moving to Canada shortly after it happened?"

Jack threw up his hands. "Around and round we go. But we are never going to find out. We have to live like most people with questions which have no answers."

"I say he and that crooked Seattle lawyer had them killed."

"Mother never said that," I said.

Threatening to take away the children and ruining his career were powerful motives but, as Jack said, that didn't necessarily mean that he had done it. Mother had never come out and out and said he had intended their deaths. He had been given a defiance and all he wanted was not a fight but for them to go away.

Not Saint Anne, the eldest, not Jack, her second child, not her youngest offspring ever dreamt that Mother would abandon the empty nest in Vancouver and run off to live in a small, plain bungalow with the garage converted into a family room, smack in the shadow of Boeing's flight path. Saint Anne's biggest reconciliation came a couple of months after Mother moved in to live with Donald. It was one of those emotional, nine-hour sessions, where, according to Saint Anne, Mother laid bare her soul. She asked for Saint Anne's forgiveness for not telling her the truth about how we had come into the world. She thought we would never find out; it wasn't important, all those years ago should have been laid to rest.

Mother asked that all her kids understand that she had never had a normal life in Canada. She hadn't had much of a life at all. She felt she had been on the run and that she had never lived just for herself. All her life, she had been lonely and shut out. The only place she ever could express herself was on the golf course. The one location where she found peace of mind in something she did well. I could see Saint Anne hugging Mother; her arms wrapped around Mother's neck, tears in both of their eyes, the mutual expressions of fondness.

Saint Anne showed her the old clippings about the death of the three women from the Seattle brothel house and watched for a reaction. When Mother looked up there were tears in her eyes.

"Did Father know how this happened?" asked Saint Anne.

Mother had a tight smile. "He only wanted them to go away. He didn't ever want any harm to come to them. To anyone. It wasn't his fault. But the guilt never stopped, even after all these years. We did the best that we knew how. It wasn't good enough but it was all we knew at the time. Now I've said more than I should. Only I ask you not to judge him too hard. He never could have harmed anyone."

❖

"YOU see, Donald loves Mother for herself. He allows her to forgive herself and forget the past," Saint Anne said. And she then turned to Alex who had just come into the room and said, "If only you could be more like Donald than Father."

"If only you could accept me for what I am," he replied. "Accept yourself for what you are."

If only he had not gone to Paris. But she was like Father and not like Donald. She wanted an abnormal life. What else can you call being famous? She would have done anything necessary to remove someone or something which got in her way. Her quest for the spotlight had caused her suffering. There were other "ifs"—if only the Harvey Trio hadn't quit just as she was to make her big breakthrough or if she hadn't married, and if only she had never met Peter Montard. A storage closet of regrets as high as the moon and as wide as the sun and the tide comes in and goes out and the beach always looks about the same.

22

Having been raised in a family of failed visionaries, there was little surprise or disappointment in finding another idea we had clung to was an illusion. Thinking we could escape from Frank Cora was about as unlikely as escaping from the reality of our past. Jack got out of the car and stood in the street performing one of those small bows I had seen him perform in Hong Kong when he greeted a Triad boss. The bow had a combination of respect and fear, but most of all it was a sign of capitulation to some greater force that had the ability to destroy him. I sat in the front seat a little longer, wishing I had the guts to climb out with the guns, walk over to the car and shoot both of those motherfuckers dead in the limo. But I didn't do that. Jack and I were like those guys in an old World War II black-and-white documentary reel: British soldiers, who, having been ordered to surrender, laid down their guns, and stood at attention, saluting a caravan of cars carrying Japanese officers into Singapore.

Frank Cora had been like bad music, turning sideways, note after note, like spokes of a wheel, looped round and round inside my mind. The facts, the arguments, the positions, the statement, none of these things mattered in the back of Frank's limo. In the brittle silence, steam rolled out of a manhole cover in the street, blew back over Heather's BMW, fogging the window. It made me think of Teddy's insulation burning under the Lincoln with the rearing mustang horse hood ornament. Of Father plotting the deaths of our mothers in Seattle. Of Peter Montard promising to make Saint

Anne a real star, a celebrity whose face everyone would recognize. Of my asking Frank Cora over a Chinese lunch for a special favor.

The basic components of each person's vision were always restricted in about the same way. By the nature and condition of their time and background. Whom they met at school, a party, a conference, in an office, on a street, or in an airport bar. All those scattered impressions were like walls. Some people climbed over them; others accepted them as they accepted home. Those who lived in obscurity and those who lived in the public eye were separated by another wall. In between was a deep and wide river infested with soul-eating sharks which had names—the no talent big mouth shark, the bad luck killer shark, the misjudgment buzz saw tooth shark, and the miscalculation razor fin shark. Saint Anne had spent a lifetime trying to find a way to cross that river. I was happy camping on the shore, same as Jack, just watching that old river run on past. Saint Anne was more like Father who dreamed of moving rivers and oceans and mountains.

No wonder that after Father's world collapsed roof into floor upon floor into the basement of his life, all that remained was the one primal question asked by Nietzsche: "Is there danger?" That was the message he wrote on paper airplanes and threw to the wind.

CHUTE frisked each of us before letting us into the limo. Jack climbed into the front seat. The rest of us got into the back of the limo. Frank Cora sat on the long, soft, cushioned bench between Saint Anne and Heather, while Teddy and I used the jump-seats, the kind of pull-down seats for people of lesser importance. Once Chute turned on the ignition, Frank slipped his arm around Saint Anne's shoulders. That set the tone for the evening. Frank insisted that we were among friends. All of us. He never explained whether he frisked all of his friends before they were allowed inside the limo. Chute had relieved me of both handguns, grinning as he showed the guns to Frank, before locking them in the glove compartment.

"What were your plans for the 38s, boy?" Frank Cora asked.

I didn't say anything. But I was glad I didn't have the guns because I would have shot the sonofabitch between the eyes.

"Were you figuring on hurting someone?"

The horrible, ugly way he had killed Parrot still bothered me.

"Why did you kill Parrot?" I asked.

Frank's head snapped around, and his eyes, wild and large so you could see all white around the pupils, seemed like they were on stalks, coming across the small empty space between me on the jump-seat and him in the back seat. He seemed angry and confused.

"Kill who?" he asked, screwing his jaw tight.

He had killed enough people with strange foreign names that he didn't remember all of them. This set him on edge, as if I knew something he had forgotten.

"Ali's dog," I said.

"The head," added Heather, chewing gum to settle her nerves.

"Oh, the dog. That was its name?" Frank asked, after the flying dog head clicked in his mind. He relaxed a little. "What kind of name is that for a dog?"

"Did you do that, Frank?" asked Saint Anne, moving his hand away. Frank took her gesture personally. "Hey, you think I killed the dog? Is that what you're thinking? Mean Frank Cora killed that animal? What was its name?"

"Parrot," I repeated softly, thinking of the King's College necktie he'd been wearing last time I stopped to cuff him around the ears.

"A yellow cab ran him down. Look at all that fucking steam. You can't see shit, know what I mean? It was hit and run. The cab killed him dead. Nearly sliced off his head." Frank unwrapped his arm from around Saint Anne. He brought his hands forward, palms up, as if swearing an oath to the heavens. One by one he met our eyes, and leaned back against the seat.

"Parrot's head made an awful mess on the floor," said Jack, half-turned around in the front seat.

"I couldn't believe anyone could do that," said Saint Anne, her hands clasped on her knees.

"Stupid. That's what it was. I told Chute he was going too far. Didn't I, Chute?" Chute's eyes found him in the rear-view mirror. "That's exactly what you said, Mr. Cora."

"The army sends these boys away to places like Vietnam. Then they come back and get into this kind of shit. They eat dog soup in Vietnam, don't they, Chute?"

"It's a favorite, Mr. Cora," answered Chute in a neutral voice.

I didn't believe Frank Cora's story about how Parrot died for a second. But what was more disturbing was Saint Anne's silence in the wake of the racial remarks about her momma's country. She had let it pass and that wasn't like her.

Chute contributed to my sense of danger and obstacles by driving north on Wooster Street—a one-way street running south—then ignored the red light on Grand, swung right onto Grand, then swung over and executed a sharp left turn onto Greene Street. The Greene Street turn was a definite omen of bad fortune; we were forging through that river I had spent my whole life trying to avoid. I had this gut feeling we were about to become famous but with the kind of fame like having your picture on the post office wall.

The fastest route to La Guardia Airport was to drive east on Grand until you reach Center Street, then turn left and follow Center until you hit Kenmare where you make another right. Kenmare becomes Delancey and that takes you right over the Williamsburg Bridge and into Brooklyn. But people from the outer boroughs and crooked taxi drivers use streets which go somewhere for sure, but the airport isn't at the end of them. In SoHo the narrow, one-way streets have names like Prince, Mercer, and Greene which are lifted from England. Chute appeared more confused than a crook as he turned around. Since I was seated with my back to Chute, and Jack, who didn't drive, knew nothing about one-way streets, Chute had little assistance.

A wrong turn in SoHo had unpredictable consequences because it was the center for the Great American Fame Machine. The neighborhood operated as a twenty-four hour location shoot for television dramas, comedies, specials, as well as for made-for-TV movies, feature films, and God only could hazard a guess about how many commercials and music videos, and combine this rainstorm of film activity with a legion of NYU student filmmakers running around with Sony mini-cams and sound equipment, the chances of running into some "film people congestion"—as neighborhood people call it—was reasonably high. Living where we did was part of the reason that made Saint Anne crazy about becoming a celebrity. From where she sat just about everyone seemed famous but us, and it didn't seem fair to her, seeing she had talent and all.

By turning onto Greene Street, Chute selected one of the streets TV and film location scouts love to put in their freeze-frames of New York. A one-way street that runs straight into the homes of middle America. Even Mr. Hedgecock had written in a letter wrapped around two packets of seeds that he'd seen one of "my" restaurants on Greene Street on TV.

The prime spot in all SoHo was the intersection of Greene and Spring. It was half a block before I saw the telltale signs of a film crew. Four Winnebago trailers the color of Westhampton sand at low tide, and they were parked end to end. Each one was as long as a mobile home. And through the lit windows, you could see all kinds of production people inside—wardrobe and make-up people, producers, continuity persons, assistant directors, the whole crawl you see running after a TV show was finished. They walked in and around the Winnebagos, making Greene Street look like a high-class trailer park. Chute took his foot off the gas. And at the same time, Frank removed his arm from around Saint Anne's shoulders and leaned forward between Teddy and me so that he could see out of the front window.

"What the hell . . ." he said, his voice trailing off.

"Another coffee commercial?" asked Jack.

"No, they have only one Winnebago," said Heather.

"I've got it! It's Hunter," said Jack.

Chute, his face half-turned, glanced at Jack. "They canceled Hunter," he said.

I figured it was a home audience made up of guys like Chute which had kept it on the air for seven years.

Heather was suddenly excited and rolling down the window. "That's Kevin Costner. All right. I love that man." She leaned her head out the window and screamed, "Kevin. Hey, Kevin. You're great, man."

Only it wasn't Kevin Costner; it was a member of the production crew wearing cut-off jeans and a Dartmouth College T-shirt with huge sweat circles under his arms, carrying a walkie-talkie, who came up to the limo. This clean-cut guy bent down and made a wide circular motion with his hand, motioning Chute to roll down his window. As he did so, a blast of hot summer air poured into the car.

"Street's blocked. You're gonna have to back up," said the college-age face, peering around inside the car.

"Anyone ever telling you that you look like Kevin Costner?" asked Heather.

"No," he said. "You're the first."

Frank stuck his head forward. "We got a plane to catch. Let us through."

"Can't. Nothing's moving in or out of here for another half an hour." He was about to walk away when he did a double-take on Saint Anne in the car.

"Aren't you Saint Anne Harvey?" he asked. "The singer? I saw your act a couple of weeks ago. Not bad."

Saint Anne glowed and was about to lean forward when Frank leaned in front of her.

"No, you're mistaken," said Frank.

The guy shrugged, eyes narrowed, and walked away.

It was rare but sometimes a customer from the club recognized her on the street, going up to her and saying how much they liked her singing. But being recognized in the limo with Frank Cora was a real stroke of good luck. Nothing bad was going to happen. Not unless he was going to kill this guy as well. Wowee, I thought. This is our lucky day. We could climb out of that river of fame and sun ourselves on the shore. But then people made mistakes like Heather thinking the guy was Kevin Costner when he wasn't; people were always mistaking someone for a star or a personality and getting it wrong half the time, proving that a lot of people look like famous people.

By the time the production guy had split, several more cars had boxed us in. More bridge and tunnel people who'd made the same mistake as Chute, thinking all streets in SoHo were created equal. Even Frank could see there was little point arguing with the production guy. Angled to our right, about half a block ahead of us, a cheer went up from a thousand or so people seated inside the intersection of Broome and Greene. Bleachers had been set up like a makeshift baseball stadium. The crowd was mostly young, black and Hispanic, the subway crowd from the city projects. At first blush, it looked as if they had been rounded up and stuck on these bleachers after the authorities had disarmed them, packed them onto buses and taken them out to some place like Meadowlands for the ultimate solution. For that fraction of a second, our own problems paled into insignificance.

"It's the Human Bullet!" shouted Jack. "Heather, remember him from the Sports Channel?" His voice squealed with delight. Jack loved celebrities.

"Hey, I remember that guy. But where is his cannon?"

With the back door open, I leaned out of the car, half stood, and craned my head above the crowded sidewalk. The Human Bullet. That was the answer. No mass deportation to the Meadowlands for the city's unemployed, uneducated ghetto kids this summer's night. Crew members rolled a large, potbelly of a silver cannon into view, and pointed the barrel skyward in the direction of a huge net two hundred feet away. Opposite the cannon, the net had been filled to the brim with thousands of large green watermelons. The Human Bullet's stunt was being shot out head first down Broome Street and into a cushion of watermelons. Television cameras had been installed on tall metal platforms behind the cannon, another camera angle was behind the net of watermelons, and two more rose on steel cranes, covering the action from the crowd's point of view.

"Beats going out to catch that airplane," said Frank, falling back in his seat. "Don't you think, Teddy?"

"What does?" asked Teddy, the blood drained from his face. He hadn't said more than these two words since we all climbed into the limo.

"The cannon. Don't be a dumbshit. Look behind you. Don't you see that cannon? Now that's a hell of a way to get shot. Know what I mean?"

Teddy didn't turn around, he just lowered his head and stared at the floor. This would have been a perfect opportunity for him to make a run for it. I had the door open and was halfway into the street myself. We were caught in traffic. The streets overflowed with people, and it would've been easy to disappear in the crowd. Maybe it was

Saint Anne's touching Frank's hand. Or the excitement in Jack's voice as he cheered the arrival of the Human Bullet. Or the unreality of a man, his costume sparkling with sequins, calling himself a bullet, being loaded into a gun. Willingly the Human Bullet slid feet first down a black hole and into an Alice in Wonderland universe where, surrounded by gray, cool steel, he waited for flight.

All I had to do was block Frank on my right, as Teddy whipped past, and we'd both be down the street. What good would that have done? Saint Anne and Heather would've been trapped inside. Frank Cora was capable of doing just about anything and he probably could get away with it. Teddy looked frightened and defeated; he was frozen solid in his seat. He would never have taken more than a few steps before Chute would have mowed him down once again. Just like he creamed in the Japanese restaurant. We lacked any means of organization, had no plan, or means of communicating. So we watched the Human Bullet fly like a two-hundred-pound moth larva spinning out of its nest and splashing against hundreds of ripe watermelons.

Within minutes of the act ending, the bleachers were cleared and members of the crew pulled back the ropes on the net. Thousands of watermelons tumbled, spilled, wobbled over the cobblestone street, rupturing against the bleachers, curbs, and were scooped up, here and there, by quick-handed kids darting out from the crowd. As if all the severed heads of the French Revolution had been assembled in one location. Saint Anne turned away from the sight. Frank caressed her hand. Teddy Eliot, Peter's accidental assassin, tensed at the sight of all those splattered watermelons. The motion and the swampy mess of red flesh and seeds of so many watermelons were painful for him. Peter's name was on Saint Anne's lips as the thousands of green heads cracked and bled into the street. As hundreds of teenagers dived into the melons, it didn't take long for the first kid to emerge besides the limo, carrying a watermelon on his shoulder. Chute rolled down his window and motioned a black kid about seventeen over to the limo.

"Hey, Yo. Yo. Bro," shouted Chute. He leaned to one side and pulled out his wallet. "Give you three bucks for it." The kid grinned, lifted a 40-lb watermelon from his shoulder, and sat it beside the limo. "Five and you got a deal," the kid said.

"Put it in the back," said Chute, with a snappish bite in his voice.

"What the fuck you doing that for?" asked Frank.

"Because I like watermelon," said Chute, looking at him with those cold eyes in the rear-view mirror.

"And so do I," said Jack.

"What about you, boy?" Frank was looking at me.

"It goes well with fried chicken," I said, understanding how some killers feel no remorse after they do someone.

Chute watched the kid roll the watermelon into the back. He shoved it, with a final burst of energy, between Teddy and me. It felt hot to the touch, this huge green melon with yellowish stripes. And it smelled ripe. The black kid slammed the car door, and a minute later the same boy emerged from the net with two more. But, by that time, Chute had slowly backed down between the parked cars on Greene Street.

THE dome light was on as Frank opened a switchblade knife. We moved slowly in heavy traffic on Grand Street. He stuck the outer skin of the watermelon with the point of the knife, then pushed the blade in little by little as the juice began running over the sides and onto the carpeted floor. The smell of the warm melon clung like a bad taste in my mouth. Frank, his hand curled in a fist around the knife, opened a king-sized slit in the underbelly of the watermelon. Still grasping the knife, he reached down to the floor and ripped the melon with his bare hands. A gnawing, tearing noise, like something living being twisted hard, with the fine-textured surface finally groaning heavily with a swift, ear-splitting crack. Frank stared at the red fruit inside; he used the knife to flick a few of the black seeds to one side.

"Kinda reminds me what good ole Mr. Teddy Eliot did to Peter Montard. Left him split open in the street just like this."

He paused for a moment, smiling, as he glanced forward at the back of Chute's head. "Great idea, Chute. We should have got a couple more." He passed him a piece of melon, the juice dripping between his fingers. No one in the car said anything as Frank took out a handkerchief and dried his hands.

"I'm a little disappointed that none of you connected up good ole Teddy to the crime. Because Peter's head wasn't exactly a piece of fruit. His head was screwed on right. I didn't know him. But that's what Saint Anne told me. Gideon, too. I read about him in the newspaper. They said he was well liked, a wonderful guy. Rich. Lived the good life. Where did it get him, huh? Teddy thought he was the Human Bullet. Right, Teddy?" He reached over, grabbed Teddy's knee, and tightly squeezed it. Teddy's tongue darted to the side of his cheek, as if to suppress the pain, as if to bite it, so that he wouldn't say what was on his mind.

"That was a great trick from thirty stories," Frank continued, leaning back.

"That's enough, okay, Frank," said Saint Anne. "He's been through enough tonight. Remember what you promised me?"

I had suspected promises must have been exchanged before Saint Anne had enough confidence to deliver her family to Frank Cora. I liked that about Saint Anne and always had. She was careful, patient, and deliberate. She was a true believer in promises; she looked at promises as some guarantee of her future fame. Visionaries always failed, she believed, because they had no faith in promises. Visionaries have been the murderers throughout history. The future lay in getting someone to pledge their word and honor. The very thing she liked about Alex. The same value she wanted him to betray, she now had cast our entire lot on the basis of Frank's promise, and the hope that unlike Alex, Frank wouldn't betray her trust.

"I know," he said. "But have you really thought about it? How Teddy just did it. Pushed that beam off. For kicks. For something to do. That's the way I hear that it happened. Of course, you can believe his bullshit if you want. That's your choice. So help yourself to some watermelon. How is it, Chute?"

"Real good, Mr. Cora."

"That's what I like to hear. 'Real good, Mr. Cora.' Think of it as one big party. And we're all pals, know what I mean?"

Jack curled his head around the seat and stared at the knife in Frank's hand. "Is that the same knife you used?"

"Same as what?" asked Frank.

"To cut off Parrot's head?"

23

One of the reasons we were in the back of Frank Cora's limo had to do with a bet between Alex and Peter. In the beginning, Peter Montard had been one of Alex's biggest fans. He had followed professional football for years, and had remembered when Alex was a star for the Raiders. Peter said—and I have no way proving he was lying—that he had been in the stadium on the day that a blind-sided tackle by a lineman who weighed over three hundred pounds ended Alex's professional football career. It had been easier for Peter to be a loyal fan when Alex was a stranger, a famous football player who lived on the other coast and who came into his life only on television. But when Alex stayed in a house three doors away from his own on Dune Road, Peter the die-hard fan became Peter the die-hard competitor. Peter said, "Alex looked bigger on television." Meaning that Alex on the tiny screen looked larger than Alex standing before him in the flesh and blood. That never made any sense to me at the time but later I learned what Peter was really saying. Secretly Peter Montard believed he had been born to be a superior athlete. If only he'd been in the right place at the right time, known the right people, received the proper training and encouragement, then he would have become a legend. It stuck in the back of Peter's throat like a small fishbone that he couldn't cough up or swallow. It was as if he blamed Alex for the fact that he had not become a household name; as if Alex had stolen the one slot which had been allotted to Peter.

Peter flipped over in his mind the kind of great football player he could have been. For hours he quizzed Alex about the other pros he had played with and against. How much they weighed; how quick they were with their hands; how fast they were, and so on. All the time, Peter rated himself against the standards these men had set. Inevitably, the competition in the abstract became arid, and Peter gradually began taunting Alex. The competition between the men had begun because Peter was bored with Alex's stories and wanted the scent of blood. Peter seemed on edge every time he was around Alex, and the tension increased with some minor dares, followed by petty insults, and then some direct challenges. Alex took all of this reasonably well. I think he understood where Peter was coming from and felt sorry for him; it had not been the first time a fan had turned nasty. Alex said it came with the territory and you could never stop someone from saying the kind of trash Peter had been saying. Their gaze and talk became a series of silences and small scrimmages. Peter went around calling Alex, "The Hot-Shot."

The illusion of civility finally and inevitably evaporated one day as it must have uncoiled a couple of centuries earlier between Aaron Burr and Alexander Hamilton. It had become evident their competition could not ever be resolved by words alone.

Peter's world had room only for winners and losers. Either you were in the Hall of Fame or you never made the team. Either a man was hung like a stud or he had nothing between his legs like a eunuch. You were strong or a wimp. Brilliant or stupid. Rich or poor, his was a black and white world with no gray patches. A man stood either on one side or the other. Every day, Peter had to prove his manhood all over again; to himself, to those around him, in particular, to those who mixed as friends around his pool, and on his wind-surfing board.

Peter Montard had made millions in the stock market in the great bull market of the 80s. A Jay Gatsby lifestyle fed by grabbing other people's money for the exchanges. He had been able to demand clients pledge no less than $10 million to their trading accounts. He made other people huge paper fortunes. He had a reputation on the Street for shrewdness, accuracy, and good judgment. That platform of success wasn't wide enough or big enough for Peter's ego. It was more a tree house built by monkeys who believed that he had magic in the jungle. Had he lived, I am certain he would have turned on Jack because he saw Jack Harvey as someone who threatened him by making too much in the Asian stock markets. I had the idea Peter wanted to flatten Jack but Jack never seemed to be worried.

Peter held himself hostage. And he could never sprint away from himself, slip through a lane, climb over a retaining wall and hide. The master voice that played at will in his head demanded an impossible ransom. Peter was hooked on one thing. The need for control. Since he lacked total control, he felt that he'd never proved himself. Not completely. Not the way that Alex had done by playing three seasons with the Oakland Raiders. In his view, Alex had, for a brief moment, control over his own life. Enough to keep him going for a lifetime.

But Peter would have transferred a large share of his wealth for Alex's three seasons. Making money was easy; but the legend Alex had created in three years was something that even money could not buy. It was maddening to be around a man who had something he wanted but he could not buy no matter how much money he made. Although Peter had socked away ten times more money than the starting Raiders offensive team would ever run their fingers through, the fact remained that the money never compensated Peter for being excluded forever from the starting line-up. If Alex had gone sloppy-looking, sluggish in mind and body, then Peter could have absorbed his past as one of those flukes of nature. But Alex's appearance had altered little since the 80s. He was one of those body types that are loaded with a natural athletic talent and know few bounds.

Except for one sport. Wind-surfing, a sport that Peter had carved out for his own, had worked on throughout the summer months until the sun washed out in the sea. Peter worked like a man in training. Like a man possessed with a deep, burning passion for victory. The first week in May, we opened our Westhampton beach house early, starting the summer before Elizabeth and Lucy flew off for their annual trip to England. That afternoon Peter walked across the beach, and threaded his way along the broken-down snow fence and long shoots of grass to the walkway which led to our house. He carried a bottle of Beck's, and had a dirty Mets baseball cap pulled forward to keep the sun off his face. He wore a pair of creased shorts that came down to his knees and made him appear shorter, and younger than his age. His appearance made Saint Anne laugh with delight. She thought Peter had walked out of one of the old reruns of the Our Gang series.

Saint Anne, tending the barbeque, waved as Peter walked up the gray, wood walkway leading to the house from the beach. He raised his beer to her.

"Great day," she called out.

"The market's up twenty points," he called back. "That makes it a wonderful day."

"So what are you doing out here?"

Peter shrugged his shoulders, lolling his head from side to side, trying to find Saint Anne's face in the glare of the sun.

"Need to recharge the batteries," said Peter.

"Why aren't you out on your board?" asked Saint Anne, as he crossed over to the verandah. He leaned forward, kissed her on the cheek, then poked a hamburger with his little finger.

"That one's got my name on it," he said.

"So why aren't you out on the Bay?"

"You probably think that's all I live for?"

"You said it, Peter," Saint Anne said, smiling as she flipped over a hamburger.

"Where's everyone?" he asked, looking over me as I stretched on a beach chair with a jazz magazine over my head. A few feet away, Elizabeth studied a play on the checkerboard, as Lucy glanced up, giving Peter a big smile.

"Hi, Uncle Peter, can you help me?" asked Lucy, waving him over to the board.

Peter crossed over and stood behind Lucy. He leaned over, his head next to her ear. He flashed Elizabeth a wink, then examined the board before cupping his hand around Lucy's ear and whispering the move. Lucy nodded, picked up her one king, and, her eyes sparkling, jumped three of Elizabeth's draughts.

"Thanks, Peter," said Elizabeth.

"Where's Gideon?"

"Over there." Saint Anne had come up from behind. She pointed a finger, greasy and glistening in the early May sun.

"I thought that was Jack under there," he said.

I had been reading an article about last year's Grammy Award winner, who had signed a multi-million contract to sell hamburgers and French fries on television, thinking about how this was Saint Anne's dream, holding up that award in one hand and a burger in the other, smiling and chewing, and all the time she is counting the money in her head. That's called laughing all the way to the bank. I lifted the magazine off my face.

"We all look alike," I said.

"Jack and Heather are in the village," said Elizabeth, putting down the checkers for a new game.

"And Uncle Alex's inside watching a football game," said Lucy, rocking back and forth on her chair.

Peter stepped through the partially open sliding glass door which led into the dining room, and walked into the sitting room. Alex, reclining on the couch, raised a hand to acknowledge Peter's presence. "I can't understand it," Peter said, sipping his beer, and watching the television set explode with a landmine, a moment later a helicopter evaporating into a large ball of orange flame. "We lost that war. What's the point of watching something that we didn't win? It doesn't make sense to me."

Alex pushed the pause button on the remote control, lifted himself upright on the couch, and looked out a double rows of windows at the sea-blue sky, and a light wind blowing the long, green dune grass like the mane of a strange, wild, sleeping animal. As I glanced up at him from my beach chair on the deck, I saw Alex shift to his feet. He had a thing about Vietnam. His older brother, Larry, had been killed at Da Nang in '68. Alex had been too young for the war. Alex only talked about Larry, as far as I know, once or twice. I wondered whether marrying a woman who was half-Vietnamese was tied up with his brother's death. Saint Anne's miscarriage had reopened the pain and brought the full weight of Larry's death back into Alex's dreams. Instinctively, Alex bowed his head against that old Wailing Wall. The new grief and the deferred grief twitched in his eyes. Vietnam had been nothing but pain for that man. His brother dead in the jungle. His wife crazy with the fame illness. His unborn child dead. It was three-strikes-and-you-are-out time only Alex was still pretending everyone was cool and he was in control.

The turbulence of the pain and guilt washed over him, as he sat for hours keeping a vigil for Larry and for Saint Anne's baby which had no name. In fairness to Peter, I was certain that he didn't know either about Saint Anne's miscarriage or Alex's brother. Nonetheless, as I sat on the deck, I felt my heart sink a little for Alex.

"It never made sense to me, either," Alex finally said, turning away from the window.

"Vietnam was the first television war. It was like a TV series that got canceled in 1973," said Peter.

"Yeah, only some people didn't make it back."

Peter drank his beer, thinking about why Alex looked so sad.

"You ever go wind-surfing in California?" asked Peter, as if it were an afterthought.

"Sometimes," said Alex, walking out into the kitchen, opening the fridge and taking out a beer. "We had clauses in our contracts that kept us away from that sort of thing."

"But you didn't let that stop you."

Alex returned to the sitting room, one hand on his waist, the other holding his beer chest-high. He looked at Peter as if to figure out what he was after. Peter didn't just arrive in the middle of the afternoon without something specific in mind. A favor, a venture, a proposition, were the kinds of gravitational pull that brought Peter off his wind-surfing board and into our beach house in the middle of a beautiful spring afternoon. On the deck, a few feet in front of me, Saint Anne flipped Peter's hamburger—or more to the point, the one he fingered—onto a toasted bun.

"Peter, your burger's ready," Saint Anne shouted through the half-open windows behind me. She was humming that damn theme from The Bodyguard, which made me want to break glass and walk over the broken shards to ease the pain that song caused me.

He gave her a wink and a funny little wave. "Be right there."

"Want to give it a try this afternoon?" asked Peter.

"What?"

"Wind-surfing. I've got an extra board. And, to make it interesting, I thought we might stage a little friendly competition." Saint Anne brought Peter's hamburger on a plate into the sitting room and handed it to him. He took a large bite, making an approving groan. Licking his fingers, he said, "Well, what do you think?"

"Aren't there easier ways to make money, Peter?" Alex asked. He leaned against the back of the couch, his beer cradled between his outstretched legs.

"Who said anything about money?" Peter shrugged and looked for support from Saint Anne. "Did you hear anything about money, Saint Anne?" She smiled, looking over at Alex, his tanned athletic body sprawled out. He weighed a good fifty pounds more than Peter, who had the body shape of a swimmer. All of 5'7" and no more than 150 pounds, Peter looked like the team waterboy next to Alex Walker. The short-man complex was written in ten-foot tall letters all over him that afternoon.

"Good," said Alex, walking past Peter, and turning into the dining room.

"You name your stake," said Peter.

"A case of Beck's." Alex slid the door open and walked out to the deck.

"Afraid you'll lose?" asked Peter, stopping Alex in his tracks.

In all the time that passed from that moment, I often wondered if Aaron Burr had frozen Hamilton in some eighteenth-century sitting room, garden, corridor of power, with a similar challenge. The muscles in Alex's enormous neck tensed for a second as if nature told him to expect a hit on his blind side. Peter threaded his arm through Saint Anne's. She looked a little embarrassed, yet more pleased than anything; she liked being the object of affection and attention. It was a well-planned maneuver intended to knock Alex off his stride. One of those gestures that sometimes loom around betting time when women are in the room.

"Let's go for bigger stakes than money." Peter Montard bounced back on his heels, his little finger plugging the beer bottle.

Alex thought for a moment before answering.

"Tell you what, if I win, then you'll give up wind-surfing for the summer," said Alex, taking back the offensive. He managed to strike Peter in the sweet, juicy spot where his ego was the most fleshy. It was Peter's turn to stiffen. He dropped Saint Anne's arm, and walked around the corner, following Alex onto the deck. They stood at the foot of my deck chair.

"And if I win?" asked Peter.

"Name it." said Alex, a gleam in his eyes, and heavy with attitude undercoated with hurt.

"To tell you the truth, I have a great idea. This morning I was on the phone to my Uncle Jean-Claude in Paris. He wants to start an American football team franchise in France. The NFL is interested. He thinks the French are ready to take the plunge. But of course, we French don't know shit about your game. So he's looking for a coach. Someone to spend the summer whipping a team into shape. Someone the League knows. A legend like Alex Walker. You design the plan to set up the first team. Say a six-month contract. Of course, he will pay you extremely well." Peter paused, and took a long drink from his beer, the suds bubbling between his teeth as his face opened into a wide smile. He knew exactly how to get to Alex.

"Yeah," said Alex. "You talk like you've already won."

"So if you lose, then you will go to France for a six-month tour of duty as Uncle Jean-Claude's manager?"

Saint Anne stopped humming that Bodyguard song; her voice, high-pitched, registering the shock of Peter's proposition, carried all the way across the verandah.

"Over my dead body are you going to France for six months," she said.

"But he might win," said Peter. "Doesn't Alex always win?"

"No, this has gone far enough. I'm sick of you acting you're still in eighth grade," shouted Saint Anne. "Bet a couple of hundred dollars. What's wrong with that, Peter?"

"But this is more fun."

From my chair, twisting back, I caught Alex's face in the window. The gears and pistons of his mind racing in ten directions. A smile finally broke over his face like a child straining to reach the last cookie in the bottom of a large cookie jar. He'd passed the hump. Peter was stubborn. Sooner or later, Alex knew that confrontation would follow confrontation, and there would be no peace until he defeated Peter on his own ground.

"What a great idea," said Alex.
Peter extended his hand. "Shake on it."

A week later, in the afternoon, on the Bay, one hundred people lined the beach to watch the race. Video cameras were set up and one of the sports channels sent a crew. It was like a duel, in a way. I played the role of Alex's second. Peter had a house guest, a Young Turk from his brokerage house, as his second. A week of planning was needed to lay out the rules, and for Peter to make a fair number of side bets.

The course was three miles. The day of the race, a southerly wind picked up the flags on nearby boats. Ten minutes were spent going over the rules. Afterwards, they shook hands before grabbing their boards. They paddled out to the starting line marked by a sailboat. The course, from a couple of practice runs the day before, took only twenty minutes to complete. To win, though, each man had to complete the course three times, and the first one to cross the finish line would be declared the winner.

After two false starts, the race had begun at two in the afternoon. The crowd, seated on blankets and beach chairs, nibbled sandwiches from wicker hampers and drank white wine from long-stemmed glasses. "If one squinted," said Elizabeth, "and held one's breath, then one might think it was the Henley crowd." They seesawed back and forth, Peter taking the lead for a few minutes, then Alex, cutting inside, would take the lead. Whatever size and bulk gave a professional football player an edge didn't give Alex a decisive advantage over Peter. If anything, Alex's frame was a disadvantage, he displaced a lot of wind which slowed him down. Saint Anne, a bundle of nerves, ran up and down the beach, her hands cupped over her mouth, shouting encouragement to Alex. Each time Alex pulled ahead, like a cheerleader, Saint Anne jumped up and down, jabbing her small fists into the air.

A quarter of a mile from the finish line, Alex was ahead by at least twenty board-lengths. He'd all but won. I couldn't believe it myself. The race was all but over. All Alex had to do was hold on tight, and let the wind blow him across the finish line. His sail billowed in the wind, and he leaned back in perfect balance as if he were running back a kickoff against a defensive line which would never catch him. As if he gazed at a different, fresh world, and found the past tense of himself tumbling out.

And he would have won, too, except that Peter got into trouble near the end of the race, he wasn't thinking well; he wasn't following through the way he was capable of doing. In executing a tack, he slipped off, hitting his head on the side of the board. Alex, maybe a hundred feet from the finish line, doubled back for him. He dove near the overturned board and pulled Peter's head above water. Peter emerged above the surface, bleeding from the nose and mouth. Blood dripping over his smiling lips and over his chin. He had a gash over his right eye. Like a boxer's wound, all bloodied. He took four stitches in a head that ultimately would have to be stitched back to his neck.

The reason Peter smiled had been immediately clear to Saint Anne. She waded into the Bay up to her waist, twisting around to shout at me directly behind her.

"What's that mean?" she asked. "Alex was ahead. So he wins, right?"

"Not exactly," I shouted back.

I'd been there when all the rules were laid out. One of the rules of the race—Peter had insisted on it—was that doubling back was not allowed. Anyone who doubled back over the course for any reason whatsoever forfeited the race. That was the deal Alex had agreed to. He had the choice of crossing the finish line first. But, instead, he doubled back to pull Peter out of the sea. As Alex helped a couple of men load Peter in the boat, I was there at his side. I saw his grim, bloodied face.

"You're gonna love Paris," whispered Peter. "Uncle Jean-Claude's gonna be real pleased, Alex."

In Peter's voice was the confidence of a man who had won. There was some question as to whether Peter had rigged his accident in order to win. He knew that Alex would always do the right thing. The exact attitude which had limited Alex's effectiveness on Wall

Street, and the absence of which had made Peter one of the most successful men on the Street. Within the core of his ambition was a bundle of many different kinds of ways to win. That afternoon on the Bay, Peter Montard had defeated Alex in athletic competition—a technical win is still a win. And Saint Anne wept and trembled, holding and then rubbing her stomach with both hands. She had lost so much so quickly. That night, alone, Saint Anne went down to our beach barefoot. She had lost her mother to the sea, and now the sea had taken away her husband.

24

As the limo slowed around a curve, Frank leaned over, opened the door, and threw out the larger hunks of the pale green watermelon rind. An oblong chunk bounced down the cobblestone street like an old tire spun off the wheel of a car. Black seeds and pinky flesh showered the parked cars. Feeling satisfied with himself, Frank Cora opened the limo bar and poured a double whiskey into a martini glass. A double shot of whiskey loosened and mellowed him; he needed the booze to settle his nerves before doing the business he had been hired to do. Then for Saint Anne, he poured a white wine in a martini glass. The rest of us were not offered anything to drink.

"I know something about show business," he said, after the first whiskey. He leaned forward and refilled his glass. "But I never got a chance to show you. So now, I'm gonna make up for that. You'll see," he said, placing his arm back around Saint Anne. She looked straight ahead, her eyes staring into the void.

"What do you know?" I asked him.

Instead of getting all huffy he smiled and pulled back his shoulders.

"All the production people are members of a union. You fuck with the unions in this town and you are dead. I can close down any shoot I want. All I gotta do is snap my fingers and the production is stopped. The producers need the co-operation of the unions. They want to fuck around with us? Then let them try, because I can put them out of business."

That had been the ace up Frank Cora's sleeve; the one he had pulled out for Saint Anne and she had shoved all her chips onto Frank's side of the table. From the confident way that Frank Cora explained his position, his power, I can't say that Saint Anne was wrong.

With everyone listening to Frank Cora no one was paying attention to where we were going. When I turned to look ahead it was already too late. Chute had executed his second misdirection of the evening, driving straight on Grand Street and missing the turn onto Center. The limo passed the old gothic police station building already half-converted into luxury co-ops, and headed into the outskirts of Chinatown. Even at two in the morning, on a suffocating, steamy July night, people in old clothes, their faces scalloped, lined, their skin like leather from cheap liquor and adulterated drugs, advanced out of the shadows, talking to themselves, shouting, begging, or staggering, sticking out thick, red, coarse tongues. One guy tried to light a cigarette butt with a match, another used a lighter flame to ignite a crack pipe. We crawled through a street, more a flea market of odds-and-ends people who were used up, thrown out like trash; only no one sent the sanitation crew to clean them off the street. We all stared at these wrinkled, crumpled, and wasted people who had no chance, no money, no family and no hope. I had never seen anything in the third world to top it. It made me wonder just how bad life in China and other places had to be with millions of illegals doing whatever they had to do to make the passage to New York City. Maybe they didn't know until it was to late to do anything about it.

As the car stopped for a red light, there were few other cars on the street; but a hundred eyes stared at us, looking down from the open windows above, out of back lanes, behind boarded-up entrances, but inside the car, the only eyes I was conscious of belonged to Chute. The ex-paratrooper panned the ragamuffin men wandering along the streets like he had been dropped deep inside enemy territory. Then, among the shadows, I caught a glimpse of his eyes in the rear-view mirror, scoring points, mapping out courses, wide and prepared. You could see the white all around the pupils. Someone once said that was an indication of craziness.

They said JFK had eyes like that. And Elvis and one of the women who read the news on CNN. If you had any brains you turned away from eyes like that because beyond the craziness was something else—not exactly evil—and if you were not careful you would be like a satellite in an orbit around that person, and they would be controlling you, telling you what to do, and when. I thought people who believed this kind of nonsense were crazy themselves, yet it made no sense to take a chance that they might be right.

Chute's eyes with that all-white look made me wonder whether Alex's brother had the same eyes when he went on patrol in the jungle. I started to think that the central purpose of war was to empty the country of all the men like Chute, ship them overseas, and keep them occupied full-time with killing foreigners. Keep those eyes off the street, out of shopping centers, away from school children. If that was true, then the central problems of peace arose once the foreign killing ended and the Chutes, by the hundreds of thousands, came home, marching home again with those crazy eyes filled with too much white.

"You don't think I have the power to stop MTV?" asked Frank Cora.

Saint Anne sighed heavily at this boast. "They have a lot of influence, Frank. Friends in government," she said.

He lit Saint Anne's cigarette with a gold lighter, and slipped it back in his jacket pocket. "I was cut out for someone like you."

Saint Anne raised an eyebrow at the generality of the compliment. The comment about his being a major media warlord rang loud bells in Saint Anne. Hadn't she wanted such power her entire life? Like a spotlight she could control and make her a celebrity? Someone whose face was on the television set? Alex had been on the television, he had the power in his hands, and he knew how it felt. He had gone to France to find the power again, she had told me. It had nothing to do with the bet he had made with Peter. He hungered for the power. He was addicted and Peter had offered him a fix, it didn't matter that he would be on television in a language he couldn't understand; he would be there. On the screen, looking out saying, "I'm back. Remember me? I didn't go away forever. It's Alex Walker, the famous one, in your face again."

"You would pull the plug on MTV for me?" Saint Anne's voice grew chilly. "I'm that important?"

"In a minute," Frank Cora said, and there wasn't anyone in the back of the limo who didn't believe what he said.

Heather's mind floated from thought to thought like light striking random clouds. She had listened to Frank's speech on how he could bust balls to get Saint Anne into the hall of fame. It was too much for Heather. She fumbled noisily inside her handbag, trying to locate the plastic bullet. She carried it loaded in the side pouch. Sometimes it slipped into the bottom of her bag and she'd empty the entire contents onto the floor, the street, a car seat, it didn't matter.

A smile flickered across her face as she raised the lost bullet from the bag. Then she covered her left nostril with a forefinger and slid the bullet up her right nostril. Heather took a deep hit. Out of the corner of his eye, Frank saw the bullet emerge from Heather's nose. With the back of his hand, he knocked it out of her hand and it flew across the back seat of the limo, falling into darkness on the floor.

"I hate that shit," Frank said in an angry voice, slipping out of the "man-of-power" voice he had used with Saint Anne.

"Hey, that's not right, man." Heather leaned down to the floor, still wet from the watermelon, looking for her cocaine bullet. It was lodged against Teddy's foot. "Teddy, can you hand it to me?"

"Don't touch it," said Frank Cora.

Teddy poked his tongue against the inside of his cheek. He squirmed. Hands folded on his lap took shape as fists.

"You like ordering people around, don't you." Teddy's sudden-found courage surprised me; I think it surprised Frank Cora as well.

"Did you say something to me, punk?" asked Frank Cora.

Teddy, his white-knuckled fists folded on his legs, slowly nodded his head. "I said you like bullying people. And I didn't think powerful guys had to use brute force like that. But maybe we don't read the same comic books."

With them sitting opposite each other, Frank's face growing red, his mouth harder and smaller, it was more like a frightening dream, one you tiptoe through, and are happy to wake up in your own bed, the blinds closed, a cool, clean wind lapping the curtains. A certain kind of hate spills out into a confined space and displaces everything else.

"And how would a scumbag like you know anything about power?" asked Frank. Eye-scratching, belly-ripping words on the streets of New York City. I saw Frank's hand beginning to slide inside his coat.

"I don't like this, Frank," said Saint Anne.

It was then that Frank saw a glint of light off the snub-nosed 38-caliber revolver that Teddy cradled in his hands. He'd picked Frank's pocket as he threw out the watermelon. One of those little tricks they teach in prison. Efficiently, without a sound, a touch, Teddy had disarmed one classy guy. I hadn't noticed and neither had Frank, until that moment, that his gun was gone. "Don't be an asshole," Frank said. "Give that to me."

"Take me to the airport. No detours. No backstreets. Just put me on a plane like you said. Then it's yours." As Teddy spoke his confidence rose and fell like an adolescent boy's voice.

The power had shifted like it always does, depending on who has the power to destroy the other. Frank gave the order to Chute and the limo picked up speed.

CHUTE half-turned and was ready to deliver a blow to the back of Teddy's neck, when a dancing red Chinese ceremonial dragon snaked directly into the path of the limo.

"Stop," screamed Jack, bracing himself for a collision.

Chute slammed the brakes to the floor, hurling Teddy and me off the jump-seats and crashing into Frank, Saint Anne and Heather. It was mass confusion with everyone shouting and screaming.

"Get the fuck . . ."

"My head, Christ, you broke my head . . ."

"I'm going to kill you, you sonofabitch . . ."

Frank rolled on top of Teddy, reached down and grabbed for the gun and after a short struggle he came up with it, smiling like a linebacker who had recovered a fumbled ball. Saint Anne and Heather picked themselves off the limo floor.

Heather looked at Frank.

"He's got the gun," she said.

"Yes, I've got the gun."

"You alright, boss?" asked Chute.

"Nice move, Chute," replied Frank.

Saint Anne stared at the gun as she lowered herself onto the seat. Heather, who had taken the opportunity to find her cocaine bullet on the floor, emerged with a wide, white-mustache smile. The red dancing dragon had cut across Grand, having slithered between some parked cars. The gun firmly held in Frank's hand, he leaned hard on his elbow, pressing it deep into Teddy's chest. Frank watched the dragon dance within a few feet of the limo. Chute hit the horn with the heel of his hand, but the dragon refused to disappear.

"What the fuck is this asshole doing?" asked Frank.

"Isn't it wonderful?" said Jack. "Such an inventive, ancient race, the Chinese. Beautiful language. The Chinese invented gunpowder and handwriting while Europeans were still living in forest caves. And what stock markets they have invented."

Wowee, I thought. Those Chinese illegals and shares had made us rich. But what did it matter? We were being held hostage by Frank Cora and a psycho named Chute.

"Shut up," said Frank. "What is that fucking thing?"

"It's a dragon," said Jack.

"I know it's a dragon. But what the fuck is it doing here this time of night?"

"Looking to score," said Heather.

The enormous evil dragon's head had bulging eyes, huge yellow teeth, a gaping mouth with a deep throat, painted blue and wooden nostrils flaring painted orange and red flames, shooting skyward with a wild, naked abandon. One man operated the head, and three others, spaced down the body of dragon, made the beast come alive with a coordinated side-winding movement. Chute leaned on the horn. And in the back, Frank Cora sat opposite Teddy with a stiff, formal smile; in that smile was the disdain that lights a moment just before the eruption of violence. What may have saved Teddy from a gunshot wound at close range had nothing to do with Saint Anne, or anyone else inside the car. He was saved by Chinese and by the hundreds of firecrackers they had thrown into the street. A loud explosion ripped through the quiet night, sending a bright fissure of light and smoke across the road. The noise was astonishingly sharp. And the confrontation between Frank Cora and Teddy Eliot dissolved into a common concern about the noise, the smoke, the dragon, which under cover of the firecrackers was closing in. A delivery van, which appeared out of nowhere, swung in directly behind and closed off the possibility of retreat. I had seen such vans, and because of Jack I knew what uses the Triads had for such vans this time of night—robbery or smuggling illegals from our building to some sweatshop in New Jersey. Once a week, such a van would park outside our building on Wooster Street, wait for the signal, then drive into the car elevator and take it to the roof level and either drop or pick up a contingent of illegals. They were orange and white checked vans with "Mario's Bakery" painted on the sides. Always smelling of buns, fresh cakes and bread.

Jack, who had been keeping quiet after the Human Bullet had taken flight, slapped the tops of his legs and stomped his feet on the floor of the limo. He swung open the door, climbed out, clapping his hands and shouting,"Bravo! bravo! You don't know how much this cheers me up."

"I'm not happy," said Frank. "Get back into the fucking car."

Frank rolled down the window and stuck the gun into Jack's back.

"I said get back into the car," Frank said.

As Jack applauded, ignoring or not hearing what Frank said, the man under the dragon's head lifted the mask from his head and shoulders, and faced Jack with an automatic pistol held hip-high and pointed at Jack's midsection. Jack went silent; he had a gun in his back and another gun in his stomach. Even in New York getting yourself double-gunned like that was rare. The man from the dragon's head was Chinese, in his early thirties, and dressed in black silk, with leather sandals. Jack started talking to him in Mandarin, sounding like someone who was a member of the imperial household. This wasn't what the Chinese guy with the gun had expected. He turned and shouted something at the dragon, and the dragon came apart before our eyes. The other three Chinese men surrounded the limo, aiming automatic weapons at the car. The lifeless husk of the dragon lay near Jack's feet, his hands raised high above his head.

"Chute, run over those cocksuckers," called Frank, who was kneeling between Teddy and me, ignoring our presence.

"Forget it," said Chute, his hands upturned, with the palms showing, on the steering wheel. "They've got M16s. You don't run over a gang carrying war weapons. Not when you're in a soft-shell vehicle."

"Is that like a soft-shell crab?" asked Heather.

Chute just stared at her in the rear-view mirror.

In an odd way, there was something funny about Frank and Chute backing down before a heavily armed Chinese gang. This was what passed for highway robbery on Grand Street around three in the morning. Part of the New York miracle of wealth distribution from building site, to pension fund, and from the hands of one criminal group to the next as if the entire city operated on an invisible conveyor belt powered by violence and corruption. The Mario's Bakery van blocked escape from behind. The gunmen covered the avenues to the front and the sides. The lead gunman nudged Jack with the short barrel of his M16. That set off a rare display of anger in Jack. From the tilt of his large head—his mark of high-pressured anger—a major disturbance was certain to follow. Jack, after all, held the wild card. And this was the right moment to play it.

JACK liked to say that he disarmed the Triad gang with words. What he really meant, and didn't say, was that there was a whole lot more to it than his words spoken in perfect Mandarin. He spoke Chinese directly to the gang leader; this melted his expression, best described as an intense, focused and impersonal gaze, into a drippy, leaking face wet with shock. Jack had caught him entirely off guard. The gang leader lowered his gun slightly. He knew and feared Jack Harvey because Jack merited the same respect as his boss's boss. Jack started barking orders in Mandarin like a drill sergeant, lining up the men for inspection. After another brief exchange, Jack walked over and put his arm around the gunman's shoulder and gave him an embrace.

Frank's eyes rolled in from the street and, like the tide, washed over Saint Anne, and then me. "How the fuck did he do that?" asked Frank.

"He has the power, Frank," I said, flashing a grin at Teddy.

"You see that, Chute?"

"I saw it, Mr. Cora. They are paying him respect."

Each man was making a low bow to Jack as if offering their heads for him to cut off if he wanted.

"I've lived in New York my whole life and I ain't never seen anything like that. What is your brother? Some kind of fucking Triad leader?" Frank was looking at Saint Anne.

"Jack knows people," said Saint Anne.

"Everyone knows people," said Frank. "He speaks their lingo. Speaks it better than they do. Know what I mean?" Frank sat back, put his arm through Saint Anne's arm and patted her hand. "You got Chinese blood?"

"No," said Saint Anne. "Some Indian blood."

"Red Indian?" Frank's eyes were big. The wheels of his mind were spinning as he tried to understand what kind of family he had hijacked, and now had hijacked him.

"Jack learned Chinese playing golf in Vancouver," I said.

Frank shot me a quizzical look, then gently pulled Saint Anne's chin around so that he could see her eyes. "It's true," she said.

Often what you don't tell someone has the real truth. For example, that the first man who had promised Saint Anne a shot at the brass ring of fame was Mr. Ling, Jack's boyhood golf instructor, who had become a highly influential person in China-town—that means he was a Triad leader, a boss, a warlord—and he had recruited Jack real young, treated him like a son. It was Mr. Ling's Asian connections which launched the Harvey Trio's career. We worked that territory for years until Jack Harvey knew every local boss in the region—Manila, Bangkok, Hong Kong, Singapore, Shanghai, and Taipei. Then after Tiananmen Square the Harvey Trio retired but didn't exactly break up. Jack and I stopped being entertainers, we had had enough of the business from the inside, knowing there isn't that much money, recognition, and you can forget about glamour in singing the club circuit in Asia. Jack, who passed for white, was welcomed into the most powerful Triad in New York. He had a business empire. He bought a nightclub for Saint Anne, and I opened a photography studio in our building. We were all doing pretty much what we liked to do and without any outsider getting involved until Saint Anne decided the priority in her life was to be famous.

FOLLOWING a few more brief exchanges in Chinese, the back door of the Mario's Bakery van slid up with sharp crack. A frail, elderly Chinese man stepped down a couple of stairs to street level. He wore beaded slippers similar to the ones that graced Teddy's feet, a white silk shirt with a pink crane stitched on the front pocket; his goatee, thin and wispy, shone pure white; his lips folded back into a smile to expose two rows of yellow gold-capped teeth. Jack approached him, bowed, and spoke softly in Chinese. The old man slightly bowed, and pointed at a building down the street. The ancient man with a hollow face and sunken eyes barked something in Chinese to the gang, and within a couple of seconds, the dragon, men, and weapons had vanished behind the closed back door of the delivery van.

Jack, walking slowly, brought the old man over to the limo. "I want you to meet a very dear friend." Jack leaned against the roof. He rapped his fingers on the back window. The tinted glass silently rolled down as Chute pushed the controls in the front. Jack squeezed the old man's hand, and both heads came into focus at window level.

"What a small world. Mr. Chang Kow Chen's uncle Lei-Yen has a cousin named Sui Dai who married a great nephew of Mr. Ling."

"Oh, yeah," said Frank, sweat beaded on his forehead as he stuck his head out of the window.

"They're all from Beijing Province. Can you imagine that? We once performed at a wedding in Bangkok for this man's grandson. Ahh, it seems like yesterday, as I was saying to Mr. Chang."

That had been our gig at the Oriental Hotel in Bangkok. Saint Anne smiled at me that she remembered how I had played the piano and she had sung while Jack had circulated among all the Triad gangsters who had come to give money to the newlyweds.

Frank's lower jaw fell open. "You mean out of one billion China-men, you know this guy?"

"Isn't it wonderful?" said Jack, patting the old man on the back. "A reunion of my Chinese family here on Grand Street. And Mr. Chang's invited us all into his house for tea. He has a small wedding gift for Teddy and Holly," Jack said, throwing a wink.

Know him, wowee, that was not half of it. Jack had business—illegals and all—with the old man's crew. Mr. Chang was one of Jack's partners, and Jack was being real modest in front of Frank Cora about this connection.

Teddy came off his seat, and his head appeared next to Frank's at the window. "What did you say?" said Teddy.

"Show him your tattoo," said Jack.

The old man had a real close-up look, smacking his lips. He spit in the street and smiled showing flashes of gold. He spit again and nodded. He seemed to like the tattoo, and like Jack, it made him look at Teddy in a different way. The old man said something in Chinese. Jack translated it, "He said it was an omen."

"Good or bad?" I asked

Jack talked to Mr. Chang for a couple of minutes.

"I told Mr. Chang all about Teddy's last night bash. With all of Teddy's New York City friends. Before his big wedding. In San Francisco." Mr. Chang slapped Jack on the back, then half-turned and said something in Chinese. Jack waved his hands, nodded, and replied in Chinese. After which Mr. Chang stepped forward and shook Teddy's hand with the vitality of a man many years younger.

"I told him that Teddy would bring much loyalty and joy to the house of Wong. That their sons will carry with them through life their Chinese names. Mr. Chang thinks that's an excellent idea." said Jack.

"Tell Mr. Chang we're late for Teddy's plane," said Frank, looking at Jack, then at the old Chinaman with the sunken eyes and small, narrow lips.

"He's invited us for tea. We can't say no without causing him to lose face with his sons."

Frank cut Jack off. "His sons?"

"The young gentlemen who dance the dragon so well," said Jack.

There it was, clear as your own face in the mirror. We had won. By accident but it didn't matter, Jack had delivered us from Frank Cora. Or so I thought. Because what I had failed to take into consideration was how Saint Anne was going to play this one through.

THE way Jack had presented the invitation left no doubt that Frank Cora had no choice but to go along with it or have his ass shot off. The men with the M16s stood behind the Mario's Bakery van and if there was any trouble, they would come out firing, riddling the limo—the soft-shelled vehicle, as Chute called it—with hundreds of bullet holes. That would have been a messy way to kill Teddy.

We stayed at Mr. Chang's apartment for more than an hour. Jack was talking mostly in Chinese, telling the host that "These running dog Italians are dangerous." I had heard him use the Mandarin phrase before. I also remembered the Chinese word for barbarian which cropped up often in Jack's conversation with Chang. The Chinese were enjoying themselves, listening to Jack talk about how the month before he had helped one of their relatives by plane from Panama. He had the man claim asylum on account of the Chinese government wanting to impose restrictions on the size of his family. The relative was twenty years old. Lately Jack had made a lot of money off that one piece of American policy. It was late and no one seemed in a hurry. But I understand that this was some kind of a slow, respect ritual which you can't hurry without causing someone to lose face.

Chinese women who could've been daughters-in-law, aunts, cousins, a wife, or any combination, silently glided in and out from the kitchen at four in morning as if it were noon. The room wasn't air-conditioned, and the smell of fish, oil, onions, and soya sauce circulated in the air with the rotating of the blades of a fan. We removed our shoes at the door. A small gun fell out of Chute's boot, and he leaned over and put it in his pocket as if he had dropped his car keys. For a while we relaxed, sitting in a circle on bamboo mats in the center of the floor.

Even Chute managed a smile, knocking back a cup of Chinese tea, as if the world that rolled you in one direction, sometimes tossed you unharmed in the opposite path, and at the end, for a fragment, time slowed and something passing for happiness seeped up through the cracks. Jack, our link to the Chinese, proved to be an excellent master of ceremonies. He knew the names of Mr. Chang's sons, who had various times driven the Mario's van to our building. Each time he rattled off one of their names, their eyes lit up with pride and a blush of excited giggles echoed across the room from the women who had never met Jack before. He had his audience enraptured with stories of China. Even the old man deferred to this honored guest. The Harvey Trio, so the old man told him in Mandarin, was still a legend in Asia. We had played for every Triad boss in the region, at weddings, in their nightclubs, opened for acts they brought in through their production companies, played background music for Chinese movies in Hong Kong. I guess, if you put it that way, we did have a moment of fame. I had heard Jack's rap before and went over to a corner of the room where some kids were watching television. I sat on the floor and a moment later there was a TV movie about Jackie Kennedy, who had died on Fifth Avenue of cancer a couple of months earlier. The TV screen filled with all the old pictures. There was the car in Dallas on the day I was born. I had seen that film a thousand times if I had seen it once. And every time, I had this same, sinking feeling that it was a hellva of a day to be born in the United States of America. The Chinese kids ate popcorn from a large bowl and watched Kennedy being blown away. Kennedy getting shot was just something no one could get away from. I got up and rejoined the group, looking like someone had kicked me in the face.

"I think we might have room for someone with your talents," said Frank to Jack.

"That's very kind," said Jack. "But you see, I've just arranged with our host here to have you and your pet gorilla shot. Nothing personal, mind you. But I am tired and a little bored. So I hope you will understand."

Chute's hand was starting to go into his pocket for the gun he had kept in his boot when he felt the tip of a knifeblade touch the base of his skull.

"You are going to do what?" asked Frank Cora, fingering his teacup.

"Have you disposed of," said Jack.

"Hey, I thought we were friends. You know. Just taking this guy out to the airport. Wasn't that the deal?"

"I don't recall having made a deal with you."

Saint Anne stepped forward between Frank and Jack.

"I made the deal, Jack."

"You can't trust this man to keep his word, Saint Anne," said Jack.

I looked around the room and noticed that all the Chinese women and children had fled to the kitchen and shut the door. All the men were holding guns and knives waiting for further orders and trying to follow what Jack and Saint Anne were saying in English.

"If I am wrong, then I will kill him," she said.

Frank Cora looked pale, his eyes glassy like he was going to vomit. Chute hadn't moved and neither had the knife at the back of his head. Sometimes making a family decision wasn't easy. Saint Anne somehow felt that Frank Cora was going to deliver her something that Jack Harvey for all his money and connections had failed to give her. It crossed my mind that maybe Jack wanted to kill Frank Cora for this reason. How much face would Jack lose if Frank did make her famous by threatening to get unions in the entertainment business to walk out? It would break Jack's face if that were to happen.

Jack was obviously thinking the same, for he said, "I'll phone a booking agent tomorrow. He's connected to MTV."

"Forget it, Jack. You aren't going to kill him. Stop being selfish. You have to let me decide this. Please, Jack. Father made us promise we would never abandon each other. And if you kill Frank, that's what you will be doing. Because I can't stand being in a family that doesn't trust me."

She had been watching me out of the corner of her eye. In Chinese culture the younger brother was required to show respect to his elder sister. Of course it was never that simple, and there was loads of exceptions. When it came to deciding to kill someone, I didn't know who had the final right to decide his fate. Since it was a split vote, Saint Anne looked serene as she turned to me, "Gideon, you are the tie-breaker. Hey, why are you so quiet and looking so sad?"

They both looked at me. The heavily armed Chinese were looking at me. Frank and Chute were so scared they didn't know who to look at. A horrified, grim expression appeared on Teddy's face. Saint Anne squeezed my hand and told me everything was going to be all right. This is what Frank's destiny had come down to; one guy who he didn't know, who had played the piano, who was depressed by what he had seen on television, keeping everyone waiting to know what he was going to say. I had this power of life and death in my hands. Wowee. A rush went through my body and head. I was tired and I hadn't eaten for so long that I felt weak. And I remembered how Frank had called me, "Boy" and worse, and how I had wanted to cut him, make him bleed for that.

The uncertainty as to how it was going to come down made Frank crack.

"Don't do it, Mr. Harvey," he said, as if he could read my mind.

I saw his hands shaking.

I looked over at Jack and didn't say anything, I just raised an eyebrow.

That did it. Saint Anne relaxed, a slow smile coming over her face. She had raised something more important than who was older or younger; she had reminded us of our blood-oath to Father who had made us promise (this was before we found out about our mommas drowning in Peugeot Sound) for our good never for as long as we lived to abandon the others like our mothers had been forced to do with us. We might have been whores' children but we would be raised to not act like whores ourselves.

"Okay, I won't kill him," said Jack. "But only because you said so, Gideon."

I thought Frank Cora was going to faint; even Chute managed a little smile.

Teddy wiped his mouth, stood up from the table with an outstretched hand.

"I still don't trust him," Teddy whispered in my ear.

"Be cool, man," I said.

Jack sighed. "Unfortunately this family has never been a democracy. What can I do? Frank Cora, you are free to go. But if you break your word to my sister, we will find you. Think of today as your lucky day. Buy a lotto ticket."

In the street, Frank Cora walked alongside of Jack. They were far enough ahead that I couldn't hear what they were saying but it seemed that Frank was doing most of the talking. Frank Cora hunched forward as he talked and used his hands. Jack was nodding his head and calling out in Mandarin to one of the Chinese who ran up beside him. Frank stopped and took out a cigarette. He looked at it, then threw it on the street unlit. Chute had fallen back between a couple of Chinese. His boss had been humiliated, out-gunned, and ended up begging for his life. On the way back to the limo, I walked beside Saint Anne, with Heather and Teddy walking together and Chute at the end.

"What are they talking about?" asked Saint Anne.

"Frank's cutting a deal," I said.

"And if Jack doesn't like it?" Then her voiced trailed off.

"Yeah, Jack will kill him before we reach the limo. Because that is the way Jack is," I said. His eccentric behavior was about the best cover any one man could ever hope for and guys like Frank Cora were always underestimating Jack and that gave him strength and power.

A half-dozen Chinese walked on either side with M16s at their sides; I think they were disappointed, and were making side-bets that Jack would change his mind and order them to kill Frank Cora. No one talked much, as if the awareness of life had sobered them, made them reflect that strangers could come out of nowhere, inside a dragon's head, and destroy them. That was America—full of surprises.

Only it didn't come to that. Frank Cora got into the limo. Then everyone else climbed inside except for Jack who leaned against the front door, as each member of the honor guard came up and gave him a small bow, showing him respect. Frank watched this ceremony, taking out a cigarette and lighting this one.

"How come I never heard of your brother before?" he asked.

"Jack keeps a low profile," said Saint Anne.

She had put her finger on one of the big contradictions in our family. She had wanted all her life to become famous, to have herself interviewed on Larry King Live and Donahue. Jack hated the limelight. Any time a reporter came into our nightclub, Jack disappeared. He had bet that Saint Anne's quest to make it big as a singer was one of those dreams she would outgrow and when she didn't, he convinced himself it didn't much matter, because she wasn't ever going to make it in the big time. This was Jack's honest opinion. He had been a member of the Harvey Trio and had heard her sing thousands of times and he said, "She's good, Gideon. But Saint Anne is not Whitney Houston. If she were, then she wouldn't have stayed in the club. She would have contracts all over town. It's no accident she hasn't gone out on her own. The reason she doesn't go is that no one is asking her." I knew what he was saying was right, but Saint Anne either didn't know that, or if she did, then she hadn't thought about it as deeply as Jack, or if she had, then she just plain could not accept Jack's conclusion—that she was just another pretty face who could sing real good but was never going to be great.

As we drove away, I thought Frank Cora might collapse, the way he had pitched forward.

"Frank, you're not having a heart attack?" I asked.

He rose back up with a 9mm handgun he has stashed under the seat.

"I have never felt better," he said, winking at Chute who was clocking him in the rear-view mirror.

Teddy rumpled a silk tablecloth in his hands, and pressed it over his nose, so he looked like a stick-up man staring at the wrong end of Frank's gun. The tablecloth had been a present from Mr. Chang.

"What are you doing, Frank?" asked Saint Anne.

He was rolling his head from one side to the other.

"I've got a knot of muscles between my shoulders," he said.

"It's from the tension," said Chute.

Jack looked straight ahead, not saying anything. This passivity disturbed Heather who was still pretty upset that Frank Cora had taken her guns away from me.

"Jack, you should have killed him while you had a chance," Heather said.

"That's what I was thinking," said Teddy.

"Saint Anne, sing something," said Frank.

She started singing How Am I Suppose to Live Without You, a melancholic tune, that if I were Teddy, might have made me a little nervous as to exactly what kind of deal Frank and Jack had struck as they had walked to the limo ahead of the rest of us. Was she thinking of Alex, or Peter, or Frank as she started singing? It was a strange song for her to choose out of all the hundreds she knew by heart.

"That's real good," said Frank.

Teddy smoothed the silk tablecloth which was hand stitched with red storks over his lap as if he were thinking about setting the table for the Last Supper. His knees were knocking together he was so scared. I could feel the vibrations going through his jump-seat and running through the steel frame which connected my jump-seat to his. One corner of the silk cloth fell onto the carpeted floor, soaking up the juice from the watermelon. I was remembering all those birds Jack had tried to release from the upper windows of the old whorehouse, and how some of them couldn't fly and fell on the ground, and others circled and came back to their catch, how the Mexicans had caught some, skinned them, and fried them up in a corn batter and ate them.

"Why did that old Chinaman give you a present?" asked Frank Cora.

"Jack told him I wanted to marry Holly Wong."

"Yeah? He gave you a wedding present?" said Frank Cora.

Frank ran his hand along the silk, smiling.

Teddy touched another corner to his face, his eyes closed.

Teddy said softly, mostly to himself, and out of what seemed pure emotion, "I wish I was marrying Holly Wong. God, how I wish you could go back."

"Anything is possible, if you believe," said Jack from the front seat. He was listening to the financial news on a portable radio he had plugged into his ears.

25

As the limo came off the Williamsburg Bridge, Chute switched into the right-hand lane, and then signaled for a turn onto a road which led in the opposite direction from La Guardia Airport. Wowee, I thought. We are in the shit. I tried turned around, trying to get some reading from Jack if he knew what was going on.

"Jack, what's happening?"

"The Hang Seng lost three percent," he said.

I wasn't really concerned about the Hong Kong stock market but that wasn't the point—if Jack was thinking about the market and not worried why we were not going to the airport, then I thought he had his reasons.

Chute chuckled as if his brain were wired into some comedy network; he knew where he was going, and this was a destination which had nothing to do with airplanes. Saint Anne turned, looked out the window, she knew this wasn't the way to the airport, too; she stopped singing. Heather slumped in the corner and stared out the window, thinking about all the money they had lost. Saint Anne blinked, twisting around in her seat, stopping in mid-turn, and looking over at me to find some sign of reassurance. I shrugged, raising an eyebrow.

"Beats me," I said. "I ain't never gone to the airport this way before."

Her eyes, all wild, expanding into that spooky full white-eyed look, she was running her hand nervously through her hair. Biting her lip, she slowly raised her head and found Frank's eyes on her.

"Why did you stop singing, Angel?" asked Frank.

That's the first time I heard him call her Angel. It reminded me of the angel on the Christmas tree at the foreman's house—Gary—and his wife who Chute had taken to some back room to quiet her down.

"This isn't the way to La Guardia," Saint Anne said, searching in his eyes for some explanation.

"Trust me, Angel," said Frank Cora, giving her a little hug. "We have another passenger to pick up. Five, ten minutes, and Teddy's on his plane."

"Why didn't you say something earlier?" she asked. Saint Anne desperately wanted to believe him. But from the grim expression on her face, she hadn't been satisfied.

"The same reason Teddy didn't tell us about his wedding plans. He wanted to keep it a secret. Right, Teddy?"

Teddy pushed forward from his seat, reaching for the door, using the silk tablecloth to cover his action.

"Why don't I take a cab the rest of the way?"

But Frank shoved Teddy back into the jump-seat with the toe of his shoe.

"The foot is the lowest part of the body," said Jack. "You should never point it at another person. It is a terrible insult."

How did Jack sitting in the front seat know that Teddy had just been kicked in the chest by Frank's size 12 EE shoe? Then I saw his head was next to mine and he had been watching the show.

"This is America," said Frank "And there are much worse insults."

Like being lectured by a short, half-Chinese guy named Jack who had him nearly pissing in his pants. That would have been my guess as to what Frank was trying to say.

"This isn't right, Frank," persisted Saint Anne. Her voice, as it constricted with doubt, slightly rose at the end of the sentence, the way it did when she was talking to some wanker who sat at a front table in the club and leered at her breasts all night.

"Just relax. Hey, haven't we had a good time tonight? Why should we spoil things now? Know what I mean? Everyone's feeling good. We are on the same side. You're safe, Teddy. Why would you want to jump in a cab? It's been a special evening. Let's not ruin things."

The streets under the Williamsburg Bridge ran like dark, empty, ugly gullies pocked with unfilled potholes. The limo sped, bouncing on heavy suspension springs, through a warehouse district. Huge buildings loomed in the dark on both sides of the road. It was an easy place to get lost but Chute drove as if he knew exactly where he was going. There was no exchange between Frank Cora and Chute, as if they had worked out what was going to happen a long time ago. I was wishing Jack had demanded that Frank give us back Heather's guns which were locked in the glove compartment. With everything going on, he had probably forgotten about the guns but I certainly didn't want to yell, "Hey, Jack, make that asshole give us back our guns."

"Think of the sort of people who would work in this sort of neighborhood," said Jack, gawking out the window. No one answered him. "You could hide a lot of illegal immigrants in these buildings and no one would ever find them."

"This is our territory, Jack," said Frank Cora.

I didn't want to be in Frank Cora's territory. I wanted another cup of tea and more of Jack's running dogs and barbarian talk with the Triad guys. But it was a little late for that. What we got were a series of broken streets with grease and oil patches and abandoned cars. The stink of industrial chemicals and sewage rolled off in poison clouds of pollution from the East River. Snot ran out of my nose and tears splashed off my cheeks as the smell filtered inside the limo. Jack rolled down his window and drew in a long breath.

"Now that is what made America great," he said.

"Close the damn window," I said.

High voltage chemicals had been illegally piped into the sea.

"Chemical disposal is one of our business interests," said Frank Cora. There was pride in his voice like when he said, "This is our territory, Jack." And there was respect, too. It wasn't so much he was sucking up to Jack but he was letting him know that Frank Cora was a man of influence, capital, resources and power. He would put his illegal chemical dumps against our illegal immigrants any day and let the cash register decide the winner.

Chute turned onto a dark lane which was wide enough for one car; it ran between two old red brick warehouse buildings. The limo headlights were on high beam and we could see the windows on the first two floors of the buildings on each side had been smashed. Acts of rage, acts of violence. Some of the windows had been boarded over with rough planks. Others had been filled in with ugly, gray concrete blocks. The neighborhood had a mean, abandoned, overgrown, violent feel like a woman exposed to sexual abuse over years, both day and night, to the exhausting, menacing thump of dangerous men in a hurry, men who were not too concerned about hurting someone who got in their way. Men like that lashed out and broke things, faces, and dreams. I thought about my mother in that Seattle brothel and in the cold water of Peugeot Sound, going down for the last time. With no one left behind to mourn them, or even remember that they had lived. She had given me life the day Kennedy was killed.

Chute pulled up tightly against one of the buildings so that no one could get out of the car except on the driver's side. Without a word, Chute switched off the engine, leaving on the headlights. He stared into the rear-view mirror until he found Frank Cora looking back, and Frank gave him a nod, then he got out and swung open the rear door for his boss. He stood with his back to one of those broken windows.

"Saint Anne, why don't you come along with me?" said Frank Cora, getting out of the car. He leaned back in and said to Saint Anne, "He's a show business type."

"No chance is she going in there with you," I said, rising out of my seat.

Jack looked calm and didn't say anything at first, looking across the blank space from the front seat. Then he said, "Go ahead, Saint Anne."

Chute pulled out a silver-handled handgun. It was the same one that had fallen out of his boot back at the Chinese tea-party. "Put the gun away, Chute. These people are family. We owe them. We are in the same business." Chute shifted the direction of the barrel so that it pointed away.

Then Frank Cora reached over and patted my shoulder. "Trust me. It's okay. No hard feelings or nothing."

"If you hurt her, you're dead," I found myself saying.

Again he raised his hand as he done with Chute. "Don't say it. No threats. Nothing's gonna happen to the Angel."

Frank Cora, as proper as a gentleman, stretched out his hand and waited until Saint Anne placed her hand into his. Then he gently helped her from the limo. Outside they locked eyes, their faces close enough they could feel the other's breath on their faces. They paused like that for a moment, then Frank lit a cigarette for her. But her hands were shaking so much that she dropped the first cigarette. Then the whole pack tumbled onto the street. Frank knelt down, the gravel crackling under his shoes, picked up one of the cigarettes, shoved it between his lips, lit it, took a long puff, then stood back up. He put the cigarette between Saint Anne's lips. That calmed her, but she was rattled. One of her arms was wedged close to her body. And her free hand, the one holding the cigarette, shook like a sail flapping from a ship's mast. Frank gave her a hug, whispered something in her ear. She nodded and tried to smile.

Then Frank leaned down, resting one hand on the limo roof; he gestured for Teddy to get out. "Trust me, Teddy," he said softly, his eyes not blinking.

Teddy, without looking back, or saying good-bye, slammed the rear door and walked over beside Frank. Chute handed Frank a flashlight and Frank led the way, shining the flashlight on the path as they walked up the loading ramp of the warehouse, Teddy behind Frank and Saint Anne in the rear. Chute sat on the back of the limo like a lizard, half an eye on the three of us inside, the other following his boss up the ramp to the loading dock door. Frank stopped, fished around in his suit jacket and pulled out a key. He unlocked two large Yale locks, and lifted the large, folding aluminum door halfway up. Leaning down in my seat I could see a car inside. The back end of a red BMW. Same year and model as Heather's, I thought, "Wowee, I know that car." There was something familiar about it. I repeated it over in my mind. BAR-483. Then I repeated it aloud, and Jack leaned over the front seat.

"BAR-483," I said.

"I am playing the lottery on that number!" Jack said, his voice excited. "Remember, Gideon. That's the car belongs to the owner of the factory. The one Teddy told us about. It burned down. Teddy told the police. I am starting to understand."

They stayed inside the warehouse loading dock for what seemed like hours, but in real time they were gone no more than a few minutes. Around five-thirty in the morning even people who work in clubs are in bed. I yawned as I rolled down the window. Chute had turned off the air-conditioning and the muggy summer air was thick, heavy, smelly. Jack did not look afraid; he was still plugged into an Asian financial news channel. He looked small, harmless in the front like a college kid who had never been away from home, who believed human rights were more important than international trade—that was another advantage Jack had over the competition. There were family obligations and obligations to authority. But rights had nothing to do with anything as far as Jack was concerned. I fanned myself, roasting in the heat swimming with damp river smells. Heather, beads of sweat on her face, moaned softly in her sleep, and stretched out a foot on the seat. Her white mustache had melted and glistened like a thin streak of icing with tiny bubbles in it.

When the first echo of angry voices broke the long silence, Chute raised up on the limo hood; he was alert, the gun he had been cradling pointed directly through the window at my head, then moved between Jack's head and mine, and back and forth. The loud, shouting, angry voice belonged to Frank Cora.

"You fucking punk," Frank Cora shouted, his voice carrying from the loading bay and into the alley where we were parked.

"No, don't do it," shouted Teddy.

"You shouldn't have talked to the police, asshole."

"Please, I'm sorry," said Teddy.

Saint Anne's voice screamed outrage into the early morning air. "You promised. You lying bastard. Don't, Frank. I said, don't."

Two loud pops echoed from inside. I knew the sound of gunfire. A brief smile lit Chute's face, as he held the gun with both hands, training it on us through the side window. Frank Cora came to the top of the ramp and motioned for Chute. "What about them?" he shouted back across what was left of the night.

"Leave 'em. I need a hand with the car."

"Jack," I said, real loud, so he could hear me over the radio plugged into both ears.

"It's okay," he said, waving me off.

Chute slipped his gun back into his boot and walked toward the warehouse, Frank Cora waited until he got to the top of the ramp, and put an arm around Chute's shoulder. I was out of the limo, and crept a few feet behind, keeping low. I saw Saint Anne standing in a corner, splayed fingers covering her face. Peeking between her fingers, she spotted me on the ramp. Parked off to one side was the red BMW and I saw a stranger, his head tilted to one side, who was sitting in the driver's seat, his body slumped over the wheel. I slipped behind some crates and knelt down and caught a glimpse of the stranger as Frank held the flashlight inside for Chute to look. A white man in his early forties with flecks of gray hair. His face had blood caked on one side and some white bone from the skull was splintered. Frank reached inside and switched on the dome light. Then as he and Chute pushed the car past, I saw the dead man's nose had been smashed flat against his face. His cheek and jaw on the right side were gone. What remained was a maze of coiled pieces of cartilage, bone, and flesh. On the passenger's side, Teddy Eliot leaked blood. Fuck, they did him, I thought. Jack was not going to like this and Saint Anne was never going to be famous at this rate except on some real-life crime show.

I grabbed Saint Anne as she passed behind the BMW and pulled her behind the crates.

"Where the fuck are you going?" I asked.

"It's okay, Gideon. I'm handling it."

"Handling what? Frank killed the man. And he said he wouldn't do that."

"I killed the cocksucker," said Frank, seeing both of us standing there.

"You did real good, Mr. Cora." Chute looked over the bodies.

"I always carry out my end of a contract."

Chute nodded. "That's your reputation, Mr. Cora." He looked at me and was going for his gun.

"Leave them," said Frank.

Chute had that look of someone all rigged up with his parachute on his back, standing in the hatch, ready to jump when the commanding officer orders him to go back and sit down. I could see him thinking for a split second about ignoring Frank, until he put his shoulder back into the pushing.

They did not have very far to go, the edge of the East River less than half a block. Frank walked along the driver's side of the

BMW, reaching through the open window, over the dead guy full of bullet holes, steering the car as Chute made his contribution the other side. Frank was in the chemical disposal business. I guess that included bodies, too.

Saint Anne was telling me the story as they were still pushing the BMW. It seems Frank Cora had taken a freelance assignment, his job was to dispose of both an arsonist and the informer. His client had decided it was better to dump all that insurance trouble in the East River and that would make just about everyone involved happy. People in the construction business, the union, an insurance executive, a politician in the Bronx, the police, the fire department, a Gallup poll of business opinion registered a high degree of approval. Life would go on, shareholders would be paid, buildings completed, new offices opened, there would be more pension funds to invest, a better than average year for all. Before they reached the edge of the river, Frank Cora pulled the emergency brake from inside the BMW, stopping the car. Chute rose upright, glanced back at the limo.

"I can handle it from here, Chute. Know what I mean?"

Chute gave his boss the thumbs-up sign, turned and took two, maybe three steps back towards the limo. As I saw him approach, I screamed at Jack. "Switch on the engine."

Saint Anne and I were standing on the loading ramp watching when the first bullet from Frank Cora's gun split open Chute's head like the ripe watermelon. He stumbled half a step forward. The impact of the bullet knocked him forward, crumpled his knees like he was doing a deep-knee bend exercise. Chute reached out with both hands, as if to break his fall, as if to hold onto the last edge of night, and then his knees buckled underneath him and he went down hard.

Blood trickled out of the corner of his mouth, running over his teeth as he tried to say something. But only a gurgling sound came out. Frank stood above him and shot him two more times in the head. The sound of a bullet going in a skull is difficult to describe, but it sounded a little like when you flicked your fingernail hard into a ripe pumpkin. Chute was about as dead as a man gets. Frank turned away from the body and walked over to the ramp. Jack was out of the car, the earplugs dangling around his neck. He walked over and knelt beside Chute's body.

"Had you worried for a minute," Frank said, a half grin on his face.

"When a man is executed in China his family is sent a bill for the bullet. Since one usually does the job, a bill for three bullets would probably upset them."

Frank Cora grinned. "Well, Jack, this is America. And that's kind of the way we handle things here. No one is going to be getting any bill for these bullets."

Jack stood up. "I know."

Teddy Eliot climbed out of the BMW. His face was pale, his front teeth pressed into his lower lip. Teddy walked over beside Frank and looked down at the bay. His hands were dug deep into his jeans pockets; his body was trembling, and then he turned, walked two steps into the shadows and was sick. He was wiping dead man's blood off his face, rubbing his hand on his pants leg.

"You lose your cookies, boy?" Frank said, glancing from Teddy over to me. He walked over to the BMW. Teddy had left the car door open, and Frank tossed his gun into the lap of the dead factory owner.

Jack went over and put an arm around Teddy.

"He was an evil man," said Jack. "Now we take you to the airport. How does that sound?"

Teddy was sobbing so much he didn't know how anything sounded but his own fearful voice. He couldn't help but notice that Saint Anne was holding hands with Frank Cora, and they were both smiling. And what is Saint Anne singing? It was about the kiss of life and the sky full of love. I remembered it was one of Sade's songs that Saint Anne sometimes sang at the club. The kiss of life. She was dedicating it to Frank Cora.

"Mama," Teddy moaned. That should have been the last woman he would have looked for comfort from.

But there was work to do. Frank kissed her on the forehead.

"We have to load him in the car," Frank said.

I said no way was I going to help stuffing Chute into the BMW. Frank and Teddy, with Jack holding Chute's feet, finally got Chute into the car and closed the door. There was a crack of light already on the horizon; if it wasn't sunrise, then it was close to it.

Once Chute's body had been dumped inside the rest went easier. Frank reached inside and took the keys out of the ignition. He pulled back on the emergency brake, then walked around and opened the trunk. He emerged with a crow bar which he used to wedge the accelerator to the floor. He put the key back into the ignition and switched it on. Then he took off the emergency brake and stood back. The red BMW with the license plate BAR-483, the engine racing, glided over the edge of the dock, and for an instant, was airborne, before it hit the East River. It hovered on the surface like a curious, misplaced object beneath the Williamsburg Bridge, in a spot beyond the first rays of dawn. The engine spluttered out, and finally the BMW, the arsonist, and Chute silently slipped below the inky surface, leaving only a hiccup of bubbles. I stood next to Teddy, the toes of our feet near the edge of the dock, and watched a few moments longer, until the surface of the grave became smooth as glass. Frank's people were in the disposal business—chemicals, srike-breakers, insurance cheaters, snitches—I had the feeling that Frank Cora's people had a diversified business.

"Done deal?" Frank Cora asked Jack.

Jack nodded and walked back to the limo.

"You were wonderful," said Saint Anne.

"Jack, why didn't you tell me?" I shouted after him

He flapped his arms and giggled.

"Gideon, it was your decision," he said, turning around.

"You cast the deciding vote," said Saint Anne.

"Meaning it was either Frank or Chute?" I said.

"You understand perfectly," said Jack, climbing into the limo and closing the door.

What I understood was that Chute had enough talent to make him useful but he was expendable, even interchangeable, like a member of a chorus or a back-up singer. You know those people who were on stage, standing outside the spotlight like furniture or props. Like the piano player for the Harvey Trio. Getting yourself famous made you non-expendable in America unless you became too famous like John Lennon and then an expendable person becomes famous simply by killing you. Fame was a tightrope walk and a lot of people schemed, plotted, cheated, and killed just for the chance to stand alone under that spotlight high above everyone, showing them, saying, "Hey, look at me. I am tall. I am someone. You're looking up here and you don't see anyone else in the world but me. So I must be someone. I beat the ordinariness of everyday life. I've beat the 9 to 5 lifetime prison sentence most people receive. I broke out of the system. I made it. I'm free. I am your dream come true. That's why I'm important. Good. Talented. That's why I'm great."

Saint Anne slipped into the back seat of the limo, and Frank, still taking off his gloves, soaked with blood in the early morning heat, climbed in after her. He held her head between his large hands and pressed his lips to her cheek. She sobbed, from exhaustion, fear, uncertainty, bone-weary, and the sobs became small spasms rising up, now and then, to make her gasp. I climbed into the driver's seat of the limo and adjusted the mirror. Teddy and Jack crawled into the front, closing the door softly. I started the engine, but before I put the limo into gear, I glanced into the rear-view mirror. And as I looked at Frank Cora comforting my sister, I tried to remember the color of Chute's eyes. I think they were kind of brown you find in the deep-sea depths on a piece of coral.

"Don't cry over him, Angel," said Frank Cora.

"I'm not," she said. "I'm thinking about our mommas."

Jack and I understood but we didn't say anything. This was a private, family matter that didn't concern outsiders.

26

A morning rain pelted the limo windshield. The streets, wet and slick, glistened like the streets in Vancouver six months a year. Out of the east a thunderclap broke the silence. Fissures of lightning made brilliant cracks leaking light against the black skyline. Everywhere along the side streets, the temporary shanty towns looked gray and broken like they belonged in a third world country and the street people scurried to find a dry spot in crowded doorways and bus shelters. Streaked with grime and dirt, the black limo was fleeing the scene, away from the bloodshed and terror, the smell of gunpowder, the smelly, black river. Jack rolled down the window and stuck his hand out the window. Even as a child he loved playing in the rain. He liked getting wet, walking barefoot on the beach, the rain in his face and hair. He pulled his hand back into the car and touched the rain water to his face and smiled.

"Sometimes I miss Vancouver, Gideon," he said. "Each and every time it rains. I love the rain. I'm mad about the rain."

"I remember, man. You were crazy about the rain. No one could keep you inside. Mother thought you had web feet and gills like a fish."

"It makes me feel so alive," Jack said, his eyes half-hooded from lack of sleep.

No one in the back was talking. I turned on the radio and found some music station which was playing Ray Charles and felt real happy. The rain didn't matter so long as you had a great player like Ray to listen to; he would get you past the black storm, the lightning, and the thunder because behind all of that, you knew there was some real beauty, some talent, and genuine feeling that survived in the darkness.

By the time I pulled into La Guardia's departure ramp it was light. The ramp was almost deserted as I circled around and pulled to a stop beneath the American Airlines sign. Teddy had the door cracked open before I had come to a full stop. He should have been far too tired for such a quick reaction. I guessed that his adrenaline pumps were still working full speed. He was worked up realizing that he was alive, he had made it, and in a couple of hours he would be kicking back on a flight to San Francisco, thinking he had gone through a bad dream. He had Mr. Chang's silk tablecloth tied around his neck, making him look like a Broome Street vendor hawking his wares to commuters lined up on the approach to the tunnel to New Jersey. After he rolled out of the seat, he spun around, as if he'd forgotten something. He knelt down with one knee on the wet pavement and stared into the back seat, finding Saint Anne's eyes, large and red like those of a nocturnal animal locked in the rays of a gray dawn.

"You can still come with me," said Teddy.

Wowee, this kid doesn't give up, I thought. He wants to join one of Frank Cora's waste disposal projects for sure. Jack looked over the front seat and fixed Frank to his seat with one of those hard looks that needed no translator to tell you what he was saying.

I thought there might be trouble. Frank Cora looked at Jack, then he looked away, his worn-out eyes glazed. He just yawned. Teddy, it seemed, no longer existed; for Frank, he was in the bottom of the East River alongside a two-bit arsonist. Saint Anne's eyes held him on the point of saying something else, but he stopped.

"You go back, Teddy. I got things to do. People to see. And I made a promise to Frank, so you see it's not that easy."

"My momma always said promises are something you got a choice about," he said. "So?"

"You know how important good character is to me, don't you? And you know that I think you have it, don't you?" After each question, Teddy gave a small nod, swallowing hard, as if he could see what was coming.

"You really think he's going to make you famous?"

Saint Anne said nothing, as she leaned forward out of her seat and reached across Jack's shoulder, and lightly stroked Teddy's cheek. "That's right, Teddy. That exactly what he's going to do. Take care of yourself, okay?"

A reddish stubble of a beard covered Teddy's face. He looked, the tablecloth around his neck, as if he'd stumbled out of a barber-shop, all confused about time and place. I thought of him wearing Alex's old battered Oakland Raiders helmet, hanging like a piece of downtown performance art on my studio wall. That seemed a lifetime ago. But it had worked out. He had been a back-up singer that the management knew was expendable but he had somehow slipped through the cracks and survived in a cut throat business. Teddy was a free agent, he could move on, find another job, keep walking through his life and hope that some fucking beam didn't fall on his head.

"One thing, Teddy. Remember you're dead. No one wants to hear from you. Change your name and keep away. Otherwise . . ." Frank Cora didn't finish his sentence, probably because he thought leaving the threat unsaid was more scary than spelling out what would happen if Teddy didn't do what he was told.

"No problem," said Teddy, giving Frank a little salute.

"That goes for contacting your mother, too."

Teddy swallowed hard. "I can't see why she would want to hear from me."

"I can't either," said Frank Cora, reaching over and shutting the door.

Teddy knelt at the curb looking inside, the rain falling on his head. What was going through that man's head? All the time, Teddy was thinking, "Maybe I'll go back and look up Holly Wong again." Why not? Sure she had married someone else after he'd gone to prison. Most prison sentences last longer than an American marriage. And look at the people in the limo, the way they had arranged their lives, their marriages, their careers and associations. Anything was possible. In the process why not look up Mr. Duncan and go back to the old job working on fancy houses in the hills outside of San Francisco? Anything was possible, anything could happen now; and maybe it might happen all over again, but this time, when the insulation bounced underneath a Lincoln, Teddy Eliot would keep right on going. And next time he saw someone burning down a factory, he would not remember anything. What did good character bring one in life? What had it brought him except going to prison and nearly getting himself killed?

As I pulled away from the curb, Teddy gave me an awkward wave. I gave him a thumbs-up sign. We were still inside the airport terminal airport when Jack turned around in his seat and smiled at Saint Anne. He extended his hand to Frank Cora, who blinked at Jack's paw, with the disorientation of one who'd missed a night's sleep.

"Welcome to the family," said Jack. "I do hope that you know something about show business because I would be really upset if you disappointed my sister."

"I'm going to do my best, Mr. Harvey," said Frank Cora.

The balance of gravity and power had shifted.

"I am sure that you will," chortled Jack.

"You want me on MTV, don't you, Gideon?" asked Saint Anne.

I smiled at her in the mirror and nodded. "I would love to see you singing your heart out on MTV."

Frank glanced at Saint Anne who stared directly ahead, her head resting on Heather's shoulder. He tapped Saint Anne lightly on the arm, and leaned over, putting his mouth close to her ear. "Why don't you sing something?"

Saint Anne blinked at him. "I'm too tired, Frank."

"Ah, come on, honey."

I changed the radio channel until I tuned in on Tracy Chapman singing, Born to Fight.

Saint Anne started singing along with the radio, then Jack and I started singing along and soon everyone in the limo was singing.

Jack beamed, bouncing up and down in his seat, slapping his hands against the dashboard. He stopped singing. "See what a bright girl you're getting. A wonderfully talented, sweet girl," said Jack, as I stepped on the gas pedal, moving us into the fast lane.

"A real angel," said Frank.

We left La Guardia Airport with a gentle rain pattering the window, singing along to Tracy Chapman on the radio. It made me think how we were all born to fight and that most of us get knocked down at the count long before we die.

27

What happened next is not exactly free from doubt and I have done the best job I can to reconcile the conflicting accounts—some private, some of them in the popular press. The way I have put it together, once Teddy got back to the Coast several significant things happened in a short period of time. He found a lawyer who, like Arnold Keene, had a judge in his pocket and got Teddy's name changed to Rod Jacobs about as quick as you flick on and off a light switch. To Teddy's credit he kept his side of the deal, despite the hellish treatment in our basement and his near death experience in the Japanese restaurant and Frank Cora's limo.

Then there was the Chinese girl, Holly Wong. This woman had been going through his mind during the entire ordeal, her face keeping him alive with hope. Jack questioned him closely about Holly Wong in the basement, taking great interest that Teddy had lived with a Chinese woman. It had not stopped in the basement. Teddy had been talking about her when we dropped him off at the airport. None of us were surprised later that he had looked her up a day after getting off the plane in San Francisco. He got a room in a cheap guest house and phoned her from the hallway phone. Yeah, she was glad to hear from him; real surprised, too. Three months before her divorce had come through from the assistant manager at Safeway. The husband had dumped her for a cashier. A white girl with big breasts, so Holly Wong told him, and she was a nervous wreck, her self-confidence running on empty. Teddy's timing, for once in his life, was about perfect. He put down the phone, packed his bag and took a cab straight to her place. Within a couple of days of leaving New York, he had himself a new name, a new apartment, and Holly Wong. He had a flame of light in his eye and a song in his heart.

His feet were on firm ground, with a new job arranged by Jack through one of his Triad connections in San Francisco. Teddy Eliot, newly minted as Rod Jacobs, had climbed out of the deeply shadowed valley of bad luck. He had found himself a life. And this new 9 to 5 life sentence would have gone on until he died, unheard, unseen, unnoticed by anyone on the East coast. A pleasant, happy obscure life so far out of the eye of anyone that Teddy and Holly, their children and friends might just as well never have existed. One small turn of the screw was all that it took to bring Teddy out of the wilderness. Holly and Teddy were planning for a small wedding; she had been divorced, he had been to prison, so they were not thinking of making a big splash on the local newspaper's society page. All the same, there were traditions to be followed and one of those traditions called for a best man, and in bed one night, she asked Teddy who he wanted to stand up for him and he was silent. Finally he confessed that his secret desire was for his old construction mate, Lloyd, to do the job. Then he explained that wasn't possible; that he had cut every connection with New York and it was kind of important that it be kept that way.

The story touched Holly Wong the way a man's suffering touches a woman. She did what you would have expected her to do—make her man's dream come true.

If Teddy wanted Lloyd to fly out to San Francisco and stand up for him at the wedding, then by God, she would see he got his wish on his wedding day. The day of the wedding Lloyd appeared dressed in a rented tux at the church. Teddy couldn't talk for a couple of minutes, sweat poured down his face which had gone pale, yellowish, making him look almost Chinese. There was the last man he thought he was going to see again—the guy he had been working with when the beam went over the side and cut off Peter Montard's head on 58th Street. Teddy managed to get through the wedding but he was shaking so much that Lloyd had to put the ring on Holly's finger and no one in the church—there were about twenty people, most of whom were Chinese—had any idea why Teddy Eliot was trembling.

250

"Are you okay, Mr. Jacobs?" asked the minister.

But Teddy had forgotten his new name.

"He's talking to you, honey," said Holly.

"I'm cool, man," said Lloyd. "No sweat, I can keep a secret."

That is the one sentence in the English language you know is a lie. We are wired to tell people what we know that they don't know if for no other reason than to show them how much better connected, informed, and wise we are, not to mention the pure joy in seeing the shocked look on their face.

A week later the crew foreman named Gary who had the ancient Christmas tree and the drunk wife saw Lloyd smiling at him.

"What're you smiling like that for?" asked Gary.

"I was just thinking about a wedding in San Francisco," Lloyd had answered.

"Who the hell you know out there?" Gary looked him up and down as if he were the sort of man whose friendship couldn't possibly range beyond the Bowery.

Lloyd shrugged his shoulders. "It's a secret," he whispered.

"It ain't gonna be a secret if I throw your ass off this site. So tell me what you were doing going to a wedding in California?"

It was a long way down and Lloyd was thinking that this was a dumb secret to start with and why was Teddy Eliot all bent out of shape because he had showed up anyway? The man hadn't done anything wrong. He didn't have anything to hide.

"Teddy," said Lloyd. "You remember, Teddy Eliot. He got married in San Francisco. And I was in church, standing right beside him. I was his best man."

THAT evening Gary stumbled into the house late and with ten beers under his belt. He belched in the living room and fell over the coffee table, breaking a couple of dirty glasses. His alcoholic wife, a watery gin and tonic in one hand, came out of the kitchen and found him laying on the floor, his face in the carpet. Broken glass all around. The television was on, a few pine needles stuck to the branches of Christmas tree which looked like it had been hit by Agent Orange. She rolled him over. She got him to sit on the

251

couch. Then she made him some coffee and sobered him up, got him talking. It wasn't like him to come home falling down drunk. Gary squatted beside his wife, leaning over and taking off one of the silver foil angels with gold heads and painted with red eyes, mouths, and noses.

"What you doing with that?" asked Linda, reaching for her gin and tonic.

"I'm remembering something, honey."

"I'd say you're trying to forget something," she said.

Gary cradled the tin-foil angel in his hand. Blinking at him several times, her brow knitted, Linda snatched the angel out of his hand, and fumbled to hang the angel back on the tree. The sympathy had gone and she had an angry expression.

"That night Frank Cora and Chute came in. Remember that?" asked Gary. "And how Frank broke one of our angels and thought it was a big joke? They were looking for that guy on the site who knocked over the beam that killed that guy. Guess what I heard today?"

"I'll kill that sonofabitch if he ever comes back here," she said, clenching her fists.

Gary took a long drink from her gin and tonic. He rose to his feet, and walked into the kitchen. She took away the glass and gave him a mug of hot coffee.

"I wanna know exactly what Chute did to you that night," he said.

Linda's body started to shake and she leaned forward, touching her forehead on the couch so she didn't have to look at him. With the toe of his boot, Gary tapped the bottom of her jeans. Slowly, her head rose, her hair uncombed. She had a look of abject terror.

"You gonna tell me about it?"

She looked at him, wondering if he was sober enough to understand; or if she were drunk enough to tell him.

"He took me upstairs," she said, real slowly, trying to keep in control. She took a deep breath. "He took me across from Jerry's room. And he slapped me across the face. Hard. Like this." Linda twisted around and swung a fist into the Christmas tree, knocking the colored balls, angels, tinsel, lights, popcorn strings and needles across the room.

"And then?" said Gary, his voice quavering.

"He made me do it." Linda stopped, looked up at her husband as if looking for some complex point of contact in his eyes. Then she looked away and began crying.

"Why you doing that, honey?"

"You didn't give a shit before. Why now?"

Gary bent down and put his arms around his wife, rocking her slightly as she cried. "He did something, didn't he?"

"The kids were sleeping in that room. At least I hope to God they were sleeping. Because that asshole made me blow him." She wrapped her arms around Gary's neck and hugged him tightly. Hot tears streamed down his cheek and chin. He kissed her, found her tongue and kissed that as well. Linda pulled back a little. "I felt so dirty and cheap, Gary. And you, you asshole, you didn't want to hear nothing."

"Frank should have done something," Gary said, his heart pounding in his throat.

"You idiot. It was Frank who told him to take me upstairs. It was Frank."

Chute had disappeared and the rumor was he had gone on a soldier of fortune run to some African country, and was getting a lot of money to help one tribe kill off another tribe. It was no use thinking about striking back at Chute; he wasn't on the scene, and all that rage was building and building. Gary had thought something like that had happened that night but kept putting it out of his mind; he didn't want to think about it or have to handle it. Now it was out in the open and he had no choice, he had do something.

That evening Gary phoned an officer in the union. They went out for a beer in Queens, and Gary explained that he heard a rumor that the mob had whacked Teddy Eliot. Then the next thing he hears from one of his construction workers, is that Teddy Eliot wasn't dead; he had just got married to a Chinese girl in San Francisco. Gary made up his mind exactly what he was doing that night. The seed that Frank Cora had planted with the assistance of Chute had broken through the surface and a stalk of hate five miles high was ripe for felling. For the first time, Gary wanted to know what had happened, because now there was something he could do about it.

I remembered well my feelings the night we arrived at Gary's house. Frank viewed Gary as a low-life sycophant; his main function was to obey and not question. And Gary's wife, a troublemaking drunk, with a big mouth. Frank had ordered Chute to shut her up. These people occupied a world walled in by insults, and the threat of beatings, blindfolds, electric shocks, weapons. A world in which a powerful man like Frank Cora determined their lives.

Frank Cora had fanned through these people who lived like urban shanty dwellers like a warlord who wanted to teach me a lesson about how you deal with such people; how to conduct an interrogation, to subvert their confidence, to steal their self-respect, to rob them of every dignity that made them human. He had power and was showing it off. Frank intended this experience to be my rite of passage. A therapy which made the process of killing possible and more acceptable. A rite of passage I needed before Teddy Eliot was handed over to me, before I killed him in the basement of our building, doing a hit that Frank had been paid for. This was the kind of joke that Frank would have liked. He thought this was his lucky day; he had a contract to kill a man and not only does he hustle someone else to do the job but he's going to get a girl out of it as well. Saint Anne's need for revenge had fallen into his life like pennies from heaven.

Frank Cora and Chute had taken me to Gary and Linda's house and into their private lives so that Gideon Harvey might learn the lesson of how to inspire fear. I was to be Frank's apprentice executioner. And Saint Anne had been on his side. She had wanted to kill Teddy Eliot. Frank Cora had committed the ultimate New York City mistake in judgment—he thought there was a free lunch.

HIS secretary said that Frank put on his jacket, and left his office at the union about six at night. As was Frank Cora's habit, he took the elevator from the tenth floor to the lobby. This evening, a car had been waiting outside for him. A chauffeur wearing a cap had opened the door as Frank climbed into the back. Before he left, Frank Cora instructed his secretary to phone his lawyer and tell her that he had some business out in Westchester and that he was running an hour late for dinner. By then, Frank Cora had moved out of his house, leaving wife and kids, and rented a one-bedroom apartment in the

Village. By ten o'clock when there was still no telephone message, Saint Anne broke down and phoned Frank Cora's wife. She hadn't heard from him either.

One week to the day after he climbed into the back of the chauffeur-driven car, part of Frank Cora turned up in New Jersey. His head and upper torso had been stuffed into a Goodwill box in Madison, New Jersey. A workman with an artificial hand, the kind with a curved, Long John Silver's hook on the end, pulled a piece of Frank Cora from the bottom of the box. The Goodwill issued a statement condemning the use of their boxes as dumping grounds for the Mob, living quarters for beggars, as garbage pits for the surrounding neighborhood. What the statement neglected to mention was the exact condition in which Frank had been found. His body had been mutilated. The bottom half was missing altogether. The head had been smashed by a heavy object like a metal pipe, a hammer or baseball bat. Fourteen bullet holes were counted in the chest and stomach. Rope burns were found on his neck. Frank had died, so it seemed, more than once.

What the Goodwill tried to hush up, but the workman with the silver hook sold as an exclusive to one of the tabloids, was that Frank hadn't been found alone. The bottom half of a goat, the hair wet and matted, smelling of mildew, and crawling with lice, had been wedged into the footlocker which contained parts of Frank Cora.

Less than a week later, two water-logged suitcases washed up on the Jersey shore near Spring Lake. The rest of Frank Cora had been carved up like a wild animal, wrapped in newspaper, and placed in twenty-gallon plastic trash bags. The suitcases rolled in with a brown tide as the sewage system in New Jersey broke down and spilled raw waste along twenty-four miles of coastline. Frank's story that week became half lost in the overall concern that pollution would destroy the tourist business on the Jersey shore.

The two young boys whose curiosity led them to open one of the suitcases, according to the newspapers which concern themselves with such news, were transported to a local hospital in a state of shock. Photographs of Frank Cora, accompanied by lurid articles tying him into the Mob continued in the press for a solid week and a half. Saint Anne was interviewed by a ranking officer of the Anti-Crime Squad. A couple of days later the cops got a full confession out of Gary. He had killed him because of what Frank Cora had done to his wife. Now that made every tabloid paper in the country.

Frank's funeral was attended by a contingent from his former NYPD detectives department, the union, City Hall, and the Mob. The New York papers remembered him as a former police detective who'd been highly decorated and won many departmental citations. As a man who'd been a victim of union in-fighting. No one was talking about Frank Cora sicking goons on union members' wives for free blow-jobs.

Saint Anne shivered each time the phone rang for weeks on end. She was getting interviews. *People* magazine did a piece about her singing career. Within a month, her fixation on fame seemed to be paying off because someone from one of the cable television stations thought she might be right for a show. She auditioned and before long Saint Anne Harvey was on the television. Frank had made her famous just like he had promised, carried her along into a new world, where she drifted in and out of all our lofts, carrying scripts, talking on the phone to possible guests. She sat with Heather and Elizabeth, who had returned from England with Lucy, who thought it was really neat that her aunt was on television. We would sit out on the roof for hours at night watching the sunset, then the lights automatically switch on over on the AT&T building, and the flapping American flag. Jack, holding a flashlight between his teeth, worked around us with his putter, sinking one ball after another. He'd hold the light for Lucy. She'd tap the golf ball a little too hard, and Jack would stop it with his foot, roll it back for her to try again.

"Teddy got his revenge for the insult," Jack said.

"Revenge, man. Why, Frank let him go," I said. "Are you going to tell about this insult?"

Jack smiled and waved his golf club. "In the limo, Frank pressed his dirty shoe against Teddy's chest. You remember that, Gideon."

I nodded, it was coming back to me.

"And I said, that is a serious mistake. The foot is the lowest part of the body. You don't touch another person with your foot."

"But Teddy's not Asian," I said. "And Frank did a lot worse than stick a foot in his face."

"Ah, maybe he told his wife, Holly Wong," he said vaguely.

"She's American."

"She has Chinese blood."

"But she married a barbarian."

"That can be overlooked. But Frank's toe in her husband's chest, that is difficult to overlook and sleep well at night, knowing your ancestors do not approve."

It was that time of August when artists failed to cart their works into my studio to be photographed. They had painted themselves out and drove out to the Hamptons to sit on the beach. So I suggested that we all go out to the beach house, and stay away from the city until Lucy started school in September. But the news of Frank's lower body washing up on a beach had put everyone off the idea of the Hamptons. At least for a while, Manhattan was the one place where Saint Anne felt in control. She had her work. The sanctuary of our building on Wooster Street.

28

Victims of Men was the name of Saint Anne's cable TV show and within a year it was playing in every major market in the United States and Canada. People we had not heard from for years in Vancouver wrote to the station, saying how proud they were to see a Canadian was doing such a great job on women's issues. And she had letters from Indian bands, the Chamber of Commerce of Seattle, womens' organizations all claiming she was one of them, and they were one hundred percent behind her. Alex wrote and said he had decided to stay in Paris, and Saint Anne crumpled up that letter, threw it in the waste can, saying, "That's the best news I've had in a long while. I don't want hanger-ons."

Saint Anne was direct and to the point on her show. She told her viewers how she had been a victim of men since the time of conception and how her mother had worked as a prostitute in Seattle and how a crooked lawyer had forced her mother to put her up for adoption. It had been a man who had paid to have sex with her mother; it had been a man mad with greed who sold her to a family. The same man who had murdered her mother. She played a tape-recording of a death-bed confession by a very old man named Arnold Keene, a lawyer, long retired, probably no longer of sound mind, but he remembered every vivid detail of having three prostitutes drowned in a sailing accident not long before our family moved to Canada. It didn't much matter to Saint Anne that Father had had nothing to do with the deaths of our mommas, at least according to Keene's account.

She looked into the camera as tears filled her eyes and you could hear all of America sniffling along with her.

Men had left her, abandoned her, thrown her away, and she knew she wasn't the only woman in America who had been abused, neglected, ignored, and thrown away by men and this show was for them. Women abusers like Frank Cora. Then his picture came onto the screen in one of those computer-generated boxes.

When Linda came onto her show that was one of her all-time highest ratings. Linda and Saint Anne handing each other tissues as Linda explained how she had been abused by her drunken husband who was serving life for killing Frank Cora and how Frank Cora had ordered his hench-man to rape her. She even said blow-job on television and no one beeped it out. As I said, Frank had made Saint Anne famous.

She even had an "Abuser of the Week" competition and women from all over the country wrote in letters with photographs, claiming that they had been kicked, beaten, burnt, struck, stabbed, shot and slapped around by a man. It was usually a husband or boyfriend. But there were uncles, teachers, preachers, neighbors, grandfathers, mailmen, and gang members. The winner of the "Abuser of the Week" competition got invited onto the show to tell her story to America. She won some prizes as well, like a holiday for two to Hawaii, luggage, kitchenware. The sponsors changed, along with the prizes.

One night Jack was watching the show and said, "She never sings."

"I don't think she thinks being a singer is serious enough," I replied.

"But she is a nightclub singer," Jack went on.

"She wants to forget about it," I said.

"She looks angry on television," said Jack.

I couldn't say that he was wrong. But I knew she had never been happier in her entire life; she had got what she wanted, and now she had the difficult job of deciding if it had been worth wanting.

After that night no one in the family mentioned that Saint Anne never sang on her television show, although she told how she had been the lead singer for the Harvey Trio, and the photographs from our days in Asia were still hanging on the walls of her loft. What she chose to remember—what I called her "television memory"—was how men had leered at her in Bangkok, Hong Kong and Singapore, offering her money for her body.

"Women have a right to revenge when they are abused. We have a right to be angry for what is done to our bodies," she said.

No one was denying that.

Saint Anne found herself leading the charge for all those women who were angry and they couldn't stand by any longer, waiting for men to change. They had to do something for themselves and she was going to have women every week who had done just that. Cut off a man's penis, poured hot wax, boiling water, oxtail soup and paint thinner on it. Saint Anne had found her niche. She had become a celebrity. Her face was in Vogue magazine, and all the tabloids. She had sponsors and she was finding her way onto the tightrope at last.

Watching Saint Anne on her cable TV show, I started to understand what it meant to be famous in America, and why going on television was about the best way of becoming a "personality." Whether the person was an actor, preacher, film star, football player, or singer, it didn't matter because they were all working for the same business. They got rich from other people spending money the way they told them to spend it. This was the basis of true power—a person shows their face on the tube and explains to millions of people that their life was going to be better, richer, and they would feel good about themselves, even think of themselves as being a little famous if only they would run out and buy what they were seeing on the television screen. With that information highway running straight to their front door, they didn't even have to run out; the highway came to them. They picked up the telephone and called the number running on the screen and a delivery van would show up with a package.

Saint Anne found her niche in the selling business, pitching all kinds of ideas about men and women, household goods, personal effects to the masses who sat all day and night before the television set.

They were a kind of human herd. People who had been educated enough so they could earn money to buy stuff but not educated enough to understand that most of the stuff they bought was stupid, worthless, harmful to their health and their soul. Or if they didn't have a job, then they could go on welfare. Or if they couldn't go on welfare, then they could steal to buy the stuff on television that promised to make them feel good about themselves. Maybe in the old days, guys like Drake could command ships, become famous and not be tempted to buy Nike shoes or Honda automobiles. But those days were long gone. Father knew that he had grown old in an age where everyone had a price and it made him go crazy. Mother knew it, too; but she decided to live with the world she was born into.

That was American capitalism. We lived in America. The whole world lived in America so there was no way of getting out, no escape to some remote outpost that wasn't linked up to a television. Fame was another product. And being famous was like being another kind of snake oil seller with perfect teeth, a nice tan, and an expensive haircut. But I didn't want to say all this to Saint Anne.

She thought that she had what she wanted; what television had taught her that she wanted. Who was I to tell her she should be happy singing at Jack's club, hanging out with the family, having a family of her own? She would have said that I was jealous and that if I had a chance of getting on television I would have run over my own mother to get into the studio. I would like to think she was wrong about me. But you never know until the temptation is there. And someone says, it is your turn to be famous. Here's a couple of million dollars that you can spend any way you want, and all you've got to do is walk out in front of the camera and sell this stuff.